For Eve, Rae, and Pip — because nothing else matters.

Kindle Direct Publishing Edition
Manuscript date: February 2024

TALES
OF THE
RISEN TIDE

BOOK I

SEED OF THE FAIR FOLK

DAVID M REYNOLDS

COBALT SEA

BOTHNEY B.

THE JÖTE

THE
TRASHLANDS

VITZAMAR

BRUTTAN

STEEL SEA

UR-UP

KARPATHIAN BELT

LAKE
HUNGER

LIMNAL SEA

BURG

LOSALFHYM

KIMPAKKA

SHOALHAVEN

GRADLON

RAZEEN

Prologue

The light down here was different. The hot red-white burn of the sun that baked and bleached the rock of her home was held at bay by the water, slowed and bent into dancing pillars of cool blue and gold. Protected from the harsh glare above, other colours dared to reveal themselves: the delicate pink of a coral, drinking in the diluted light; the velvet midnight blue of an anemone, waving slowly in the gentle currents of the lagoon; even the rarest of all — green — in the distant crop of sea-palm that was tended by her uncles.

But it wasn't the light and colour that brought Nix into the clear water of the lagoon today. Today was a pilgrimage. An honour to Ol'wen, the closest thing she'd had to a grandmother; and the woman who had first shown her this place. The woman who had taught her how to swim, and in so doing find a world unlike the echoing caves of home. A world where *nobody* could hear, where she wasn't a burden. A world where things were even.

She'd stayed for as much of the old woman's funeral rites as she could manage, but the moon-song was too much. She'd attended one before. Stood there like a foreigner while her people raised up their voices in the Lunehall, all weeping and holding hands and chanting in the pale light of the Mir-Trees. 'Acoustics'. 'Resonance'. Her friend Syra had tried to find the hand-sign to explain what it felt like: *like bringing a hundred candles into a hall made of mirrors, only the candles were voices*. All Nix felt was a vibration in her chest, and a deep sense of unbelonging.

That time, it had been for a boy she hardly knew. One of the Eastlock kin had fallen from narrow-rocks and died. She couldn't face feeling like a stranger again, not at the ceremony for someone she loved so well.

Her lungs began to plead for air as the pain in her heart burned through her oxygen. Pushing against the rusted wreck that was her perch, she kicked gently for the surface, breaking it slowly and without disturbing the water. Everyone would be below in Lunehall, she knew, but the stealth was long baked into her by now. She wasn't supposed to be out here, and a big enough splash would attract attention. It was strange, living in a world dominated by sound. She knew what it *was* — what would make it and how to stop it — but she would never really *know* it. Never *hear*. Even the island itself could hear, protected as it was by a network of devices that could hear a ship's engines from way out on the horizon and raise the alarm — another sound she could only sense on the panicked faces of others.

She skulled the water and looked around at the lagoon. The half moon hung low and bright in the clear morning west, and she saw clearly the long straight scars cut into its surface by the ancestors. It would be visible from Lunehall soon — timed so as to match the old song's ending. Time for her to go.

Sipping the warm air, Nix slipped under the water again — it was quicker and quieter to swim below the surface — and glode back to shore with strokes made confident by years of solitary practice.

Something caught her eye. At first it seemed like the moon peering up at her from the very bottom — impossible — but it *was* a silver disc. Kicking both legs in unison, she drove herself down, deeper and closer.

Lungs burning again from the unexpected effort, she pushed on. As she drew closer the curious object began to resolve itself: a bright metal puck, only a little larger than her eye-socket, with a thin chain attached. Snatching it up along with a handful of seasoil she kicked for the surface, abandoning stealth this time in favour of quicker air. Bursting from the water, she flung her hair back and kicked for the shore, still clutching her prize in hand.

Panting, and without even pulling herself from the water, she inspected her find. Her breath caught in her throat as she rinsed the soil and turned the thing over in her hands. The back face of the puck had been bright metal — salt-steel she guessed, from the lack of rust — but the front face was dark, with symbols she didn't recognise and a dull window of grey-green she did. It was a display.

Teck. Unshielded, relic teck.

Nix glanced around guiltily. Even here on Losalfhym, teck was forbidden outside the heavily shielded deep-caves. But this gadget, or gizmo, was long-dead. Any ounce of trace would have faded centuries ago, and had obviously not attracted any predators to the hidden island.

But there *was* a button. Smooth and shallow — almost flush with the edge of the disc — begging to be pressed. She teased it gently with her finger, felt it wiggle under her touch. But she dared not push. Not out here. If by some miracle this relic still had life in it, she would have no way of knowing if it made noise. Not until someone came to investigate.

Stashing the relic in a nook of the rock, Nix pulled herself from the water and patted herself dry with her bundled clothes. She could already feel the sun penetrating her ivory skin as she began to apply the thick, grey sunclay that would protect her.

Movement caught her eye, and as she flung herself instinctively behind the cover of the rock, the jar of sunclay slipped from her grasp, smashing on the ground. Nix groaned inwardly. *That* would have made a sound for sure. Sheepishly she peered over the rock searching again for the movement, and sighed with relief as she saw Syra. What was her friend doing away from the moon-song?

The two girls locked eyes, and Syra beckoned urgently, signing with exaggerated gestures to compensate for the distance.

The alarm sounds. They are sealing the gates. Come.

Abandoning the sunclay, Nix pulled on her clothes and dashed toward her friend, replying as she scrambled over the rocky ground.

A ship nearby — question?

Syra shook her head. *Perhaps nothing, not an engine. But close by.* She took a shawl from her shoulders and draped it protectively over Nix's exposed skin — already burning in the morning sun. Syra would burn just as fast, of course, but she was a full six months older and was fiercely protective of her 'little sister'.

Nix hurried alongside. They would seal the gates and hide, as always, until the sound passed. Their island would appear to be just another barren rock — some hilltop or ruined building protruding from the flood-sea — not worth investigating. And then, when it was safe once more the Goodmother would send the search parties out, checking the island over.

Nix halted as she remembered the trinket. She couldn't have anyone else find it. Spinning on her heel she darted back towards her hiding place, throwing a quick sign to Syra as she did. *Go — I follow quickly.*

Syra might have objected, but Nix didn't turn back to give her the opportunity. Hurrying across the uneven ground, she sprung down lightly behind the rock-hide, snatching up the stashed teck-relic and flinging the broken pieces of the sunclay jar into the water with her foot. Looking around to make sure she'd left no other clue to her misadventure, she hesitated. There was *another* glint of light, a little further away this time. The same bright gleam of metal, only this time on the rocky ground.

Glancing back to check that Syra was out of sight, Nix crept closer. It was rare enough to find an ancient thing deep in the lagoon where perhaps the tides of a hundred years could have moved it, but out in the open? Within the protection of narrow-rocks and the gulley? She'd walked this way a thousand times before, she could never have missed this. A spiral of bright steel, with a short wooden handle — not teck, just some trinket — but nothing she had seen before among her people.

The breeze brought foreign smells: sweat, mixed with the distilled tree-spirit they used to clean old gears. Her hair prickled against the shawl.

There was movement at her side, and she whirled about.

An outsider — oily clothes barely covering his rough, sun-poxed skin — grinned at her with a mouth full of metal teeth.

Another closed in next to him, this one taller, and wiry, and looking right past her. She turned — panicking now — and saw a third man, thick as a tree, stooping to collect the steel spiral from the floor. His eyes never left hers, and his lips moved, though she couldn't read them.

Forcing her trembling body to obey, she charged right at him, darting suddenly left to narrowly avoid his grasping hands. A heartbeat, and she was past him, heading for the path that would take her to inner-sea. She could swim then, perhaps, or make for the northern gate before...

Something caught her feet, tangling, slamming her to the ground. She felt her chin split on the rock. She tried to scramble back to her feet but found herself enmeshed in a coarse web of ropes as the three men — now four — approached.

Desperate, Nix screamed, feeling her voice breaking from lack of use. She pushed the air ragged from her lungs, felt the resonance in her hoarse throat and chest. Wincing, the wiry man shoved a rag into her mouth, stifling her cry.

She was carried, kicking and biting, and thrown into a small boat, its inflatable sides patched and bulging. She was forced down by many hands, and felt the water moving under her. There was the biting smell of gazleen, and cool salt-spray fell upon her face.

Nix tried to calm herself, to think. There was a motor, but a boat this small couldn't have made it to Losalfhym alone, they were a hundred clicks from the nearest land. With the sensors triggered, her people would be hiding behind sealed gates. She was alone.

The boat turned hard and thudded into something. The hands released their pressure and she felt them snatching, dragging at the nets that bound her. Suddenly she was lifted clear of the boat and up...

...up to a much, much larger boat. A *ship*. Too big to have made it here unheard. Bigger than any she'd ever seen up close. Bigger even than the *Archon*, the only one that had ever been allowed within the confines of inner-sea.

Hands from above groped down, and she was hauled onto the rusty, fly-eaten deck. Blinking against the light and the pain, she saw a dozen pairs of feet crowded around her. More groping

11

hands, and the nets were torn free, and Nix dragged unsteadily to her feet, her arms held.

The dozen pairs of feet were shared between more than a dozen men, each more vulgar than the next. The mingled pungence of oil, sweat, spirits and fish was nauseating. They looked almost more afraid of her than she was of them, crossing themselves and muttering as they leered at her alabaster skin. Nix read the same familiar word on many lips. She jutted her chin defiantly and tried to appear uncowed. *Fairey.*

The cleanest among them — a false-toothed man with a wide green hat and an intricate black beard — stepped forward appraisingly. He carried a note of lavender oil above the stench of the crew. He spoke, and Nix managed to read a clutch of his words. 'You are _____ our ship. _____ and I have _____. What are your _____ inside?'

Nix tried to move her hands, to sign something — even just to point to her ears, but her arms were held fast. She realised that — through all this — she still clutched the metal puck-relic as if her life depended on it.

Green-hat tried again, slower 'Do you understand? I need to know that _____ _____ alone? Are you _____ age?'

The arms holding hers twisted roughly, trying to squeeze an answer from her. Desperate for options, and seeing her chances of rescue slipping away, Nix felt out the button on the teck-relic, held her breath, and pushed.

Nothing happened.

The pirates seemed to hesitate, and Green-hat must have given an order to the thick arms holding her — as they wrenched her fist open and took the relic. Green-hat held out his hand to receive it, chuckling. He pushed the button once more, then pulled a close fitting copper shield-mesh from his pocket and slipped the puck inside, polishing it on his waistcoat and fastening the chain to a button-hole.

A path cleared in the mass of bodies, and a hunched figure made his way forward. Molten scars licked across his cheeks and brow from behind a dark bandage that covered both eyes. He gripped a long staff with bony fingers and felt his way forward. All eyes among the crew were on him, even Green-hat made way as he stepped forward.

Green-hat gestured impotently at Nix and muttered something, but the blind man swatted his words away and handed the man his staff as he drew closer to her.

His bony fingers clutched at her face, prodding and poking. Then her shoulders and chest. Nix swallowed back a pained gasp as he groped her small breasts roughly. She could smell decay on his breath, the same scent she'd caught on Ol'wen in the days before the end.

He took a half step back and spoke, his parched lips close and slow enough for her to read. 'Deaf. Flowering, but young enough yet to be called a child. She'll do. Haste, now, or the devil take us all.'

Green-hat yelled orders, but the crew were already rushing for their posts. Great makeshift oars were snatched up and thrust through freshly cut holes in the gunwales, two men to each, and soon the great ship started to move across inner-sea. So *that* is how they hid from the listeners, Nix realised with a detached admiration. The same way the Tsar came for his blood-mixing, by rowing.

The arms still clutching hers dragged her to a post and bound her there, while a small shrivelled man sprayed her with a clinging rust-oil that stained her pale skin red-brown like theirs. Her eyes began to sting fiercely from the oil-fumes, and the tears she had been holding back began to tumble unchecked down her cheeks. She watched as the steep walls of narrow-rocks began to slide past the ship, the hull groaning where they passed too close.

Nix had grown up on a diet of Ol'wen's stories about the voyagers on the open sea, and soon grown hungry for more, persuading Syra to sign-repeat every word of Inkäinen's tellings when the Archon visited. She'd spent many hours dreaming of a life beyond the caves of Losalfhym, where she could be more than the curious deaf child. But now that she found herself — on the day of the old teller's funeral, no less — face to face with the characters from those stories, she wished for nothing more than to be back inside the safety of the sealed gates.

There was a blur of red-green as a young fezzard swooped across the bow of the ship and back toward its perch atop the gulley. She watched it go, and longed to fly after it, free of her bonds.

Nix felt a tremendous rumble in her chest, and the rock wall to their right exploded, sending shards of shattered stone crashing down to scatter across the deck. A wave of panic tore through the crew. Some abandoned their oars, ducking for cover from the unknown assault. Nix's skin tingled. Only one thing could do damage like that…

She looked to the high cliffs at their left, saw the still-smoking barrel of one of the great sentinel-guns ratcheting down towards them. She glimpsed the ivory-white spectres of Uluwe and Nankin — guard men who should have been sealed away inside with the others.

Another gun rolled forward from its cavity in the cliff — then another — and Nix's heart leaped as she saw familiar figures in the shade of the cave tunnels. Her father, and Syra clinging to him, sobbing. Syra! She had raised the alarm and brought help.

The Goodmother strode forward into the light, her ivory skin dulled by hurried sunclay. She bellowed something and raised a hand.

Nix's captors were arguing now — some cowering behind the gunwales; some wrenching the oars to free the ship from the gulley; others bellowing orders and fetching weapons. One raised a rifle and fired, the ball smashing into the rock inches behind the Goodmother, but the old chieftess did not flinch.

From amidst the chaos, the scarred blind man hobbled toward Nix, a curved knife in his hand. Squirming to get away, she found her bonds suddenly cut, then her neck in a vice-grip as she was thrust forward towards the sheer cliff.

The old man ripped the shawl from her head revealing the salt-white hair, now incongruous with the red-stained skin. He forced her head upwards, holding her out like a trophy, a warding stone protecting the ship against further attack.

Syra wailed and clutched at her father in the shade, while the sentinel-gunners looked on, ready to fire, but the Goodmother was impassive — a statue upon the high platform, arm raised.

Nix's eyes streamed from the vapours of the oil-dye. The Goodmother's hand moved an inch, then hesitated. Nix saw her father yelling something, but it was too far, too dark to read. A fezzard landed on one of the sentinel guns beside the Goodmother, and raised its head in the long sorrow call Nix would never hear. The old woman hung her head, and slowly lowered her arm, unable, or unwilling, to give the order.

Syra wailed, as the ship's crew cheered and returned to their posts, guiding the hulking vessel clumsily free of the gully. Nix watched as her home slipped away past the sides of the ship, and too soon she was on the open water, alone and afraid, prisoner among pirates.

I

Every Day Aboard
Is Two Days off Your Life

'For then, at the height of man's arrogance, he began to believe that he was able to change the whole of the world. He saw the coming floods and said 'lo, this mighty thing is of our own doing!'. He saw the fires and famines and cursed his fellow man and said 'look now what we have done to the Earth! See now how we must change our ways!'.'

Undeterred by the droning of the Par's sermon, a tiny magfly crawled across the steel plate, two of its eight legs prodding and testing the new joint for weakness — any break in the metal surface where it could begin to gnaw at the rich ferrous within.

Jymn Hatcher watched, studying the creature, his good eye squinting at the jerking mechanical movements that would reveal any flaw in his work — any void or cavity in the weld-bead that held fast the latest patch in the great steel patchwork that made up the ship's hull. Out of habit, he rubbed a thumb over the sooty lens of his tinkered eyeglass, but his bad eye was not much help in the gloom.

'But the floods and the famines were not of man's making, but of the Lord's own command, and they could not be averted by any arrogance of man.'

The old cleric's voice had grown muffled and distorted as it reverberated up through two full decks of the ship, but Jymn heard the words as clearly as if he'd been in the chapel himself, beside the masters. He'd sat through the *Gospel of St Stephen* more than half a hundred times now, and the sermon had etched its own groove in his mind.

'For it was man who, envious of God, tried himself by infernal devices to create life and so be as a god himself. But he was not God, and man could not hold sway over his creation, and so it was that the Lord called forth the Sword of Fire, and the Flood, to cleanse the Earth of the heresy.'

Frustrated, the magfly spread its tiny fibre wings and buzzed noisily away in search of an easier meal. Good. If the little creature couldn't find a mistake, neither could the Bo'sun, and there'd be one less reason to add days to Jymn's debt. He coughed. A harsh, barking cough — his lungs caked with the same soot that clung to every surface up here — belched from the weld-torch each time the airline choked. *Every day aboard is two days off your life.*

Jymn relaxed, uncoiling himself from his perch and worming his way back into the void between the hull and the superstructure. His muscles protested angrily — stiff and knotted from the efforts of completing his twelve hour shift in just over ten — but with the work done, he'd have time aspare to get some air, and look out over Gradlon before bunk.

It took almost a quarter hour to work his way back down to Sixdeck, stopping every two levels to lower his weld-torch and tanks before scrambling down after them, sandwiched between the crisscrossed frame of the *Trossul's* superstructure and the sun heated patchwork of her hull. Jymn wondered, as he climbed, if people had been much smaller back when the ancient ship was built — or if they too used children like him for repairs. Or machines perhaps — they'd had machines that could do anything — there was probably a machine that would do his job, back in the old times.

Jymn always found Sixdeck eerie and unfamiliar when the engines were idle. It wasn't the stillness of the great crank — you could hardly make that out in the dim light of the lamps anyway. It wasn't even the smell — the place stank of oil and fuel just as bad even now — it was the quiet. Right now Jymn could hear barked orders on Fithdeck above, and boots scurrying to obey. He could

17

hear the spanking of air trapped in the soil pipes that pumped the crew's waste out to sea. Even the rhythmic chanting of Par Carrek, blessing the ship against contamination from the many tecks and heresies of Gradlon. With the *Trossul* underway, he'd have heard nothing. Nothing but the endless howl of the engines as they shunted the great hulk through the water, day after day, between ports. The din was so loud, so unrelenting, that Jymn and the other boys that bunked down here with the engine would be forced to go days without speaking. Sometimes it got so bad Jymn couldn't even *remember* his own voice, nor even conjure its sound in his mind. But today the engines were off. Today he could hear.

Footsteps. Behind.

'Hatcher! Done already?' — the voice was falsely kind, oily. Myke.

Jymn turned to see the older boy swaggering towards him, his searching eyes giving lie to the wide smile he wore.

'Done? No I'm heading back up, just came to change tanks,' Jymn lied. It had been a few days since he'd had cause to use his voice, and it cracked a little as he spoke.

'No tussle, no tussle,' Myke smiled, spreading his hands innocently and signing the words as he spoke them, out of habit, 'just need a swap, that's all.'

Jymn turned to his rack, hoisting his tools onto his appointed stash-hook. 'No swaps, Myke, remember. My gear's all marked, anyway.' Being the smallest boy in the enginer's bay, he'd taken great pains to etch patterns into all his posessions, specifically so this sort of thing wouldn't happen.

Jymn flinched as Myke's fist slammed into the rack, gripping a charred weld-torch.

'You'll just have to mark this piece of *zhū-shǐ* too then, won't you…' he reached forward and flicked the lens of Jymn's eyeglass, hard. '…Squint.'

Jymn's good eye darted to the torch. The mixer valve was janky — he could see the soot and scorch marks all around the base of the grip. Getting caught with broke kit was a month extra, minimum — and that's if you managed to keep on top of your work — but

18

he could fix it. And Myke knew it.

'Okay, Myke, sure,' he sighed, 'no tussle.'

Myke was already unhooking Jymn's good torch from the stash. 'Yeah, that's what I thought. Good lad, Squint,' he thrust the bad torch into Jymn's chest and swaggered off towards his bunk.

Jymn sagged against his rack and forced his breathing back under control, wiping sweaty palms on his scorched leather bib. His mind raced with a dozen things he should have said to Myke, things he *could* have said, if he were older, or stronger.

He looked at the janked torch with a sigh. It wasn't too bad, he could fix it up top while he got some air.

Scrambling up into his bunk-hole Jymn retrieved the small roll of tools he kept in a stash beside his pillow. Makket squeaked excitedly when he heard the disturbance, sniffing the air and scratching at the glass of his makeshift cage.

Pulling the bunk curtain shut behind him, Jymn lifted the old rat out of his little nook and scratched at his neck. 'Sorry Mak — no dinner yet — I'll be back later, I promise.' But his words did no good, of course, and the greying rodent continued to sniff around excitedly, searching for the treat that wasn't there.

'Okay, okay! Tell you what — how about some fresh air? But you'll have to be quiet or you'll end up back in the bilge!'

He tucked Makket carefully behind his leather bib, and swung back down from his bunk-hole, clutching the tools and broken torch. There were a half-dozen open routes to Topdeck from here, and a dozen more that only he and the other enginers knew — climb-paths in the superstructure, or shortcuts through unpatched holes in the internal walls. Jymn always preferred to stay out of sight — his deformed eye and small stature made him an easy target for the rest of the crew — and the last thing he needed was the Bo'sun figuring out he could finish a day's work early.

The first time he'd finished up before the claxon — way back when he was first learning the trade — he'd rushed off proudly to find the Bo'sun and tell him. Jymn cringed at the memory. Not only had his workload almost doubled, but so had the workload for half the boys on Six. He'd almost gone unnoticed until then, even with the disfigured blue eye, but no longer. He'd suffered beatings for almost a month after that, and extra if one of the boys couldn't keep up and got beaten himself by the Bo'sun.

He'd learned a hard lesson that day, and so — even as the various tricks and skills of the trade had revealed themselves to him, improving his craft — he made sure to never again be caught on deck afore the end of a shift.

But today was an exception today there was something to see — Gradlon.

He'd seen it only twice before. The first time he'd only glimpsed the island's walls through a wide hole in the hull he was fixing, but then last year he'd managed to hide up on Topdeck and see beyond the seawall and into the compound itself.

What he'd seen had taken his breath away. Life, as close as it came to the old times. People living — healthy and happy — away from the pains of the broken world. There were plants everywhere, and children eating from them — just pulling fat red spheres from the trees and eating them raw! The people of Gradlon smiled, and were pale, and dressed in loose clothes — not haggard, sun-cooked, and desperate like the ragged folk everywhere else.

And the teck — they didn't even try to hide it — there was teck just out in the streets. And not just scraps. Jymn had once seen a wealthy passenger sneak down to Sixdeck to use a cobbled device no larger than a bowl of rice, but here… he remembered there was one piece — a great jagged, black panel mounted to a courtyard wall — that was taller than three men! He'd never seen it do anything, but the whispers were that at night it would light up and show bright pictures that could move around by themselves. Jymn only half believed the rumours, but it sounded magical nonetheless.

With his heart beginning to race with excitement, even at the memory, Jymn planned his route up top. He needed to avoid the other enginer kids, and the Bo'sun, and especially the ship's Cleric. Par Carrek would whip him for a week if he were caught looking at teck. So — he'd climb to Four, then scurry down the starboard side of the hold and take a ladder to Twodeck. Along to the bows, and then through a rust-hole and up to the top from there. That spot should be deserted while the ship was moored, and would likely give him the best view.

He wasn't wrong. The sun was low in the sky when he reached his perch, and the grey-walled compound beneath him was bathed in orange light that rendered it breathtaking in its majesty. Jymn closed his eyes for a moment. The wind was blowing out of the west, and carrying the smells of Gradlon up to him — he smelled the plants on the sea air, and cooking. Real food. He didn't know what it was, but his stomach growled all the same. Makket smelled it too, and started to scrabble at his confines. Jymn pulled him gently from beneath the bib, and set him down on the deck next to him.

'Smells good, huh?' He asked as he scratched at his rat's fur. 'One day maybe. Two more years and we'll be all paid-up, and then we can start saving for a real meal. Think you can last that long, Mak?'

Jymn had pulled Makket out of the bilge when he was just a runt — near-on eighteen months ago now — and he already seemed like an elderly rat, his movements slow, and his brown fur shot through with bristly grey hairs. Jymn wasn't sure he had two more years in him — their diet of nothing but salt-rice was supposedly enough to keep you alive and well, but there was a reason rich folk supplemented it with other food when they could get it.

Jymn loosened the string of his eyeglass and worked it free, huffing warm air onto the lens and cleaning it on the hem of his shirt. Without the protection of the glass the warm salt air made his bad eye weep and sting, but he carried on. He wanted the lens good as new. He wanted to see everything.

Gradlon was even more majestic than he remembered. The island was a full two clicks around — it would take half an hour to walk the sea wall — and yet it seemed only about fifty people lived there. And most of those were servants or security, most of the space was reserved for Leer — the rich-keep whose kingdom this was — and his family. Jymn thought about his own bunk-hole — barely big enough to stretch out or sit up in.

As he stared out over the compound below, his hands worked nimbly at the broken weld-torch. He still remembered – back when he was first taken on — how the gear all seemed so complicated and frightening, how he thought he'd never understand it. But now. Well, now it was as easy as breathing. He found the source of the blockage — some flux-crud that had made it into the methane valve. He pulled a pick from his tool-roll and stripped the valve down. He'd need to make up a new gasket with scraps from his bunk   but it was an easy enough fix. Sometimes it would frighten the other boys, seeing him fix things so easy. They'd make the sign of the cross and sometimes tell the Par, who would beat him some. But it wasn't teck, just gear — no heresy — so he could only be punished so bad. If it was teck, he'd have been flogged, or worse.

Leer and Gradlon were above such concerns, of course. The teck here was out in the open, for all to see, and the Church could do nothing about it but stew in their righteous anger and hope that his shielding failed, and the teck called down destruction upon them for their sins. But of course, the shielding in Gradlon was second to none. Jymn marvelled at the elegant cages of pure copper — you would almost mistake them for handsome display cases, or protection for the ancient relics. Armour to stop things getting in, rather than their true purpose — to stop the trace getting out. Out here in the open sea there were Raptions — hungry machine creatures — listening for any sign of the ancient teck, and even Leer and all the might of Gradlon would be powerless against them.

Jymn shuddered at the thought and crossed himself. Teck fascinated him, but not as powerfully as the thought of the metal monsters terrified him. He'd have thought they were just another story made up by the Par, but he knew the way grown men crossed themselves whenever they saw the water move uncannily. And besides, there wouldn't be so much shielding at Gradlon if it was all just part of some hokey superstition. The rich were beyond such things.

He saw some women laughing together as they strolled across the courtyard below, eating the round, colourful fruits that grew here on the carefully tended trees. It wasn't often he saw women

— they brought the badluck onto a ship something terrible — but whenever he did he couldn't help but think of his mother back in Razeen. He only had the one memory: her lifting him onto a ship, full of worry and fear. But her face was always changing — a collage of features from his imagination and those he borrowed from the women he'd glimpsed on shore. Perhaps she looked like these women once, beautiful and carefree. And happy.

No. These women wouldn't have a child like him — with a deformity. Their genes would have been fixed by a splicer generations back. And they would never have to make decisions like she had — to give your child up to a rescue ship. To burn your whole crop when the rice-blight came. They were safe here, protected.

He noticed one of the guards patrolling the wall near the seagate where the Trossul was moored. He was dressed all in white, in loose, but well fitting clothes. He smiled and joked with the Trossul's crew as they hauled the great steel containers back to the ship, now emptied of the precious nitrammite fertiliser. A weapon hung from a sling across his chest — it looked like one of the guns the deck crew carried when they were in bad waters, only this one wasn't cobbled together from scrap — this was real, a relic from the old-times, like so much in Gradlon. Jymn wondered how much it was worth, wondered how anyone could amass so much wealth that he could afford to hand out relics like that to his crew, rather than keeping them locked away in a vault.

He tried to imagine himself atop that wall. Wearing those clothes, carrying that relic. He'd get good food to eat at night, and probably have friends, too. Folks liked people like that — confident and in control — he could see it on the faces of the crew. He wondered if he'd have to bravely defend the walls against pirates, and save the day, just like in the stories.

But how could you get a job like that? First he'd have to work off his debt here — another two years at least. Then he'd start getting a wage, and if he saved up enough, he could transfer to another workship. There were better ships, working safer seas with less pirates and calmer water. He'd heard that working on the HuoZhen Fleet or the Smitt Line 'prentice enginers got a weekly ration of meat *and* two days shore leave once a month! With money saved, and shore leave, he could try to get a job on land, away from the constant din of engines and the confined spaces. He was thirteen now — if his counting was right — so by the time he was seventeen — if he kept out of trouble — he could be on land. He could have a *home*. There, he'd be free to roam around in his off-time. Free to find people like him. Friends.

His eyeglass started to fog up as the air began to chill. He should head back to Sixdeck ready for the claxon, and feed time.

He scooped up Makket and stood, stretching his stiff legs. People were beginning to congregate in Gradlon's central courtyard below. He saw a man move among them — drawing their attention as he went as if by some invisible force — and decided that it must be Leer, the man whose uncountable wealth funded this oasis.

The group were gathered around the huge, shielded black panel — the jagged shard of salvaged teck that was rumoured to conjure pictures that moved. Jymn peered around the deck. There were crew starting to filter back up from below already, but it was drawing dark, nobody would see him if he kept still and waited.

He found himself holding his breath. It was almost dark enough now, and there was a chill in the air. Makket fidgeted impatiently in his grip, but Jymn absent-mindedly stroked him calm. A robed tecksmith appeared from a hatch near the panel, brandishing a small box with a long trailing wire. He pushed a button.

There were murmurs of appreciation from below as the darkening courtyard burst into light. Jymn gasped. Even from up here he felt his bad eye ache at the power of the teck-light. There were colours he'd never imagined — squares and rectangles of vibrant green and blue and red and white — and vivid in-between colours he didn't know the names for. He felt his eyes begin to sting and water, but he didn't blink. The pattern gave way to a picture — more detailed than he'd have thought possible — of a huge smiling woman surrounded by sunlit grass and trees. She was more beautiful than Jymn had thought possible.

Then the picture moved. Jymn's mind swayed as it struggled to process what he was seeing. The woman laughed, then turned and ran — very slowly — *into* the panel, but somehow was still right there, on its surface. She turned back to the crowd, and an arm appeared holding a glass bottle towards her. She took the bottle and drank from it slowly, still smiling. The liquid looked dark — like engine oil — but somehow also cool and refreshing. The woman wiped her mouth and beamed at the crowd with pearl-white teeth. The screen turned to red, shot through with white, and the onlookers applauded gleefully. Jymn blinked at last, his mind catching up, eager to see more.

He swayed again and this time fell forward, catching himself on the rusted railing. Gradlon began to drift slowly away and to the right. It took him a moment to process.

The ship was moving. He'd stayed too long. He'd be caught.

Rushing back down with all haste, Jymn abandoned his former route in favour of the most direct path. Being seen wasn't the pressing problem now. If the engines were running, that meant he'd long missed the claxon, and trouble was waiting for him down on Six.

He heard the roar of the great engines before he even made it below. By the time he reached Threedeck it was overpowering, and by the time he hit Fithdeck, it was all he could hear. The noise always made him nauseous at first — but after a day or two he'd adjust.

When he reached the engine bay on Six the stash-hooks and gear-racks were already full, but the other boys were nowhere to be seen. Feed time. Jymn cursed under his breath, barely able to hear his own voice above the engines.

Dashing to his bunk-hole, Jymn replaced the tool roll, and carefully dropped Makket back into his nook. If he could get to the back of the line without being noticed, he might have a chance at slipping under the Bo'sun's nose — he was probably distracted with all the cargo changes anyway.

Jymn dropped back to the deck, spun to return the damaged weld-torch, and gasped involuntarily in shock.

Sneaking about after claxon?

The Bo'sun was leaning against the gear-rack, half stooped as always down here. His bristled, sun-dried face contorted back and forth as he chewed a length of rubber medicable. He had to use hand-sign, of course — it was far too loud now for speaking, you would simply shout yourself hoarse.

Not sneaking. It took a long time to climb down today. Jymn replied, tucking the broken torch under his arm to free his hands.

Lie. Your tanks and regs were here already. The Bo'sun's gestures were aggressive, cutting. He'd never been able to sign as effortlessly as those that learned young like Jymn and the other boys of Sixdeck, for whom there was no alternative amidst the roar of the engines. Nobody remembered who taught it to them first, each generation of kids just passed it onto the next.

My torch jammed. I stashed the tanks and went to find better light to fix it. Jymn signed, brandishing the half-fixed torch as evidence.

The Bo'sun snatched the tool from him and inspected it, sniffing at the scorched plastic of the grip. He jabbed a finger at it, and then at Jymn, making the crude sign for questioning: *This yours?*

Fixed now — no problem. I finished all my work.

The Bo'sun eyed him suspiciously, chewing the lix-infused cable that stained his teeth oily-brown, and scratching at the beginnings of a sunpox lesion on his neck. He thrust the torch back at Jymn. *Prove it then.*

Taken aback, Jymn stepped past the Bo'sun and pulled the lines from his tanks, trying to stop his hands from trembling as he attached the torch, hoping the damaged gasket would hold out.

The Bo'sun's copper beater clanged against the gear-rack, forcing Jymn to turn back.

Not here. There are strut-welds to do on Three. Port sides. Braces three to twenty-eight.

Jymn couldn't quite keep the outrage from his face. *That's a whole day's work!*

Yes, you are right. Perhaps we add it to your debt instead. He pulled his ledger from his vest-pocket, and fished a pencil from behind an ear.

Okay — okay — I'll do it. Jymn interrupted, waving his hands over the ledger. *You said three to twenty-eight?*

The Bo'sun closed the ledger and snarled his oily-brown smile. *I said three to thirty-two.*

Jymn swallowed the indignant anger that swelled in his throat, and hoisted his gear from the stash-hook. Better to work now, than pay for it later. *Every day aboard is two days off your life.*

———————————

The old gasket held out for almost two hours, after that it took all his focus to avoid the spouts of flame that would spit from the valve with no warning. By the time Jymn dragged his tanks back to the gear-rack, he was exhausted, dizzy with hunger, and wore a half dozen fresh burns across his forearms. It was full-dark now, the cabin lights were doused for the night and would not be relit until the dawn claxon in a few hours time.

Food. Ditching his gear against the rack, he felt his way in the dark to the ration room. The smell of boiled salt-rice made his stomach growl like an angry dog, and he found himself groping around in the blackness — scooping mouthfuls of pot-stuck rice from the bottom of the great pans. It was cold, thick, and burnt, but it was food, and after a while he felt his hands stop trembling. He drank some of the pot water, and pocketed a small ball of the rice-scrapings for later.

He collapsed into his bunk, without even the energy to stash his gear back into the rack. Only Makket's squealing and scrabbling kept him from falling unconscious right where he dropped.

'Sorry boy' he muttered, knowing full well the rat couldn't hear him over the unceasing roar of the engines 'I didn't forget you, just had some more work to do. Here'

Fishing him from the small nook, Jymn set Makket down next to the ball of salt-rice, pulled the bunk curtain closed and hung his eyepiece on its hook beside his pillow. He pulled a scrap of stolen medicable from his stash nook and placed it under his tongue. The lix would help with the pain. He closed his eyes.

Laying there, motoring across the ocean while the old rat licked at his wounds, Jymn Hatcher fell into a deep, dreamless sleep, utterly unaware of what awaited him with the dawn tide.

II

The Dawn Tide

Jymn sprung from sleep to wakefulness in a heartbeat as the world lurched to one side. Instinctively his hand shot out and caught the edge of his bunk-hole before he could topple out to the decking below.

The ship was turning. Hard.

He pulled back the curtain, blinking the grogginess from his eyes. A handful of the oil-lamps had been lit, but the place was empty. He felt the thick tar of medicable on his swollen tongue. The lix-sleep must have made him miss the dawn claxon, but why hadn't he been dragged from his bunk and flogged for oversleeping?

He felt a scratching at his elbow, and found Makket there, anxious for reassurance. Jymn fished the last few grains of salt-rice from his pocket and laid them down for his pet. 'It's ok Mak, you stay here, alright. I'll be right back, I promise'

Sliding down from his bunk-hole, Jymn set his feet unsteadily on the deck. The ship lurched again, turning hard the other way, and forcing him to leap over his unstashed tanks as they rolled across the floor, slamming heavily into the bulkhead. He couldn't hear the impact over the scream of the engines, but he felt it through his feet.

The ship turning that hard once could be explained — maybe a chart-looker made a mistake and was now being flogged while their course was corrected. But *two* turns?

Jymn stood alone in the enginer's bay, unsure of what to do.

Suddenly aware of his exposed eye, he retrieved his eyeglass from its stash-hook and headed cautiously for the stair to Fithdeck.

The light on Fithdeck was scattered and broken by the thousand low pipes and chains that carried heat, fuel, and gearing power to the rest of the ship. Jymn peered around for someone. There was always somebody on watch here — monitoring the various gauges and temperatures, Usually enginers would get a cuffed ear for talking to a crewman, especially while he was working, but that was a small risk to take. He silently prayed that he found a crewman that knew hand-sign — not many of them did — but if they had regular shifts down on Fith they'd probably know at least *some*. It was too loud down here to *think* clearly, let alone speak.

He spotted a silhouette up ahead and ducked under a broad pipe to head towards it — almost tripping over something in the process. Catching himself before he fell, Jymn saw the outline of the obstacle — a foot.

The Bo'sun lay sprawled across the decking, face down and still, a pool of oily-brown lix-spittle flowing slowly from his slack jaw. His copper beater rolled around nearby with the swaying of the ship. Jymn moved towards his master's head and felt for a beat in the leathery neck — there it was — he wasn't dead then, just out cold. There was blood on his cowl — perhaps he'd fallen when the ship lurched. Jymn's brain caught up with his situation — he needed to find help, fast, lest he was discovered like this and assumed guilty.

A movement caught his eye, a figure crouched behind a standpipe across from the body. Another enginer kid — Myke.

Jymn signed to the older boy — *What's happening — was this you?*

Myke shook his head slowly, wearing a grim expression. He raised a hand to his face, covering one eye, in a sign that Jymn only knew from the stories…

Pirates.

Jymn's blood turned to ice in his veins. His lix-swollen tongue felt suddenly dry, and would not let him swallow. Pirates would kill them all… or take them as slaves… or set them adrift on the sea toward starvation and madness.

Myke reached from his hide and snatched the heavy copper beater from the floor as it rolled towards him. Then, sneaking a last look above the standpipe, he disappeared in the direction of the silhouette.

Jymn crept over the Bo'sun's body and hurried after Myke, his palms sweating. The older boy whirled around wild-eyed, the beater raised to strike, only just stopping himself from dashing it into Jymn's skull. *What are you doing?!* he demanded.

Jymn moved his hands apart and then together, and added the sign for questioning. *We should stick together?*

Myke shook his head. *You should hide — leave this to the full-growns.* And with that, he slipped away.

Jymn did as he was told. For what felt like an eternity he crouched — frozen still — behind the standpipe, straining hopelessly for any sound from above. Eventually his imagination and curiosity got the better of him — he had to at least *see* what was happening — and who better to move through the ship unseen than an enginer?

Stealing back down to Six, Jymn collected his rope and hooks, and headed for a port-side access panel. There were few better hiding places than the narrow cavity between the superstructure and the hull, and there were unpatched holes aplenty that he could use to spy on the action.

The climb up was interrupted by the engines giving out. Whether deliberate, or by sabotage, the Trossul was no longer under power, and with the departure of the power, so returned Jymn's hearing. He heard the unmistakable crack of gunfire from somewhere above, and a grinding against the outside of the hull — just inches from where he hid.

Careful now not to give himself away by the noise of his climbing — Jymn continued upwards towards an unpatched hole in the hull no larger than his own head. Magflies buzzed hungrily around the lip of the opening, gnawing and widening it a mouthful at a time. Jymn swatted them away with a whip of his rope, and settled himself against the superstructure.

It took a moment for his good eye to adjust to the bright sunlight streaming through the hole, and a moment longer for his bad eye to catch up, but soon he was able to cautiously bring his face to the jagged hole and peer out.

Great ropes were laid against the hull, reaching up further than he could see. Craning his head downward, he saw their anchorage: a boat barely one fifth the size of the Trossul, with a half dozen such ropes clinging to the sides and top of the larger ship, like an octopus grappling a larger prey. The ship was queerly made: she had huge white sails for power — odd enough — but stranger still she seemed to be made almost entirely of wood. Jymn squinted at the peculiar vessel, discerning the figures of pirates on her deck, dashing between cover as gunfire rained down overhead.

There was a yell from above and a terrible scraping sound, then a great mass of scrap metal plummeted from the Trossul, hitting its mark and smashing into the wooden pirate ship below, tearing sails and snapping ropes as it went. There was a great cheer from the crew above, as the pirates below leaped to secure the broken lines.

Jymn froze as he heard movement directly above him. Stealing a glance upwards, he saw boots stepping across the superstructure through a larger hole in the hull. Boarders. Jymn's mind raced — he was level with Threedeck, so the pirates were coming aboard on Two, right beneath the fighting on Topdeck.

He had to find a master — or even just a crewman — they'd know what to do.

Jymn mapped the scene in his mind — from here the quickest route out of the hull-cavity and into the ship proper was through the large rust-hole directly above him. But that was no good — the boarding pirates would surely be watching their backs, guarding their escape. But there were many other holes on Two. Repairing the damage inflicted by the swarms of hungry magflies was a constant battle — but the lower decks were always the priority, being that much closer to the water, up here there were holes aplenty.

Jymn hurried towards the bow of the ship, climbing nimbly

between the steel struts of the superstructure. There, above him, familiar rays of daylight speared through the hull — old bullet holes now widened by magflies — and opposite, the air intake he'd repaired a few months back.

He climbed up, inspecting the grating around the air-duct. Just as he'd remembered — a shoddy bit of welding by one of the other boys — right next to a damaged section of the hull. Magflies had made short work of the thin metal, which was now barely hanging in place. Jymn peered through to Twodeck, checking the coast was clear, then braced himself against a strut and kicked against the damaged grate, tearing through it like cloth.

Scurrying through, Jymn found Twodeck deserted. The oil-light up here was augmented by shafts of daylight filtering down from Topdeck along with the sound of footsteps, gunshots, and the cries of battle.

Jymn rarely spent time on Two — it was mostly accommodation for the masters — and when he did, it was best to stay out of the way. Today he needed to find someone, though it went against the instinct of many years on board. He pulled open the first few dorms and found them empty, some immaculate, some clearly evacuated in a hurry.

Then — bathed in a pool of light from above — a body. A wiry crewman sprawled across the deck at an awkward angle. Jymn crept closer and felt for a beat — it was weak, but there. His skull had been cracked by a bloody stone lying nearby. Jymn tried again to swallow, but found his tongue still refused.

Suddenly a hand clamped across Jymn's mouth, dragging him back into the gloom. Panicked, he lashed out, and bit down hard. His attacker cried out, dropped him, and struck him across the face with the back of a hand. Jymn fell hard to the deck and felt the lens of his eyeglass shatter beneath him. He whirled around, his head reeling from the blow. Par Carrek stood over him, his image broken and refracted through the shattered lens. He reached down once more, and Jymn braced for the punishing blow — but it never came. Instead, Jymn found himself dragged into a dark dorm, and felt the hot stale breath of the Par on his face.

'Heretics — they're here, on this deck!' He rasped, an inch from Jymn's cheek.

Jymn squirmed away from the old man 'I know, Par. I came up to tell someone but th-' Jymn was hushed by a thick finger pressed to his lips.

'What's your name?' Rasped the Par.

'My name… Jymn. Jymn Hatcher, Par.' He answered, a little off guard. He'd been on the Trossul now eight years, and couldn't remember ever saying his own name aloud.

'Go above Jymn — you must tell them we're down here. If they take the ship we'll all be killed! Find someone.'

And with that, the old Par thrust him from the dorm, pulling the bulkhead door shut between them.

Jymn steadied himself against the wall, squinting through the broken lens that split each shaft of daylight into three. His cheek burned from the Par's blow, but now — *now* he had a task. The old priest had charged him with saving the ship from the pirates, just like in the stories.

Summoning his courage, Jymn crept towards the broad Topdeck stair, slinking from one hide to the next along the way. The sounds of gunfire were loudest here, and as he drew near he saw the figures of two armed men in the oily-grey overalls that marked them as the Trossul's own crew. They were crouched almost to their bellies at the top of the stair, and were firing out across Topdeck from behind the scant cover it provided.

But before Jymn could sprint up the broad steps and warn them of the danger below, a movement in the darkness beyond the staircase froze him. A heavy-set bearded man was creeping towards the defenders from below. His face was hidden by a deep hood, but his thick tattooed arms were bare, and he carried a heavy beater in one hand. His gait was lopsided as he crept — Jymn had to stifle a gasp as he saw the man's right leg was missing from the knee-down — a bright copper prosthetic taking its place.

The pirate nodded across the foot of the stairwell, and Jymn followed his gaze to another figure lurking in the darkness — a woman this time. Young — barely older than Myke — and handsome. She had a dull purple sash bound around her left arm, and carried a tall staff in her right. Peering up at the Trossul's defenders upon the stair, she reached into a satchel and withdrew a smooth stone, couching it in a strip of fabric at the top of her staff.

Jymn's mind raced. He couldn't catch the crewmen's eyes from down here, their attention was fixed firmly on the fighting above. And even if he could, they were Topdeckers — they wouldn't know the hand-sign to read his silent warning. And he couldn't reach the stair — not without running *between* the approaching pirates. But he had to do *something...*

Before he could make up his mind there was a cry of pain, and one of the two defenders was thrown backwards down the stair, to crumple in a twitching heap. A spear protruded from his chest, capped in a fat cylinder which spat bright sparks of blue light. Jymn's eyes widened and he felt his jaw grow slack — *teck.* The pirates had teck.

The woman-pirate — still hidden — lowered her staff and began to swing the stone back and forth, her gaze still locked on the remaining crewman. Jymn's head swam with the accumulated lessons of a hundred stories. Brave heroes, defending their homes and ships from the scum of the sea. From heretic pirates. The stone began to spin faster.

Marshalling his nerve — Jymn darted forward from his hide toward the stair, screaming over the din of gunfire. 'Down here — they're down here! Pirates!'

Just in time the Trossul's remaining gunman threw himself to the side. The slung stone exploded against the steel stair where his head had been just a heartbeat before. He fell to his back and whirled the gun around, spraying a hail of fire down into the deck below. The two pirates dived for cover as bullets ricocheted all around, slamming into the body of the twitching crewman and sending sparks into the darkness. Jymn blinked, checking himself over — but he was miraculously unhurt.

As the smoke cleared, the gunman locked eyes with Jymn and for a moment looked like he might fire again — then, a blur from above — and from nowhere a third pirate appeared behind the man, pressing a crooked blade to his throat.

'That's enough — easy now.' This third pirate was young, only perhaps Jymn's age, but his voice was full of confidence and calm. 'Down she goes.'

'You'll... hang for this, you know that? Hang as murderers!' the crewman stammered, but a prod of the knife persuaded him to obey. He let the weapon clatter down the steps, and raised his hands.

A gruff voice came from the darkness at the foot of the stair 'Murderers, is it?'

Jymn turned to see the peg-legged man step into the light, yanking the spear free of the twitching body. The twitching stopped, leaving only a limp corpse, riddled with bullet wounds. 'It was you as killed your friend, fakwit.' He looked at Jymn for the first time, the spear-tip still arcing with the blue light of teck. 'And you, eh? Some sort of fakk hero? Could have got us all shot up!' He raised the arcing spear tip, and in the blue-white light Jymn saw that the beard was in fact not a beard at all — but a swirling tattoo across his lower face. The metal leg clanged against decking as he lurched forward, grinning cruelly.

Jymn backed away, then turned to run — to find somewhere to hide in the darkness, or...

'Oof!' — he slammed right into the sling-woman, immovable as a wall, and a full hand span taller than he was. She raised an eyebrow.

'Haha — shouldn't't'a made her miss, bro,' jeered the peg-legged pirate, now close behind him. 'Don't like to miss, do ya Daj?'

There was a brief flash of teck-light, and pain erupted in his back, spreading until it seized his whole body in an agonising rigor. He saw the copper peg-leg, and the floor close-up, and wondered how he got there. A heartbeat later, and he was swimming in blackness.

———————————

Daylight pierced the darkness as he woke — split three times

36

and refracted through the thick shattered lens of his eyeglass. Every muscle ached, and he felt the hot pang of the Par's blow swelling beneath his good eye. The burns on his forearms chafed painfully against a rough rope behind his back, and he realised he was bound. A fresh sea-breeze blew over him, free of the usual diesel tang. He blinked into the light, trying to process everything.

He was on Topdeck. There were other enginer kids kneeling nearby, also bound at the wrist. He saw Loklin and Buss, and a handful of others whose faces he couldn't make out. Myke lay nearby, still but awake, his left eye split and bloody. Instinctively Jymn tried to sign, but his hands were useless behind him.

Rolling to his back, he strained and tried to sit. Pain flared between his shoulder blades and he collapsed — remembering the sling-woman, the one-legged pirate, and the arcing blue-white light. That was it — he'd been struck with the teck-spear. Gritting his teeth against the pain he tried again, and managed eventually to struggle to his knees.

'Should've stayed down, Squint' whispered Buss, next to him. 'Might've left you alone, runt like you.'

'What's… what's going to happen?' Jymn rasped through a dry throat.

'The'll sell us, prob'ly. Kill those they can't.' Buss spat blood onto the ground, and indicated the high ship's railings above them 'They already threw the captain overboard.'

Jymn's palms began to sweat. So they *were* killers, just like the Par said. He scanned the deck, weighing the state of things.

The Pirates were clearly in charge now. Jymn saw the one-legged man strutting around a group of the senior crewmen, his heavy beater prodding them here and there. The man's hood was drawn back now, revealing more of the swirling tattoos that covered the lower half of his face. Not the face of a man — not quite — in fact he couldn't have been any older than Myke.

In fact, as Jymn looked around, not one of the pirates was full-grown. He saw again the knifeman that had appeared from nowhere, now turning out the pockets of the prisoners with a grin. A huge Eastner boy with bright, narrow eyes — thick arms crossed over a barrel chest — smiled and joked with the other pirates as they went about the business of sorting, searching, and binding the Trossul's crew.

A firm voice carried on the breeze. 'Found a cleric.'

Jymn turned to see the sling-woman emerging from below, even more striking now in the daylight. Daj, she had been called. She shoved Par Careck before her, moving confidently, and handling the old preacher with a ruthless, iron strength.

'He was hiding below.' She added, pointedly.

The Par bristled with indignation, but on seeing the state of things on deck, seemed to swallow his pride, and stayed put when he was shoved to his knees to be bound alongside the others. Jymn — filled with shame at having failed in the task set for him by the Par — tried not to meet his eye.

Daj whistled a low call at another pirate on the quarterdeck, before tossing one of the Trossul's rifles up to him. The boy that caught it was small and frail-looking, his skull thickly bandaged, though he appeared unhurt. He caught the weapon clumsily, then wound up and flung it well clear of the hull and into the water below. Jymn saw he had a pile of a dozen similar guns already at his feet.

Jymn pictured the captain being flung overboard — discarded like those guns — and tried not to think about what would happen to *him* if he was deemed too small, deformed, or runty to sell. He longed to adjust his lopsided, broken eyeglass — to appear more normal, strong — but with his hands bound he was helpless. He swallowed. Overboard. That was the worst way to go, for sure. None of the enginers could swim of course — swimming was forbidden. No surer way to keep your workers from escaping, than to have it so they couldn't make it to shore.

'Captain on deck!' called Daj, and — as one — the pirates stood to attention, as if jerked upright by unseen strings.

A boy with rusty red hair strode onto the quarterdeck above them, leading someone by a rope. He wore a short waistcoat over a ragged purple tunic, and looked to be unarmed, though he moved with a supple strength. This 'captain' couldn't have been any older than seventeen. In fact, Jymn wondered if there were any full-growns among them at all, and how they functioned without. The red-haired boy tugged the rope roughly, and Jymn saw at last the man at its other end — the Bo'sun — gritty and coarse, but defiant still.

'What are you to do with me then, scum?' barked the old master, spitting lix over the rail to the sea below.

'Nothing at all,' said the captain simply, removing the rope from the Bo'sun's neck and indicating the railing, and the short ledge beyond it, 'just stand yourself up there.'

'You must think me dim. You're angling to throw me overboard — you're a murderer.' The Bo'sun thrust his chin out. 'Well I won't make it no easier for you.'

'I'll do no such thing,' the young captain shook his head, 'you're going to throw yourself overboard, see.'

The Bo'sun laughed, but Jymn could hear the defiance in his voice begin to falter. 'Why in the Nine Floods would I do that?'

'Well, the alternative is that I let Daj count up every scar she finds on those boys,' the captain pointed down toward Jymn and the other captives. 'She started out with slavers, you know. You can imagine the sort of things she's seen. Not keen on your type.'

'We aren't slavers… this is a workship — the lads work a debt… look,' he fumbled in his pocket, withdrawing his ledger and blustering through the pages. 'Here — Myke — two hundred seventy-three days, err... Busslyn! Just eighty six days left! It's just what they owe, tha'sall!' He rapped a finger on the page, brandishing the ledger as if the case for his emancipation couldn't be simpler

The captain's temper flared for the briefest moment, and he snatched the tattered notebook from the Bo'sun's hand. 'You want to talk about debts owed? Ok…' he turned to look down at the deck, 'Daj, start counting.'

'Aye, Cap,' Daj nodded, striding toward Myke and kneeling. He resisted, at first, but her firm grip and hard stare soon warned him to keep himself still.

The Bo'sun watched in horror as she lifted his shirt, revealing a strong chest riddled with old burns. 'No no no — ok, ok,' he turned to the captain, 'what do you want?'

'I'm starting to think I want to see all those burns paid back. Eye for an eye, isn't that how it goes, Par?'

But Par Carrek kept his head down. Sensing his allies thinning the old Bo'sun began to clutch at the captain's tunic, his defiance all but forgotten. 'Come on, please — there must be something, anything,'

'Well…'

'Just tell me! What is it you want?'

'I always wanted to learn how to swim.'

'...what?'

'Never did learn, growing up. Bet you did though, eh? Different times, and all that.' The captain drew close to the Bo'sun — pointing out at the horizon, 'there's a rock out there — you see it? Just shy of six clicks, I'd say. Imagine being able to swim that far. Just to pick a spot on the horizon and get there all under your own power. So freeing. You'd like to be *free*, wouldn't you?'

The Bo'sun seemed to catch on, '...you're not serious?'

The captain called back over his shoulder, 'where are we at, Daj?'

'Twenty seven lashes,' She replied, now on her fourth subject. 'Eight burns, two broken noses. One lad claims he was given to the captain for the night…'

'Loklin!' the Bo'sun raged, then turned to the captain again, pleading, 'that's not true — it's not bloody true!'

'Of course not. Strange that you knew the lad's name though, without being told,' the captain mused.

'Oh God — oh God!' the Bo'sun wailed. Clutching the railing now, he began to weep, shaking his head against the injustice of it all. For all his cruelty, Jymn couldn't help but feel a pang of pity for the old bully — even now at his reckoning.

The captain patted him on the shoulder, 'come now, there is a way out of this, you know.'

The Bo'sun looked up, shaking his head 'It's a trick. You'll… you'll *shoot* me the minute I hit the water!'

'I will not. All your guns have been tossed over, and we don't carry them. I'm not fond. Clumsy, random things.'

'So… so I just have to swim?' the Bo'sun looked out at the water, a glimmer of hope in his eyes 'Truly? That's all?'

'That's all?' the captain laughed, 'it's six *clicks*, man, come on! But yes,' the young face hardened then, staring coldly at the old master, 'it's probably wiser than sticking around here and facing up to what you've done.'

The Bo'sun nodded, and seemed to summon his courage at last. The old back straightened, then all of a sudden he pulled off his bloody cowl and loosened his heavy belt, letting it clatter to the deck. Scrambling over the rail and out onto the narrow ledge he stopped to raise a leg and tug at a tired old boot.

'Wait!' called the captain — halting him. 'Probably want to keep your boots on. There's sharks, see? A good boot gives you a chance to kind of… *slip free*. The first time, anyway.'

The Bo'sun glanced down at the water, then back at the captain — fresh horror on his face 'Wait, there's…? But…'

And with that — the captain *shoved*. The old Bo'sun fell backwards with a scream, the boot still clutched in his hands. His howl of terror was cut short — punctuated by a splash of water far below. The other enginers gasped and stole looks at one another, fear in their eyes.

'Have courage boys,' the Par rasped, drawing himself up.

The pirate captain swung over the near-side of the rail and climbed nimbly down to the deck alongside Daj. He flicked through the ledger, reading names as he went 'Right — Myke, Buss, Loklin…' He flipped a dozen more pages. 'All of you. Listen up. Any of you that want no more of this — you make yourself known.'

Some of the boys glanced at one another, but none spoke. They all knew, from a young age, to expect this kind of trickery from pirates.

'Courage, boys!' called the Par again 'They are murderers. They have heretical tecks aboard, and females. This boy is Godless. You'll be found by the machines! Or sold as slaves!'

'They already *are* slaves, idiot', Daj thrust him back to his hands and knees with a sharp shove of her staff.

'Some would sell you, surely. But your preacher doesn't know me,' spoke the captain calmly, 'work for a time and — on my word — you'll be put ashore — if you wish,' He looked around at the boys for a response, but none came. Jymn stared at the floor. He desperately wanted to be ashore, but it was a terrible risk. Whatever this boy said, slavery *was* worse than what they had here. Here at least there was an end — they would pay off their debt and be free to work for coin.

'None of you?' The boy shook his head in astonishment. 'Truly you are the best kind of slaves'. He turned, and with a smooth, supple motion flung the ledger up past the quarterdeck and overboard.

He looked around for any hint of reconsiderance, but seeing none, turned to leave. 'Very well — may your next master be less cruel than the old Bo'sun.'

'Cap, Wait!'

As he turned, one of his companions called out and dashed over to whisper in his ear. This pirate was slender, his uncommonly kind face crowned with a purple bandana. He gestured down towards the queer wooden ship below, leading the captain to see. The captain strode to the grab-rail and peered down, then turned back to the captive enginers with a frown.

'Change of plan. It seems your lot damaged our shielding in the fight. Who among you is the best weld-maker?'

Jymn's chest constricted. He stared at the ground so hard he thought he might bore holes in the hull. He'd never worked on shielding, of course, but none of the other boys could weld as neatly or as fast as he could, and they knew it. In other circumstances they would never admit it, not in a thousand tides, but…

'Squint,' murmured a voice behind him.

'Yeah, Squint,' agreed Buss quickly, beside him. 'It's Squint,' nodded Myke. Soon there was a chorus of overlapping mumbled answers — 'Squint.' 'It's Squint,' — none of the boys meeting his eye, or that of the Captain.

'Well…?' growled the captain, 'which one of you is bloody sq… oh. I see.'

The captain crouched before Jymn and took his chin in a firm hand, guiding his gaze upwards. The face beneath the shock of rusty hair was stern — but still somehow childlike. Dark eyes seemed to take in every detail of Jymn's face, lingering on the eyeglass and the weeping blue eye beneath.

'You got Skand blood, lad?' he asked coldly, pulling a knife from his boot, tossing it, and catching it nimbly by the hilt.

Jymn shook his head emphatically, his mouth suddenly dry, his tongue slack for words.

The captain looked at Jymn's dark skin and hair, and seemed to accept this for true. 'Name?' he demanded, reaching around to cut Jymn's bonds.

'Jymn… Jymn Hatcher, sir.'

The captain grunted a laugh, and pulled Jymn to his feet — shoving him toward the wily young pirate with the crooked knife.

'North - take *Jymn Hatcher sir* to the Archon.'

III

The Archon

'What's with the smikken eye then, you spliced or something?'

The young pirate with the crooked knife had been put in charge of making sure Jymn didn't 'try anything funny' while they finished up business on the Trossul. He'd introduced himself simply as 'North' — which was no kind of name Jymn had ever heard before.

Jymn looked around nervously at the rest of the Trossul's crew, still bound and kneeling nearby.

'Hey — don't need to worry about them any more. Won't be your problem soon.'

Jymn touched his shattered eyeglass nervously. 'It's not a splice — just a bad eye. I was born with it.'

North shrugged. 'It happens. Half the crew here are spliced, some ways back. You see Gam there?'

He indicated the frail looking boy with the bandaged skull, who waved awkwardly back at North from the far end of Topdeck.

'He can hear everything we say, all the way over there. Got some monkey blood there. Gets in his head sometimes. Great lookout though.'

Jymn wondered what it would be like — to have hearing that sensitive — they must have heard the Trossul coming from clicks away.

'What about... *him*?' Jymn asked, indicating the stairway. The one-legged tattooed boy had been sent down to Six to fetch up Jymn's welding gear, grumbling as he went.

'Caber? Him, no. That's all natural, home grown, rice-fed bad attitude, there. Though I wouldn't be surprised if it came out he had some Donkey in him.' he chuckled.

Jymn heard Gam blurt out a laugh from the far side of the deck. North smiled.

There was a grunt below, and one of Jymn's tanks flew out of the stairwell, clattering heavily on the deck between them.

'Whoa — calm it down, Ass-face!' cried North, leaping away from the rolling tank.

Caber came grunting up the stair, with a half dozen weld tanks gripped in his thick arms — letting them all clatter to the deck at his foot. 'Get the ones with the swirling pattern he says.' Caber panted, his hands on his knees. 'They've all got fakk patterns on them, eh?' He looked up at North, breathlessly 'Hey, what'd you call me, bro?'

Jymn pulled his old pattern marked weld torch from the pile of gear, stealing a guilty glance back at Myke. 'What about the rat, you found the rat, right? Makket?'

'Yeah — you didn't tell me it was still alive, though — little 'theek bit me!' He sucked on a finger. 'You did a good job fattening him up, but catchin' and slaughterin's worth some too. Here, I'll split it with you.'

Caber pulled a handful of limp fur from his belt and held it out towards Jymn. Makket. Dead.

Jymn felt all the colour drain from his face, and his knees began to buckle. A heartbeat — and then he was charging at Caber, slapping at his bald head.

'Whoah — what the fakk…' Caber stepped backward over the pile of tanks, his copper peg-leg clanging and slipping, and he fell heavily to the deck, arms raised against Jymn's blows.

Roaring, Caber flung Jymn backwards. Pain exploded again in Jymn's back, and he found himself unable to breathe as Caber clambered awkwardly to his foot, glaring at the other pirates who were now laughing all around. Snatching up one of the weld-tanks in a fury, he stepped over Jymn and raised it high.

'Hey — how far do you think we'll get exactly with no shielding?' Spoke a calm voice.

Caber stopped, the tank still raised above his head. 'He started it — and it's an eye for an eye Slip — articles say so, don't they?'

Jymn twisted, and saw the slender, kindly looking boy with the bandana, hands on his hips. 'Aye — and it'd be you gave him that dirty great hole in his back, would it not?'

Caber hesitated 'That's different, that was battle, this is tussle,'

'Battle was it? A great lump like you sticking a scrap like him in the back? Maybe North can write a song about it, eh North?'

'Sure thing Slip,' Grinned North 'I've got some new metaphors I've been saving up.'

'Ugh' groaned Caber, dropping the tank back to the deck angrily. He kicked Makket's body at Jymn's chest with his metal foot. 'Here — I hope you choke.' And with that, he stomped away.

'Jymn, is it?' asked the kindly boy they'd called Slip 'I need you to come with me.'

Jymn cradled Makket's limp body in trembling hands. The old rat looked peaceful, almost as if he was sleeping. But it was clear his neck had been broken. Jymn had promised he'd come back for him, and instead had sent that awful brute to kill him.

He felt Slip hover over his shoulder. 'Captain don't like to be kept waiting, Jymn.'

Jymn nodded, and curled Makket up gently on the deck, wiping his eyes on his sleeve as he stood. Slip smiled sadly at him, before motioning for him to follow. He led the way across Topdeck to the great open cargo bay that dropped two floors into the belly of the ship. The captain stood with the huge, barrel-chested Eastner boy, who was pointing down into the hold.

'We've got a ton of plastics and some scrap metals. Some of the lads claimed weapons as first spoils. But no sign of any nitre.'

The Captain cursed. 'You're sure?'

'We opened everything in the hold. Could be she's got stash-lockers — but it'll take a day or two to search. She's a big lass.'

Cap shook his head 'No, this one's too fat for smuggling tricks. You —' he turned to Jymn, 'What do you know about the cargo?'

'I'm just an enginer… I don't really...'

'There was supposed to be four-hundred square of nitramite on board. Fertiliser. Crop food. You know anything about that?'

'Fertiliser — yeah, that's what we took to Gradlon.'

The Captain swore again, long and loud.

Slip spoke next 'When did you leave Gradlon, lad?'

'Sundown yesterday.' Jymn checked the sun to orient himself and pointed 'It's that way, maybe three-hundred clicks?'

'I know where it is!' snapped Cap. He kicked one of the weld-tanks hard. It looked like it hurt his foot more than he let on. 'Fakk Tsar! That pox-ridden son-of-a-pig-eating… *bastard*.'

'Pig-eating bastard,' repeated Slip thoughtfully. 'It's not your best Cap, but it's got a certain rhythm, for sure.'

'Finish up.' The captain instructed Slip, before turning angrily back to Jymn 'You — stash your gear, we're gone,' and with that, he whirled away in a rage.

Slip (he introduced himself as 'Wil Slippener') helped Jymn heft two full sets of weld-tanks and a spare torch, and together they dragged them to a pallet that was being loaded with gear and injured pirates to be winched over the gunwales and down to the wooden ship below. Despite his slender frame and kindly manner, the other pirates took orders from Slip without question, and set about their tasks with casual efficiency.

As the last of the gear was loaded and secured, Jymn heard a long, musical whistle from the top of the quarterdeck and turned to see Cap perched there, staring down at the bound crew of the Trossul.

'Listen. We are finished here. You must know we could have killed you, or taken some as slaves,' he called, his voice cold, and commanding. 'Trade no more with Gradlon and the other rich-keeps, or next time we will not be so gentle-handed. There's other folk that will buy from you. Folk who need it more.'

47

He looked around at the prisoners, giving his words time to sink in.

'Now. Tecks have been used here, unshielded. Be underway with haste. And do not follow us — or next time we'll hole you and leave you to the fish.'

With that the Captain climbed the railing and threw himself clear of the ship. Jymn rushed to the grab-rail and gasped as he saw Cap fly through the air — headfirst — splashing into the water between the two vessels, fifty feet below. As Jymn stared open-mouthed, there were jubilant calls and battle-cries to his left and right, and a dozen other pirates leaped from the ship — some headfirst, some feet-first — some elegant, some chaotic — but all slamming gaily into the water below, laughing and calling as they swam back to the queer wooden ship. Jymn's palms were slick with sweat, his knees weak at the very idea of plunging into the water. Of drowning.

Jymn turned to Slip, aghast, and found him chuckling and shaking his head.

'But… the sharks?'

Slip laughed, 'There *are* no sharks, lad — come on. Shark-infested waters?' He chuckled again at the notion, and yanked a lever on a mechanical winch. The platform jerked into motion, lifting up from the Trossul's deck and then slowly down and away. Jymn saw, arrayed, the sour faces of the Trossul's crew, the Par, and the other enginer kids who had sold him out. Some tried to stand, and fight against their bonds, but most just stared and seethed. When the platform was a few feet clear of the deck and descending, Slip opened a satchel and tossed a half dozen long knives up towards the prisoners, followed by a wry salute.

The outside of the Trossul's hull slipped past them, all holed and repaired, and rusty. Jymn tried to remember if he'd ever seen it from the outside. It had been his home for nearly all of his life, and he felt a sudden pang of anxiety. They drew level now with the tallest mast of the wooden ship, and Jymn saw a black flag rippling in the wind, emblazoned with a white winged hourglass. He wasn't sure if it was the queer swaying of the platform, but he felt suddenly nauseous. It must have shown, because Slip slapped him on the back, hard.

'Cheer up Jymn — life's about to get much more interesting.'

The wooden deck of the Archon could not have been more different than that of the Trossul. There were ropes *everywhere*, and bundled sheets of mismatched patchwork fabric for the sails — which he now realised seemed to be made of sun-bleached old clothes. When the platform finished its descent, they were met by a knot of wet, grinning pirates all working swiftly to untie and unload the haul. Jymn's tanks were whisked away and lashed to the gunwale, but he himself was left quite alone.

A pretty boy with dark eyes and sharp features rushed to check over the injured pirates — handing out short lengths of medicable to those that could wait, and herding those that couldn't below.

'Balder — give me a hand, dear,' he called as the recipient of the worst of the injuries — a gunshot wound to the shoulder — stumbled and fell to the deck. The huge Eastner boy with the barrel chest stopped what he was doing and gently scooped the injured boy up in his arms, ducking to follow.

Jymn felt his chest constrict as Caber strode across the deck with the teck-spear in his arms, but he marched right past, tossing the tangle of broken parts to a fraught, chubby boy in a long, grubby robe. 'Not strong enough, porks.'

The robed boy struggled to catch the bundle of broken shafts, and some of the parts clattered to the deck around him. 'Uh, right, yes. Strong.' he nodded, but then doubt seemed to catch him, 'wait, you mean the charge? Or the build?'

Caber kept walking, but looked back at the pile of broken components, raising an eyebrow, 'what do you think?'

'Hey Cay — is it true you've got Donkey-splice, bro?' called a giggling boy from half way up the foremast. Groaning with rage, Caber stomped off to quash the rumour.

'Right, yes. Ok Caber, I'll fix it, no er… tussle.' The wheezing robed boy bent to retrieve the dropped lengths of spear and lost two more in the process.

So, the pirates had a tecksmith. Jymn had never seen one of them up close, the heretic enginers that fixed up the ancient teck.

49

He wasn't sure what he expected in a tecksmith, but this sweaty, fat boy was not it. Jymn wondered what other tecks were aboard, and shivered as he remembered the broken shielding he'd been brought here to fix, and the metal creatures that it was supposed to keep at bay.

First he'd need to fix his eyeglass. The broken, thrice-split image was making his head throb, and doing nothing for the knot in his stomach. He loosened the string from around his head and pulled the old tinkered monocle from his bad eye, inspecting it. The frame was made to sit flush with his cheek, hiding as much of the deformed eye socket as possible — while the lens went some way to correcting the vision in his eye. The frame was buckled and bent where he'd fallen — and the lens was cracked in three places. He could fix the frame easy enough, but grinding the lens by hand had taken weeks of experimentation. He'd need to find a block of glass, or…

There was a blur — a streak of red-green — and suddenly the eyeglass was gone, his hand left scratched and shaking where it had been.

Jymn cried out and followed the streak — a brightly coloured bird with a snaking, long neck was powering its way upward through the rigging, his eyeglass clutched in its talons.

A half-dozen pirates nearby fell about laughing as Jymn looked about, aghast. 'What… what was that?'

'That's Puggle. She's a fezzard.' said a small bare-chested boy as he heaved a crate of plastics away.

'Lesson one — no shiny stuff on deck, or she'll have it!' added an identical boy, grinning as he hefted the other side of the crate.

'Fezzard… fezzards aren't real.' Jymn said, as confidently as he could manage. 'They're just from Fairey tales.'

'Aye, you can tell her that when you climb up to fetch it,' laughed Slip from behind Jymn. 'And you can bring back the captain's hat when you do.' He was stood with North, checking off the cargo as it was taken below. 'You're free to try, but I'd get used to the ship first. Sails move a thing differently to that motor of yours. Go see Balder, he'll fetch you a hammock.'

'He's for the Brig, Slip' said the captain simply, appearing from the stern of the ship with Daj and Caber in tow.

Slip hesitated, looking at all the gear that was being carried below. 'But, the brig's full Cap. Ain't no space with all this gear.'

The captain hesitated for a moment, weighing Jymn with a hard stare. The other pirates looked on, silenced, and waiting for his response. The captain seemed to make up his mind, and turned back to Slip 'The gibbet then.' he said coldly, and Caber grinned gleefully over his shoulder as he spoke. 'Articles are clear. No exceptions. He had his chance to volunteer, decided he'd be better off on his workship. That makes him our prisoner.'

The Gibbet was every bit as uncomfortable as Jymn had feared. A small metal cage — barely big enough for a full-grown to curl up inside — that was lashed five feet up the mainmast. Jymn was small enough to slip his feet through the bars and dangle his legs free, but it didn't help greatly.

His bad eye streamed and stung in the salt air, unprotected as it was, but he had forced himself to watch as the mismatched crew worked in surprising harmony to hoist and set the great patchwork sails. Unlike the Trossul's crew, who all wore greying overalls, there were not two pirates who looked the same — save the twins. The only sense of conformity between them — besides a lack of tidiness and cleanliness — was that each seemed to wear a small scrap of purple about themselves. For some it was a bandage, for others a handkerchief, all different — and yet the same.

From his position facing back from the central mast he'd watched the crippled Trossul disappear slowly toward the horizon as North worked the helm and held their course true. Slip was right, sails did make the ship move differently to the Trossul — the *Archon* heeled over every time she manoeuvred, and would stay that way — leaning to port or to starboard — for hours, buffeted and bucked occasionally by the gusting of the hot wind. The crew seemed to take the rocking in stride — Caber even seemed to walk straighter under sail than he did on a level surface — but lashed to the mast as he was, Jymn began to feel violently ill, and couldn't face the generous ration of salt-rice when it was brought to him — much to the amusement of the crew.

The pretty looking boy they called Kelpy had appeared while the others were eating below. He looked tired, and now wore a bloody apron that looked like it had forgotten all memory of its original colour. But he — alone among the crew — smiled warmly, and Jymn felt a genuine affection for him despite everything. He had applied a salve and bandages to Jymn's burned forearms, drained the swelling beneath his good eye, and even given him a weed to chew that he promised would alleviate the sail-sickness. It worked, and Jymn found that the salt-rice — though cold now — was spiced and flavoured cunningly.

Kelpy showed especial concern for the aching wound between Jymn's shoulder blades, and muttered darkly about teck burns and irresponsible bullies. It was awkward with the confines of the gibbet — but 'Kel' gave Jymn a length of medicable to bite down on, and set about scouring the wound with a cool liquid that burned horribly.

'That's enough of that,' he'd said, taking the medicable back, 'I'll speak to the Captain — we'll need to get that wound seen to,' he gave a tired smile, before turning to retire below deck. 'Oh and here…' he remembered, handing Jymn a small strip of clean cotton bandage and gesturing to his bad eye 'this will help the weeping'. Jymn bound it around his head, slanting down over the shrunken socket.

The gentle rocking of the night-breeze, the brief dose of lix, and the full-stomach helped Jymn eventually find sleep, though it was uncomfortable and disturbed by dreams.

The work started at dawn. Jymn had been released from the gibbet to find that all the weld-gear that had been liberated from the Trossul had been fetched ready for him. Wil Slippener — who it seemed was the Archon's equivalent of the old Bo'sun — had led him to the tall raised structure at the stern of the ship they called the 'castle', to inspect the damage.

The Trossul's defenders had dropped a huge lump of scrap steel down upon the Archon, and it had torn right through an array of blue sun-glass panels and into the deck below. Jymn peered into the cavity, and saw bent copper bars and splintered wood. The chubby dark-skinned tecksmith was hunched over in the ruins of the shielded room, salvaging scraps from the wreckage.

'We've had to shut everything down,' explained Slip, 'Lots of trace coming out of there. Can you fix it?'

Gritting his teeth against the pain in his back, and trying not to vomit from the sail-sickness that was fast returning, Jymn clambered down into the cavity to inspect the damage. The room was cramped — with the wreckage there was barely enough space for Jymn and the sweating tecksmith — but every available space was crammed with teck. Jymn gasped as his eye adjusted from the bright light on deck — there were wires trailing like spider's webs across the shielded walls, dark panels — some broken and some whole — clustered together in one corner like fragments of a shattered mirror. There were wide boards covered in buttons each with their own arcane symbol, angular mechanical arms hung from the ceiling, there was even a glass tank full of live magflies — less dangerous now, on a ship made of wood.

The tecksmith was blinking nervously at Jymn, and wiped his face with a purple neckerchief. 'What do you think?' he asked, eagerly.

'Yeah… it's quite something. I've never seen teck up close. Is it… you know, safe?'

'Oh quite safe — yes — all powered down. I'm Weylun, by the way.' He stuck out his hand briefly, but then seemed to think better of it and pulled it back anxiously, 'I meant the shielding though.'

Jymn had quite forgotten the shielding — the whole room was cunningly lined with thick copper bar, which formed a shielded cage against the teck-trace. The space within would be like an invisible bubble — except for the holes now ripped through the floor and ceiling.

'I have solder, I wondered, perhaps if we brazed them… but my tools are not hot enough...' the 'smith trailed off expectantly.

'Jymn' Jymn said, struggling to keep up with the boy's disjointed train of thought. 'And no — brazing them won't work. You need a straight run of copper — that's how it's designed, I think.' Shielding was alien to him, but he was already beginning to see the intent behind its construction.

Weylun slapped himself on the forehead 'of course — I'm so stupid. Wil, do we have copper?' he called up through the hole in the ceiling.

'I'll go check yesterday's haul — hold on.'

Soon Slip returned with a heavy casket of copper pipe and the huge barrel chested pirate they called 'Balder'. The next several hours were spent sorting the splintered wood from the broken teck, while Balder wrenched the bent and buckled copper bars back into shape with the help of a snatch-block and line. Even through the rising nausea, Jymn felt a tingle of guilty excitement every time he found a scrap of teck-plate among the debris — almost like his childhood fantasies of becoming a salvager, digging up the ruins of the ancients.

'I know what it's like by the way, on a workship' Weylun said, when he saw Jymn stop to fidget with the itching bandages on his forearms. 'It must have been horrible.'

'You're from a workship?' Jymn asked, trying to hide his surprise. Enginers came in many shapes and sizes, but fat wasn't one of them. Long hours, small spaces, and even smaller rations simply didn't allow for it.

'Oh, well yes — I was born on one.' Weylun nodded sadly, scooping up the neckerchief that always seemed to be escaping from his neck.

'Your *mother* was on a workship?' There was no hiding the surprise this time. Even stranger than a fat boy, was a *woman* on board. Unless…

Weylun seemed to see the calculation happen in Jymn's mind. 'My father was the owner.' he explained, clearly wishing he'd kept his mouth shut 'My name is Weylun Smit.'

'Of the Smit Line!?' Jymn gasped. The Smits weren't *Leer* rich — not *Gradlon* rich — but with almost fifty workships in their fleet, they were heading in that direction.

'It's called that now, yes. I was cast out when it was still just a small flotilla. Dad got in with the church, and they didn't approve of the teck too well.' Weylun perched against a worktop and mopped his brow with the abused neckerchief. 'In the end the Pars were more useful than family, and I was… well, I had to go. Where are you from? Before, I mean.'

'I don't really remember it. My parents… well they got me out before it got real bad. It was called Razeen. It got bad there — famine, I think. I always thought, one day I might...'

Weylun stiffened and nudged Jymn with his foot — following his gaze, Jymn found the Captain was stood in the doorway, staring fixedly at Jymn with a grim expression on his face, but as Jymn met his eyes he shook it off, blinked and looked away.

'Nothing left for you in Razeen, kid. Just parched earth and death.'

Jymn blinked — taken off balance by the captain's words — and swallowed the sudden knot that twisted in his throat.

'Kelpy tells me that wound in your back needs tending. He's not often wrong.' The captain said stiffly, staring at the splintered door frame 'We're putting 'shore at Shoalhaven in three days. We'll have you seen to then.' And with that, he turned to leave.

But that wasn't enough for Jymn — not nearly — and without pausing to think it through, he yelled after the Captain. 'That's where you'll sell me, then? Shoalhaven?'

The captain stopped, then slowly turned and met Jymn's eyes for the first time. 'I told you before — we aren't selling you.'

'So, what, I have to stay here living in the gibbet?!' Jymn snapped.

'Jymn…' Weylun whispered, tugging at his shirt.

The Captain shook his head 'Oh no — you're not cut out for this life. We're not selling you, because you don't belong to us.'

'But... you *stole* me from the Trossul...'

'Yeah — well you didn't belong to them either.'

And before Jymn could process his words, the Captain raised a hand, forbidding any reply, and whirled away.

It took two days to fix up the shielding. Once Balder had bent it all back into place Jymn set about fusing the rods back together, using hammered strips of the copper pipe as filler. It was slow and awkward work, but Jymn found Weylun to be gentle company among the rough pirates, and the hard work made sleep come easier at night and the sail-sickness fade — though he fumed over the captain's words often: *not cut out for this life.*

Most of the crew avoided him and Weylun — who Jymn was starting to realise was only barely more popular than himself — but sometimes Gamuwam — the quiet boy with the acute hearing they called 'Gam' — would descend his lookout atop the foremast and sit with them while they worked. It turned out he was Daj's younger brother, though where she was stoic and confident and tall, he was shy and small and anxious — flinching at any sudden noise. But as the days went on he grew used to Jymn's company, and began to reveal a mischievous sense of humour to match North's. Jymn felt more comfortable at night, knowing that Gam was up there atop the Foremast, keeping watch over the ship.

There had been no warning from Weylun before he connected the power again, reattaching the remaining sun-glass panels that fuelled the workshop. Jymn had been clearing the last of the weld-skag and broken glass from the floor when a great whirring began, and a thousand small lights started to blink. Not the tremorous flicker of an oil-lamp — but rhythmic pulses of green, blue and red teck-light. Out of habit Jymn crossed himself as the cluster of dark panels began to wake into life, displaying scrolling glyphs and arcane shapes. Weylun began his work again immediately, fixing the many relics that had been broken in the battle — utterly trusting in Jymn's handiwork — but it took a full day for Jymn's

56

anxiety about holes in the shielding and monsters on the horizon to die down.

On the third night after his capture, Jymn was allowed down from the gibbet in order to help Weylun with a task. Some of the pirates — it seemed — were still anxious about the proximity of teck and would avoid the castle wherever possible, spitting to avert evil if they were forced to get too close. But faced with the choice of spending the evening cooped up in the gibbet while the others made merry on deck, or hauling some teck around for Weylun, Jymn decided he would take the heresy and risk of damnation any day.

This was the last night before bringing a haul ashore — and tradition dictated that there should be a celebration. Celebrate too early, and you risked temping the wrath of the sea and failing to bring the loot home. But leave it too late, and you could find yourself accosted on shore before you had a chance to party. So tonight there would be drinking (North had converted an old saltwater still for the production of hooch), stories, and music. Weylun's aim was to 'capture' the music, using some forbidden teckking that would allow them to listen to it again and again, without the musicians present. Jymn didn't understand, or even truly believe him — but his task was just to unspool long cable drums from the castle towards the raised platform on the front of the ship they called the 'foke'.

The work was harder than it sounded, and the wound in his back protested angrily. The cables were heavy and stiff with plastic sleeves along their length, and there were a thousand obstacles — critical for the rigging of the ship — that needed to be avoided. Only when he had laid the first, did Weylun explain they needed one for *each* instrument, and Jymn found himself still sweating under the weight of the heavy cable drums long after the band had struck up their first tune, while Weylun wrung his hands and beseeched him to hurry.

Wil Slippener led the band, singing in a clear voice while bowing a deep, hypnotic instrument with three coarse strings. Balder produced a droning double-pipe, Caber struck up a beat on a frame drum, while North played a high metallic fist-whistle that

57

sang out above the rest like a calling bird. The twins capered about on deck, dancing when the tune called for it.

North's latest attempt at hooch was passed round for those brave enough to try it, and soon the mood was one of carefree abandon and joy. Even Daj — stoic and immovable until now — giggled with her brother as the twins began to wrestle after tripping one another mid-dance.

This whole while, the Captain had not appeared among his crew. Jymn — keeping to the outskirts of the party lest he be discovered and locked back in the gibbet — spotted him sat cross legged way out upon the bowsprit, staring out over the moonlit water ahead of them, with a scabbarded sword in his lap. Jymn watched, puzzling at the boy with the pale skin and rusty hair, who seemed so much older than his face.

Weylun appeared from the castle, offering a cup. 'Oh don't worry — it's not hooch, just stilled-water' he added, as Jymn sniffed the cool liquid cautiously. 'Thanks for your help Jymn. It's not perfect, but we got the drum and the pipes pretty good.'

Jymn nodded, and sipped at the water, still watching the Captain, who was now absently feeding scraps to the red-green mast-bird that was circling nearby. Weylun settled in next to Jymn with a tired sigh.

'She really is a fezzard, you know.' Weylun said gently. 'I didn't think they were real either, when I came aboard. Same with the Fair Folk — thought they were just stories.'

Jymn turned to him and raised an eyebrow sceptically. Faireys were even more absurd than fezzards.

'I know, I know,' he held up his hands defensively. 'I'd have called it all mad too, upon a time.' He sipped at his water and looked up at the moon and her criss-crossed scars. 'Oh, but there's a lot out there, Jymn. A lot.'

IV

Shoalhaven

Jymn woke to the sound of gulls. He blinked the sleep from his eyes and tried to focus on the movement above him. He recognised Puggle's long-necked silhouette flying in tight circles around the mast to ward the smaller birds from her territory.

On instinct, he stretched — cautious of the wound in his back — and realised for the first time that he wasn't cooped in the gibbet but rather sleeping on the Archon's deck. Someone had covered him with a spare sail for a blanket.

Pushing himself to his feet with surprising ease, Jymn realised the ship was no longer moving, but was now anchored in a wide, misty bay, littered with great rocks, and nestled in the arms of dry, craggy cliffs. It was early dawn — from the dull light — though a handful of the crew were already going about their business.

'Longboat returning!' Cried Gam from the top of the foremast.

His words spurred those of the crew that were still suffering last nights' stupor to rouse themselves from lying down to sitting, from sitting to standing, or from standing to giving the appearance of work.

Jymn — having no task to pretend to — instead peered out into the mist, trying for a glimpse of his new home. Gam's eyes were almost as keen as his hearing — especially in dull light — but eventually Jymn too spotted the wooden rowboat that was usually hung from their stern, now heading back toward them from shore.

By the time the captain climbed back over the gunwale, all the crew were at least vertical and mostly crowded around, eager for word from port.

'Metals are shifted, and Vess bought the trinkets we dug up in Epsulom' the Captain announced, taking a small sack of jangling metal from Slip, who had climbed up behind him. 'No luck with the plastics.'

There were groans from the crew; the plastics were by far the bulk of the haul from the Trossul. The captain held up a hand, 'No matter, we've got enough to get us to Croklev with a good wind, plenty of cycleworks there. We'll take the night at anchor, leave on the tide at noonbell tomorrow. Got some business to attend on shore,' he glanced sideways at Slip, before adding, 'Tsar is in town.'

At this, there was uproar among the crew, ranging from alarm and fear to outright anger. The captain held up a hand, 'it's no tussle — we just leave a light crew on board, keep her moving in case he decides to try his luck at winning her back. We'll draw straws for shore leave. Now — shares.'

Daj banged her staff on the deck to silence the crowd, and with Slip's help, began dolling out small knots of bar-coin to the crew while preparations were made for going ashore.

Jymn stared out toward the land. As the morning drew on, the hot sun began to burn off the mist. All about him the water was littered with what he'd first taken to be huge rocks, but that he soon realised were in fact ancient ruined buildings. Great mounds of angular, crumbling concrete jutted from the water — magflies buzzing around exposed steel bars. A great city, perhaps — now drowned. And there on the shore, that place that fate had decided would be his new home — Shoalhaven. A crowded stone jetty reached out into the bay, beyond which the sounds of trade and industry carried across the water. He felt dizzy from the speed that his life was changing — three days ago he'd been indentured on a workship, dreaming of the day when he could work ashore — now here he was, about to set foot on land. A wave of anxiety hit him, unbidden. He was technically still the property of the Trossul, what if they had people here, what if he was taken, flogged, and shipped back, or worse?

He took a deep breath. He'd never been to Shoalhaven in all his years aboard. If the Trossul had people here, they'd never recognise him. There was no way they could have gotten word out this far already. If he was honest with himself, they'd probably not even care that he was gone.

'Hey — we go ashore on the bell, grab your things.'

Jymn whirled around to see the captain, who was climbing down from the mizzenmast and clutching a tattered bycock hat.

'I don't *have* any things, remember…' replied Jymn, coldly.

'The weld-gear. We've no use for it.' The captain said, dropping to the deck. 'Oh, and here.' he tossed a small jangle of metal to Jymn.

It was bar-coin. A small knot of frayed cord threaded through a half dozen two-inch long ingots of copper, tin, and even silver. He'd never had any of his own before, though he'd seen plenty change hands. There was enough here to eat for a week — not salt-rice, but *real* food. He looked at the captain, puzzlement on his face.

'This isn't a workship. You work, you get paid.'

'But…' though before Jymn could respond, the captain was halfway across the deck giving orders to Balder, North, and the rest of the reserve crew.

'Oh he does that. Don't take it personally.' Weylun wheezed, dragging a sack of wreckage from his workshop. 'He's too busy to listen to me most of the time.' He gave a weak smile and stooped to collect his much-abused neckerchief from the floor, before mopping his cheeks 'Come on, I'll help you with your gear.'

Between the two of them, a pair of the Trossul's weld-tanks were hoisted over the gunwales and down to the longboat bound for shore, but when Jymn made for the ladder, Weylun didn't follow.

'You're not coming?' Jymn asked, one leg already over the rail.

'Oh…' Weylun peered over the side anxiously 'I'm not… *brilliant* with the water…'

'Come on, Porks, don't play it down, eh?' Caber barked a laugh and shoved Weylun roughly toward the gunwale, before clambering down himself.

Weylun clutched the wooden rail tightly and steadied himself, smiling sheepishly at Jymn, 'don't like the small boats much, is all.' He pried one hand free of the rail, dried it on his robe, and held it out towards Jymn. 'Fare well Jymn Hatcher. It was a pleasure meeting you.'

Jymn took the clammy hand and shook it firmly. 'Good luck Weylun Smit. Try not to attract any monsters, yeah?'

The chubby boy smiled, and Jymn departed the Archon, a free man.

The shore party had split up by the time they reached the end of the jetty, eager to spend their bar and enjoy the pleasures of port before they set sail again. Kelpy waved to Jymn, and so did the twins, but most of the crew seemed to have forgotten him the moment their feet were on dry land.

And he couldn't blame them — Shoalhaven was an assault on the senses. He knew it wasn't the biggest town he'd seen — not even close — but it was the first time he'd set foot *inside* one, rather than just peering down longingly from a hole in the Trossul's hull. Everything was bigger and more daunting from down here. There were full-growns everywhere; even they seemed larger now after spending three days surrounded by the Archon's young crew. There seemed to be a different smell around every corner — some sweet, some foul, and some that made his stomach growl angrily — but all were alien to him, and he didn't have the words to name them.

If he'd have been abandoned to his own devices Jymn felt that he might have drowned in the press of bodies, or become lost in the maze of leaning shacks and shanty. But as it was, he was led — half dragged — through the port by the captain. Jymn half imagined that this might be it — that now the crew weren't around, the act was finally up, and that he would be sold off after all. But soon the leaning buildings began to spread out and fall into disrepair, and they were following a small track away from town.

'Um, sir… captain? Where are we, err…'

'I'm not your captain, kid. I'm taking you to Syrincs. She'll patch up your back.'

'She's a medicker?' Jymn had always imagined expensive healers would live in fancier parts of town.

The Captain glanced over his shoulder as he strode, 'she's an Algenist. A splicer.'

Jymn tried to swallow and found he couldn't. He'd heard of splicers, of course, but had never met anyone who admitted to even having *seen* one. Every town had them, supposedly. A mad old witch or hermit you'd go to if you didn't trust prayer to make sure your crops didn't succumb to the blight, or to make sure your child was going to be born all proper. His hand went to his bandaged eye. Not just teck, but teck meddling with life. Only the ancient thinking-machines were a greater heresy than that.

Jymn's step faltered as he followed the captain down the track, which was now soft and bogged with saltwater, and he crossed himself for protection.

The Captain seemed to find his superstition amusing. 'I wouldn't do that in front of her if I were you. She might splice you with a frog.'

The path led them into a small copse of mangroves that clung to the sandy soil and sucked at the water. Jymn could have sworn something croaked at him when the path subsided and his foot slipped into a murky pool. A squat square of crumbling concrete stood at the centre of the grove, the trees seeming to keep a respectful distance. A door of ill-fitting steel sat in its centre, magflies buzzing at a rusty hinge.

The captain waved at a small dome above the door. There was a click that scattered the magflies, and he stepped through, beckoning for Jymn to follow. The urge to cross himself again was strong, but he wrung his hands and stepped inside.

The interior was even worse than Jymn had imagined. There were flies — organic ones — buzzing around bowls of a foul smelling sludge. Oil-candles burned, giving off a thick and acrid

63

smoke, and every surface was covered in trinkets of knotted wood, threshed reeds, and bone. Jymn's good eye stung and watered.

'Cap, my back isn't so bad, you know,' he whispered, 'maybe we should…'

'Gil Makkanok. You 'ad us worried… *chile.*'

A woman emerged from behind a curtain made of thin copper chains that sang as she passed.

'Worried, Rincs? Come on, after all these years…' The captain took her hand and bowed deeply, removing his hat. His rusty red hair was suddenly the brightest thing in the room. *Gil Makkanok* — Jymn wondered at the name, it had never occurred to him that the captain couldn't just be called 'Cap'.

'Jymn Hatcher, I'd like you to meet Syrincs Ren, finest splicer for a hundred clicks.'

'Please. Four hundred, least' The woman peered at Jymn with keen eyes that seemed to take him in all at once. Her hair was wrapped inside a rich fabric that sat atop her head, and her face was dark and noble, adorned with intricate lines of even darker ink. Jymn decided she didn't fit with her surroundings. She seemed to make her mind up about Jymn and turned her attention back to the captain.

'Thought they 'ad you this time, Mak,' she said, shaking her head slowly, 'came to me with a vial o'blood, made me read it. Detailed too, not just a skim. Even came inside to watch — all praying and crossing themselves and spitting at ma' gear.'

She glanced at Jymn, then leaned closer to Cap, 'thing is — this blood — it looked like *yours,* Mak. Just like. I thought it *was*, till I looked deeper and saw true.'

'Well, I'm still beating,' he laughed and thumped his chest, 'not mine, Rincs, no worries.'

She turned and led him through the copper curtain. 'No worries for *you*, as may be. But they've got some other poor soul with the tinkered blood, eh?'

Jymn hesitated, then decided to follow them through the heavy chain-curtain. His breath lodged in his throat as he stepped into the room beyond. It couldn't have been more different to the filthy shack outside. It made Weylun's workshop look like a child's play-room, but where his teck was of trinkets and beeping gadgets, here was a trove of illuminated tanks, bubbling pipes, and curious lensed devices clamped to the worktops. The walls were shielded with beaten copper sheets, which bent and warmed the cool light of the tanks, giving it an otherworldly hue.

An old white man was slouched in a corner, his long wispy beard and hair accentuating his drooping frame, but he perked upright upon seeing the captain and tried to stand. 'Gilly! Gil, my old friend!' he croaked.

Cap laid a hand on his shoulder and crouched beside him, 'hello Loken. Don't get up. Is she treating you well?'

The old man gurned and looked sidelong at Syrincs, who rolled her eyes and shook her head. 'She keeps me locked up like a dog, filthy pretender. Always wants to know things. Secrets, yes? Won't let me out to swim.'

'They been 'assling him,' Rincs explained. 'Last time was bad. Started asking him about old Skand stories from his childhood. Sends him backward.'

'Still, you're supposed to keep him comfortable, Rincs,' the Captain admonished. 'He's no use to anyone like this, poor fool.'

'Oh come — he's been no use for years. His secrets are long dried up, chile.' She helped the old man into a chair and fixed Cap with a hard stare. 'What's *fool* is they started asking these questions after gettin' hold'a some old Skand relic. Something that got 'em all buzzing like bees wit' no queen. Asking about *Thule*. Asking about *Fair Folk*.'

'Lots of relics around, Rincs, world's a big sea,' the Captain shrugged, not meeting her eye.

'Thing is they got this one from Vess,' she raised an eyebrow and pursed her lips, 'eight weeks a'back, hmm?'

'Oh... right,' the captain mumbled, sheepishly.

'Gotta be careful with them bits of the past Mak. It's one thing sellin' to a rich-keep, but thought you knew better than hawkin' secrets where the church could buy 'em.'

65

'Ah, past is the past Rincs, none of it's coming back. It's just cot stories and stupid dreams. *Thule!*' he laughed, 'They're welcome to it — if they're off chasing some made up island, there's less of 'em here hassling us.'

'Hmm, and the Fair Folk too eh? Just another made up island you think?' she said, sucking her teeth and raising an eyebrow at him sceptically before turning her gaze to Jymn, who suddenly felt two inches shorter. 'So, what have you brought this one for, eh? He the newest *Archonaut'!*

'He's not crew, just a kid. He got hurt by one of mine, I'd see him patched, if you're able.'

'Hah! '*if*' he says, knowin' full-well,' she tsked, and appraised Jymn anew, reaching for the bandage over his eye. Jymn flinched and stepped away.

'No it's my back, miss! Sorry, my back.' He turned, lifting his shirt as much as he was able. He felt her hands near his, and she gently lifted it clear, tutting as she inspected the wound.

'Burns, some dead flesh here too.' She muttered. 'You've been in some tussle, lad, haven't you eh?'

'It was a teck-thing, miss.' Jymn explained nervously, realising this was the closest he'd been to a woman since his mother. There was a gentle hand at his mouth, and a cloth. He mumbled into it, but no sound came out, only darkness crept in.

When he woke, he found his face was pressed against a firm cot. He moved his head and realised he'd been drooling.

Pushing himself to sitting he found his chest was bare, but bandaged, and the grubby dressings on his burned forearms had been replaced. There was the familiar tang of lix on his dry tongue. As his senses returned, he realised his bad eye was no longer bandaged.

He looked around, trying to find the makeshift covering, and locked eyes with the old white man they'd called Loken — who stared at him wide eyed past bushy eyebrows.

Loken sprung towards him with surprising vigor and thrust his head towards Jymn's, fixated on his shrunken, pale eye.

The old man, he now saw, had blue eyes himself — the first Jymn had ever seen, excepting his own reflection. Jymn watched as he reached up with arthritic fingers and pulled back the wrinkled skin of his lower and upper lids — making the tired blue orbs appear wild and bulging.

'*The Ice Cat roams atop the hill, In search of blue-eyed young to kill*!' Loken sang in a shrill, childish voice. Covering his face with his hands he span away and capered about the room, still singing.

> *The Ice Cat waits, up there on high*
> *Don't go up — she'll scream — you'll die!*

'Loken, time for a swim, dear, hurry now!' Rincs had appeared again through the chain-curtain, which she now held aside for the old man, who cavorted through the doorway and out to the sandy swamp beyond, still singing to himself.

'I am sorry, chile. If I had known, I wouldn't have left you with him. He's harmless, just… older than any man should be allowed to get.'

'His eyes — is he a *Skand*?' Jymn asked hesitantly.

'Blood is. Parents were. But he barely remembers that life. Spent most of it by himself in a ruin, till Mak saved him and brought him to me.' Rincs sighed and looked out towards the open door.

'I never met one before. *My* eye is just… it just went wrong. I'm not...'

'I know, chile. I can read it. Here,' she handed Jymn a glass of water and produced the bandage for his eye — now cleaned. He pulled on his shirt and realised that for the first time there was no pain between his shoulders.

'Thanks. For my back, I mean'

'Ain't no thing — all I did was grow you some new skin. Next time you're in port I can fix up that eye — if you have the bar.'

'Oh, I'm staying,' Jymn drained the glass thirstily. 'I'm looking for work in town. But thank you, I'll think about it.'

He found the captain outside, sitting upon a fallen mangrove and attempting to smoke a bowl of herbs Jymn recognised from Sryrincs' outer room.

> *Oh Ice Cat! we hear your call,*
> *But won't climb up — we'll die — we'll fall!*

Loken's rhyme echoed eerily around the swamp, and the Captain watched as he cavorted in the shallow sandy pools nearby. He looked up as Jymn stepped out into the daylight.

'All done?'

'Smooth as a newborn toad,' Rincs replied from the doorway, giving Jymn a start. The captain fished out a jangle of bar-coin from his pocket and tossed it to her.

'Next time, Rincs,' he bowed, set down the bowl, and took off again along the track for town.

Jymn hurried after him. 'So, that's it, am I done now?'

'You're done,' the Captain nodded, then glanced at him. 'Free. So the next thing will need to be a favour.'

'The next… what's the next thing?'

The captain pulled his hat back on and nodded toward town, 'I need you to come to the tavern.'

The Smikken Sun was the first tavern Jymn had ever set foot in. He almost hadn't been allowed in — a sour gap-toothed sailor with too much skin had barred his way and grunted, 'no kids!', until he recognised Cap and chuckled some unintelligible words of greeting, before beckoning them inside.

Once inside, Cap had handed him over into Slip's care — though Jymn had hardly recognised the young bo'sun beneath an odd drooping hat pulled low over his purple bandana. He was whisked away to a grimy table beneath an even grimier window. There was a stranger at the table who turned out to be Daj — only now she wore a high-collared coat with a deep hood. A questionable looking drink was thrust toward Jymn, and he took a moment to look at his surroundings while he weighed whether he should drink it or not.

A tangle of rusty compressor pipes hung on one wall, all frosted with a thin film of ice, which seemed to be cooling the stuffy room to a bearable, almost pleasant level. The place was dark — the bright pillars of noonday sun that beat in through the dull windows barely made it past the outer ring of tables before being slowed and stopped by the heavy air that was thick with herb-smoke, oil-tang, and humid sweat. The patrons seemed to share only a handful of limbs between them, and even fewer manners. Near the centre of the room, the bar was fashioned from the hull of an upturned boat, supported on steel posts, from which hung jars, bottles and barrels of all shapes and sizes.

Cap — Jymn wasn't sure what else to call him, now that he wasn't working for him — was standing at a table in the middle of the crowded room. Across from him was a huge man sweating into a heavy coat, his long thinning hair slicked back to the collar. He chewed a length of medicable, and a bowl of blueish smoke burned in front of him. It seemed almost half of the patrons were watching the table — though few were doing so openly.

'That's Tsar,' Slip whispered, nudging Jymn's drink towards him. 'He's the one told us where your old ship would be, and when.'

'How'd he know?' Jymn asked, raising the plastic tankard and sniffing its contents.

'Tsar's got half a hundred ships under him. Lots of coin, lots of ears. Used to own the Archon too, 'fore the Captain took it from him.'

'Used to own more than the ship,' Daj added, scowling in the opposite direction. Jymn realised it was the first time she'd actually spoken to him — albeit without eye contact.

'The Tsar's all business, no heart — deals in workers fair often. Slaves you see?' Slip explained. 'There — that's your cue Jymn

— off you go!'

Slip shoved Jymn towards the centre of the room, where Cap was now seated across from this 'Tsar' and beckoning towards him. Jymn turned back hesitantly, and saw Slip urging him on, already sipping at Jymn's drink.

'You must'a missed it — that's all. Or got the wrong vessel *again,* son,' Tsar folded his arms.

'Well it just so happens I've got a lad here *from* the ship who says that's a crock of *zhū-shĭ,'* spat the Captain, turning to him. 'Jymn?'

'Uuuum,' Jymn hesitated, staring at the imposing figure of Tsar. His heavy coat was open, revealing a half-dozen sun-pox lesions across his hairy barrel-chest. He leaned through the veil of blue herb-smoke and peered at Jymn, smiling a lix-brown smile.

'Jymn, is it?' he said in a thickly accented voice, snatching Jymn's hand and shaking it firmly. 'You'll have to excuse old Mak, here — no sense of decor, manners.' He mimed lifting his hat from his head, though the hat itself was currently upon the table next to him beneath an obese, sleeping cat.

'Jaglion Tsar, third to the name. Captain of the *For-More,* and Chairman of the Rougian fleet, pleased to make you, Jymn lad.'

Cap snorted, 'Tsar here was just telling me again about all the Nitre that was supposed to be on the Trossul, Jymn. That same Nitre you saw them deliver to Gradlon a day and a half *before* we got there.'

'Ar — now — let's mind the facts, shall we?' Tsar held up a thick finger, 'Jymn, the ship *was* full of Nitre, were it not?'

'No. Well, I mean it *was* but…'

Tsar turned to Cap, 'an' the ship *was* where I said it would be? You boarded her?'

Cap rolled his eyes — 'Obviously we did — but…'

'Well it seems to me everything I told you were true. I told you what she carried, and where she'd be and when. Don't recall specifying what would be on board the day you found her. Yer joining the two facts, so to speak.' He spread his hands wide, as if no case could be simpler. 'Now it were plastics you found on board, you said? Just happens so that I'm in the market for plastics,' he smiled, a twinkle in his eye. 'Make you a fair price.'

'Not in a hundred years,' Cap thrust his chin at the old man and made to stand, but Tsar grasped his hand.

'Oh, come — you know I ain't got that long Mak, not *young* like you,' he grinned, scratching the cat's skull, 'but sure, while we're on business. I got a better offer for you.' He lifted the herb-bowl to his face and inhaled deeply, sending the blue-smoke rolling across the table and surrounding them like a mist. 'Got a whole ship, for you. Bigger than the Archon, faster too. Needs a new captain, a whole crew in fact. Finds herself suddenly… lacking for hands.'

The tavern fell abruptly silent, all eyes turning to the door where a trio of clerics in their uniform rough tan robes had entered. They were met by a shady, nervous looking figure who guided them to a dark corner.

Pushing the cat aside, Tsar slowly lifted the corner of his hat and withdrew a silver chain, upon which dangled a thick silver puck in a tight fitting copper cage. He studied the curious teck-relic for a moment, before dropping it into a deep pocket, and glancing at the dark corner where the clerics now sat.

'Got to be careful,' Tsar grumbled, seeing the look on Cap's face, 'up to no good that lot. Got themselves all fired up lately under some new fanatic.' Slowly the conversations began to start up again — though Jymn noticed they were quieter and more guarded now.

'So, this ship. Come work with me, she's yours — no franchise — not like the others. You'd be your own boss this time, pick your own jobs, all the support of the fleet.'

'I already pick my own jobs,' said Cap, standing up.

'Do you?' The Tsar asked with a smirk, his eyes atwinkle.

'And nothing's as fast as the Archon — not when the fuel runs out.'

'Arr, but the sneaky bastards went and fitted oars to this one. Oars!' He leaned in close and raised an eyebrow meaningfully 'Oars so they can't be *heard*, see?'

The captain went suddenly still, concern etched on his face.

'Don't worry, I let them all… *go*. Won't be spilling no secrets.' He tapped his nose, 'and now everyone remembers why you don't go against old Tsar. So how's about it? For old times' sake, eh?'

Cap leaned over the table. 'I'd rather swim naked through the Cobalt Sea with a steak clutched betwixt my cheeks.'

Tsar laughed and spit a glob of lix-spittle to the floor. 'I don't doubt you'd survive it, neither. Never been too good at stayin' in trouble, have you Mak?' He turned to Jymn, 'what about you, son? No purple on ya — you looking for work, then?'

But before Jymn could answer, Cap had seized his arm, whistled to the others, and they were leaving.

The baking noon-light outside was all the more oppressive after the cool of the *Smikken Sun.* Daj quickly abandoned the coat, and the four of them crossed the dirt-packed street towards a janky square lined with stall-vendors and walking merchants. Daj rubbed absentmindedly at the purple bandage over her left bicep, while Slip retrieved Jymn's weld-tanks and wheeled them over to him on a cart. Jymn spotted Caber haggling over a delicate scarf, his broad neck already hung with a half-dozen pieces of intricate knotted jewellery. Slip chuckled, but Daj just shook her head disapprovingly.

'What was that about?' Jymn asked when they stopped at the edge of the square.

'Oh he's just buying gifts,' laughed Slip, 'there's girls in town, Jymn — girls you'd do well to avoid unless you want a case of the port-scratch.'

'No — I mean with Tsar.' Jymn turned to Cap, 'he offered you a *ship?*'

'A whole ship this time, was it?' gnarled Daj, raising an eyebrow at Cap.

'He had her crew killed,' Cap said, 'for going against his word.'

'By fitting *oars*?' Jymn exclaimed, disbelieving, 'surely...'

'By *using* oars,' Cap corrected him grimly, 'using oars to go places they aren't meant to go.' He looked between Daj and Slip,

his face full of a meaning that Jymn couldn't read. 'Come on —
we've a lot to do before the noon-bell tomorrow.' He held his hand
out, 'thank you Jymn. Remember, you're no one's damn property
now.'

Jymn nodded, struggling for the right words as the trio walked
away. 'Oh, say goodbye to Gam for me,' he called, 'I forgot!'

Cap just pointed at the sky, 'don't worry — he can probably hear
you. Oh, that reminds me. Here!' He turned and tossed something
bright towards Jymn, who caught it clumsily.

Opening his hand, he saw his bent and broken eyeglass — the
lens cracked in three places, and now with some scratches Jymn
suspected were from Puggle's beak and talons.

He looked up to thank the captain, but the pirates had already
disappeared into the crowd.

V

Work

Jymn's stomach growled, the smell of breakfast wafting up through the rickety timbers of the Inn and tempting him cruelly. But he couldn't face it, he was too nervous. A good night's sleep on a real bed had done nothing to make the prospect of presenting himself at the workhouse any less daunting.

Since parting ways with the crew yesterday, he'd been at his leisure to explore Shoalhaven — at least as far as the clutch of bar-coin in his pocket would allow. He'd considered sleeping rough to preserve coin, but feared for the safety of the weld-gear he dragged around behind him like a crippled pet. In the end he had found a humble inn on the outskirts of town — *The Bent Bow* — and taken a small room on the top floor that promised a view of the bay. He glanced at the small, high window, and saw gulls wheeling, out above the water. If you stood on the bed, you could make out the tops of the masts of the ships in harbour, but no more. He'd tried.

A half-day in Shoalhaven yesterday had left him with more questions than answers about his new home. He'd never understood how people lived when they weren't on a ship — who provided their food, or a bed for them? A night in the Bent Bow and a simple bowl of salt-rice had cost him half a copper-bar. He had enough from what the Captain had paid him to live like this for perhaps a three-week, if he were careful, but then he'd be on the street and hungry again. But these people couldn't all be staying in inns, and they couldn't all be indentured, either. Jymn supposed they must have built small homes for themselves, perhaps. It was all so confusing.

He'd seen children playing, while he sat downstairs to eat his salt-rice. They were mostly younger than him, boys *and* girls playing together. They had a ball, and a wiry old dog like the ones that used to catch rats in the bilge of the Trossul. Jymn had worried for them, to start with, but had soon seen that this dog wasn't vicious like those. This one was playing too, yapping and leaping as the children laughed and tossed the ball between them. Jymn marvelled that a creature could be so different here, and remembered Makket. He had longed to step outside and watch them, perhaps even join in their game — the rules seemed simple enough — but he dared not. He'd only scare them, he was bigger, and older, and frightening to look upon with his smikken eye.

His gear stowed safely away in his room — locked with his own key! — and his confidence buoyed some by a full-belly, he'd decided to take a stroll through the streets before settling down for the night. A dizzying variety of people hurried about their business, mostly carrying, fetching, buying and selling. He tried to imagine their stories. That heavy man in fine polycloth with the entourage of servants carrying crates — he was shopping for rare creatures like monkeys, fezzards and cats to sell to his wealthy friends as pets. That wild-eyed drunken sailor, always looking over his shoulder — he was hiding from former crewmates, out to rob him of a precious map. Those women, perhaps sisters, never letting each other out of their sight — they were searching this foreign port for a child, lost to them many years ago. And everywhere — clerics. Always in pairs, and always slower than the other visitors. Strolling like they hadn't a care in the world, but always *looking.* He had stopped to hear a Par preaching on a corner — a threadbare old white man that reminded him of Carrek.

'Even now the Lord permits the legacy of man's sin to abide — wicked contraptions that plague the sea, and the sky, and the land — descendants, all, of that original heresy: man's attempt to work his arts upon simple wire, and from it create a facsimile of life. I say to you, though — are these not fitting punishment for the sinful? Do they not indeed hunt down the unbeliever and the hypocrite? Do they not seek out those that would attempt to invoke the old rites?'

A handful of people listened, their eyes closed in prayer as Jymn had been taught, but most just bustled past, busy about their work.

For all the puzzles and questions of Shoalhaven, Jymn had at least found one answer. Following a wiry, sooty looking boy towards the east side of town, he'd come at last to a workhouse. Somewhere he would fit.

He'd lurked for the best part of an hour, sometimes strolling past to get a better view — but always watching, trying to summon the courage to go in and beg for work. The place seemed to be a glass-works. Jymn saw children with hand carts deliver old bottles and dug-up scraps of fibre, which were then washed, checked, melted down and pressed into new forms. An exterior wall displayed all manner of products, from looking-glasses, to window panes, to a great variety of bottles and drinking vessels. Some of the children within wore burns and scars from the kilns, but all in all it appeared to be a much finer place to work than the belly of the Trossul.

Several times, Jymn almost marched himself right up to the foreman — a stoutish, middle-aged woman, with no more hair upon her head than there is upon a rock — but his courage failed each time. Studying himself in one of the looking-glasses and realising with horror that he looked halfway-pirate, he decided that a good night's sleep and a wash would prepare him better for the task. He had parted with a full bar-and-a-half of copper on his way back to the inn, availing himself of a new linen shirt and some lye-soap.

Jymn looked at his old shirt on the bed, the burnt hole gaping between the shoulders, then at his reflection in the crude polish-mirror in his room. The bags under his eyes had faded, and the soap had pulled a lifetime's worth of weld-soot and oil from his skin. He *almost* looked like a respectable member of society, rather than a runaway slave who consorted with pirates. He was halfway to the door before he remembered his eye-bandage — hastily stuffing it into his pocket and fastening his bent and broken eyeglass in its place. Who knows, maybe he could fashion a new lens for it at the glassworks.

Hurrying past breakfast, Jymn made his way through town towards the workhouse. The streets were labyrinthine, but he'd rehearsed the route half a hundred times last night before falling asleep. He was almost on autopilot when he nearly collided with a tall, hooded figure.

'Watch where yer going, chile!' She snapped, catching him before he fell to the dirt. It was Syrincs — and she seemed even more out of place here in town than he did.

Jymn righted himself and looked at her. She wore duller clothes than yesterday, and had covered them with a grey hooded shawl. Her hair was no longer wrapped atop her head, but braided and clasped at her neck. Even her noble countenance had changed, where confidence and command had been writ, now was anxiety, even fear.

'My, and don't you look different already' she said, raising an eyebrow sceptically and taking him in — shirt, eyeglass, and all. 'Not a trace of *pirate* on you, eh?'

Jymn smiled, though he wasn't sure it was precisely a compliment. 'I'm going to apply to work in the glass-house today. If they'll have me.'

Sryincs just took a breath and nodded, looking around the street with worry written on her face.

'Can I help you Rinc… *Syrincs*?'

She returned her attention to him briefly. 'It's Loken. He's missing again,' she drew the hood close to her cheek as two clerics strolled out of a nearby house. 'If you see him, bring him back to me, yes? I would be in your debt, chile.'

'Of course!' he called, but she was already scurrying away in search of the old man, one eye always over her shoulder.

It shook his confidence, seeing such an imposing figure acting so, but by the time he'd reached the glass-works he'd forced all thoughts of yesterday — of Loken, Rincs, even Weylun and the Captain — from his head, focussing on the task ahead.

He stepped inside the workhouse, and into the bright, airy space where the scrap glass was collected, checked, and washed. The conditions could not have been more different than what he was used to, cramped in the Trossul's engine bay, or sandwiched between her hull-plates. Even the workers here were mostly clean, some even sang as they worked.

'Hey — outside if you're buying, gone if you're not!' yelled a rough, firm voice behind him.

He turned to see the forewoman, her bald forehead wrinkled angrily at the intrusion. Summoning his courage, he marched right up to her and held out his hand.

'I'm Jymn Hatcher, I'm here to work for you,' he said, smiling.

She frowned, taking a half-step back and sizing him up. From her expression he suspected he was coming up short.

'I'm a weld-maker, and fixer,' he pressed on, 'I've been working on ships for nine years. Learned all kinds about metals, engines, fixing just about anything that…'

'Ok. Follow me,' she grunted, marching past him towards the back of the room, and somewhat taking the wind from his sails.

Taken aback, Jymn lowered his un-taken hand and hurried after her. 'Fixing anything that has moving parts, see? But welding, that's my strongest skill, really. Steel, alum, copper even.'

She held up a burn-scarred hand as she walked 'I said ok, already. Just need a fixer to keep on top of the ovens.' Rounding a corner, she took a long key from her belt and unlocked a heavy steel door. The heat hit Jymn like a physical blow, and he held his hands up to shield his face. The forewoman just squinted, as if she could beat back the heat with a hard stare.

Inside were a half-dozen children, bare chested but for the heavy leather aprons and long gloves they wore to protect themselves from the trio of glowing furnaces that dominated the room. Jymn watched as one child would feed the fires with everything from old tyres, to crop-scraps and charcoal, while another would shovel great piles of broken glass into its roaring, orange mouth. Glass littered the ground, and great lumps of hissing ember belched from the furnace-fires to tumble skittering across the sandy floor.

'Keep them running, there's work here for you,' she growled. 'You can do that?'

Jymn looked at the furnaces. There were no moving parts, but the stress upon the metals would be staggering. He could already see a score of ways to improve the design to focus the heat better, or load the glass without getting the workers burned in the process. 'I can do that,' he nodded.

She closed the door and locked it again, then made to head back to the sorting room, indicating for Jymn to follow. 'You'll have a bed out back with the others, but you'll need to find your own sheets. Two square meals a day, plus a day of leave once a month — but no leaving the town.'

That life flashed before Jymn's eyes in a heartbeat. He'd lived it before. The captain's words floated back to him, unbidden, and he stopped walking.

'I'm nobody's property,' he said, firm enough to stop her in her tracks.

'What?' she said, her bald head wrinkling.

'I'm not an indenture, like the others,' he said as she closed on him, 'I'm a free worker. Got my own gear and everything. *I* work for... for pay.' This last word barely escaped his lips, so close was the forewoman now.

She appraised him anew, sucking her teeth and folding her arms. 'Fine. Two coppers a week. Less if a furnace goes down. You got your own *bed* too?'

Jymn shook his head, unable to meet her glare. He hadn't got this far in his rehearsals. 'No. I'd need to bed and board here,' he admitted.

'Less a half copper for food, a whole for bed,' she announced, 'and you're a *free* worker, so your injuries are your own to worry about.'

This time it was her turn to hold her hand out, and Jymn took it with only a heartbeat's hesitation.

Jymn strolled through the streets of Shoalhaven a new man. Employed. A real *job!* The half-copper-bar a week he'd have left was less than he'd hoped for, but he wouldn't have to worry about affording the inn, or buying his own meals. He could save nearly all of that, add it to the clutch of bar from the captain, and soon he'd be able to afford… whatever it was he wanted.

His stomach growled at a passing whiff of cooked food, and his appetite — now freed of his anxiety — returned with full force. He weighed the metal in his pocket and decided now was a good time to celebrate. The day before the port — just like the pirates did.

Following the smell to a small row of food-sellers, Jymn found himself confronted with a dizzying array of options, and ill-equipped to choose between things he'd never before eaten: corn-mash — all lumpy and thick and grey; kelp grillets — ribbons of flavoured seaweed skewered on metal spikes; and a variety of stews, each promising 'real meat' — though none venturing so far as to confirm the source. Eventually, Jymn settled for mussels — he'd seen crewmen scrape them from the hull of the Trossul before, and watched hungrily as they'd come to the engine room to boil them in secret.

The pot-keep clipped a quarter-bar from one of Jymn's coppers in payment, before scooping a generous clutch of the blue-grey shells into one half of a plastic bottle. 'Here,' he popped a few more shells into the pot with a wink. 'They're a devil to shift when the church lot are in town. And they don't keep well, see? Don't be getting caught with them, mind, or you'll have a cleric lecturing you about all the ways they'll cook *you* in the afterlife,' he winked, 'worth it though, if you ask me. It's the garlic, see?' He licked his lips with a smile, and shuffled back to his pots.

Jymn perched on a stack of old tyres and tore through the shells like a man starved. Each contained a small fleshy morsel that tasted like it had been cooked in seawater, and there was a rich savoury flavour that caused him to groan in pleasure. Jymn suspected that was what the pot-keep had called 'garlic'.

Finishing the mussels, Jymn drained the oily broth that remained, letting the grease dribble down his chin to the pile of spent shells at his feet. With a half-bar of copper aspare, he could eat like this twice a week! He giggled, giddy at the thought of living in such luxury, and drew strange glances from the street children that were once again out playing with their mangy dog. He didn't care.

The noon-bell rang, and Jymn thought of the Archon. With her business in Shoalhaven now finished, she would just now be sliding out of port onto waters new, her crew barely older than these children playing in the street. He thought of Weylun and Gam — so quiet and timid. Of North, and Kelpy, and Slip, with his uncanny ability to get everyone on side. Daj, and Balder, and even Caber — toughened beyond their years by life on the water. And the captain. Somehow the thought of them soured the taste of the food, and he saw a vision of himself ten years from now — older, and burn-scarred, with nothing to show for it but an even greater pile of shells at his feet.

> *The Ice Cat roams atop the hill,*
> *In search of blue-eyed young to kill!*

Jymn snapped from his reverie as the sing-song words snagged in his mind. Loken's song! Only it wasn't the old man singing it — but the capering children.

Jymn sprang to his feet and rushed towards them. 'That song — where did you learn it?' Jymn asked, as calmly as he could, making sure to keep his bad eye closed. The last thing he wanted was for them to equate his blue eye with the grisly rhyme. They were wary of him, but the dog — smelling the grease — licked happily at his hands and face, which seemed to settle the children some.

'The funny man,' ventured one of the young girls. 'He danced with Moby and sang it,' she indicated the dog, who was now investigating the pile of discarded shells.

'An old man, blue eyes? Where did he go?'

The girl clammed up, fearing she'd said something wrong, but Jymn reassured her.

'He's my friend, I'm trying to find him. He's lost.'

This seemed to resonate with the girl, who simply raised a finger and pointed down the street, towards the main square where Jymn had bade farewell to the crew just yesterday. Jymn thanked her and took off in search of the old man, soon finding himself caught up in a flow of bodies all heading the same way. There was a chatter in the air, especially among the sea-folk, and more than once Jymn heard the mutter of 'reward' and 'fortune'.

When he finally made it to the square, he found it transformed. The stalls had been moved aside, and a crowd was pressed about a raised wooden storefront which seemed to have been commandeered as a kind of stage by a group of clerics. Mostly the Pars had seemed to be ignored or avoided by the ragged motley of Shoalhaven, but today something was achange.

Pressed and jostled by bigger men that blocked his view, Jymn found himself scrambling halfway up a lantern-post to get a look at what was going on. The storefront had been cleared of its goods to make way for the clerics — crates of recycled metal tools shoved to the sides or hefted to the floor. Jymn saw all manner of characters in the crowd — merchants, seamen, local crafters, even indentured kids had stopped to listen. Even the windows around the square were filled with onlookers, hoping for a better vantage from on high. Jymn saw a thickset man in a heavy coat peering from a shaded, grimy window, and recognised him as Jaglion Tsar.

A great wave of whispering rippled through the crowd, with silence on its heels, as a neat man in fresh-pressed Par's robes climbed the stage, pushed past the assembled clerics, and raised his hands for silence. He kept them raised until an absolute and uncanny quiet had descended, and even then a moment longer, before speaking in a deep, mesmeric voice.

'You have come for riches. How easy it is to bring a crowd when the promise is of easy coin.' He tossed a silver bar-coin into the congregation, who snatched and squabbled at it like dogs after a morsel. He waited for them to settle again, looking around imperiously before continuing. 'This is what we have become, scurrying about in the dirt, hoping to raise ourselves from squalor. Living with blighted crops, foul water. Malformed young. I am here to tell you: there will be no salvation for us. Not without the Lord. And — rest assured — the Lord will not come back to us, not while the old ways survive.'

There were groans from the crowd, feeling they had been tricked into another sermon. But the Par raised his hands again and continued. 'Fear not — I'm not here for your scraps of broken teck. Greater sins abide. I seek the *true* heretical knowings. Those secrets that brought the wrath of the Lord down upon us and left us here in this... tainted world.' He gestured at the square in disgust, as if just being here had somehow infected him. 'And to that end, I wish to purchase your help.'

Once again the promise of coin had lured the crowd's attention, and the immaculate Par seemed to know it. He paced back and forth across the makeshift stage, his gaze sweeping across the assembled dregs of Shoalhaven, waiting until he was sure every eye was upon him before continuing.

'When Man committed the ultimate sin — mocking the creation of life with his thinking machines — the Lord, in his wisdom, sent both the flare of the sun and the great flood to purge the Earth of this blasphemy. And yet we find ourselves still unclean, kept apart from the paradise that should have followed. For not everything, it seems, was cleansed. There remains holy work for us to do. Legend holds that a mote of this heretical knowledge yet survives. Stories speak of the Skand who, fearful of the coming floods, hid their heresies deep within a mountain-island,' he paused, letting his words sink in, 'I am speaking, of course, of the story of *Thule.*'

Amused muttering shot through the crowd. No Par had ever come so close to admitting as much — that the old secrets were still out there — or that something as outlandish as the lost island of *Thule* could be real. There were laughs and sceptical jeers, and even a snatch of shouts, deriding the Par and his companions as fools.

But the man held his hands out and bellowed over the braying crowd 'Yes, yes — just a children's story. A magical island with food abundant, and riches, where the secrets of the world before the flood survive, and the sun never sets! A fantasy, of course. But within every story is a grain of truth, and this one is no different.'

A pair of clerics behind him were dragging someone to the front of the stage now, a frail, bloodied figure with a coarse sack-hood pulled over his face. They halted next to the Par, forcing their prisoner to his knees.

83

'We have come to learn that the Skand really *did* try to preserve their knowledge. And that they entrusted the secret of its location to a group of genetic deviants they called Leucans, or Albinos,' he reached out and clutched the hood, 'or more commonly — *Faireys.*'

With this last word he ripped the hood free, revealing a girl's face — impossibly pale, with fair salt-white hair and wild eyes. She was slender, and sagged forward onto her bound hands, as if with weeks of abuse. Jymn was put in mind of a butterfly with crushed wings — graceful and delicate, manhandled and broken.

There was a collective intake of breath as the crowd struggled to accept the truth of their own eyes. The Fair Folk were not real. They existed only in tales told to children about the world before the now, along with the creatures who had scarred the surface of the moon, and wizards who could conjure things from thin air with their machines. Yet here one knelt, burned terribly by the sun, and blinking back at them. Jymn tore his eyes from the girl and looked among the crowd — every eye transfixed. Though the grimy window above, where Tsar once stood, was now empty.

'One freak don't mean Thule is real, does it?' sprung a heavily accented voice from the crowd, 'can't get paid if these legends of yours turn out to be a crock-full!'

'Leave Thule to us.' The Par smiled, though there was ice in his words as he turned toward the voice, 'no, your task is not so… ambitious. I'm promising a very *real* fortune to the man who can simply take us to the home of these… *Faireys,*' he gestured at his prisoner with a sneer. 'Thirty thousand pieces of silver.'

This time the gasps were shot through with excited chatter, as objections were forgotten, plans were made, alliances forged, and the money was spent a hundred times over. The crowd surged forward, reaching out for the Par's attention, clamouring to be heard with every rumour or tidbit they had learned or invented. The Fairey girl stared blankly past the groping crowd into the middle-distance, almost catatonic. Jymn couldn't take his eyes from her — there was something about her that seemed remote, untouched even by the hands of her captors. It was as if not all of her was really here, but had retreated inside to a deep cave, a place of safety. Only her bound hands moved, almost subconsciously, a habitual prayer perhaps. One hand, a fist with thumb extended, resting upon an open palm.

Jymn almost lost his grip on the lantern-post when he realised. That was no prayer — that was hand-sign.

That was '*help*'.

VI

Help

Jymn gripped the lantern-post with his thighs and freed his hands. He mirrored her sign and held it ready. Her eyes drifted above the crowd vacantly — but with a little luck, she'd spot the movement. He held his breath, his thighs and arms aching, but the sign held firm.

There — her eyes drifted past him, and he thrust the sign towards her, then quickly the sign for questioning.

Help?

It was as if a spell was broken. Suddenly the glaze fell away from her eyes and they met his. She glanced at her hands, being careful now.

You know sign?

Jymn nodded, his skin prickling with goosebumps. He looked around to ensure nobody was watching. The girl's hands moved again.

She jabbed a finger at him, curled it like a hook, then made the sign for help again, drawing it in close to her belly.

You must help me.

Jymn swallowed, his mind racing. Her eyes never left his, and he felt that she could read his thoughts, sense every fear and weakness. He looked at the square, the makeshift stage, the half-dozen clerics fielding submissions from the pressing crowd.

How? He asked.

She raised her wrists, displaying the rough bindings and the sore, bloody welts where she had strained against them. She wanted to be untied, that was all. He could do that. *How* could he do that? They'd see, they'd *all* see. He should never have come to the square.

He tried to focus, this was just a mechanical problem. He was good at those. They weren't scary. If you couldn't undo a knot, you simply cut the line. He scanned the crates of recycled metal tools that had been shoved aside to make way for the clerics. There had to be something there. He had a vision of himself dashing up onto the stage like a Yupa knight, wielding a wood-saw for a sword, snatching her up like a princess and charging away on a steeder-bike. No — he couldn't get onto the stage. They'd both be caught, and probably killed. But perhaps he could toss something to her, something that would help. Something sharp.

Sliding down the lantern-post into the crowd below, Jymn held his breath, feeling as if he were slipping beneath the surface into a crush of bodies larger than his. Pushing between them, he found himself fighting against every other sea-rogue who had come to clamour for the clerics' attention and a chance at the offered fortune. He worked his way sideways, trying to contain the panic swelling in his chest, eventually coming within sight of the crates again. What was he doing? This was madness. He saw glistening chisel-tips bristling from one of the crates, just out of reach. He would have to lean forward and snatch one, hope he wasn't seen. Of course he would be seen, he'd be taken for a thief!

Breathing through the fear, he tried to steady himself. It was simple, the crowd around him were distracted. He just had to reach forward, snatch one of the tools, and disappear back into the press.

'Come on…' he whispered. Then, darting his hand out, he plucked one of the tools from the crate and slunk back into the crowd, a thief. His heart beat against his ribcage and he glared around anxiously at the crowd, but nobody seemed to notice the stolen tool in his hand. The wooden handle was already damp from his sweaty palm, but he tested the tip and found it sharp. He'd need to be careful not to cut her when he threw it.

Shoving his way toward the front of the crowd, Jymn caught

sight of the girl again, this time through a forest of reaching arms. Most of the attention was on the clerics now, the Fairey girl almost forgotten. If he could just toss the chisel, have it land within her reach, his part would be played, and he could disappear before anyone knew what had happened.

Slipping the chisel from his left hand to his right, he shouldered some space around himself — enough for a quick overarm throw.

'You can do this,' he muttered to himself, his hand slick against the metal blade. 'Come on. Think like one of the crew. Think like you're an Archonaut. You can do it.'

In one hurried motion he raised his arm over his shoulder and *threw*.

Only nothing happened. His arm was arrested in mid-throw by an uncannily strong hand, gnarled with arthritis, the chisel toppling uselessly to the ground.

'You can do *what*?' snarled the keeper of the hand, peering at him from within a deep hood. Jymn's throat restricted as he perceived the face within — a horrifying visage of old molten scars, creeping out from behind a bandage that covered both eyes.

'N… nothing, I wasn't doing anything…' Jymn stammered. 'I was just…'

'What?' the blind man drew Jymn in closer — so close he could smell the decay on his breath — and peeled the bandage back with his free hand, revealing empty sockets horribly disfigured by acid. 'You think I don't *see* what you're about?'

Jymn pulled himself away, the sleeve of his new shirt ripping from the shoulder as he fell backwards into the dirt. The chisel stood there in the packed earth, point down, but his courage was spent. Rolling to his belly, Jymn crawled — dignity forgotten — between stamping feet, putting distance between himself and the old man.

As he tried to stand, a stranger's boot collided with his temple — hard — and he collapsed, the floor spinning and wheeling beneath him. Fighting back nausea, Jymn righted himself and crawled onwards — pushing through a thicket of legs toward a glimpse of cover ahead.

Scurrying beneath a low wooden platform, Jymn found himself free of the crowd at last. Breathless and afraid, he felt like a wild animal cowering in a cave that was too small for his predators. He looked back at the stampede of ambitious sea-folk, all pressing forward against his wooden shelter. Forward. Something about that didn't make sense... his head was still fuzzy from the blow. He was running *away*.

Looking up through the warped beams of the platform, Jymn's good eye widened in shock and realisation as he saw someone pacing back and forth above him. A Par. He must have gotten turned around — he hadn't crawled *away* at all, but beneath the makeshift stage. Panic gripped him.

He turned back to the way he came — trying to spot a way to freedom — some gap in the pressing crowd. But there was none. For the briefest moment he glimpsed the chisel — still embedded point-down in the packed earth — almost twenty feet from him now. Just as the parting in the sea of legs flowed shut again, he caught sight of an old, gnarled hand — closing about its handle.

A chill shot through Jymn's veins. The blind man was coming for him. To kill him. Putting his back to the crowd, Jymn retreated deeper beneath the stage. He crawled over years of dirt, decay, and scrap, scrabbling for some way out on the far side of the platform. It was dark, the only light filtering through the gaps in the creaking boards above. Two sides of the square platform were blocked by the pressing crowd, and one by the tool-maker's workshop, but that still left hope, somewhere behind the piles of accumulated filth and detritus ahead. Jymn dragged rusted steel aside, sending up a cloud of young magflies to buzz angrily about his head. He quarried with his hands through a rotting mound of wood-shavings, eventually working enough space to squeeze through — through to the other side, and freedom.

Only it wasn't freedom. He could see past the platform, a narrow alley beyond it, and beyond that the street outside the square. But the view of his escape was obstructed — he was looking through the gaps in an old chain-link fence, not five feet from the edge of the stage.

Squeezing his way free from under the platform, he crouched

beside the fence and peered back at the reverse of the scene playing out above him. The half-dozen clerics were still dealing with the clamouring crowd, filtering the offered leads before passing them on to the immaculate Par who listened solemnly to a handful of sailors off to the right. The two clerics closest to him stood shoulder to shoulder, and Jymn could just make out the Fairey girl kneeling before them, looking hopelessly for help somewhere in the mass of onlookers. Chancing a look at the crowd, Jymn inched himself higher. He saw their hands, and then arms, and then heads, but his nerve gave out before he got to their staring faces, and he ducked back into the cover of the platform.

Turning his attention to the fence he wondered if he might dig under it, but the earth was packed too hard and sun-baked. He could climb it easy enough — but he'd be in full view of the crowd. The blind man might not be able to *see* him, but he would come all the same. Jymn could feel him drawing closer, the chisel gripped in his fist, his empty eyes staring.

One of the magflies he'd disturbed buzzed around him, snapping him out of the fear-grip. It flew toward the fence, testing the old steel for rust. Steel — the strongest metal, and the hardest to maintain.

Crawling forward, Jymn inspected the links. The metal was weak, and rusted. He gripped a link in both hands and began to work it back and forth, back and forth — feeling the heat accumulate at the stress-point. His palms were sweaty by the time the narrow wire gave out, but it was a start. Tracing the wire up the fence as far as he dared, Jymn started to work at another link, repeating the process of fatiguing the metal.

There was a gasp in the crowd behind him and Jymn whirled around, fearing he'd been seen. But all eyes were forward and toward the left of the stage where an old, cloaked figure had sprung to the platform, brandishing the chisel! Jymn's blood turned to ice — his killer was coming. Whirling back to the fence Jymn worked furiously at the metal, caution now forgotten. He felt it give way, and started frantically to untangle the wire, widening the hole. There was a cry of pain behind him as the killer closed in.

'Unhand her you cowards!' demanded an unsteady old voice

from the stage.

Jymn paused. He recognised the voice…

Loken.

Jymn turned, his mouth falling open as he saw the old Skand man, his cloak thrown aside, now wielding the chisel like a sword, raking it back and forth to keep the clerics at bay. One of the Pars already lay on the platform, his grubby white robe stained wet red. Fearful of being seen in the commotion, Jymn sprung back under the platform, peering anxiously up through the cracks.

'The Fair Folk are not for hands such as yours, *Skitstövel*,' Loken spat, his eyes blazing blue as he lunged for the Pars who guarded the girl. The boards groaned under the weight of the tussle, and Jymn thought they might fall through.

Suddenly there was a blur of white robe, then hands and a face fell hard against the platform right above him, staring. Scrabbling back, Jymn saw that it was not white cloth at all — but white skin. The Fairey girl's eyes widened, recognising him as he cowered beneath the stage.

She glanced back towards the fight, then back to Jymn. Through the crack, he saw something change in her then — a resolve harden behind her eyes — and before he could stop her, she sprang down from the platform.

Gasps rippled through the crowd, though whether at her sudden disappearance, or the ongoing fight, Jymn couldn't tell. He blinked at the girl — now crouched low between him and the fence, hands bound, and looking at him eagerly for their next move.

Jymn froze, his mind racing. He spoke as quicky as his dry mouth would allow.

'Go — there's a hole in the fence behind you,' he urged. If she fled, he could stay hidden here. Until nightfall if necessary.

She cocked her head quizzically and squinted at him — jabbing a finger urgently at her ear. She couldn't hear him. She couldn't *hear*. Pushing past her, Jymn pointed at the narrow gap in the fence, pulling it aside and gesturing frantically. Understanding, she scrabbled through the hole, the sharp metal tearing at her skin as she went, leaving red welts against the salt-white. Jymn glanced at the stage as she went, and froze in horror as a hundred pairs of eyes locked on him, mouths agape. Loken — now pinned to the ground by three pars — giggled with toothless delight 'Well done, my boy!' he crowed.

The neat Par in his immaculate robes strode forward, rage burning in his eyes, as he bellowed at the crowd. Jymn was already halfway through the fence by the time the words caught up to him and registered in his mind:

'A thousand silver to the man that brings her back alive!'

I have only been here one day, I don't know anywhere! Jymn signed desperately. They had put three broad streets between themselves and the square — darting down narrow alleys and zig-zagging as best they could — but breathlessness had caught up with them here, forcing them to stop and rest between the leaning timbers of a woodmaker's shop.

The Fairey girl's eyes were wide and wild, and darted about, but still she appeared calmer than Jymn felt. She'd managed to cut her bonds with a shard of broken bottle, and had signed urgently — demanding to know where he planned to take her, what he planned to do. He'd never got *nearly* that far in his imagined plans. He still wasn't sure how he managed to end up fleeing alongside her like some sort of criminal. But there was something magnetic about her. She shouldn't exist. She was right out of a story book, and he couldn't quite bring himself to stop turning the pages.

He tried to calm himself and think. Syrincs' lab was out of the way and well-hid, but with the mysterious splicer out looking for Loken — and what with Loken's sudden intervention in the square, he suspected it would be crawling with clergymen already. The *Bent Bow* — perhaps he could sneak her in there… but all those eyes had seen him — it would only be a matter of time before someone connected him to his room there.

If there is nowhere to run, we must hide. She signed simply. *Hide, wait.*

Jymn shook his head. *He offered a thousand silver.*

That is much?

Jymn nodded. *A year of work. Maybe more. They will look for a long time.* There was a yell in the street outside, then a response, and another. A search party. *We need to keep moving.*

Together they crept along the alley — always away from the square — and dashed across the neighbouring street. The girl streaked like a white comet against the grime of Shoalhaven.

We must cover you… Jymn signed as they ducked into the next alley, gesturing at the whole of her, the impossibly pale skin — already burned red with sun-rash — and the salt-white hair that stood out like a white fire even in the noonday sun. She could be recognised at two hundred paces.

Snatching a mouldering blanket from a pile of junk on the floor, Jymn cried out in alarm as a toothless woman beneath it hissed at him and snatched it back.

'Thief! Molester of the old!' She cried, staring at the intruders with feral eyes. Jymn let go the blanket and backed away — holding a finger to his lips, pleading for quiet.

'Thief! Thief and a freak!' The wild woman continued, louder and more frantic still. Jymn fished the knot of bar-coin from his pocket and tossed it to her — silver and all — begging for silence, but it was too late.

A new voice. Deep. Gruff. 'Right! Now quiet, eh? No need for hurtin'…'

Jymn spun toward the voice and saw a grim, wiry silhouette squeezing into the narrow alley behind the Fairey girl, hands outstretched in a gesture of calm. Following Jymn's terrified stare the girl turned too, and wasted barely a second before ducking low, and throwing all her weight at the intruder's waist, folding him double.

The tackle hit him hard, and threw him backwards to the ground, but he held fast, grasping the back of her neck in a sinewy vice-grip. She kicked, trying to push over him and away, but he clung on like a man overboard to a life-line. He raised a fist and brought it down hammer-like against her kidneys, sending a whoosh of air from her lungs. Taking advantage of her lapse he rolled, pinning her to the ground and kneeling astride her waist. She kicked out and clawed at his face but the wiry man was too tall, her fingers scrabbling uselessly at his neck and chest.

'Got her!' he yelled, delirious with the promise of riches 'I've got her! Ha ha!'

Jymn — shaking himself from inaction — sprung forward, wrapping his arms around the man's neck and throttling the yells that would bring the whole town upon them. The gasping man reached up to his new assailant, finding Jymn's head alongside his own. Jymn watched helplessly as the man's right hand curled into a wiry fist — like a steel ball inside a leather pouch — and pounded into his face. The first blow struck him in the jaw — splitting his lip — then the temple. Sparks exploded inside his eyelids but he fought to hold on, fought to open his eyes, at least, and see...

The third blow caught him right in the eyepiece. He felt the delicate metal give way, and the already broken glass dig deep into his cheek. Jymn cried out groggily, squeezing tighter still as the man stood up to his full height, clutching desperately at Jymn's arms — then at last he toppled forward, bringing Jymn — bloodied and winded — crashing down above him. Jymn managed to peer through his swollen eye to see the Fairey girl scramble to her feet, free. He longed for her to run — to get away and to leave him here. She seemed to read his thoughts, and turned to the open end of the alley as if to flee, but backed away as another silhouetted figure squeezed between the narrow walls before her. Jymn saw a deep hood, and imagined the blind man, returned to finish the job.

Wrenching his arms free from the unconscious man's neck, Jymn scrabbled to his feet, dragging at the girl — crying out uselessly for her to follow — pulling her back, and away from that dreadful hood.

'Hush chile — you don't have long' hissed the silhouette. As she squeezed closer, Jymn recognised the face of Syrincs within the hood's blackness. There was a yell from the street behind him — back towards the square and the way they had come. Then excited responses. Jymn heard the words 'freak' and 'rich' echoing through the jumbled streets.

Syrincs pushed herself past him and the girl, putting herself between them and the hunting voices. Pulling her hooded cloak from her shoulders she tossed it at Jymn.

'Cover her, for Chryst' sake, chile.'

Syrinc's eyes lingered on the Fairey girl for a moment, and Jymn thought he read a childlike wonder in the lines of the stern face. 'Get her out of here,' she urged, before pushing past the gawping homeless woman and into the street beyond.

As they fled, Jymn heard the splicer's deep, rich voice raised against their pursuers, but it did not cry out for long.

With the girl wrapped in Syrincs' cloak, they made a less conspicuous sight as they scurried across streets and down alleys. Jymn tried not to think of the price Syrincs would pay for assisting them — a thought embittered by the creeping realisation that it would all be for nothing, for the streets were already thinning, and they were rapidly running out of places to flee — soon they would be caught between their pursuers and the sea...

The idea struck him like a blow, and he stopped mid-flight, dragging the girl back like a dropped anchor. The Archon. The captain. They knew about the Fair Folk. They would know where to take her.

He glanced up at the midday sun, tried to remember the noon bell — how long since it had rung? He swallowed, hoping against hope that they still had time. The Fairey girl tugged frantically at his arm, dragging him towards the nearest alley as a gang of rogues down the street began to notice them, but Jymn shook his head.

To the sea, he signed, and took off at full speed right down the middle of the wide street.

By the time they reached the dock, the barking calls of chase were thick in the air behind them, spurring them on. Clutching the Fairey's hand, Jymn sprinted past the bewildered fishers, the woodmakers, and the gawping selkie-girls draped in the jewellery of their patrons. Together, they sprinted out across the shanty-street and leaped to the long stone jetty.

The Archon was easy to spot, the lone wooden hull among the rusting steel hulks, her white sails full and pulling.

She was already leaving. They were too late.

'Mak! Captain!' Jymn cried, desperately 'Come back!'

She was already far away — almost two hundred feet — too far to hear perhaps, except…

'Gam! Gam, if you can hear me you need to come back! Tell the captain!'

The Fairey girl stared at the ship despairingly, then back toward the town. Even from here, Jymn could hear the noise of the pursuing rabble — they would reach the dock soon, and it would all be over.

A familiar long, musical whistle carried over the water, and Jymn saw the captain stood on the railings of the Archon's aftcastle grasping a rope.

'I'm sorry Jymn — I told you this life isn't for you,' he called, as the ship cut away through the water.

'It isn't *for*… UGH!' Jymn wailed in frustration and strode towards the water's edge. He dragged the girl closer, and pulled her hood back — her salt-white hair shining like a flare in the noonday sun. 'It's for HER!'

Even from here Jymn saw the change come over the Captain, who hesitated for the briefest moment before spinning on his heel and yelling at the crew. Within moments, the great ship began to come about, heeling hard to one side with the effort of the turn.

Together Jymn and the girl charged right to the end of the jetty, spending what little was left in their legs. The Archon was making a swift course, but the turn wasn't enough, she was going to pass almost twenty feet from the end of the platform. She would have to turn again and make another pass.

Jymn whirled around. A great rabble had assembled at the foot of the jetty, and were pressing over one another to pursue them. More than one rogue ended up in the water, scrambling onto small boats rather than fighting the crowd.

We have to jump, signed the girl, throwing off the bulky cloak and stepping nimbly to the edge.

The Archonauts must have seen this, for lines were tossed into the water, trailing alongside the hull as it charged towards them through the spray.

Jymn's chest constricted as he looked down at the waves. The rocks. The surging hull. The leap was fifteen feet into the water. The Fairey girl looked back at him, desperation etched on her face as she prepared to dive.

I can't he signed. He longed for her to understand. For more time, so he could explain. Swimming was forbidden.

He glanced back at the crowd. The clerics were among them now. He saw proud Syrincs, beaten and bloodied, her feet skittering along the stones as she was dragged bodily between them.

There was a splash, and the girl was gone. Jymn edged towards the water and saw her — a streak of white gliding beneath the waves, quick as a fish.

'You can't escape us, we have ships!' cried the immaculate Par, and Jymn felt he could feel the heat of the man's rage even from here. The crowd was twenty feet away, now. Fifteen. Syrincs looked at him through swollen eyes. Ten.

Holding his breath, Jymn stepped out into thin air.

The waves rose up to meet him. Enveloped him. He surfaced once, spluttering and churning at the water long enough to see bodies leaping from the jetty after him.

He felt a rope drag past him like an eel. Tried to grasp it too late, and felt it snake away through the water, and he was under again. He saw the belly of the Archon tearing through the foam as he flailed and floundered.

A hand grasped his — impossibly white against the blue — and suddenly the water was rushing past him. He kicked, and came up for air, and saw the line that dragged them, and the faces of the crew that hauled it in.

As the water drained from his ears, he heard something above the roar of the water.

The crew of the Archon were cheering.

VII

The Bridge

The Archon was already turning again — her sails snapping and cutting against the wind — when Jymn toppled to the deck of the aftcastle in a shivering heap. A dozen hands lifted him to his feet, while others clapped him on the back in vigorous praise, though most of the crew seemed to be urgently working the rigging.

Jymn stood there — wringing wet — staring back at faces that had seemed so indifferent to him before, but now wore a motley-mix of respect and amusement. He was suddenly acutely aware of his bad eye — exposed and bloodied as it was. He fished the wet bandage from his pocket and worked it into place.

'You saved her Jymn,' Weylun said simply, 'that was… that was very brave.'

Jymn smiled, though a knot of guilt twisted in his gut. He didn't know what it was that had dragged him kicking and screaming through each obstacle. Fear? Cowardice? Whatever it was, it wasn't bravery. Rincs was the brave one, and the girl, and Loken, and here he was taking the credit like some sort of hero. He glanced guiltily at the Fairey girl, and his eyes met hers, though he couldn't read them. She was already wrapped in a blanket, with Kelpy busily checking her over, applying salve to her sunburned skin, while Puggle plucked happily at her wet hair. Here on the Archon she didn't seem to cause the same alarm as among the people of Shoalhaven — though not everyone was pleased with the new passenger...

'Ok, ok — sure — well done. Well done Squint. But she's still

98

a *girl* eh?' Caber hissed, jabbing a finger at her. 'Terrible badluck — girl on a ship. And now we've got all hell chasing on us, eh?'

This realisation seemed to spread through the crew, prompting a smattering of nods and muttering.

'But… *Daj* is a girl?' Jymn answered, pointing at the striking figure that looked on, unreadable and impassive as ever.

'Daj don't count!' Caber yelled, striding closer to Jymn — his copper leg clanging on the deck. More murmurs from the crew, accompanied now by anxious glances towards the Fairey girl.

'Of course she doesn't, and nor does the girl,' the captain said, appearing through the knot of onlookers. 'The badluck don't apply to the Fair Folk — Goodmother told me. Isn't that right, dear?' He turned to the Fairey, who met his gaze but didn't respond.

'Oh — uh, she can't hear you, captain. She's deaf, I mean,' Jymn explained clumsily.

The captain stared at her, thoughtfully. 'Right… Malvor's girl, yes.'

'Wait, you know her!?' Jymn exclaimed.

The captain turned to him for the first time, raising an eyebrow. 'Yes, and I *was* hoping to get some explanation for why half of Shoalhaven is chasing us.'

'Well I can talk to her,' Jymn offered '*For* you I mean.'

He wants to ask you questions he signed, demonstrating.

Yes — he is _____ I will tell all I know, the girl replied, using a sign Jymn didn't know — fingers dancing atop her head. He mirrored it back to her, with the sign for questioning.

It means his name — then she spelled *i-n-k-a-i-n-e-n* — *He is the Captain of the a-r-c-h-o-n,* and again used a sign he hadn't seen before, a ship, along with the sign for time passing. An hourglass. Of course — like the Archon's flag. *And I am n-i-x* she spelled, then made a sign like legs kicking through water, and again spelled *n-i-x.*

He'd never thought to ask her name, this girl that had saved his life. *I am j-y-m-n* he spelled, and he hesitated, before making his own sign-name — a legacy of life upon the Trossul: a squinting

99

eye.

She looked puzzled, then shook her head. *J-y-m-n* she spelled, then rested one hand — a fist with thumb extended — upon an open palm. The sign for help. She twisted it, changing it into the sign for *boy*. Then repeated the new sign and spelled *j-y-m-n*.

Boy Who Helps. Jymn smiled at her, swallowing the emotion that swelled in his chest. His hands flexed as if to reply, but he couldn't find the shapes.

'Right then — you two, Daj, with me' the captain barked, pointing clumsily at each of them and then himself, before turning on his heel and striding down the steps toward the quarterdeck. A knot of crewmen followed with him, taking orders as they went.

'Slip — you have the conn. They'll be after cutting us off, using their shallow draughts against us by heading over the sandbar. You know what to do — find me if there's a problem'

'Cap.' Slip nodded. 'Where are we headed, Mak?'

'That's what I'm after figuring out. Open water for now — through the sunk.'

Slip nodded again, and the knot of crew peeled off with him as he began to yell new orders. Jymn, Nix and Daj followed Cap beneath the aftcastle, past Weylun's workshop and into the captain's quarters.

Daj closed the door, and the captain turned, leaning on a broad, worn table in the centre of the room.

'Right — let's start at the beginning. How did she get here?'

Jymn turned to Nix and signed the question, relaying her words to the captain as they came, stopping only for her to explain the many signs that were alien to him.

I was taken from Losalfhym by pirates.

'How did they get past the Cove's defences? Why weren't they heard?'

They rowed a great ship right into the inner-sea.

'Oars. That's what Tsar was talking about,' Daj growled, 'the ship he offered you.' The Captain nodded, and motioned for Nix to continue.

There was a funeral, but I was out swimming. I did not hear them coming for me. Then the Goodmother did not fire upon them, because they had me on board.

There was shame on Nix's face as she signed, and regret. The captain's expression changed upon hearing the word *funeral*, and he seemed not to hear the rest.

'Funeral — whose funeral?'

Ol'wen. She was very old. You knew her?

'I knew her when she was just 'Wen', dear.' The captain smiled, sadly. 'Now these pirates — what did they look like? What was the ship called?'

There was a man with a long beard that he seemed very proud of. He smelled different to the others. Wore a green hat. I did not see the ship-name.

'It was the *Mirror*. That man was Captain Narcis — though he was just called Narce when I knew him. He brought you to Shoalhaven?'

No. He seemed eager to have me gone. Sold me at the first land we met. Then I was sold again, and then to the Godsmen.

'Alright — now this is important. When they sold you, was there an auction? Did they look for many buyers?'

Nix thought for a moment and shook her head. *No — they met at a beach. Handed me to another ship that was waiting.*

The Captain and Daj exchanged meaningful glances — the implication lost on Jymn.

'Why? What does that mean?' he asked.

'It means it was not a chance raid.' explained Daj, 'they had a buyer lined up. The whole thing was planned.'

The captain pulled his hat from his head and scratched, frustratedly at the flame-red hair beneath, 'and they knew not to use their engines near the Cove, which means…'

'Tsar,' spat Daj, the venom clear in her voice.

'No,' Cap shook his head. 'He'd never risk other people finding Losalfhym. Narce used to sail under Tsar on the *For More*, it's possible he knew how to get there undetected. I think Tsar *killed* Narce and his whole crew when he found out what they'd done.' The captain turned back to Nix. 'When the church — the *Godmen* bought you, what happened then, what did they do to you?'

Jymn hesitated before signing the question, but the captain urged him on. 'This is important, Jymn.'

When the... Godmen — he mirrored her sign — *took you, what did they want?*

I had to read their mouths — and I did not get everything — but they asked many questions about old stories. About the old-teck and the Skand, and Thule. They had some old relic, with old Skand words. They are searching for something called the 'seed of the fair folk' — they believe it holds the secret to finding Thule.

'What did you tell them?' demanded the captain.

Nix hesitated, and Jymn saw her fight back a wave of emotion. *When they realised I was... broken* — she gestured toward her ears — *and of no use, they wanted to find my home. I think I would have told them everything in the end — but they did not have the hand-sign.*

'We must take her home,' said Daj simply, seeming suddenly less hard, and cruel.

'No,' Cap shook his head. 'We aren't going to the Cove, we'd lead them right there. We need to drop off the map for a while. Just until they give up the follow.'

Jymn struggled to process the moving parts — this Captain Narcis had captured Nix, and sold her to the church by way of an intermediary. Then Tsar — his old boss — had him killed him for it. Now the church were after finding the girl's home.

'They offered thirty *thousand* silver,' Jymn said, his mind still struggling to fathom that amount of money, 'if Tsar knows where the Faireys are, he'll take them right there himself!'

The Captain shook his head, 'that in-particular secret is safe with him, trust me.'

'I do,' Jymn blurted — realising the words to be true as he said them, 'just not *him*.'

'He had Narce killed to keep the secret. That and to make sure folk think twice before disobeying him again.' Cap glanced at Daj, whose eyes bored into Jymn, before continuing 'Tsar visits the Cove every year Jymn. They treat him, in exchange for his silence. You saw his sun-pox?'

Jymn nodded, remembering the leathery black sores that covered the old pirate's bare chest — his skin, like everyone's eventually, slowly losing the battle with the sun's burning heat.

'It's bad. Would've killed him years ago, were it not for the Fair Folk. He'll not give that up for any amount of silver. They'll look for a while, follow some false leads — but nobody else knows how to get to Losalfhym.'

'But… how do you know that?'

The Captain glanced at Nix, and smiled ruefully. 'Nobody else knows, because *I'm* the one that found it, Jymn.'

'Cap!' The door burst open, and suddenly Slip was there, wide eyed and urgent, a scope clutched in his hands. 'We've got a problem up here!'

The problem was actually a dozen problems — fully twelve ships were chasing them out of harbour. Not the small boats from the jetty — so easily outpaced or swatted aside by the Archon's defenders — but great charging vessels that dwarfed the Archon, and came crashing through the spray towards them, gaining, as they sailed through the jutting remains of the great city that once stood here.

'Looks like every freelancer in town is after us, and a few of Tsar's franchise, too.' Slip said, collapsing his brass far-looker and shaking his head at the small fleet that gave chase.

'You must have really pissed them off, Jymn' groaned North as he struggled with the ship's wheel, tacking the Archon to and fro against the fierce headwind that robbed them of their speed and set the deck heeling violently to one side and then the other.

Jymn and Nix had been confined to the deck of the aftcastle, where they would be the least obstructive while the Archonauts worked frantically at the sails. Together they watched in awe as the crew climbed ratlines, sprinted the length and breadth of the ship, and gathered together — seemingly on instinct — to haul on a line or hoist a yard when needed.

Jymn checked behind them again. Of the dozen ships that pursued them it seemed ten were closing in — two of them rapidly — a pair of fiercely angular vessels that belched black smoke from rows of tall chimneys.

'I thought we were supposed to be faster?' Jymn yelled as they turned again, the deck lurching beneath him.

North jabbed a hand at the oncoming wind, 'we would be — but not with a headwind. Only thing worse is *no* wind. On a reach we'd be flying!' He grinned, gesturing at the side of the ship.

Jymn marvelled that, for all the peril, North was actually enjoying himself. In fact most of the crew were. Even Gam, clinging to his basket atop the foremast that tipped from side to side with every turn — Gam who was so anxious and afraid — even he wore a smile.

'They're gonna have us, Mak!' Called North, as the captain sprung up the steps to the aftcastle and peered after their pursuers, then at their surroundings.

The sea was littered with ruins — great crumbling mounds of concrete that jutted from the water like the broken teeth of some drowned giant. Their course — already problematic with the headwind — was further complicated by weaving between them, and giving a wide enough berth so as to avoid the treacherous hidden wreckage that lurked below the tide. The obstacles thinned as they made away from land — but at the rate their pursuers were gaining, they'd be caught long before reaching open waters.

Cap sprung lightly onto the gunwale, staring back past their pursuers. 'Turn us about, North — put us on a starboard beam.'

North held the wheel steady, glancing nervously over his left shoulder at the suggested course. 'Cap — that'll buy us time, but there's no…'

'Do it! Now!' yelled the captain, freeing a line from the rail and loosing the rearmost sail. 'Today's not the day they catch us!'

North put two fingers to his mouth and whistled a trill, before throwing the great wheel hard to the left. Jymn stumbled as the deck listed, but Nix caught his arm and together they staggered to the port gunwales. Puggle screeched and protested loudly as her nest atop the mizzenmast swung violently with the turn.

What happens? Nix signed, managing to free her hands from the rail momentarily.

I don't know. Jymn replied, staring over the rail toward their new course. The Archon surged forward, her sails suddenly full and pulling as the wind swept across the breadth of the ship. There was nowhere to go — ahead of them the water was thick with jutting ruins, and beyond — the coast again. Not Shoalhaven — but the same shore. There was an island ahead — a channel of water separating it from the mainland — but it was connected by a huge, ancient bridge — far too low to be sailed under.

'Cap?' prompted Slip, appearing at the top of the steps, concern written on his face.

'Slip — get everyone who's not holding something to the shrouds.' the captain yelled. Puzzlement registered briefly upon Slip's face, and then he was gone again, down the steps and running the new orders along the ship.

'Alright, we've got some speed now,' yelled North, looking back over his shoulder, 'but we're cutting right across their path — there's only going to be a hair in it,'

'A hair's all I need' said the captain, grinning as he strode to the wheel.

There was a crack of cannonfire, and everyone flinched instinctively, though the range was too great, and the shot dropped harmlessly into the water, sending up spray.

'There's eight still with us!' yelled Caber from the port-side gunwales, and Jymn found that the anxious note in the older boy's voice sent a shiver down his spine. 'Eight on one…'

'We've had worse odds,' snapped the captain, silencing him.

'I don't want to know what happens when we run out of sea, do

I?' asked North, quietly.

'They'll try to box us in, make us land.' said Cap 'But what do we do, North?'

'Never land, captain'

'Never land.' Cap smiled and clapped a hand on his helmsman's shoulder. 'Just keep us pointed at that bridge. I want them to think we've misjudged it.'

A detachment of crew clambered up the steps and rushed to the great ladder-like ropes that connected each side of the ship to the top of the mizzenmast. Jymn could see similar teams lined up alongside the mainmast and foremast, further up the ship. The smiles were now tempered with anxious glances, and Jymn could see some of the crew plotting the course in their minds, trying to weigh their diminishing lead over the pursuers, while others looked ahead anxiously at the coastline, the bridge, and the island.

Someone cried, 'Chain-shot!' — and there was a hissing and again the terrible crack of cannonfire, and suddenly the Archon shuddered. Cries of alarm echoed around the quarterdeck, and bodies scattered — then a heartbeat — and the top third of the mighty central mast came crashing down in their place, tangled and knotted in lines and sails. The great splintered wooden trunk began to slip into the water, slowing the Archon and starting to drag her around — but a dozen pairs of hands quickly sprang into action, cutting it loose and letting it topple free, overboard.

Jymn saw something flash in the captain's eyes. Was it rage? Uncertainty? Fear? With nearly a third of her sail lost, the Archon slowed, and the angular ships behind them began to gain once more. Slip quickly redeployed the shaken quarterdeck crew to bolster those waiting at the remaining masts, but everywhere were nervous glances back toward the pursuers. Even Puggle came swooping down to the relative safety of the main deck to nestle among the low ropes.

The captain sprung to the rail before the wheel — the better to be seen by the crew. 'Archonauts!' he yelled, 'when I give the signal, you're all to climb, as fast and as high as you can — and hold on!'

Near forty pairs of hands grasped at the ropes aside each of the two remaining masts, and some crew even climbed atop the gunwales to get a head-start. Jymn saw Kelpy, alongside Balder. Daj. Slip. Even Weylun, already wiping sweaty palms on his Tecker's robe, ready to obey. Jymn turned to Nix and signed — *I climb, you stay here* — and dashed away before she could reply. Rushing to the nearest shroud he reached for the lowest ratline before a thick, tattooed arm emerged from the knot of crew, and a sharp shove thrust him staggering backward.

'He said *Archonauts*, Squint. That ain't you,' growled Caber, one arm pointing at him, while the other grasped the rope.

Jymn tried to summon the will to say something back, to assert himself, or to climb anyway — but he found that any wisp of courage was long since spent. Instead he just stood there, unable to meet Nix's eye, until North rescued him from his shame.

'I'll need a hand with the wheel, Jymn,' he called, and Jymn — glad of the excuse — trotted over to him.

'When the time comes, we'll need to turn into the wind — hard and fast. Here —' and he showed Jymn the action of the wheel, 'though she'll resist much more than this, ok?' Jymn nodded, and grasped at the rough wooden handles.

There was the cracking of gunfire, and Jymn ducked instinctively — but the range was too great yet for close fighting.

'Hold fast!' yelled the captain, who alone among the crew stared forward — his eyes never leaving the great bridge. Jymn followed his gaze. The bridge was mighty — made in the old-times, and by some miracle still standing, though the waters below it had risen enormously. Huge steel cables — as thick as the Archons's masts — were draped between two tall concrete towers. A treacherous, crumbling road spanned the channel between the shore of Shoalhaven to their left and the barren island to their right. Jymn thought he might have misjudged it from way out there — but no, the bridge was far, *far* too low. Both of the remaining masts would be torn from the ship and they'd be left adrift, *if* none of the ancient road toppled down on them first.

But they were running out of room to turn aside. The angular, belching ships behind them roared, and were closing in now, for the kill. Their guns spoke again — and this time Jymn heard the hissing of bullets and saw tears begin to appear in the sails.

'Climb!' the captain yelled — 'Climb like they are already beneath you!' and all as one, the crew flew upwards. Some whip-fast and nimble, others slow, but all surging up the long, taut lines toward the mast-tops. The bridge was nearly upon them now, and still they had not turned aside. Perhaps he meant for the crew to climb to freedom — escape on the bridge while he and the others went down with the ship. Jymn's palms grew sweaty at the thought, and he gripped the wheel tighter. Suddenly there was another pair of hands — impossibly white — gripping the wheel next to his, and he turned to see Nix, but she too was staring up at the mighty bridge.

'Little to the left…' the Captain whispered to North, and Jymn felt the wheel turn away from the wind. Chancing a look back, he saw the charging steel armada behind them, closing inexorably. More gunfire, and this time Jymn looked up anxiously at the exposed crew, though miraculously none of them were hit.

'Hold…' the Captain said — raising a hand ready, his eyes still fixed on the great bridge, '...hold!'

It was too late — with their momentum, they'd never turn aside, they'd be dashed against the...

'Now! Now North, hard to starboard!' yelled the captain — throwing his arm down and sprinting for the port-side shrouds himself. The wheel flew — Jymn and Nix adding to North's strength, heaving and grasping as the spokes spun and groaned and then stopped. It fought against them — fought to turn back — but together they wrestled with it, hanging their weight upon the spokes as the ship listed.

And list, she did. The sharpness of the right turn threw her over to the left, and then the weight of the crew — all now clustered at the mast-tops — took over, and she kept going, leaning further and further still until the port-side gunwales dragged in the water below them.

Jymn looked up, and saw the underside of the bridge — the crew clinging to the mast-top passing harmlessly underneath with barely a yard to spare.

A heartbeat — and they were clear. The crew exalted as North righted the wheel, and the Archon lurched back to upright. There was a terrible iron braying as their pursuers' engines screamed into reverse. The steel ships slammed into one another in their vain efforts to halt, and were forced to watch, as their quarry sailed into free water beyond the bridge.

The Archon had escaped.

Days passed as they sailed open water, occasionally glimpsing land off one bow or the other, but still they fled. Of the dozen ships that had pursued them out of Shoalhaven, it seemed two were low enough to pass beneath the great bridge once the crush of larger vessels had cleared. A pair of low-sitting ironclads haunted them, their great steam paddles tirelessly trudging after the Archon — slower, but immune to the whims of the capricious wind.

By day, the cunning of North and Slip would out-sail them — even with one mast lost — widening the lead until they were barely visible plumes of smoke on the horizon. But with the stillness of night, they would claw back their losses and by dawn, would be dark and threatening shadows once more.

Despite the damage, and the constant state of pursuit, life aboard the Archon was markedly more pleasant than before. No longer confined to the gibbet, Jymn was afforded space to hang a bunk below deck, while Nix was granted a small cabin of her very own. They weren't treated quite as Archonauts — Jymn often felt the familiar sting of conversations falling quiet when he entered a room — but they were also not expected to work as hard as the others, and had more time to leisure. The sun was cruel and unrelenting, and Nix was forced to choose between wrapping herself in a heavy shawl, or confine herself below decks to protect her impossibly pale skin from its burn. But Puggle's constant presence reminded her fondly of home, and Jymn found some joy in introducing her to Weylun and Gam, translating for them as they asked about one another's lives. It seemed both Weylun and Gam had visited this 'Losalfhym' — or 'The Cove' as they called it — many times, though they still had questions aplenty, and answered twice as many as they asked. As the memory of her captivity subsided, Nix began to revel in finally being aboard the Archon — the only ship, until recently, that she had ever seen up close — and one that she had grown up on stories about. She was hungry for details about the real-life heroes of those stories — the wily captain, the loyal bo'sun, the deadly first mate (Gam delighted in telling her all the ways his big sister was in fact *not* deadly, but actually quite goofy, when the mask slipped).

At first, Jymn had been reluctant to venture below deck — he'd only been as far as Weylun's workshop and the captain's quarters thus far, and they weren't really *below* below. He'd spent his whole life confined below decks, and was enjoying the novelty of fresh air, and being able to see more than a hundred yards in a straight line. But he need not have worried — life below deck on the Archon could not have been more different than that of the Trossul — except perhaps for the confined space. The first thing he noticed was how ever-changable the space was: of an evening great swinging tables would line the upper deck where the crew would eat together, these would then be cleared away and a dense forest of hammocks would be hung for the night, and by following morning, the space was again cleared and readied for the day's task — be that fighting, looting, or trading ashore. Always at one end, the galley stove burned, maintained by the ship's cook — a stout, soft spoken boy called Scup, his arms — like Jymn's — criss-crossed with burns. Day and night he would tend the pots — soft boiling salt-rice, adding whatever ingredients they'd managed to scavenge, and somehow making it interesting, new, and plentiful enough to feed a crew of fifty-two.

Jymn learned when to speak and when to listen, when to help and when to leave well alone. He learned who to avoid, and who to share a joke with, who could spin a good tale, and who would teach him — if he needed it. Kelpy was ever a kind face — his attentions for the most part focussed on those who still bore wounds from the fight for the Trossul, and those handful that had been grazed by stray bullets in the flight for the bridge. But he found time to wander the ship, checking in with the various teams and cliques, and helping where he could. More than once, he changed the bloody bandage over Jymn's bad eye, and re-dressed the padded bindings beneath the purple sash that protected Gam's sensitive ears from the noise of daily life.

On the third day after leaving Shoalhaven, Jymn found himself in Weylun's workshop, chatting with Nix and the tecksmith, when the captain strode in with Slip at his shoulder.

'Weylun — map please.'

'Oh — uh, yes… of course,' blustered Weylun, glancing at Jymn and Nix awkwardly. Usually they would be sent out before any of the Archon's secretive tecks were used, but today their presence was ignored.

Slip helped Weylun remove the heavy wooden tabletop from its pedestal in the centre of the room, stowing it to one side and lashing it fast. Beneath, set into the top of the pedestal was a great, dark glass panel — almost an arm's length across. Weylun busied himself with a trio of small devices in the corner of the room — sliding a small plastic card into one, before connecting it to the plinth with a twisted braid of cable. Jymn gasped as the panel burst into life, glowing with an eerie white teck-light, and then crawling with strange shapes and glyphs. A curious image flashed upon the screen — a great blue-green sphere — which then vanished, giving way to a jagged yellow and blue shape, criss-crossed with red lines, dots, and small writings.

'Okay, out — and east,' commanded the captain, staring at the screen. Weylun clutched a makeshift box — connected to the others by a fragile wire-braid of its own — and prodded at the salvaged buttons that covered its surface. The image shrank, and suddenly more of the shape it described was visible — then it began to crawl slowly across the panel. The yellow gave way to blue and then back to yellow again.

'There — that's Shoalhaven,' Slip said, pointing to a great red circle set deep into one of the yellow shapes.

The captain traced a finger diagonally away from the circle, and tapped a finger on a new spot. 'That puts us... here.'

Jymn's brain seemed only now to understand what he was seeing. He knew about maps, of course — but they were little more than a collection of sketches annotated with trade routes, and were fiercely guarded by the captains of great shipping lines. This was something wholly different.

'Right. We need somewhere to hide, maybe find a new mast,' Cap went on, 'there's a calm coming, and we've not shaken those two steamers yet. They'll have us if the wind dies.'

'What about here —' pointed Slip, 'south of Railer Bay. There's that clutch of small islands?'

The captain shook his head, 'we'd have to motor, and their engines are better. What else?'

What is this? Nix signed to the room, and Jymn translated hesitantly. The captain and Slip didn't even register their presence, but Weylun gave a whispered answer.

'We think they used to use it to tell them where to go. It doesn't do that any more, but it still has a map. Everything for a thousand clicks, from the Cobalt Sea, through Burg, to the edge of the Limnal Sea.'

'Only it doesn't *show* the Limnal Sea…' grumbled Slip.

'Ah, well no — it's from before, you see,' explained Weylun 'before the, uh… before the Flood. We have to figure out what's still left. Although...' he trailed off, heading to one of his small screens, his fingers dancing across one of the many panels of glyph-buttons.

'If I may, captain?' he coughed, interrupting their study of the map. 'I've been working on some code. It seems the map doesn't just contain shape data for the old-land, it actually has something they used to call *elevation* — which I think is a measure of how high above the sea the land used to be. I've been experimenting with a way to redraw the bit-map by altering those numbers.'

Everyone stared at the wheezing tecksmith, waiting for him to arrive at his point, but it seemed he had. 'And that helps us because…' prompted Slip.

'Well, watch — if I offset the sea level…' he prodded a button repeatedly, and the map began to change. Slowly the blue areas bled into the yellow, pushing back their edges, redrawing the coast. Yellow islands formed as areas of high-ground held out against the rising blue. Suddenly it would swallow whole areas — red circles, lines and all. Jymn imagined roads, towns. People. Bit by bit the yellow was drowned, less than a third of it survived the onslaught of the sea, and most of that which was left was disconnected from its former whole. Jymn felt fingers grip his own, and turned to see Nix staring at the simulated flood, her eyes wet with tears. He squeezed her hand.

'That's it — stop there!' The captain rapped on the panel excitedly staring at the new coastline.

'Weylun, you're a genius,' whispered Slip, peering at the altered map, his mouth agape.

'There — that's Shoalhaven, Railer Bay, fakk — you can even see the Cove here…' the captain shook his head in disbelief, and looked up at Weylun, gravity in his eyes. 'Nobody can see this, Weylun. You understand?'

Weylun nodded sincerely, and mopped his brow on the much-abused neckerchief. 'I'll make something,' he said, solemnly.

'So where do we go?' muttered Slip, peering in awe at the new map. Where once had been a solid block of land, now they stared at a thousand islands and archipelagos.

The Captain turned his attention back to the map, his face so close to the panel that his breath misted the surface. They all watched, as his head hovered over the virtual sea, as if sailing. Then all of a sudden he tapped hard upon the glass 'There! There's cover, and timber aplenty. Slip, tell North to set a course: east-south-east,' he looked at his bo'sun, a devilish smile splitting his face. 'Kimpakka. We're going to the Graveyard.'

VIII

Fruit

Jymn watched as a cloud of magflies swarmed from one of the rusting hulks below, the black mass bulging and rolling through the air before settling on the rotting hull once more.

It had taken a full day and night of sailing — their small lead over the indomitable ironclads always diminishing — but they had finally reached the islands of Kimpakka, or as most of the crew called it, 'the Graveyard'. Jymn had asked why, upon first hearing the name, but all he'd received in place of explanation were amused smiles and 'you'll see'.

And see, he did. He was atop the foremast sharing a watch with Gam when they had first made sight of land. Half a hundred ships, wrecked and ravaged upon rocks, lay rotting in the heat. There were islands, too, almost as many as the ships. Great towering stacks of rock, lush and green, rising from the water like spurs upon the crown of some mighty sea-god. Jymn could not tell why — or how — so many ships had met their end here. Perhaps it was the promise of shelter, or the scarcity of fertile land. Perhaps each ship simply came to scavenge the others that had come before, like vultures — each venturing into the lion's jaws after the last.

Whatever foolishness had driven them, the same madness seemed to have gripped the captain. Slow now, moving only under the power of the foresail, they drifted among the wrecks, while Puggle soared ahead, occasionally diving into the clear water after a fish. Jymn peered down to the foke, where crewmen lined the bows of the ship, some watching the waters beneath them, others armed with great fending-poles to ward off any wreckage that came too close. Jymn saw brightly coloured crabs — each the size of a handspan — scuttling about on the rocks, or chewing at exposed wires on the hulking wrecks. Clouds of magflies swirled about the deck of the Archon as she passed — but found no feast upon the curious, wooden vessel, and soon, they were past the worst of the wreckage. The ironclads — so close now Jymn could almost make out individuals on their decks — seemed at last to have reconsidered their pursuit and had halted beyond the ring of festering ships. A swarm of magflies like this would take years, perhaps even decades off the life of a metal hull — and that's if they had good weld-makers aboard to repair the damage. It seemed, finally, that their prize was not worth the risk.

Gam appeared to hear something from below, and peered down at the aftcastle, giving a thumbs-up.

'They want us to watch the route ahead,' he explained, turning back to Jymn and pointing at the bow of the ship. 'Terrible dangerous, these islands, even at this speed. Shallow, see? And strange channels.'

'Is that how all those ships were wrecked?' Jymn asked, peering down at the clear water ahead of the bow.

'Some, I guess. That's why it's safe here. Too shallow for ships like *that*.' He indicated their pursuers, lurking back in the deep water. 'But most of these would have been left here on purpose.'

'On… on *purpose?*' Jymn exclaimed, 'why?! We're clicks from anywhere. How would they…' he trailed off, looking back at the wreckage and trying to imagine what would possess someone to abandon a hundred tonnes of good steel to the flies.

'Came here to live, didn't they.' Gam shrugged. 'Thing you've gotta understand about these islands, Jymn, is they are perfect. Golden sand, great forests, cool air. Fruit, as big as your head, just hanging there for the taking — look!' He pointed toward the closest island, drifting slowly past them as they went. Jymn squinted, and though even his good eye was not half as sharp as Gam's he made out the shape of great ovals, weighing heavily upon the branches of the trees.

'Fruit…' Jymn gasped. He'd never seen — never even *heard* of fruit growing. Not outside of one of the great compound-islands like Gradlon, where it cost a fortune in maintenance and fertiliser. Fresh food, healthy and ripe, just hanging from trees, free for the eating. 'How… I mean, why… why aren't there people? Whole *cities* here?'

'There are. People, at least.' Gam said, simply. 'But not for long. It's all bad, see? The stuff that grows here, all of it. It's all poisoned. Something in the soil, maybe, or the water.' he shrugged.

Jymn looked back at the fruit. They were closer now, he could see it clearly — red and orange and ripe-green. He half imagined he could smell it, imagined he could *taste* it — though he couldn't conjure the flavour. 'So the people die? Why doesn't anyone tell them?'

'They know. They come anyway. For some of them it's too much — the promise of a home, or paradise. Maybe some of them think they'll survive it, I don't know. I suppose for some of them it's better to live for a year, or for five, like a king, than spend their whole life living like a slave, working for a handful of salt-rice. If the blight doesn't get it first.'

The thought sickened Jymn, though whether it was the idea of people being willingly poisoned, or the realisation that he could relate to their decision, he couldn't tell.

Slowly, and with much care, the Archonauts guided the great ship up the narrow channels between the islands. Sometimes they passed so close to land that overhanging trees scraped the rigging, and other times Jymn was sure he felt a juddering in the mast as the belly of the ship grazed the sand beneath them.

At a deep channel between two of the towering islands Jymn saw a number of the crew peering over the port gunwales, and leaned down to follow their gaze. A great creature lay motionless in the clear water, and fear gripped him as he perceived the glinting of metal pistons latticed across its back. He gasped.

'It's dead, don't worry.' Gam reassured him. 'It was a bearfin. We reckon it was lured here by the trace off of all those ships, and got stuck.'

116

'Then they *are* real,' Jymn whispered, as much to himself as Gam. He'd grown up on stories of Raptions - the great metal monsters that would follow trace — hungry remnants of the old thinking-machines, scouring the oceans for teck that would replenish their bodies. 'Aren't you worried? That something like that will come after us?'

Gam shrugged 'I guess. But we have good shielding, and the teck helps keep us safe from men. Men are worse than the machines. Harder to understand, anyway.'

He held up a hand before Jymn could reply — apparently hearing orders from below once again, then nodded. 'They want us to look out for smoke — find an island without any.'

'Why?'

'No smoke — no people,' Gam said, his expression grim, 'sort of folk that come here, live here for a while — not the sort you want to share an island with.'

Eventually an island was selected — large and steep with strong trees for a mast — but free of smoke and other signs of the fruit-eaters. The Archon was guided carefully into a narrow inlet that hid it from view, and the crew assembled on deck.

'Right — we're safe for now,' called the captain, who was sat casually in the rigging above the crew, 'we'll all go ashore and find ourselves a new mast, make any repairs we need to. Weylun — we'll spread out, so we'll need your speak-wires on the beach. And remember — ship-rations only! I don't care how good it looks…'

'*Don't eat the fruit!'* chorused the crew, as one.

The captain laughed his musical laugh and swung down to the deck. 'Alright! I guess I've told you often enough. Let's go.'

The long rowboat was put to work ferrying the crew back and forth to the narrow beach in gangs of a dozen at a time. After the fourth trip, it returned for Jymn and Weylun, who had been busy manhandling the great cable-drums, and Nix and Gam, who had waited aboard with them. The great cylinders of wrapped wire were a good deal easier to lower into the boat than Weylun — who protested hotly until North had insisted 'The captain said *all* crew ashore. Not *all crew who aren't scared of a little water*. Or do you want me to check with him?'

Weylun didn't, and now sat low in the belly of the rowboat, clutching one of the cable-drums for support, while Nix — wrapped in a heavy shawl to ward off the sun-rash — affectionately rubbed his back.

'How come we can use this stuff on shore anyway? What about the trace?' Jymn asked, trying to take his friend's mind off the gentle tipping of the boat.

'The speak-wires? It's all shielded,' Weylun mumbled, 'would be a *lot* easier to use *ray-dee-ohs* to talk, but they stop working as soon as you shield them. It's like they *need* trace.' A thought seemed to occur to him, and he spoke mostly to himself. 'I think maybe the talking *is* the trace, somehow. But not with these,' he patted the great spool of wire. 'With these we can send people ashore, or split up, and they can keep talking as if they... aah!' Weylun squeezed his eyes shut as the small boat lurched violently to one side, but North just laughed.

'That's *land* Weylun, come on — for pity's sake. You're a *sailor!*' North shook his head as he sprung out of the boat and splashed into the foam. Jymn followed, marvelling at the beauty of the beach. The sand was fine and golden, and the small cove was encircled by steep forested slopes whose mighty trees spread their branches to provide shade.

After much fussing and tinkering with delicate connections Weylun had attached one end of each of the four great cables to a small crate on the beach, and affixed a curious curved handset to the other. Tests were performed, and by some ingenious teck-spell of Weylun's the four gangs of crewmen were able to speak to each other *through the wire* as if they were standing next to one another. Even Nix, unable to hear the productions of the teck, seemed to understand what was happening, and eyed Weylun with astonished respect.

The great drums were hoisted onto poles and each gang set off up the beach, unspooling the wire behind them as they spread out toward the dense and humid forest.

Slip, who had been overseeing the arrangement of broken spars, yards, and mast-fragments that would serve as templates for the newly harvested wood, led Caber and Daj to collect the last spool.

'Weylun — you'll stay here to keep an eye on the teck, ok?' Slip laid a hand on his shoulder, 'Gam — I want you keeping watch over the ship. Don't let her out of your sight. Any problems, you call us right back.' Gam nodded solemnly and winked at his sister.

Slip turned to Jymn and handed him the farlooker. 'We shouldn't be long — you and the girl stay here. Don't eat anything, try not to get into any trouble this time, yeah?' Slip patted him on the shoulder before hoisting his pack and turning away.

A bird squawked loudly in the trees, and suddenly Jymn was acutely aware of the danger. He imagined the bearfin returning to life and charging the beach, or fruit-eater cannibals lurking in the trees, waiting for easy prey. 'Err… Slip?' he called after the gang, 'what if there *is* trouble?'

The crew just laughed. Caber, already unspooling the wire with Daj, produced a small knife from his belt and tossed it right at Jymn, who sprung back, the blade landing point down in the sand at his feet. 'Well, scare it off, hero!'

It turned out, far from being terrifying, keeping watch on the beach was tremendously dull. The four friends snacked on rations of dried-kelp, but they didn't last long. Weylun fussed with the teck-crate for a time, eventually conjuring a hissing, crackling noise from it, through which the crew could be heard as they spoke with one another across the jungle. This was interesting for a time — but once the joking and chatter died down, the teams fell into silence, only occasionally checking in to report on a suitable piece of wood or other. Once the teck-crate had lost its novelty, Nix retreated to the shade of the trees where she could finally be free of the dense sun-shawl that protected her fragile skin. Gam seemed overcome by a sullen mood, and climbed into the branches of a low tree where he silently kept watch over the

Archon, as she rocked gently in her shallow hide.

Jymn felt an uncanny weight of responsibility for the others as he sat staring out at the other islands across the water-channel. Weylun and Gam were Archonauts, and had been at sea almost as long as he had, but ever since his return to the ship, with Nix in tow, they had treated him differently. It was *her* that had rescued *him*, as he'd explained a half-dozen times — they'd seen her pull him from the water — but still they shook their heads and smiled approvingly. And the truth was, he did *feel* different somehow. He looked at the knife. It was a wrench once — one end still bore the circular jaws and the maker's mark — but the shaft had been heated and hammered into a hard, curved blade. Enough heat and pressure, and you could transform anything. Change it to fit the demands of the environment.

Something moved in the breeze, catching his eye. Sun-bleached fabric — purple once — trampled and half-buried in sand. Snatching it up, Jymn recognised Weylun's much-abused neckerchief. It seemed once again to have slipped its knot and made a bid for freedom, and perhaps a less sweaty keeper.

Weylun was bent double, leaning down into the rowboat and scrabbling around for something, when Jymn handed it back to him. 'Ah — there you are...' he groaned as he took it back, thanking Jymn and mopping his brow once more. 'Thought I was in trouble again, there.' He wrapped it about his neck once more and fussed at the knot.

'What's with these, anyway?' Jymn asked, stepping forward to fasten it for him, 'You all have them, is it uniform or something?'

'Yes, I suppose,' Weylun flustered, straightening his robes. 'It all started with Daj. Well, and Gam of course — though he was only very small back then, I think.' He glanced at the trees and waved a hand in Gam's direction. Jymn had noticed this — whenever anyone spoke about Gam, they would look for him and wave, as if to reassure him they weren't talking behind his back.

'It was when the captain first saved them. He stole the ship from Tsar, and the child-slaves too, but something went wrong,' Weylun explained, and started to stroll along the beach alongside

Jymn. 'There was a fight — and the captain would have been killed — but Daj fought beside him. She wasn't as… scary, as she is now, only small herself. But she saved him, and he saved her. And everyone, really. Anyway, she was shot — in the arm, see? And Cap tore a strip from his lovely long tunic to bind it for her. And she kept it — still wears it now. It just became a thing from there. There's not much of the tunic left now!' He tugged affectionately at his wayward neckerchief. 'Course that was before my time. I got mine after they found me on a prison ship, headed for Vitzamar. But that's a whole different story,' he smiled as they completed their lap of the beach and found themselves back at the silent crate once more.

Nix dashed excitedly from the trees and waved for their attention. There was a thick grey-brown film over her hands, and she was wet from the knees down.

There is clay here, she signed, with a broad smile, *In the stream. Clay to stop the skin from sun-rash. Come. see.*

And before they could respond — she turned and led the way back into the shade of the treeline. Jymn followed, Weylun trailing behind. Thirty yards into the trees, at the foot of a low cliff, was a stream. The water spilled down the side of the rock face, forming a shallow pool that wound its way through the trees and away to the sand. Nix crouched beside the pool, cupping handfuls of water, then letting it drain away again. She turned back to them, rubbing the slimy residue between her fingers and holding it out to show them. She grinned, and wiped her hands on her face, leaving a thin grey streak over the burned pink-white.

What is it? Jymn asked. *Healing?*

She shook her head. *We have this clay at home. Thick layer on skin, blocks out the sun. Stop the burning before it happens. Protect, not heal.*

Jymn nodded his understanding. *That's good. You can collect it?*

She glanced up at the cliff. *This is just the show of it.* She struggled for the right sign, then used the one for *trace*. She pointed at the top of the low rock-face. *I need to find the source. Thick clay.* And with that she set off, along the foot of the cliff.

Jymn turned to Weylun, who was just now catching up. 'We need to go with her, find out where that clay is coming from so we can collect it,' he explained.

Weylun wrung his hands and peered back at the beach anxiously, 'I don't know, Jymn.'

'I don't think it's far — just up there a ways,' He pointed up at the rock face.

'But… we're supposed to keep in sight of the ship, remember?'

Jymn tossed him the farlooker and smiled. 'Well, better keep it in sight, then. Come on!'

Gam appeared, clutching two empty ration-jars. He held them up in response to Jymn's questioning look, 'well what's she gonna do, *carry* the clay in her arms?'

Jymn smiled, and wondered if he'd ever get used to having Gam around, always listening, unable to switch it off. It was like having a skinny, shy, guardian angel.

Together the three boys set off after Nix. She'd found a spot where the cliff was lower and less aggressive, and had managed to scramble up on her hands and knees. Weylun struggled, but with some help the four friends soon found themselves high above the beach in an area of dense undergrowth and ferns rising to shoulder height. Nix struggled to find the source of the water, but Gam followed the sound of its trickling, and soon led them to a shallow stream that cascaded down from even higher ground.

Together they followed the stream uphill through the undergrowth — Weylun stopping every now and then to anxiously spy the Archon with the farlooker. He could only make out the remaining masts, and rigging, and the black hourglass flag through the trees, but it seemed enough to reassure him the ship had not sailed away or burst into flames without their oversight. Jymn smelled an overripe sweetness that made his stomach growl, and followed it to a clutch of rotting fruits that lay nearby, the juicy flesh home to a hundred small insects that buzzed and whirred about it like magflies. Looking up, he saw dozens more of the great oval fruits — swollen and heavy, and hanging there temptingly for the taking. His mouth watered.

There was a splashing sound, and Jymn was snapped from his hungered trance to see Nix crouched beside the stream, slapping at the water for their attention. She pointed eagerly toward a patch of exposed sand. Only it wasn't sand. As she wode through the water and dug her hand deep into it, she withdrew a thick fistful. It was clay.

Jymn followed, and marvelled at the texture — it was smooth, like thick mud, but also tough like rock. Gam crouched nearby, and together he and Jymn began to slough handfuls of the grey clay into the ration-jars, while Nix eagerly rubbed it on her exposed arms and face.

How long will it last? Jymn signed, after rinsing his hands in the cloudy water.

Many days. Maybe more. I use a lot at home because I love to swim, and the water washes it off.

He remembered her name-sign — legs kicking through water — and also the confidence with which she saved him at the jetty. He hesitated before replying, but decided the hand-sign was secret to the two of them, and private. *I never learned how to swim.*

She seemed to think about this for a moment. *Your parents, they are dead?*

Jymn swallowed the lump in his throat. He didn't know if it was the Fairey way, or the economy of signing, but she had a habit of cutting right to the point. *Maybe. Probably. They gave me to a rescue ship when I was very young. There was a great hunger.*

She nodded sadly. *Our story-teller taught me. Under the water — nobody can hear, so swimming was good — for me.*

Not all Faireys are deaf?

She shook her head vigorously. *Only me, and one other much older. But my parents know the sign, and a friend.*

And the story-teller? Jymn ventured. It was fascinating to

123

imagine this glimpse of Fairey-life, like stepping inside the pages of a child's story.

Yes — she taught us. She is dead now.

Jymn made the sign for sadness, not knowing what else to say.

'Ok, she's still there.' Weylun announced, collapsing the farlooker once again. 'We should head back though, I don't…'

Gam threw up a hand for silence, his eyes screwed shut, concentrating. He fumbled at the thick bandages that protected his ears, peeling one back briefly before looking at the others with alarm.

'There's someone else on the island,' he whispered, tugging at Weylun's robe, pulling him into a crouch beside them.

'Fruit-eaters?' Weylun gasped, glancing about the ferns nervously.

Gam shook his head, 'no — I don't think so. I heard an engine. A small one.'

'We should tell the others!' Weylun hissed, making to head downstream toward the beach.

'Wait — we should find out what it is first,' Jymn said, holding up a hand. 'Don't want to raise the alarm over nothing.'

'I don't know Jymn…' Weylun said, 'it must be *something.*'

'But we need to know what to tell them. We need to at least know *where* it is, in case they come back right into it! Gam — where was the sound?'

Gam pointed across the slope, away from the beach. 'Over there — next beach over, I guess.'

What happens? Nix signed, squinting at their hushed lips, *there are people coming? An engine?*

A boat — this way, he replied, pointing. *Quiet.*

She raised an eyebrow, and he realised the stupidity of the instruction, but she followed him all the same, as Gam led them crawling through the undergrowth.

As the slope crested and began to descend, they saw bright sand again — the very next beach from the Archon's hiding place. A small inflatable boat — orange originally, but patched a hundred times with black and blue — bobbed in the shallow water. Three men crept across the beach, each armed with long guns, and peering up at the trees that encircled them.

The four friends looked aghast at one another as they lay hid among the ferns.

'What are they doing?' whispered Weylun, worry knotting his face.

'Looking for us, I think. I can't hear them over the engine,' Gam said. 'They must have followed the ship through the Graveyard.'

'They'll find it!' Weylun hissed, 'it's only there!' he pointed behind them, past the tall bluff of rock that separated this beach from the next.

Jymn took the farlooker from Weylun and spied down on the men. They were rough — cruel and piratical looking — but anxious. They muttered and argued amongst themselves, gesturing up at the trees with their makeshift guns.

Nix jabbed his arm with her fist and made the sign for questioning. Jymn handed her the farlooker, and she too squinted down at the intruders. She watched for a good while, adjusting the lens more than once for a clearer look before turning back to him.

They are scared of the island. They spoke 'cannibals'.

Jymn frowned in confusion, but Nix gestured at the farlooker, and then her lips. *I read them. It is hard, I don't see much.*

'Come on, we need to tell the others!' Weylun whispered, shuffling backwards into the ferns. The others followed, hurrying back as quickly and quietly as they could manage. They scrambled down the cliffside, and by the time they reached the beach, were at a full run, racing for the small, hissing teck-crate.

Weylun grasped the curved handset that sat atop the crate and pushed a button. 'Errr… everyone. Archonauts. There are pirates coming. *Other* pirates. They are on the next beach over, to the… uhhh…. west.' He looked at the others desperately, unsure of what else to say. 'Come back? They have guns.'

Weylun let go the button, and the four friends waited for the

125

crackling response. But nothing happened. Gam dashed off into the trees, following the direction the crew had taken.

'No no no....' Weylun fiddled with the wire connections and rapped upon the button again 'Hello? Anyone? You need to come back *right now.*'

But again there was no reply, only an empty, hopeless hissing.

A cry carried out of the treeline. 'Uh.., guys? You better come see this ..'

They ran toward Gam's voice, and found him twenty yards into the trees, clutching a cable and backing away from something. Jymn saw movement in the undergrowth — a dozen crabs, each the size of a handspan, with brightly coloured shells of swirling blue, orange, and green. They were swarming around the cable, tearing at the plastic sleeving with their claws and mandibles — Jymn saw exposed wire, then a break in the wire. He looked at Gam, who clutched another free, broken end in his hand, panic on his face.

There was no way of reaching the others. They were alone.

IX

Fruit-Eaters

'So wait — you and Gam are going back there? With the box?' asked Weylun, running the hurried plan through, in his mind. 'That means…'

Jymn nodded, 'yeah — it means you need to row back to the Archon.'

Weylun's eyes bulged as he looked out at the water, his face growing pale. He wiped his palms on his robe and nodded toward Nix, 'alright, I guess we can do that.'

Jymn hesitated. 'Uh… Weylun, I need Nix to stay here on the beach, for the fire. But you can do it, mate. It's not far, and the water is calm.'

'But the cable? I can't row *and* hold the cable,' he flustered, pacing now, and staring out at the ship.

'We'll tie the cable to the boat,' Gam reassured him, 'it'll unspool from here.'

'Then you just connect it up and send the captives down it,' Jymn explained again, as Gam darted away to fetch the salvaged wire.

'Captures. Sound *captures*,' Weylun corrected him absentmindedly.

'See, that's why it has to be you, mate. Nobody else knows how, do they?'

'Alright, Jymn. If you say so.' The tecksmith swallowed, and clambered awkwardly into the small boat as Gam returned with a long coil of cable looped over one arm.

They had dragged each of the four cables back to the beach — kicking at the hungry crabs that clung on — until they had found the longest remaining length. One end, Gam now tied to the prow of the rowboat — the other was coiled near the treeline, and connected once more to the teck-crate.

'Is the talker as loud as it will go?' Gam asked, adjusting the thick bandages that protected his ears.

'Speaker. It's called a speaker. But yes — it's all the way up.' Weylun grasped for the side as Jymn and Gam heaved the boat into the shallow water, sending their terrified friend drifting slowly back toward the Archon.

'Is he going to be alright?' Jymn muttered to Gam as they watched him fumble at the oars.

'He's going to have to be. Come on!'

Together they dashed back up the beach toward Nix, who had stacked the wooden spars and mast-scraps into a loose tower, and was now draping them with green ferns.

They will make it smoke more. Lots of smoke, She signed. Then something seemed to occur to her, *how will I start the flames?*

Jymn pulled the wrench-knife from his belt and handed it to her, grip first. *Use this. There are rocks near the cliff you can strike it on.* He looked at the makeshift bonfire. The wood was thick, the ferns damp and green. A spark would never catch. He pulled the grubby bandage from his head and held it out, being careful not to look at her with his exposed, smikken eye. *This will catch the spark and burn well.*

She took the bandage and teased the cotton fibres apart, nodding. *When it is burning, I will find you.*

Jymn shook his head earnestly *No. You swim for the Archon. Find a way to signal the crew.*

Before she could object he grasped her arms firmly and pulled her into a hug. Gam waved at her bashfully, and managed to half-make the sign for *luck*, and then he and Jymn were off, sprinting for the trees.

The plan had been thrown together in minutes as soon as they had faced the cold reality that the rest of the crew were unreachable. The pirates were afraid of the fruit-eaters, only there weren't any on the island. Every minute that passed, they would grow more confident of that — and then it was only a matter of time before they found the Archon. But not if they could be persuaded that there *were* fruit-eater cannibals here after all…

First of all, Nix would light a great smoking fire on the beach. Whatever gods looked over the Archon — or perhaps those that were worshipped in Kimpakka — had obviously smiled upon them, and a fresh breeze was blowing right from the Archon's hide toward the pirate intruders, to carry the smoke.

Next came the hard part — Weylun's contribution. Jymn and Gam would carry the teck-crate into the trees, up the cliff, and as close to the pirates as the salvaged cable would allow. Then Weylun would activate the sound-capture he had made of the ship's band — specifically Caber's drumming — and send it down the cable from the Archon to the *speaker* in the crate.

Then came the final piece of the illusion. With the pirates smelling fire and hearing drums, Jymn and Gam would throw the poisoned fruit from the trees, and see them off for good.

At least that was the plan.

The crate was heavier than it looked, and they had to run the cable off the ground, hanging it in the low branches for fear that more of the colourful crabs would show up to feast upon the sleeving. Eventually, as they reached the crest of the hill that overlooked the pirate-cove, the wire ran taught. Together they wedged the crate carefully in the boughs of a tall tree so that the sound might carry better.

They dared not shake branches to dislodge fresh fruit — the movement might alert the pirates, or scatter noisy birds to the wind — but there was fruit abundant lying on the ground, mouldering and fermenting in the sun. Together, Jymn and Gam collected it into a wet, pungent pile of ammunition, and crept down the slope toward the beach.

But they had taken too long. By the time they spied the pirates they were already wading back to their inflatable boat, the small engine coughing and spluttering.

'They're heading for the next beach…' whispered Gam. 'That's the Archon. Weylun, and Nix!'

Jymn could smell the first tinge of Nix's fire upon the air, but the blessed breeze had died away, and no smoke was yet visible. What would the captain do? They had to hurry, and do without. Grasping Gam's arm, Jymn dashed back toward the speaker, lifting the curious curved handset that would connect him to Weylun.

'Now Weylun — play it now, hurry!'

There was a terrible crackling sound, and Jymn thought he could hear Weylun's voice, distorted and garbled over the noise. Then drums — Caber's drums — terribly loud, reverberating through the trees, but broken up — hissing and fizzing and obviously false. Panicking, Jymn fumbled with the dials until the sound dropped down to a low whisper. He held his breath.

The boat engine stopped.

Gam hissed for Jymn's attention a dozen yards away where he'd found a cast of the hungry, multicoloured crabs marching up a tree-trunk, tearing strips off the wire's plastic sheath. He swung at the creatures with a branch, swatting them aside and kicking them into the undergrowth, but they had already savaged the cable.

Suddenly an ear-splitting crack rang out, sending half a hundred birds squawking and fleeing the trees. Overcome with pain, Gam cried out — dropping the branch and clutching at his ears.

'Right — show yourselves!' came a gruff response from the beach, along with the splashing of water, and the re-cocking of a long gun.

Jymn peered through the ferns and down to the sand. One of the pirates was stalking right towards them, gripping a handgun. The others had trained their long guns on the trees, toward the source of the speaker-sound and Gam's cry.

He tried to breathe through the fear and *think*. The crabs had eaten through the cable — so there would be no drums. There was a faint whiff of smoke on the air, but not nearly enough to scare them off. All he had left was the fruit. Would it be enough by itself?

It took all the nerve he had to creep back toward his pile of mouldering fruit, belly crawling beneath the canopy of fern and not daring to look up. He grasped a pair of the rotting projectiles. The pungent juice dribbled down his trembling hands, staining his skin red. He could hear footsteps now, drawing closer. He would have to stand, in order to throw. If he burst out of the undergrowth in view of the pirate it would all be over — he'd be shot in a heartbeat. But if he hesitated, or waited too long, the pirate would reach Gam, or find the teck-crate.

The footsteps grew closer, crashing through the ferns ahead. Jymn tried to place them — was he fifty feet away now, or only ten? It was impossible — he longed for Gam's hearing. Gam. His friend was right at the source of the noise the pirate was heading for. Jymn had left him there, clutching at his sensitive ears. After the thundering gunshot he might already be deaf — like Nix — and unable to hear the approaching killer. Jymn *had* to do something. He couldn't let cowardice paralyse him this time. Forcing himself above the canopy, Jymn peered through the ferns.

Right into the face of the pirate.

The face was gaunt — the bones beneath the skin and stubble clear to see — the nose unusually large and hooked. The man's eyes widened at the sight of movement in the undergrowth — and suddenly Jymn found himself staring down the barrel of the handgun.

The gun barked just as Jymn threw himself aside and into a roll. 'Oi!' cried the pirate as Jymn disappeared from view, and the gun spoke again, this time spattering Jymn with scarlet. His ears rang out, and he looked down at himself fearing a wound, but instead finding the remains of one of the fruits.

There was an agonised cry from Gam a short way up the hill, and the pirate whirled the gun around, striding towards the spot where the teck-crate — and his friend — were hidden.

Clambering unsteadily onto reluctant legs, Jymn charged forward to intercept — or tried to — only his feet didn't move. He tried again, and found that he was rooted to the spot, and trembling violently. He knew, in that moment, that he was going to stand here — coward — half hid in the undergrowth while his friend was found, and killed.

A movement caught his eye — and with it a terrible warbling cry. Something was crashing through the trees — a horrifying figure running right at the pirate, arms raised. Their skin was grey and thick and cracked — blood smeared in primitive spirals over war-paint.

A fruit-eater.

The pirate spun to face them and tried to train his gun, but the intruder darted left and then right, screaming in a foreign tongue and brandishing a bright blade, thrusting it toward the pirate, who seemed struck with fear — not knowing whether to shoot, or to run. A chill shot down Jymn's spine as he recognised the blade as his own wrench-knife.

Suddenly the deafening rhythm of drums erupted, echoing all around the trees, and at last it was too much. The pirate dropped his weapon — and fled.

'Fire! There's a fire!' cried the gunman's companions as he burst from the trees, and finally Jymn saw it — a great column of black-grey smoke rising like a pillar from the beach beyond the hill. Regaining control of himself at last, Jymn hurled the bruised fruit that was still clutched in his arms, then another, and another. Some of the missiles exploded against trees, others crashed down to the sand, sending the panicked pirates charging through the shallow water to throw themselves inelegantly into their boat.

Breathless, and still trembling from fright, Jymn turned toward the fruit-eater, trying not to think about what they must have done to Nix to win the knife from her. If they were lucky, she had only been taken prisoner, and could be bargained for. As he approached the bloody figure, his palms raised in a show of peace, he tried to remember who it was that had first described the island's inhabitants as *cannibals*.

As he drew near, he saw that the fruit-eater was watching the pirates' inelegant flight, and laughing. They seemed skinnier and less terrifying, now that they weren't screaming and brandishing

132

the knife. Almost familiar.

Pretty good — you think? They signed. *Think I even scared you for a moment there.*

She tossed the knife to him, then swatted at a small cloud of flies that buzzed about her, and Jymn realised at last that the blood was not blood at all, but the juice of the poison-fruit — painted in crude patterns above a thick, cracked layer of clay. He shook his head in disbelief and rushed forward to wrap Nix into a hug.

Mid-embrace, he realised awkwardly that more than half of her clothes were missing, and stepped back bashfully. *Gam* — he used the name-sign they'd invented — a hand cupped to each ear. *He is hurt — come.*

Together they rushed toward the sound of the drums, and found Gam slumped between two trees, hunched over the cable. Blood stained his ear-bandages, and his eyes were screwed shut. As they moved him, the drumming suddenly abated, and the cable slipped out of his hands. He had been holding two broken ends together, his fingers twisting the copper fibres within, his hands unable to protect his ears. He smiled feebly upon seeing Nix, and waved away their concerns. 'I'll be fine,' he whispered, 'It happens — just need to heal, rest.' He winced at some distant sound and added 'help is coming.'

Moments later, Puggle appeared high above them, and soon Slip came charging through the undergrowth, snatching the farlooker from Jymn without a word and spying after the fleeing pirates.

'Oghan and Nott — some of the Tsar's old crew,' he said, collapsing the spyglass, and looking round at Daj and Caber, who came crashing through the trees behind him.

'You were right, all the wires were cut,' Daj panted, noticing the knife in Jymn's hand.

'And someone set fire to all the rigging on the beach!' yelled Caber. 'Some sort of signal.'

'What happened Jymn?' Slip demanded. 'Where's Weylun? We told you not to let the Archon out of your sight!'

'We didn't! Well not at first — but Gam heard them, see? Oghan and Nott? And a third one. And we tried to call you all back, but the lines were dead. So we tried to scare them off.'

'It's true, Slip.' Gam spoke, his voice hoarse and strained. 'We pretended to be...' but he trailed off, as Daj stooped over him, shushing him and inspecting his bandages tenderly.

Slip studied Jymn for a while, frowning, then turned to Caber. 'Fetch the captain. Tell him what's happened.'

Caber grinned wickedly, and disappeared back into the trees.

'I hope you're telling it true, Jymn.' Slip sighed. 'The captain isn't fond of being disobeyed.'

Jymn found his palms suddenly clammy, and the trembling began to return. 'Weylun is on the Archon. You can ask him.'

Slip didn't reply, but crouched in the undergrowth and plucked the pirate's handgun from the dirt. Moments later the captain strode into the clearing, with Puggle coiled on his shoulder and Caber hurrying along after, a rope now clutched in his hands. Slip handed Cap the discarded handgun.

'Whose doing was this?' Cap demanded, looking between them, and following Gam's nervous glance towards Jymn. He fixed Jymn with a hard stare, and Jymn was again painfully aware of his exposed bad eye. 'I gave you specific instructions, and when it mattered most, you ignored them.'

'No, I… we didn't…' Jymn looked to Gam for support, but his sister blocked him from sight. He looked at Slip, but the kindly bo'sun wouldn't meet his gaze. Nix frowned between them all — struggling to read the scene. The captain shook his head in disgust and turned his back.

'Caber — tie him up.'

Nix stepped forward to intercede, but Slip put himself between her and Jymn, shaking his head. Caber eagerly bound Jymn's wrists, and then dragged him to his feet.

The captain nodded to Slip and strode away, and Jymn found himself dragged along behind — Caber on one arm, Daj on the other.

'Cap, I'm sorry!' Jymn called, 'we were just trying to scare them off. I should have left someone in sight of the ship, I see that now- *ooof!'* The air rushed out of his lungs as Caber's fist met his abdomen, and he found himself barely able to breathe.

'Captain's made his mind up,' Daj growled sternly. 'No changing it now.'

They dragged him up a steep, rocky path and eventually to an outcropping of rock that hung over the water. Jymn could see a dozen islands from here, the smoke trails of the fruit-eaters on some, and could even glimpse the rotting hulks of the Graveyard, beyond. The captain tossed the handgun over the edge, and Jymn felt his heart beat many times before he heard it splash below.

The captain's eyes blazed as he turned back to Jymn. 'Kneel.'

'Wait, Cap?' Caber protested. 'You're sure you want to do this?'

'Caber!' hissed Daj, and Jymn felt her foot in the back of his knee, sending him sprawling to the floor before the captain.

'Jymn Hatcher. You have rushed into danger without thinking,' the captain pronounced. 'You have stolen, and profited from that stealing.'

Jymn's mind raced. What had he stolen? *The weld-gear — but that wasn't me!* 'But…' he stammered, but the captain went on.

'You have done violence against your fellow man.'

Jymn remembered the man in the alley. *It was self defence!*

'You have endangered yourself and your crew.'

No… well yes, but we had to do something…

'You have been told what to do. And have disobeyed.'

Yes. Yes he had, but… it worked. The plan worked. Surely that counted for something?

The captain paused, letting his judgement sink in, then nodded sadly at Daj and Caber.

Daj leaned down, checking his bonds, and then with savage strength, ripped his new shirt from his back. Jymn's eyes watered, and he barely heard the lapping of water fifty feet below over the pounding of his heart. Before he knew what was happening, he felt strong hands lift him, and he was thrown — clear of the cliff — plummeting to the waves below.

135

The impact stunned him, and suddenly he was kicking at the water, fighting for the surface that could have been anywhere. His lungs burned, and he strained against his bonds, and found to his amazement that the thick rope fell free. He scrabbled, and suddenly his ears roared and he was clear of the water, gasping for air. He found the waves were not so tall after all, and the cliff above not so impossibly far away. There was a laugh beside him, and he turned to see grinning faces in the water with him — splashing him. Archonauts. Kelpy was there, and Balder, and the Twins, all frolicking in the water and smiling as he choked and spluttered. Mighty Balder scooped Jymn in his arms and lifted him clear of the waves — carrying him to the beach.

Slip stood in the sand smiling, with Gam alongside him, and Nix washing the clay and 'blood' from her skin. Behind them, the captain was striding down the beach with Daj and Caber in tow — his stern gaze replaced now with a wide, devilish grin. He held his hands up and shrugged.

'You'll have to excuse the theatrics, Jymn. It's something of a tradition,' he smiled. Even Daj smiled beside him — only Caber seemed unable to enjoy the moment. Taking the wrench-knife from Slip, the captain sawed at the short purple fabric that barely covered his ribs, tearing a narrow strip free.

'Jymn Hatcher. You have rushed into danger without thinking,' he repeated, the words solemn now. 'You have stolen, and profited from that stealing. You have done violence against your fellow man. You have endangered yourself and your crew. And best of all — you have been told what to do, and have disobeyed.' He leaned in close, pressing the purple sash into Jymn's hands, 'welcome aboard, lad. Seems you might be cut out for this after all.'

A hush fell over the gathered crew, who studied Jymn expectantly. He looked at their faces — all seemed anxious to see what he would do next. Then it came to him.

Reaching up, he tied the fabric aslant about his head, covering the bad eye — as the bandage had once done. As he turned to face the crew, gathered in the shallow water before him, they cheered — whooping and splashing and rushing to congratulate him.

As the crush of jubilant crewmates dissipated, Jymn saw Weylun standing — pale and unsteady — next to the rowboat, with North at the oars. He looked around at the grinning sailors — and at Jymn, shirtless — puzzlement knotting his face.

'Wait… what did I miss?'

———————————————

The next days were as close to happiness as Jymn had ever found himself. It turned out that despite the failure of the speak-wire, one of the teams had identified a suitable mast, and a great labour was taken up to fell the tree and drag her down to the beach to be carpentered. Now a fully-fledged Archonaut, Jymn found himself sharing in the chores — or 'watches' as the crew called them — but rather than resent the work, he revelled in the sense of camaraderie and purpose that had always been lacking in life aboard the Trossul. His shirt was returned — and one of his first jobs was to stitch it into the fabric of the patchwork sails alongside all the others. It was another of their curious traditions — and a task from which he came away with bloody, sore fingers, but also a tremendous sense of belonging.

And for all the work, there was just as much play. It turned out that the crabs that wreaked so much havoc with the cabling, were in fact working on pure instinct. It seemed they had long ago been spliced to seek out and digest plastics — indeed their thick, mulicoloured shells were made of the stuff. Weylun took a pair of the newly christened 'Polycrabs' to his workshop to study, but the rest of the crew found great joy in racing the colourful creatures across the island, using scraps of plastic as lures. For exercise, a pair of sand-masts and ropes were erected on the beach, and Jymn soon learned the rules to the game of 'Kassel Ball' — an athletic and tactical game played between two teams of five using a large 'monkey's fist' knot for a ball. On the third day, North fabricated a short mast and sail for the rowboat, and taught Jymn how to sail her in the narrow channels between the islands. It was tremendous fun — being so close to the water but still dry and fast — one time they even had to see off a raft of real fruit-eaters that paddled out to appraise them.

137

By night, the work abated, and the crew would gather around fires on the beach to sing, play music, drink North's latest distillation, and make merry. Nix answered many questions about her home, and quickly established herself as a wondrous teller of stories — aided by Jymn's translations. Before long, most nights ended with her fireside tales of the Faireys, and especially of the fantastical traditions they clung to — of their ancestors who walked upon the moon, and of the wizards of ages past who flew through the skies like birds. Jymn faltered often — Nix having to explain the curious signs for *ancestor, teckromancer,* and *astronaut* before he could convey them to the enrapt crew.

He felt a bitter guilt that — once again — he had taken all the credit for an act of courage that was almost entirely her doing. Just like in Shoalhaven — he had spent most of the time paralysed with fear, while she charged the enemy headlong — but the crew lauded him with praise and reward, while she was overlooked. But she simply shrugged when he confessed his guilt. *I won't tell them*, she laughed, wickedly. *It will be our secret. Besides, they can't make me an Archonaut, can they!*

Indeed they couldn't, for the ship's 'articles', which Jymn was now forced to memorise, were quite clear on the matter of women aboard — though somehow nobody seemed to think this applied to Daj. There were laws detailing the limits of the captain's control, and the votes that would take place outside those limits, laws detailing the punishments for stealing from the hold, or galley, or for tussling with your crewmates, and even laws for the 'proper' way to take a ship from a fellow captain. And pages — whole pages that Jymn had to struggle through one troublesome word at a time — that detailed in specifics the allocation of treasure and profit among the crew, including a bonus of 'first spoils' for those that came across the bounty.

On the fifth evening after the 'routing of the reavers' as the events of the first day had been dubbed, Jymn found himself translating the tale of Nix's capture and subsequent imprisonment.

My old teacher and storyteller Ol'Wen had died, and it was her funeral. A Fairey funeral involves much singing in the deep moon-caves, and it makes me sad to not hear, so I was on the surface —

138

outside, swimming, as she taught me.

I found a curious teck in the water — I think it was a time-teller — and took it to the shore. My friend came to fetch me. Losalfhym is protected, as you know, by great listener devices — and they had heard something, and the alarm had been sounded.

But I was curious, and went back for the teck — and I was caught! Snatched by a great pox-ridden pirate with metal teeth!

'That's Jonny Hull!' chattered one of the Twins excitedly.

And I ran — but then his friend — a terrible man, thick as a tree, cast a net over me.

'And that's Blaken!' shivered the other twin, 'he's awful,'

'*Was* Blaken,' corrected Slip, crossing himself. 'Tsar had them all killed, remember?'

And then I was stuffed into a boat and taken to their ship — the Mirror. And they all looked upon me with fear. The captain, a slimy man with a green hat...

'Narce, may he rest in piss!' chimed North, drunkenly tipping a measure of drink to the sand.

Well, Captain Narcis couldn't decide what to do with me, you see? So he called upon a fearsome old pirate. Ancient he was — with scars across his face where his eyes once were...

Jymn stopped translating, a shiver running down his spine. He turned to Nix. *A bandage, across acid-scarred eyes?*

Nix frowned, then nodded. Jymn's mind raced.

'What's the matter, Jymn?' called the captain, over the impatient clamouring of the audience.

'She's describing an old, blind pirate. Bandage — scars…'

'Yes — he was called Jon Cane,' nodded Cap, 'nasty piece of work, used to sail under Tsar himself. Good riddance too.'

'Yes… only — only he's not dead, captain.' Jymn stammered. 'I saw him in Shoalhaven, when they had Nix. He nearly caught me trying to help her.'

'You're sure?' the captain demanded, suddenly stern.

Jymn nodded, swallowing the iron lump in his throat and

glancing at Nix. 'If he escaped Tsar, that means…'

'It means he can take them back to Losalfhym,' the captain finished, the colour draining from his face. 'And we've been here five days…' Turning to the merry audience, he yelled clear above the noise, 'everyone back to the ship — right now! We're leaving.'

X

The Cove

Jymn stared out at the darkness ahead, straining for any hint of the wreckage he knew was all around them. He gripped the wheel tight, his palms sweating into the rough wood as he guided the great ship through the Graveyard.

'Starboard! Hard to Starboard!' — Gam's voice carried out from the darkness above, barely audible above the din of the engine, just as Jymn saw a hulking mass of rotten metal appear in the dim lantern light ahead.

He wrenched the wheel to the right — but too late. The Archon groaned as it grazed against the festering metal, grinding and ripping, and sending a cascade of night-dormant magflies scattering across the deck.

There was an angry bang from beneath him, and he heard the Captain's voice bellow from below, 'easy, Jymn!'

He wasn't ready for this. North was supposed to be the helmsman. Jymn looked to his left, where North was slumped with a coil of tarred rope for a pillow — blind-drunk on his latest batch of distillate. In fact, more than half the Archonauts were similarly afflicted, and now the great ship was being crewed by just thirteen, and not thirteen of the best. The wind between the islands was against them, and they were permitted to fire up the terrible old diesel engine, which was a mercy, as they would never have managed the sails between them. The grinding whomp of the motor put the captain in a terrible mood, and even seemed to rouse the inhabitants of the other islands. Jymn had seen more than one

141

fire flare up on the small beaches, or among the trees — queer silhouttes staring back at them in the night.

North groaned beside him and muttered in his drunken slumber 'larboard — or is it stars… uhh', before rolling over and passing out once more.

The captain was below with Weylun, trying desperately to perform a dangerous teck-spell called 'hayling' — by which they could somehow send a warning across the sky to reach the Cove before the Godsmen did. Weylun had panicked at the suggestion — apparently there was no surer way to attract the attention of the Raptions, so strong was the trace involved — but the captain had insisted, pointing out that they would be long gone from the source of the signal by the time anything came to hunt them.

While they worked, Jymn had been tasked with the first watch at the helm. There was no time for subtlety — once they were out of the Graveyard he was simply to point the ship right at the Cove, and let the crew figure out the setting of sail when the wind finally came.

'But, the map? I don't know where to go!' Jymn had protested, as the captain had turned to hurry below.

The captain threw one arm about Jymn's shoulder, pressed close, and pointed at a star ahead. 'You see that star? The left foot of the Rigger — just off the starboard bow, you've got it? Now to its right — there. That second star on the right. You just point us there Jymn, and hold the course straight until morning, ok?'

Jymn had nodded feebly, trying to fix the star in his mind, lest he lose himself and all the crew upon the open sea. But the constellation of the Rigger was easy enough to spot — and though he lost it behind a low cloud every now and then, he managed to doggedly keep the Archon trudging her course until dawn came, and he was relieved by a pale-looking North.

There had been no response to the 'hayling', a fact which set the captain on edge, though Weylun consoled him by pointing out that the Faireys would have to be truly desperate in order to send word back — it was their home, they were not so fortunate as to be able to simply sail away from the trace it would create.

A full day and a night passed like this — and despite a fine wind, the crew remained solemn and almost grim, subdued by the urgency of the voyage. Nix, rudely awakened from her brief daydream of happiness on the island, had again retreated within herself, and sat — caked in sunclay — always staring over the bowsprit, or silently sharing the foremast with Gam.

Jymn tried to help Weylun plot their course across the new map as they went, taking North's reckonings of their speed and bearing, and translating them into a crooked line that bore ever onward, toward the small speck of yellow that marked the Fairey home. And so it was that at first light on the third day, at dawn, they looked to the East and saw Losalfhym.

And it was burning.

Distress spread like a muttering wave across the deck as the sighting was made — a clear tower of dark smoke carried north on the wind, the small, precious island Cove beneath it.

Nix was below refreshing her sun-clay when Gam's call carried down from the foremast, and it was not until one of the twins was sent to fetch her that she learned what was going on. The smoke was the first thing she saw as she rushed above deck.

A resolve came over her then — Jymn had seen it happen — it was as if through the set of her jaw and the clenching of her fists, she had managed to conjure a suit of armour to protect herself from feeling. There was no signing for *help* today, and Jymn didn't know the right words to show her.

Once the shock of the smoke had faded, the Captain ordered Slip to beat to quarters. Caber's great frame-drum was roused in a steady rhythm, and the crew rushed into action, preparing themselves for close fighting.

Jymn — unpracticed at battle — tried to help where he could, and found that the labour at least managed to keep the feeling of sickening dread at bay. He, and Scup, and Kelpy cleared the tables from the upper deck, and prepared a space for Kelpy to work upon the wounded, but the sight of the medicker's instruments and bloody rags was too much for Jymn — who excused himself and dashed for air above deck. There he found all obstructions had been cleared away, great boarding nets had been rigged, and the crew had outfitted themselves with all manner of arms — swords, beaters, and knives, crude bows and mismatched armour. Even Nix had availed herself of a wicked spear that looked as if it had been hammered from a solid rod of bronze.

Weylun called for assistance, and Jymn soon found himself helping to distribute the various teck-weapons among the crew. The long spear was familiar — with its great sparking tip that would immobilise its target — but there were also quivers of charged steel rods that could be shot from bows, bandoliers of handheld cylinders each with a pair of sharp probes, and wooden beaters ringed with steel bands that hissed and fizzed in the morning air.

Only when there were no more tasks to distract him, did Jymn find himself crouched behind the gunwales alongside the others, clutching his small wrench-knife, and trying not to picture having to use it. His anxiety must have been clear, because mighty Balder came alongside and offered him a short single-handed crossbow and a hip-quiver of the sparking bolts.

'Here — it will help keep the fighting at a distance,' the huge, gentle boy smiled, then added with a shrug, 'at least until the darts run out...'

Jymn thanked him, and fitted the small quiver to his belt with trembling hands. An eerie silence fell over the ship as she glode toward the island. The closer they drew, the more Jymn could make out of the fabled Fairey home. On all sides the Cove was unbreachable — all but for a narrow chasm that yawned black on its western shore, and for which they headed.

'The sentinels are gone,' Balder said quietly, a grim expression on his broad face as they drew closer to the gully. Jymn followed his gaze and saw a half-dozen great alcoves in the high rock walls, each the height of two men. The cliff face looked as if it had been beaten half to death by a great giant of the sea — though Jymn suspected cannonfire was the true cause. A mighty field-gun lay crippled and broken — its rent barrel protruding from one of the alcoves, but the rest were empty. Others among the crew began to notice, and confused glances and whispers began to spread along the Gunwales as the ship slid deftly between the narrow cliffs.

144

Jymn searched for Nix — and found her near the bow, gripping the wooden railing so hard he thought she might snap her own fingers.

There was a screeching cry, and Jymn saw Puggle streaking above the mast, tangling and coiling high in the air with another fezzard, though whether playfully or violently, he couldn't tell. Nix turned to him, confusion and worry etched on her tired face. *Can you hear the fighting?* She demanded.

Jymn paused for a moment to listen. *No — there is nothing*, he signed. He had taken the eerie silence for granted, not thinking through what it meant. Whatever had happened here, the fighting was over. Nix swallowed, and turned back to her vigil.

The gully was so close on either side of the ship that Jymn felt he could have touched it with the tip of Nix's spear. Two of the Archonauts were ready at the bow with the great fending-poles, but North's expert piloting guided them silently through the channel, and suddenly out into a wide, curving lagoon, surrounded by craggy rock.

The signs of battle were all about. The pillar of smoke, it seemed, came from the far side of the island, but there was wreckage aplenty here in this inner-sea. Three great steel ships protruded from the water, sunk and burnt and abandoned — already buzzing with magflies — and a pile of pirate-dead lay heaped and smouldering upon the steep shore. The Archon's sails were let out, and she drifted slowly among the wrecks as the crew scanned the rocks, fearing some trap or ambush.

'Who goes there?'

The voice echoed all around the protected cove.

'Speak — or suffer the fate of these others!'

The ships — the voice was coming from the wreckage of the steel ships. The captain sprung atop the gunwales and faced them, pulling his cap from his head and calling 'Gil Makkanok. Inkäinen. Friend, and captain of the Archon. I bring home Nix, of your kin, daughter of Malvor.' The captain beckoned for Nix, who — still clutching her spear — strode to join him.

'Prove it.'

The captain hesitated, looking round at his ship, 'prove what?

145

That she is Nix? That I am Inkäinen? Or that this is indeed the Archon? Have you seen many wooden vessels of late?'

A face appeared in the wreckage of the nearest drowned ship. Grim, and greyed with sunclay, the white hair almost black with the grime of battle. 'Prove that you are a friend,' spoke the face, 'let the girl go.'

'Uluwe!' called the captain — 'I have known you since you were a boy.'

'Let her go then,' insisted the voice, 'and prove that the friendship holds.'

The captain turned to Nix, helping her up to the gunwale. He struggled clumsily at the sign — pointing at her, then the water, then made a crude swimming motion and pointed at the grim face across the water.

It seemed to be enough. With a nod, and a quick glance back toward the crew, Nix handed him the bronze spear and dived from the ship with barely a splash. Jymn rushed to the side after her, and saw only a white streak gliding through the blue, leaving a trail of sunclay behind it, like smoke in the water.

The release of their 'captive' seemed to be enough to demonstrate the intentions of the crew. Soon more Faireys began to emerge from the wreckage, and small boats were rowed out to the Archon to ferry the crew to the rocky beach — though great care was taken to ensure no weapons left the ship. The captain was on the first boat ashore, and called for Jymn to join him, that he might translate for Nix if the need arose.

Jymn felt like he was wandering into a daydream, as he climbed out of the curious boat and onto the island alongside Slip and Daj. Nix had been the first and only Fairey he'd seen — she was slight, and silent, and wilful — it was easy to forget that she was not some magical sprite blown in on the wind, but part of a race of others just like her. And yet not so like her, it seemed. These Fairey men wore the same impossibly white skin under their crust of sunclay, but where she was slight, they were strong and muscular. Where she was silent, they spoke with deep guarded voices, as if they were always listening at the horizon.

146

Despite the standoff on the water, Uluwe greeted the captain with a fierce embrace, apologising for his lack of faith. It seemed the attackers had breached the Cove with a similar ruse — pretending to have brought Nix home — only to then summon reinforcements and take control of the island.

'The Goodmother — she listened to some rogue pirate?' The Captain asked in disbelief. 'She opened the gate without seeing proof?'

'Ah, but it was not just any pirate,' sighed Uluwe, 'It was the bloodletter Tsar himself that came, with some poor harbour girl dressed up like Nix, and the head of the captain that had taken her.'

The captain's face grew dark at hearing Tsar's name, and he strode beside Uluwe along the shore in silence.

Throughout this exchange, Nix had been treated like little more than a trophy — surrounded by the strongest of her kin, dried and wrapped in a sun-shawl, but unable to speak, unable to understand what was happening.

Eventually she shouldered her way free of her bodyguard and found Jymn. Bypassing everything she reached simply for the sign for questioning.

Jymn tried his best to fill her in — tried to explain what little he understood of what was happening here — but for everything he told her, three new questions arose, and he was soon of little help.

Eventually the party reached a sheer face of rock, jagged and rough, pockmarked and scorched by recent gunfire. Uluwe stepped forward and banged a heavy steel staff against the floor.

'Uluwe — Feinal's son,' he boomed.

Jymn flinched as a voice echoed through the rock, seemingly from a dozen places all at once. 'What is hidden in snow...'

Without hesitation, Uluwe answered, 'is revealed at thaw.'

There was a pause, then a great wrenching of steel from within the rock, and a portion of the stone swung outwards toward them — a great circle, as wide as a man's reach, backed with steel and hung upon mighty hinges. The sounds of mournful singing flooded out of the door like a wave, and though the inside was dark against the bright morning sun, Jymn saw many lights sparkling within. It reminded him of a stone that a passenger upon the Trossul had shown him once — dull and unremarkable on the outside, but that when split open revealed a tiny cavern of jewels.

A knot of Faireys stood in the doorway to receive them — Jymn counted five. There was a couple — or perhaps a brother and sister — it was hard for him to see past the identical colouring. They looked fraught, and tired, and seemed to lean upon one another for support. There was a pair of Fairey men that looked like they too had once been powerfully built like Uluwe, but time, and no small share of recent wounds, had sapped them of their strength. And before them all — an ageing, white spectre of a woman. She was short, and appeared hunched by some invisible weight, her locked hair reaching almost to her knees, but still she held her head high, and there was a solemn dignity in the pools of her eyes that Jymn couldn't help but be drawn to.

Nix shoved past him and darted to the couple, who dropped to their knees and wrapped her into a weeping, trembling embrace. Jymn felt a pang of envy at the sight of the reunited family, though it was swiftly drowned by a wave of guilt at his own selfishness.

The old woman stepped forward and surveyed the newcomers, her big, dark eyes reflecting the daylight without. She nodded gently. 'Inkäinen. You come to us at a time of great sorrow.'

The captain strode forward and, removing his hat, knelt at the old woman's feet. 'I am sorry Maitryn, we were too late,' he said, staring at the ground.

'Respect, boy — she is named Goodmother,' growled one of the old warriors, but he was silenced with a wave of the old woman's hand.

'You tell a kneeling man of respect, Uthan? When was it *you* last kneeled for me, hmm? Come Gil, on your feet,' and she pulled the captain upright with a surprising vigor, and embraced him. 'Better late, than not at all. And bearing such sweet gifts, too,' she added, turning to Nix, who was signing urgently with her sobbing parents. Jymn looked away, fearing to intrude upon their privacy.

'Make space for our guests Uthan, and see that they are fed.' The

Goodmother pulled back from the captain, her nose wrinkling, 'and bathed too, I think.'

'I'm sorry, it has been a long voyage.'

'Less of this *sorry* hmm?' she tsked. 'It is not a coat that fits a captain, I think. Now come, we have much to speak on.'

Taking his arm, the Goodmother turned to lead deeper into the cavern. Slip laid a hand on Jymn's shoulder and whispered, 'welcome to the Cove!' and together they followed deeper into the Fairey home.

Losalfhym was, it seemed, a network of sea caves that had long ago been joined and bored out by the work of men. It seemed almost that a timeless war was being waged — smooth, precise passages cut by ancient machines giving way to cavernous chambers of natural rock, jagged and knife-like, and wet, sculpted by the sea. Everywhere glassy pools of water reflected a twinkling starlight that was trapped in the vaulting ceilings above — though whether from some artificial teck-source, or a natural phenomenon, Jymn couldn't tell.

He wasn't sure what he'd expected — pale creatures sitting in moonlit trees, laughing and playing harps, perhaps — whatever it was, it wasn't this. Far from being gay and happy, this place felt like an imprisoned memory of the past. There was a terrible sense of sorrow among the Fair Folk, and it seemed magnified — echoed and rebounded — off the rock walls, like their longing, mourning songs. And everywhere, among all the ancient grandeur, there were signs of the battle.

Jymn overheard much of what was said between the captain and the Goodmother, and what he missed he managed to piece together later. It seemed Tsar — desperate as he was to keep the Cove a secret — had realised the hope was lost, and had thrown his lot in with the church, providing them with a small army in the form of his 'franchise' Rougian Fleet. He had sailed the *For-More* to the Cove under engine, and then with only a rowboat and knot of his crew to guard their false prisoner, had approached the gate as he did each year for treatment, this time presenting Captain Narcis' head as proof of his intentions.

The moment the gate was opened, hell broke loose. The *For-More-ians* killed the girl, and then the gatekeepers, and by the time the Faireys had assembled some resistance, the rest of the fleet had arrived. The Sentinel guns held off most, but a half-dozen made it to the inner sea, flooding the shore with pirates. Some brave Faireys holed and sunk three of the invading vessels, but it was too late — they were outnumbered a hundred to one. The whole thing lasted less than an hour. The battle, at least. The occupation of Losalthym had lasted many days more while they searched for their answers.

'The *seed of the fair folk?*' The captain asked, adding 'they tried to learn it from Nix'

'Yes,' the Goodmother gritted her teeth. 'Though I would speak those words with caution, here. Much suffering has been borne for the sake of them.'

The column had drawn closer to the epicentre of the mourning — a vaulting chamber in which a dozen bodies were arranged, laid each beneath a white sheet. Fairey full-growns knelt beside some, weeping and swaying and calling out in their long, undulating grief-song.

'No, Nix!' her father called uselessly as she shrugged free of her parents' grasp and ran to one of the bodies. Letting out her own discordant cry of anguish, she collapsed, clutching at the form beneath the sheet. The couple already knelt beside the body wept all the louder for this fresh grief, and drew her into a sorrowful embrace.

'They brought a relic with them,' the Goodmother continued. 'Not teck — not even an artefact of the Skand, but some of their descendants, perhaps. A panel of beaten copper, etched with the old tongue. There were many ramblings, talk of a return to glory, of food inexhaustible, and a sun that never sets. But among it all, they obsessed over one passage:

Leyndarmál feðranna verða að koma til barnanna
Leiðin er falin í fræjum álfanna

150

It translates roughly to: *The secrets of the fathers must pass to the children. The way is hidden within the seed of the Fair Folk.'* She stared darkly at the young dead before her, weary with grief. 'All that death and pain, all because of one word, misunderstood. Mistranslated. The Godsmen are so obsessed with their heresies and their sins — blood, and death and lust — they read 'seed of the fair folk' and thought of nothing but breeding, sex, offspring...' she fought to stop her voice from breaking, '...our children. They had a splicer with them — despite their laws — and one by one they brought our young to her, searching in their blood, and flesh, and bone for their secret while we looked on, helpless. Only on the third day, after all this, did they come to me and reveal the relic. *Leiðin er falin í fræjum álfanna* — not *offspring*, not *children* — That is a trick of their language, not ours — *fræjum* to us literally means *seeds.*'

'Seeds?' The captain repeated, turning the problem over in his mind. 'What seeds do you have?'

The Goodmother nodded toward the West. 'None. Not any longer. You saw the smoke when you arrived? It comes from the Lunehall. They found their answer in the splice of our Mir-Trees. Moments, it took them — so clear was the message — hidden right in the genes of our sacred trees. A Map. Now, it seems, we begin to see the mind of our creators, and why those trees were made to be so revered.'

'A map to Thule,' Jymn gasped, overhearing. The Goodmother turned to him and seemed to weigh him with the light of her deep eyes. At length, she nodded.

'And the smoke?' asked the captain.

'They burned every tree. Every leaf, every root. All to ensure the map would be erased.'

'So it's over, then. They've done what they came to do.'

The Goodmother shook her head sadly. 'No child, for them it has just begun.'

151

XI

Council

Jymn washed, letting the cascade of hot water pour over him, drumming against his back and shoulders, and easing his knotted muscles. They had only been in Losalfhym a few hours, but already he felt strangely rejuvenated, and safe. The captain had taken leave to seek out some old friend among the Faireys, while the rest of the crew had been shown here, to their lodgings — a wide cave whose sandy floor fell away toward a pool of blue-green water, fed by a handful of small streams that tumbled down over the rocks. Steam rose from the water, and choked the narrow beam of daylight that pierced down from a cleft in the rock high above. Fezzards, occasionally, would screech down through the hole — bright streaks of red-green that seemed to ride the column of sunlight into the gloom, their loud calls echoing all around. But the Archonauts paid no mind, and being familiar with the place, lay bedrolls upon the sand to sleep, or played at slate-cards, or stripped and bathed in the falls of hot water. Jymn caught himself staring at Kelpy, whose gentle frame seemed so incongruous with the hourglass tattoo that was now revealed, spreading its broad wings across his chest. Balder had splashed him then, and yelled in mock protectiveness, and they had all laughed for the first time since leaving the Graveyard.

Jymn dried himself, and dressed. His skin was sore from the onslaught of the sun, and he lamented the loss of his shirt. This shirtlessness, it seemed, marked him as a newcomer to the crew. The twins — the most recent addition besides him — had only purchased their new tunics a few months back, having been similarly shirtless for the best part of a year. He hoped to find something sooner than that — he felt awkward, and clumsy, and vulnerable in his bare skin.

The crew of fifty were swallowed by the enormity of the cave — it almost felt like they were encamped on a beach at night, so far away were the walls. Only the echoing gave it away. Whispers were hard to conceal in the hot, damp cave. He heard it confirmed that the Splicer the Church had brought here was Syrincs — and that she had been forced to do awful things against her will. He also heard tell of this 'Fairey friend' the captain had gone to see. A woman, or girl. And she was quite clearly pregnant, it seemed, if the whispers were to be believed.

'How long since you were last here?' Jymn asked Gam, who seemed to hear everything, whether he chose to or not. 'Is it the captain's child?' It seemed impossible to think of the captain siring children — he could only have been perhaps four years older than Jymn.

Gam shook his head, 'I don't think so. Myrgrét and the captain, they were involved for a long time, but he's too young for her, now. Or she's too old, I'm not sure. It's been a year since we were here, besides, and they fought last time.'

Jymn thought of Nix, and of her wailing and clutching at the body beneath the sheet. He should find her, make sure she was ok, though he worried his signing was too clumsy and practical for such a conversation.

He wandered the caves of Losalfhym alone, stopping to ask once or twice for Malvor — Nix's father. But not all the Fair Folk were as trusting as the Goodmother, and most refused to answer him directly. Eventually, lost and alone, he had come across Weylun struggling with a chest of tools. It turned out that the Faireys had never received the Archon's warning, and though it wouldn't have helped anyway — for it was sent far too late — Weylun was still mortified that he had failed in his task. And so, had determined to pull the offending teck from the ship and repair it in one of the great shielded chambers of the Fairies. Jymn, of course, was enlisted to help.

'Hand me the melter, will you?'

Jymn plucked the hot steel wand from the bench and handed it over cautiously. The young tecksmith was hunched over a tangle of wires and circuitry, a pair of thick lenses over his eyes as he squinted down at the thing he called a *ray-dee-oh*.

'Ok — try now,' he called across the room to the Fairey boy who had been appointed to watch over them, but now was serving as a third pair of hands to their tinkering. The boy nodded, then turned back to his instruments — a dizzying array of lights, switches and dials set into the ancient worktop before him. He wore a curious device upon his head that covered both ears, and he closed his eyes, listening as he fiddled with a pair of dials. He opened his eyes again and shook his head apologetically.

'Ugh. Well — that's it then,' Weylun threw his hands up in frustration. 'The tyksaryx is fried.'

Jymn peered at the ship's radio on the bench. It looked like a creature that had been caught by some predator — its hard outer shell cracked open to expose the wires and precious components within. Weylun reached in and teased a circuit board from the heart of the device, holding it up for the Fairey boy to see.

'You have more of these? I need a new one.'

The boy crossed the room and took the small board, turning it over in his hands with a frown. He shook his head, 'no, I think. Not here. There might be one inside the machines, but...'

'...but it is forbidden to touch them, I know,' muttered Weylun, bitterly. Jymn got the impression he had been longing to get at the Fairey teck for some time.

'What's it for?' Jymn asked, taking the part and squinting at the intricate silver wires tracing across the green teck-plate, 'power?'

'Power? No — look...' Weylun pointed out a pair of threaded gold cylinders affixed to the board, and Jymn saw the letters Tx-Rx engraved alongside them. 'Tyks-aryx — it's the part that converts trace into words. You speak into here...' he indicated a makeshift

154

plastic handset that trailed from the device, 'and then this part twists your words up within the trace. Then someone with another *ray-dee-oh* can sort of 'catch' the words and untangle them.'

'Very dangerous,' muttered the Fairey boy darkly, as he did whenever the word 'trace' was uttered. Though Jymn understood his fear — there was enough old teck in here to bring every Raption for a thousand clicks — but these weren't relics, not salvaged scraps from the ruined world — these devices were the birthright of a people who descended directly from the teck-makers of old.

'So what's the answer?' Jymn asked, sniffing at the circuit. It smelled faintly of burned plastic.

'Question.' Corrected Weylun, 'always questions. *The scientist is not a person who gives the right answers, he is one who asks the right questions* — That's what my teacher used to say. *Whenever you're stuck for an answer, Weylun — try to reach for the right question instead!*'

'What's a scientist?'

'Oh, they were like splicers and tecksmiths in the old world — *before* — you know. The ones that built all this.' He gestured around at the Fairey teck lining the chamber.

'Oh, ok.' Jymn thought on this for a moment, before adding 'well, what's the question then?'

Weylun took the broken circuit back and frowned. 'Where do I get another one of these, I guess.'

While Weylun took the broken radio back to the ship, along with some scraps of plastic to feed the crabs, Jymn set off once again in search of Nix. Night had fallen, and the occasional shafts of light that pierced the caves from above had faded, leaving only the orb-like teck-lights that were festooned along the walls, and the curious 'stars' — set high into the vaulting ceilings, mirrored in the glassy pools below.

Jymn thought of Nix's name-sign — fingers kicking, like legs through water — and remembered her love of swimming. None of the hundred pools within Losalfhym had been deep cnough to swim, and so he sought out the main gate and took his leave to stroll outside, along the banks of the 'inner sea' in hope of finding her.

Not a glimmer of artificial light escaped the caves, though the moon was waxing toward full, and hung low in the evening sky. The water was clear and dark, and Jymn felt sure, as he clambered along the overhanging rocks, that he would be able to see her, shining like a white beacon in the deep pools, but there was nothing.

He strolled by moonlight to the western edge of the island, beneath the wispy column of smoke that still drifted lazily into the night sky. The smoke of the mir-trees. He'd heard of them in the Fairey stories, too — magical trees that took in light during the day, and gave it back at night. He'd imagined scenes of beautiful twilit forests and fertile soil, not some jagged rock beset by the flood-sea, but it was still strangely comforting to know that not *all* his childhood wonder had been false, though he might never be able to see the trees now. He climbed jagged and perilous rocks toward the smoke hoping for a glimpse of the burned orchard within. He knew, of course, that it had been put to the torch by the Church and their pirate army, but some part of him hoped he might see something, some remnant sapling that had survived the fire, against the odds.

The opening was wide — perhaps ten feet across — and seemed like a gaping, bottomless void against the moonlit rocks without. The smoke was thin and eerie as it caught the light, and Jymn half imagined the dust of the trees still glowing as they drifted upward in death. Cautiously he clambered to the edge, putting his back to the low moon and squinting down toward the patch of ground that the light struck.

He heard voices below, barely discernible amidst their own echoes, 'Oh, come child. You knew it as well as she — it was never to last, this thing. It was time she took someone her own age.'

Fearing he'd stumbled deep into privacy, Jymn made to turn and

156

leave, but there was a noise, and suddenly a sharpness and pain at his throat, something grasping his hair.

'One move and your blood will mix with the ashes, útlander.' The voice was deep, cold.

Jymn fought every instinct to squirm, kick, and run. He felt the cold bite of a blade at his neck — and the hot breath of his attacker against his ear.

A figure appeared at the edge of the hole, springing out of the darkness in a blur of white, a long blade catching the moonlight. The features were hard to make out — though Jymn recognised the strong set of the frame.

The blade lowered. 'One of yours, Inkäinen,' spoke the figure, and Jymn recognised the voice of Uluwe. There was a quick hand gesture, and suddenly the knife at his throat vanished, his hair released.

'You should tread careful, boy. There has been much faith broken, here,' Uluwe spoke, as his blade disappeared into its sheath. 'What is your business?'

'I'm…' Jymn found his voice stuck in his throat, and coughed, 'I'm looking for Nix. The girl we brought back?'

'I know who she is,' snapped Uluwe, 'she isn't here, boy. Be off.'

'Bring him down to me,' came a call from the chamber below, and Jymn recognised the voice from before — the voice of the Goodmother. Jymn's mouth was suddenly dry. He'd heard something he shouldn't have, and he didn't like his chances of lying about it to the old woman.

Grumbling, Uluwe took Jymn firmly in hand and led him into the void and down. The climb was steep, and treacherous, and without Uluwe's strong arm and guidance he would surely have slipped and been dashed against the rocks below, but as it was he soon found himself standing — shaken and damp with fear-sweat — among the burnt ruins of the mir-grove. The moonlight shone down from the opening like a searchlight, cutting blue through the dusty, smoky air. Though the night was cold, Jymn was sure he could still feel the remembered heat of the fire radiating from the floor and walls of the chamber.

The Goodmother stood, arm in arm with the captain, among the black and crumbling boughs of the trees, her eyebrows raised toward Jymn expectantly.

'I believe thanks are in order?'

'I'm sorry, yes. Thank you,' Jymn mumbled, eyes fixed on the ground. 'I wasn't trying to…'

'Your captain has told me how you rescued the girl,' the Goodmother went on, 'thank you, Jymn Hatcher, for bringing her back to us.'

Jymn looked up into the huge, dark eyes, reflecting the moonlight now. They were smiling. 'Oh, well I didn't really… it was luck, mostly. And she saved me, besides, so we're even.' He glanced at the captain, trying to weigh whether he had said the right words, but the rusty-haired boy was lost in the past, and paying no mind to the present.

'Hmm, that is good.' The Goodmother bobbed her head, setting her locked hair swaying, 'lífsskuld. The debt is paid then.' She continued her walk — arm in arm with the captain — and motioned for Jymn to follow.

'Settle an argument for me, if you will, Jymn,' she said, gesturing at the ghastly blackened trees all around. 'What is the difference between a secret that is meant to be found, and a secret that is meant to be forgotten?'

Jymn turned the puzzle over in his mind. He'd heard some riddles from foreigners upon the Trossul before, and in stories, but none like this. The confusion must have been plain to read, because she continued:

'Let us say you have a secret, some treasure or other, and you want to make sure somebody, one day, will find it. But not today. What do you do?'

'Hide it, I suppose?'

'Indeed you would,' she smiled. 'Now let us say you have another secret. A dark one, perhaps. And you want to make sure nobody finds it. Not *ever*. Would you hide it also?'

'Yeah, I think so.'

The captain threw his hands up in triumph, but the Goodmother stopped to turn to Jymn — her gaze penetrating.

'Unless…' Jymn hesitated.

'Go on…'

'Well wouldn't it be better to just... destroy it?'

She smiled and spread her arms, indicating the scorched trees all around. 'It seems so, does it not?'

'This was different,' the captain spoke at last, 'this was close by — and the secret hard to keep. Nobody would go to the end of the Earth just to destroy something that's already hidden — that's not how people work.'

'*They* would. They *are*, child. This leader of theirs — Rasmus, they call him — he's not like the old Pars. For him it's not about the money, or the power, or the violence even, though God knows he's no stranger to it. This man *really* believes the reason the world is this way is because of teck, and that the only way to get back to 'God's grace' is to stamp it out once and for all. That's why they will go to the end of the Earth — and all the preserved knowledge of a thousand years will burn if they get there first.'

The captain hesitated. 'First? What do you mean *first*?'

The Goodmother glanced mischievously at the captain, her dark eyes twinkling.

'Oh no…. no way!' the captain shook his head. 'I've got a crew to feed — we haven't made a good haul in weeks. We need coin for that, not honour. Maitryn, I hate the church as much as you, but I can't be taking the boys off on some crusade.'

'Plenty of coin in old teck, as I understand?'

'Not if it's burned to ashes when we get there, there isn't!'

'Fastest ship on the world-sea, that's what you used to say, isn't it?'

'They have a head start! And we don't even know where they're going,' he jabbed a finger at the nearest mir-tree. 'They *burned* all the maps, remember!'

Even in the dark, Jymn could see the Goodmother's eyes close as the two pools of reflected moonlight winked out. 'The old ways

159

and places are still known to a few. When I was a child there was a man that came here trading stories for teck. A white man that spoke the elder tongue.'

'I'm done with the Skand...'

The Goodmother shook her head, 'not Skand, Magi.'

'That's worse! Teckromancers!' the captain scoffed. 'Mad old wizards. They all got hunted down by their machines, or burned as blasphemers. There are none left.'

'He is left. Rumours of his name still blow in the West. Node he is called. You must find him if you are to learn the way.'

'This is all just... madness!' the captain turned away, exasperated. 'Finding Thule, hunting for wizards! Fooling around with the past isn't going to make anything better for today, is it? It's too late.'

'All the secrets of all the codewrights of the ancient world, buried beneath Thule, they say. All manner of past-fixes for present-problems, I should think. For the world, and for each of us.' She reached out and gently touched the bandage that covered Jymn's eye socket, and he was surprised to find that he didn't flinch away. 'Might even find some medicker code, too. To change things back to how they ought to be.' She looked at the captain and Jymn sensed that some meaning passed between them — but it was hidden to him.

Cap caught Jymn staring, 'what? You're crew now, you have a voice — speak your mind!'

'Well... it's just what Syrincs said, isn't it? This whole mess started *because* of ignoring the past. And they've still got her, haven't they — prisoner, like? Don't we owe her our help?'

The Goodmother smiled. 'A wise one you've got here, Gil. Sometimes one eye sees clearer than two.'

The captain sighed, relenting at last. 'You know we have to vote on it, it's not just my decision.'

The Goodmother smiled, the deep pools of her eyes twinkling. 'And you know as well as I, those boys will do whatever you ask of them.'

Beyond the constant blur of red-green comets, Jymn spotted the small, wiry outline of a Fairey — white against the black rock — huddled in the corner of the tall chamber. He'd found her at last. The Goodmother's guess had been good. She had told him 'you seek to find someone who wants to be alone. Try going where nobody wants to be.' And nobody wanted to be here. The fezzardry was a permanent cacophony of screeching birds, spinning and whirling like feathered darts around the moonlight at the centre of the cave-shaft. Jymn darted forward into the light, narrowly avoiding a collision as he sprung past the wall of diving birds. The noise in here was deafening — but unlike the suffocating engine-roar of his old home on Sixdeck, the fezzards were a discordant choir, ever rising and falling and predictable only in their inharmony. It was music, but made by different, perverse rules. Impossible to ignore or drown out.

Nix, of course, didn't care. He'd thought at first that she'd even managed to find sleep here, and was about to retreat, but the young fezzard that nestled at her feet had nudged her then, and she had stirred, opened one eye and had seen him there cowering within the whirlwind of screeching birds.

Sadness seemed to overwhelm her then, as his presence disturbed her peace, and he felt guilty and selfish for having sought her out. Only one sign came to mind.

Sorry.

Nix forced a smile, and shuffled to one side as if to make space for him — though she sat upon the floor, and there was space aplenty.

Jymn bade his time before crossing the wall of streaking birds again. He almost lunged twice, but sprung back — clipped by wingtips, and prompting outraged squawks from the birds.

Slowly — walk slowly. Nix signed.

Jymn hesitated, staring up at the whirlwind of moonlit birds, some almost the size of dogs. If he went slowly...

Trust. Nix gestured as if she were grasping a rope with both

161

hands, clinging on for dear life. *Trust.*

He shut his eyes and stepped forward, expecting to collide with at least a dozen of the birds — so great was their speed. But nothing. He opened his eyes, and couldn't help but laugh. The birds were flowing around him on both sides like a river parting around a stone, barely slowing their pace as they rejoined the spiralling flock. He grinned at Nix with wonder on his face, and the smile she returned was no longer forced.

They are amazing, he signed as he reached the far wall and sat beside her, *how do they know to do that?*

Her smile faded and she fussed at the young bird at her feet. *They don't, it is just programming.*

Jymn's mouth fell open as looked back at the wall of birds, *they are machines?*

Nix shook her head — *No. Spliced. They are not from nature. Our creators took things from beasts they liked and mixed them. That is all fezzards are.*

Amazing. Jymn signed, looking at the young bird with renewed awe.

It is? Nix asked, with an eyebrow raised. *It's not just the fezzards, everything here is fake. The mir-trees. Even us.* She rapped a hand hard against her chest.

Jymn hesitated, then made the sign for questioning.

They built us, just the same as the birds. Nobody says it, but everyone knows. The creators tried to make a whole race of their own. We aren't like you — we aren't part of the world.

You aren't fake, Nix.

You don't know.

It hurts, doesn't it? Your friend? She didn't reply, but he could see that it was true. *That is not fake.*

She swallowed, then brushed something that might have been a tear from her eye and took a long breath. Suddenly the forced smile was back. *You are leaving?*

I think so. Jymn signed, accepting the change of subject. *There will be a vote, but I think we are going after them.*

She sat bolt upright then, as if he had slapped her. *Take me with you. I must come.*

I don't think… why?

Her eyes lit up then, and she signed slowly. *Revenge.*

But you are home now. They will not let you, I think. The Goodmother will not…

She will. Nix interrupted. *You must tell her that you saved my life, and that I am owed to you as payment.*

Jymn's throat constricted as he remembered the old Fairey's questions in the mir-grove. *I cannot.*

You must. Her sign was vigorous, as insistent as it had been the first time he'd seen her, in Shoalhaven. *It is an old tradition, but…*

I have already told her. You saved me. The debt is paid, she said.

Nix's mouth hung open, then she balled her firsts and pressed them to her eyes, turning away from him. She might have groaned, but Jymn could barely hear his own mind over the screeching birds.

Suddenly she was facing him again, staring fierce into his eyes. *The captain then. You tell him it was me that scared off the pirates on the island. You tell him you were scared and I saved you.*

I… I can't. What if he takes this away? Jymn gestured at the purple sash bound about his head. *You said it would be our secret.*

You have to! You didn't see what they did to Syra — they cut her, Jymn. All over. All to try and find a secret that wasn't even there.

I know, but…

You're afraid. Again!

Jymn hung his head then, ashamed. The truth was already in his head, but it hurt terribly to see it on the face of another. Eventually he marshalled the strength to look at her. *You are home now, Nix. Your parents are here. I haven't got anywhere else to be, I'm sorry.*

She just shook her head, and screwed her eyes shut with such force Jymn half-imagined he could hear them close.

I'm sorry. He signed uselessly. He tapped her on the leg, shook her, but her eyes stayed firmly shut. The small bird at her feet snapped at him angrily, protectively, and he backed away.

'I'm sorry' he spoke, but his words were lost in the clamour.

The argument kept him awake through most of the night, and he could barely keep from yawning as stood on the deck of the Archon at sun-up. The vote hadn't taken long. Some of the crew understood the importance of Thule, and the need to get there first, but most were drawn by the promise of fathomless riches, or the desire to exact revenge upon Tsar and the Godsmen. Once it was decided, Jymn had skipped duties, searching for Nix while the rest of the crew stashed their gear and made ready for sail. But it was no use. Eventually, he'd given in and joined the other Archonauts as they watched the captain speak one last time with the Goodmother.

A great many Faireys had spilled out of the gate to see the Archon off, though whether through gratitude, or a wish to be rid of outlanders, Jymn couldn't read. He searched the crowd, hoping to see Nix among them, that he might apologise — find some sign to repair the damage — but she was nowhere to be seen.

Eventually the Goodmother embraced the captain, and he bowed, pulling on his hat before striding up the gangway and motioning for Slip to weigh anchor. Soon, the great ship began to drift across the inner sea and towards the narrow gully that defended it. Jymn's eyes never left the assembled Fair Folk, straining hopelessly for some glimpse of his friend, until Puggle let out a long, lamenting cry overhead. He looked up then, and saw her wheeling alone around the mast-top. Only now she wasn't alone. Jymn smiled sadly as he recognised something tangling in the air with her — a new addition to the crew — a small, young fezzard, sailing away with them to the west.

XII

West

The going was hard. While the rushed journey from Kimpakka to Losalfhym had been an exhausting blur of hurried focus, it had at least been brief, the end always in sight. This voyage west was relentless.

Jymn was used to hard work, of course — life aboard the Trossul had been one unceasing task from dawn-bell to bunk-time — but while it was tiring and sometimes brutal, it had never been as physically demanding as the life of an Archonaut. Each night he'd clamber inelegantly into his hammock with numb, trembling arms, and awaken next day to a crippling soreness of limb and back that never seemed to abate. Slip laughed and assured him it would pass, that his body would adapt — and Kelpy gave him an ointment that made his muscles burn and his eyes sting. Sure enough, after a week the soreness started to subside, and he noticed lines of definition on his shoulders that had never been there before. Even his brown skin seemed to have darkened, resisting the sun's burning heat. He was becoming a sailor.

Between the punishing watches, there was still time for play. He was inducted into the game of 'Stok' — played by four players armed with North's deck of curious wood-slate cards that were painted in cunning designs of the old seasons. He would most often team up with Scup, the ship's cook, to face off against Balder and North — though he rarely won, more often finding his small store of round pebbles or 'stok' depleted by North's shrewd raids and Balder's stalwart defence. It was great fun, and he played as often as he could, though Scup was often too busy cooking in the galley. The Faireys had supplied them with many provisions for their journey west — lamp-oil, bolts of heavy cloth, great stores of salted seaweed — but best of all was the fish. Jymn had never tasted fish before — they were scarce, and often dangerous to eat — but the Faireys somehow managed to cultivate a clean, healthy flock, the meat of which would last months if dried properly. They didn't have many, but Scup was no stranger to stretching resources as far as possible.

Today the fish-meat was grilled on a bed of salt-rice, and sprinkled with crushed seaweed, though as Jymn reached the front of the queue Scup scratched his head in confusion, his trusty iron ladle idling in the pot.

'I'm sorry Jymn — I'm out of fish. Never happened before, must be low on sleep. Here, let me make you somm'et else,' and he fretted about with a fresh pan, tossing in scraps. But Gam took Jymn by the arm, agreeing to share his portion, and together they climbed the foremast to look out over the west, and the sunset they chased each night.

As well as the provisions, Losalfhym had also provided *Sparks* — the young fezzard that had taken up residence on the mizzenmast with Puggle — so named because her bright feathers shone like a sliver of rainbow in the noonday sun, and like fire at sunset. They had always expected her to fly home, an hour from the Cove, or perhaps a day, but she'd never left. Jymn watched her drifting lazily above the ship as they ate, and his thoughts went — as they often did — to Nix. A familiar shame and regret swelled in his belly, and it must have showed.

'I miss her too,' said Gam, offering a smile. Jymn sometimes wondered if the boy's uncanny hearing extended to words unspoken.

He tried to return the smile, and rubbed at the purple sash that covered his eye. 'I should have spoken to the captain, she might still be here now.' He hadn't told Gam, of course, what she had asked him to do. It would mean admitting that he was a coward, that he had watched an armed pirate headed right for Gam while he stood there rooted to the spot.

'You know, we meet a lot of people, Jymn. On the ship. Passengers and such. Some are good, some are bad. Some are great, like Nix. But we take them where they want to go and we set them loose, all the same. You know what they'd be if we didn't?'

Jymn shook his head.

'Prisoners,' said Gam, simply. He tossed a scrap of fish-bone into the air for Sparks and Puggle to fight over. 'She's home now, where she ought to be. And we'll see her again, Jymn. That won't be the last you'll see of Losalfhym, I'm sure.'

But Gam didn't know the truth of it. He didn't understand, after all. Nix had *wanted* to be here, and instead Jymn had taken her place. He was only an Archonaut because of a lie. She was trapped at home with her anger, and he was trapped here with his shame. He stared ahead, as the red sun grazed the horizon, setting the water on fire.

The lands of the west were strange, even to the older Archonauts. The hardships endured by those who lived out here were unique and native to them — but the resulting hunger, sickness, and fear was familiar nonetheless. The rice-blight, little more than a whispered anxiety in the east, was a daily reality here, and more than once Jymn saw great salt-water fields being put to the torch, while hollow-eyed locals looked on. Raptions, too, seemed to weigh more heavily on the western mind, and many a door was guarded by charms or wardings. But despite their hardships, there were always people to be found who clung dearly to the life they found themselves in, however trying. These folk could be found singing on the small boats that tried every morning for fish, or in the small towns and villages that avoided the worst of the raids. But though they stopped many times in the days after leaving Losalfhym — hoping to collect rumours of this Magi named 'Node' — the Archonauts found naught but whispers, and old fingers pointing always west.

Jymn remembered a huge rectangle jutting from the sea, visible from almost twenty clicks out. Drawing closer, they had come to a great encircling ring of rope, attached to oil-drum floats. Each of the blue steel barrels was daubed with a red X. A border. The monolith had begun to glint, as if with the reflected light

167

of spyglasses studying them. Slip had used their own farlooker then, describing great flags billowing from the top of the ancient building, its sides draped with bright banners. And guns. Every window, every hole or crack in the great structure bristled with the long barrel of a gun, defending the scrap of crumbling concrete from imagined invaders. They had turned away then, continuing west.

There had been a long, flat island, barely proud of the tide, from which the unmistakable, foetid tang of a seaweed farm drifted. A long hall had been erected from stone and driftwood, and gaunt people could be seen working the weed-pools and harvest lines. A team had gone ashore with the aim of bargaining for food to restock the galley, and for rumours, but they had returned empty handed — turned away by the lord of the hall who instead tried to sell off some of the youngest islanders, grumbling about 'too many mouths to feed'. Something in Jymn boiled to the surface at the thought of the helpless children being sold for a snatch of coin, though he couldn't deny they would have enjoyed a better life aboard the Archon than the strange island they called home, and when the unsettled landing party had returned, there were whispers about the curious people of the island — slim almost to the point of malnourishment, but all seeming to share the same face.

On the fourth day out of Losalfhym, Gam had called down a warning to the helm — flotsam in the water ahead, and risk of collision. The sails had been let out then, and the fending poles brought out to ward off the trunks of a dozen felled trees that floated together in the water, clicks from any land. Gam had quickly seen their source — a cloud had passed before the sun, and in the dulled light he made out the hull of a great ship, just a few feet beneath the surface. Anchor had been dropped then, and the decision made to investigate — if this had been one of the Tsar's fleet, they could already be on the right track, Node be damned. A handful of volunteers were armed with Weylun's sparking rods (which were apparently excellent at warding sharks) before diving from the gunwales, eager to claim the right of 'first spoils'. They were fair swimmers, though Jymn couldn't help but compare them to Nix, and wish she were here, not for the first time. Their terrified faces, upon surfacing, made him reconsider. It was not, as it turned out, one of the Tsar's Rougian fleet, but a simple timber-haul, half of its cargo — and crew — still trapped below. But the most frightening thing was the bow of the ship — or rather the lack of a bow. It seemed the great steel vessel — almost twice the length of the Archon — had been rent in two below the waterline by some terrible force. Scraps of a bent and broken shield-cage were winched out of the water to the deck of the Archon. There had been teck aboard. They didn't even wait to salvage the timber, but weighed anchor, and fled those cursed waters as fast as the wind could carry them. *Raptions.* The word crept past the lips of many a crewman that night, and for the days that followed. Jymn thought of the dead bearfin, rusting in the channels of the Graveyard. It was huge — perhaps twenty feet long — but not nearly huge *enough* to have ripped a ship in two.

The beating sun, full winds, and open waters did nothing to soothe the worry from their minds, and despite Scup's careful rationing, the foodstocks were running low, which further sapped morale. Soon all that would be left was the dried food.

The waters they sailed now were queer and foreign, and known to few besides the Captain. Jymn spent time with Weylun, studying the teck-map, trying to track exactly how far they'd come, and how much further they'd have to go before finding this 'Node'. He could see that they had travelled far from the dense archipelagos of the east, putting island-cities behind them, and a sparse, barren sea ahead. A chain of distant islands skirted the far edge of the map, and Jymn had suspected it could be their destination, but Weylun shook his head and drew a solemn finger across the western waters. 'No Jymn — that's Bruttan — that's the Cobalt Sea.' A chill had run down his spine then. He'd heard of it of course, the great poisoned sea that suffered no life for long, but he'd had no idea they were so close. As they drew ever nearer, the evening stories that entertained the crew — usually so hearty and dashing — began to turn darker. Jymn heard many tales of the ancient war in which a Queen of Ur-Up had caused a winter that lasted fifty years, poisoning the land beneath what was now known as the Cobalt Sea.

But it wasn't the Cobalt Sea that set Weylun on edge — after all, every captain knew the signs of it and when to turn back — it was the last great island-city that lay ahead of them that worried him. The port at the world's edge: Vitzamar. Weylun, like so many of the crew, knew it by rumour alone — it was the slave-port where he was to be sold years ago, before he was freed and became an Archonaut. Only the Captain and Slip had ventured this far before, and assured the others it was their best chance to restock and cast a net for rumours. And so the great galley fires — now at a loss for fresh food — were repurposed to melting down the salvaged copper shielding from the wreck, and casting it into a great stock of new bar-coin. The crew, of course, expected a share of the plunder — especially the divers who were still shaken by what they had seen — but Slip had commandeered it all for the resupply — 'we don't know how far we've yet to go, and I don't need you lot spending it all on fancy knives or another case of the port-scratch.'

Next day they smelled, and then sighted another vessel, making the same course for the island-city. She reeked of foul sewerage, sat low in the water, and lacked both the plume of dark oilsmoke that marked a motorship, or the mast and spars of a sailboat. Drawing closer, they saw she was some manner of cattle-barge, crowded with a herd of two dozen sad looking, emaciated beasts. Her crew seemed to consist of one leathery old woman, who was frantically alternating between bailing water and inching the barge forward with a single long oar. The cattle already stood ankle deep in their own filth and seawater, and if their keeper were to stop bailing for more than a few minutes, Jymn suspected the whole barge might slip beneath the water. The order was given to come alongside, and lines were thrown to secure the two vessels. Jymn — close now — stared wide-eyed at the cattle. He'd seen beef cargo before, on occasion, but always carcasses, or all ground up and mixed with padding, never alive to look back at you. He watched their wide, rolling eyes and wondered if they knew their fate.

Only when the Archon was within spitting distance did the old woman stop bailing, quickly lashing her barge to the larger ship with hands practised by decades.

'You need help?' called the captain, smiling down from the

Gunwales.

'Help?' The old woman looked up, puzzlement squinted on her face. 'No. You need cattle?' Her voice was coarse and heavily accented.

The captain laughed 'These? There's barely a mouthful on them!'

'Ah, but what a mouthful! Bet you've never had it *live*, have you? Just dry old scraps.' She spat over the side of the barge, eyeing the Archon's crew that had appeared, peering down over the gunwales. 'But it's true. Not enough meat on one for a crew of strapping lads such as you've got here. Best take the lot, eh? Good price.'

The captain laughed again, louder this time. 'And where exactly do you think we'd fit two dozen head of cattle then?' He gestured at the crowded deck behind him.

The old woman shrugged, nonchalant, as if the thought had barely crossed her mind. 'Well, you could tow the barge I suppose… until you get somewhere with a slaughterhouse.'

'Tow? Ah, yes...' the captain said, her designs coming clear in his mind 'and the nearest would be…'

'Oh, Vitzamar?' she shrugged, stooping to bail another bucket of slop from the barge. 'I'm going there myself, see, only the motor's gone and died.'

'Well, why don't you come aboard so we can agree a price, and we'll tow you behind in the meanwhile? Unless that's... inconvenient?'

'Well, I suppose I could spare an hour, if it means that much to you.' She grumbled, grasping the roll-ladder that was lowered for her.

Her barge was tied to the stern, and two Archonauts set to the task of bailing the sea water that endlessly found its way into the shallow hold, while Sparks circled overhead, spooking the cattle. Jymn tried to figure at the old woman's manner. She was clearly in difficulty, it would have taken her days to make Vitzamar with her lone oar — and she looked like she could easily have died from the effort — but she acted like, far from saving her, the captain was

171

inconveniencing her with his arrival. Western ways were strange, it seemed.

The hour of negotiations had become three, and had then adjourned for dinner — a meagre portion of seaweed-wrapped rice that the old woman ate slowly, though Jymn couldn't mistake the hunger in her eyes. It became clear quite quickly that the captain had no intention of buying the cattle, but was simply humouring her in spite of her hollow protestations.

In this manner, an hour after the sun hid behind the western horizon, they saw the lights of Vitzamar begin to hold the dusk at bay. The waters for clicks around the port-city were dotted with bright floating buoys that glowed with an unmistakable blue teck-light. There was much muttering and even some crossing among the crew, who still remembered the broken-hulled wreck and its rent shielding. These buoys seemed to have no shielding at all, but just floated there, draped in salvaged teck for all to see. Weylun had taken the farlooker and studied the devices, taking notes of what he saw, though even he seemed to grow pale at the sight of such lures.

'Offerings,' was all the old woman had said, when pressed for an explanation. Offerings. Jymn tried not to think about who — or what — would collect such a gift.

The lights of Vitzamar seemed to grow to envelop them, and soon they were sailing into the arms of the bustling, foreign port. There was an excited clamour from the crew as a great steel vessel passed them, crowned with cranes and winches, and crewed by grim men wearing oilskins and weathered faces. There was a great churning in the water behind the ship, and Jymn gasped as he saw the metal body of a bearfin slumped heavily over her stern, leaking hydraulic fluid into the harbour, its back bristling with long harpoons. The old woman spotted the catch and closed her eyes, making a queer hand-gesture and muttering 'bless the taker and his water'. But her reverence soon passed, and by the time the cattle barge was cut loose, she was trying to sell her entire vessel — cattle and all — to the captain, praising its apparent virtues with a straight face, while all the time bailing slurry from around her ankles. Jymn suspected the barge would never again leave the port.

Jymn was assigned to Slip's gang, and ordered ashore to barter their fresh stock of copper bar-coin for food. He anticipated a hike across the dark and sprawling city, but in truth they barely had to step from the jetty before being harassed by traders from lands Jymn had never even heard of, in a dozen languages at once. There was fermented crab meat that, once smelled, seemed to follow you for hours. There were bulbous shellfish, still alive, magnified and warped by the glass tanks they tried always to escape. Jymn saw hot spiced spirits dripping from a copper still into glasses no wider than his thumb — and made a note to describe its function to North. Roasting meat-sticks, fish broths, and oil-brown stews infused with pure lix-root.

'You can taste it all on your own coin next time we are in port,' insisted Slip, dragging the twins away from a seller who was offering long strips of pickled bird meat. 'Last thing we need is the whole crew getting belly sick on foreign food. The gunwale's not long enough for you all to shit at once!' Eventually, and with much grumbling, a price was struck for a good deal of cornmeal and salt-rice, and they set about hauling it back to the Archon. On the third trip, they stopped — gaping at the sight of the bearfin which had been craned from the hunting boat and was now hung by the tail while the grim Vitz crew set about hacking and grinding its components from the mighty steel spine to be sorted into great bins of teck.

Jymn crossed himself out of habit — though of course the Church had no presence here in these exotic, dangerous waters. Other gangs had tried for rumour of them, but it seemed neither the Godsmen nor Tsar's fleet had been seen in these parts for years.

Rumour of Node, however, was more fruitful. A mad old man matching his description had been seen not one week back — wild eyed, muttering about signs and claiming to follow a star to the south. 'In a wee catboat he was, too,' the fishers had laughed, 'hardly big enough for open water, but off he went. Bad weather coming in though, mind. You'll want to wait a threeday or some for it to blow through, 'fore goin' after him, if that's your thinkin.'

But the Archonauts couldn't wait. If the church fleet hadn't been

173

through here that meant wherever Thule was, it was not this way. Time and tide were against them, pursuing Node their only hope.

The fishers' warnings proved true. The storm came the next night, and caught them eighty clicks south of the city. Jymn had experienced storms before, of course — the boiling seas to the south and the chilled winds from the north made it such that barely a week could pass without one. It was a frightening thing — being huddled below deck on the Trossul while she was tossed about on an angry sea — but there was never any sense the great ship could falter, it was too big, too strong. The Archon on the other hand, was built to be affected by the weather — pushed across the wide ocean by the wind — but not such a wind as *this*.

The first Jymn knew of it, he was being roused from his bunk and sent above to help prepare for its coming. The gale caught him like a slap in the face the moment he appeared on deck, and he saw the brooding grey reaching down before them to whip up the sea. Even Puggle and Sparks had come down from the mast and were huddled together, sheltering near the aftcastle.

Weylun was peering up nervously through the thick lenses of his goggles when Jymn came alongside him.

'What are we doing, are we turning back?' Jymn asked, his mind still struggling to shake off the sleep.

Weylun wrung his hands, 'No. *Some things are too big to run from,* that's what the captain said. I guess it's moving faster than us anyway, so we could-'

'You two!' Slip yelled, spotting them without purpose, 'fetch rope — fifty foot lengths — tie one end to the gunwales and toss the other over. As many as you can manage.'

'Will that... is that for drag, or...?' Weylun asked, frowning.

'It's in case you're thrown overboard,' Slip said darkly, 'now hurry!'

Hands trembling with nervous energy, Jymn and Weylun hurried

174

back down below, pulling armfuls of knotted lines from the stinking rope-locker and lobbing them up through a grate to the deck above where Sparks would peck at them as if they were great worms emerging from the ground. The ropes were tired, frayed and coarse — some even looked older than the ship itself — but Jymn supposed anything was better than floundering in the water and watching the Archon drift away through the storm without you. He pulled a tangle of rope from the bottom of the locker and brought a pile of fish bones up with it.

Something moved, scrabbling beneath the rope, and Jymn spotted a grimy rat's tail worming its way deeper into the pile. On instinct he snatched at it, trying to pull the creature free.

There was a yell, and a hand snaked out, grasping the lock of matted hair Jymn had mistaken for a tail. Jymn shrieked, almost jumping out of his skin as he clutched at the bewildered Weylun for support.

Fearing some Vitz stowaway, he snatched the wrench-knife from his belt and held it out toward the mound of ropes that now writhed. 'Show yourself!' he yelled.

A pair of hands appeared from the back of the locker — palms forward in a show of peace. Pale hands. Jymn's mind swam as he recognised the figure emerging from the cramped hide.

Nix.

She was filthy, and stank of the food scraps she'd been sneaking from the galley-stores, but Jymn clambered into the locker to embrace her all the same. There was a blur of feathers, and Sparks appeared through the deck-grate, flapping and flustering all around, before getting distracted by the fish-bones.

They drew apart, and both began to sign at once.

I'm so sorry — Jymn started, just as Nix signed:

I shouldn't have asked —

Abandoning signing, they embraced again. Weylun, forgotten until now, coughed 'Err — Jymn? You might want to tell her about the storm...'

The reunion was cut short, and Jymn and Weylun enlisted Nix's help in tying the lifelines. Gam almost fell from the ratlines in his hurry to clamber down from the foremast and greet her — though his embrace was rather bashful and awkward. North, too, embraced her — but the rest of the crew whispered about the return of the Fairey, and Jymn heard mutterings about bad omens, but superstitious worry soon gave way to very real danger as the first great waves began to crash across the bow.

The storm was like nothing he'd ever experienced. All hands were either on deck, furling the sails and lashing down anything that could move, or were part of the great chain of crew that bailed water from the bilges below and carried it upward to be thrown back to the sea. Rain lashed across the deck in great torrents that felt like hot shards of glass cutting at his exposed skin. Waves tossed the great ship about causing her mighty timbers to shiver and groan, and broke across the deck sweeping cannier sailors than he from their feet to crash into the gunwales. Wind screamed through the rigging, whipping the lines into a snapping frenzy. They were only spared the lightning, which lanced down all about them in blinding flashes, but seemed to find no target among the wooden masts.

Jymn spent most of the time clinging white-knuckled to the ratlines of the mainmast — trying desperately to summon the courage to climb further, to help the brave crew that were edging along the highest yard in an effort to furl the garnt'sail. It had ripped from its buntlines and was billowing full-open in the gale, hauling the ship left and right as if the very hand of God had reached down to grasp the ship by the mast-top, and toss it about like a child might play with a toy.

But he was too late — with a great howl the old sheet had ripped in two, its freed ropes whipping savagely through the air and cutting the nearby sails to ribbons. North was hit by one of the snaking lines and thrown fully ten feet backward across the aftcastle. Blood spilled into the rain-soaked deck then, and the captain carried him below, while Jymn was summoned to take the helm in his place. The great wheel had a mind of its own, and though he enlisted Weylun's help, it was all they could manage to stop it from simply free-spinning and tearing itself apart with the rest of the ship.

Blinking through the stinging rain, he'd seen Nix stooped alone on the deck below, struggling with a stray line that seemed possessed with a life of its own. There was a terrible groaning crack above, and at once a dozen faces whipped round to yell at her, screaming at her to move — but their cries fell on deaf ears. Abandoning the wheel to Weylun, Jymn flew down the stair, but he was too late. Suddenly from the ranks of desperate sailors, huge Balder charged forward, tossing Nix aside like a doll an instant before the great spar fell, crushing him in a tangle of wood and ragged sail.

Together they swarmed to lift the broken rig, dragging it aside to find Balder, hunched and trembling beneath the wreckage. Jymn moved to go to him, to help him below, but Scup grabbed him by the arm and shook his head, warning flashing in his eyes. Balder slammed a great fist against the deck, the blow ringing out like a hammer even above the storm. He jerked his head violently, groaning in a mixture of pain and rage, and the assembled crew took a step backward.

Kelpy appeared from below, his apron stained in fresh blood. He took one look at Balder and darted forward, any thought of self-preservation forgotten. Dropping to his knees and grasping the huge boy's face, he pleaded with him. Balder's jaw was clamped so hard Jymn thought his teeth might break, and he blew hot air into Kelpy's face like a bull readying to charge, but still the smaller boy spoke, stroking the gurning face with no thought for his own safety. Eventually the rage seemed to abate, the trembling turning to a weakness of limb, and he was led gently below deck. A collective sigh of relief seemed to ripple through the crew, and the wrecked spar was lashed down tight against the wind, lest it was lost overboard.

Cap appeared from below, his hands and chest covered in North's blood, and Jymn hurried alongside as he fought his way to the wheel.

'North, is he…?' Jymn yelled, through the rain.

'He'll live. Though he'll not be half as pretty,' the captain joked, though his bloody face remained grim, his jaw set.

'I… I don't know where to point us. There are no stars. Are we turning back to Vitzamar?'

'I doubt we could even if we tried, Jymn,' Cap looked up at the great swirling tower of cloud above them, 'she's all about us now. All that's left is to find the way out, if she'll let us.'

In truth the worst had already passed, but still — drained as he was of energy, and shaken by the sight of blood among friends — Jymn found the next hour more punishing than the first. He gripped the wheel with hands numb from the wind and squinted always ahead into the tempest. He felt like a statue — like the bitter rain had flayed his flesh from his bones and he stood there, fighting the wheel as he piloted the ship into the underworld. Then, at last, a call rang out over the screaming wind.

'A star!' Gam's voice carried down from the foremast. 'A star in clear skies!'

His eyes were true, a fiercely bright star hung off their port beam, and together the shivering crew slowly guided the battered ship toward it. The going was hard — much of the Archon's rig was damaged, and the smaller sails they needed for such delicate work were shredded, but eventually, inch by inch, they found their way free of the storm and out under clear skies.

Having no better option, they limped after the guiding star that seemed always to fall toward the southern horizon, until with the coming of dawn it dipped behind a scrap of land ahead of them. Exhausted and battered, they ran at the small island — summoning one last burst of speed to beach the great ship upon the sand at last to rest a while.

They had survived.

XIII

Unlucky for Some

'What do you mean *there isn't an island here*?' demanded the captain, pointing at the sand beneath the gunwales, 'there very much *seems* to be an island here, Weylun.'

'Well — of course, yes.' Weylun swayed against the mast and looked like he might vomit again. 'I just mean it's not on the map, is all.'

'And you're sure you're not looking in the wrong place? Got awful turned about in the storm…'

'North seems to think not,' Weylun mopped his sweaty brow with his neckerchief, 'we're definitely south of Vitzamar — and Gam got a good look at the stars before sun-up. We're pretty sure we're...'

'Look, I don't know what to tell you, kid. Either *you're* wrong or your map is, alright?' He leaned over the gunwale and cupped his hands to his mouth. 'Ram! Nuckle! Give him a hand with the stove, for pity's sake!' And with that, he swung his leg over the railings, and dropped to the beach below to join the rest of the crew.

Jymn patted Weylun gently on the shoulder, eager not to make his sail-sickness any worse. 'Don't take it personally. He's been like this ever since they brought the sail down.' It was true — it turned out that the garnt'sail that had so dramatically ripped last night was the oldest on the ship — and the tear had run right through Cap's own shirt, sewn as it was into the canvas. The superstitious

179

among the crew — which was most of them — had taken this as a terrible bad omen, which along with the presence of a hidden female on board was quite enough to both explain the tempest, and foretell of danger ahead. Of course Caber was a strong proponent of these beliefs and had called for Nix to be left ashore here while they went on alone — though fortunately this was too drastic for most. The rest of the crew were polite enough to their new guest, despite their superstitions, but made sure to keep their distance all the same, lest they attract some of the *badluck* themselves.

They had been careened on the beach now most of the morning, and spent much of it untangling lines and stripping torn sails from the rig as they watched the great storm retreat into the north and east. Driftwood and brush had been collected from the beach and tussocks beyond, and were now burning in an old stove they had set upon the sand. Above the stove the best of their cargo of plastic was now being melted, spun and extruded into a thick thread with which to repair the ripped canvases. But the work was slow, there was never enough thread to go around, and a great many of the crew were hurt, or — like Weylun — still sail-sick from the storm.

Balder had staggered about briefly on deck, taking some air on Kelpy's arm before being ushered back below to rest. He appeared remarkably unhurt, given the great mass of timber that had crashed down upon him, but his pride seemed desperately wounded, and he muttered bashful apologies to all he met. North, on the other hand, was in terrible pain. The wound to his face was savage, and prevented the chewing of medicable to bring him some relief. In the end, Kelpy had to administer a small bottle of neat, oil-brown lix directly into the open wounds. The cries of pain were terrible, and did nothing to raise the crew's spirits.

Early on, Jymn had been given the unpleasant task of translating while the captain chastised Nix about having stowed away. Jymn did his best to soften the words, but the captain's anger was plain to see. They were too far gone now to take her back, and Cap assured her the recent tragedy at the Cove was the only reason he didn't have her tossed overboard, though he did agree not to punish her stolen rations in accordance with the ship's articles — which demanded that she be stranded ashore. Instead, she was sentenced to three nights in the gibbet, to be served once they were repaired and underway. Jymn had tried to comfort her after, reassuring her that the captain was just angry about the ship, but it had not done much good, and she'd kept herself scarce ever since. It had taken some looking, but eventually — after chores — Jymn found her atop the foremast with Gam, peering out over the curious island with the farlooker. Gam had now begun to learn some of the handsign himself, and managed to struggle through their interactions with a queer motley-mix of sign and pantomime.

It's small, only a mile across, Nix signed, handing Jymn the farlooker as he appeared at the crowded mast-top. *Tall hills to the west, trees to the north of them*, she guided the farlooker with a hand, aiming him at the large copse of trees that skirted cliffs at the base of the steep hills. He scanned the rest of the island as best he could, though the morning was damp and foggy. Long dunes of tussocky sand gave way to dark soil, where a fertile heath extended across the central plain. But no sign of man.

'Buildings?' he asked, signing at the same time.

Nix shook her head, and Gam answered, 'nothing. No sign of anyone, but…' and he leaned over Nix to point south. 'Look this way — when the mist parts… there!'

Jymn saw it — smoke, dark and thick, hung in the southern reaches of the small island. Jymn checked with his naked eye to be sure it wasn't some smudge on the lens.

You see it? Nix asked.

Jymn nodded.

'That's right where that star touched the horizon, Jymn,' Gam added meaningfully, taking the farlooker.

'Stars go behind the horizon all the time...' Jymn said. He couldn't read the stars like some of the crew — but he knew enough to pick out some of the Xii-Zodiac.

Gam shook his head, 'not in the south they don't. Always west.' He pointed across toward the mountains. 'I think this one *fell,* Jymn. Fell right out of the sky and landed there! And Node was following a star, wasn't he?'

What do you think? Nix signed, excitedly.

181

'Have you told the captain?'

'The mood he's in?' Gam laughed, 'I've heard him chewing people out all morning!'

Jymn noticed that Nix was looking at him again, her eyes — like her words — always finding a way to pierce the surface and find the core of things.

'Ok, I'll go talk to him,' Jymn said, holding his hand out for the farlooker.

The captain squinted through the spyglass from the top of the nearest dune, though the view wasn't so good from down here.

'You're sure?'

'Pretty sure,' Jymn nodded. He'd not mentioned Gam's 'falling star' theory, figuring instead that smoke on the horizon was noteworthy enough. The captain studied him, then looked to the plume of dark smoke from their own stove with a frown.

'Well, if you can see their fire — it's a pretty good chance they can see ours. And even if our repairs were finished, we can't leave until this damn tide shows up to lift us.' He collapsed the farlooker and handed it back to Jymn. 'Ok Jymn, pick a half-dozen crew, go take a look.'

'Wait, *me?!*' Jymn sputtered, as the captain turned to head back down the beach.

'Yes, you. You're an Archonaut, aren't you?'

'Yes, but…'

'And you're not hurt, or sick, or busy?'

'Well… no…'

'There we are then. I can't spare Slip or Daj, and Kelpy's still tending the sick. Beyond that, they're all yours. You're just looking, mind — you come right back and report.'

And with that, he tugged the peak of his bycock hat and strode away down the sand. Jymn found himself saluting, and wasn't sure when it had happened. He brushed his hand through his hair

182

and hoped nobody noticed.

Gam and Nix were his first picks, of course — it was their discovery after all. There was no finer lookout, besides, and Nix had proved her worth time and again. Weylun had nearly vomited over his tools when Jymn had asked him, and had to dash from his workshop for the gunwales just in case. Jymn rubbed his back and told him not to worry about it, to get some rest. That still left four, then. He needed a fighter — just in case — and with Daj off limits, and Balder still weak, the only obvious choice was Caber. There was simply no way he was bringing Caber. Scup was thickset and strong enough — and though he'd hesitated at first, he quickly decided that cooking cornmeal was a simple enough task to be managed without him, snatched up his iron ladle, and joined Jymn's small posse, eager of the change. Running out of viable choices, Jymn decided that — in the absence of experience — enthusiasm should count for something, and agreed to let the twins sign up, too. He tried to tell himself it wasn't simply because he feared the shame of not being able to gather a mere team of six among a crew of fifty-two. But the rest of the Archonauts were still nervous about the unlucky stowaway, and so with one space left, he decided to count himself among them — as if that was the plan all along — and finally the gang of a half-dozen was complete.

They armed themselves with small knives, packed some seaweed rations and foraging sacks, and were underway within the hour. The tussocky dunes were hard going, but soon gave way to the heath where they found narrow tracks running between the scrub. The tracks were curiously straight, and intersected one another at severe angles, and though they never seemed to lead precisely south, even zig-zagging between them was faster than trying to struggle over the brush. Gam led the way, having the best eyes against the fog, though the whole group seemed to defer to Jymn for decisions. The group was seven after all — for though they tried to send her back to the ship, Sparks hovered twenty feet above them in slow circles, refusing to let Nix out of her sight, and extinguishing any hope they had of travelling undetected.

183

The track widened as they headed south, and Jymn fell into step alongside Nix, finding the silence between them unusually awkward. He fished a strip of seaweed from his pocket, ate half, and offered the other to her.

It is nice to eat something that isn't dried fish. She signed, tearing at the smoked kelp with her teeth.

Jymn laughed and pointed at Scup, *he thought he was going mad, there was never as much food as there should have been.*

Nix covered her mouth and stifled a laugh.

You ate my supper one day! Jymn signed, mock anger on his face. *And you still stink of fish!*

Sorry, sorry, she chuckled, smiling at him.

No, I'm sorry. Jymn signed. *I should have spoken to the captain in Losalfhym. Set things straight.*

He is angry, I think.

He is angry at everything, Jymn signed. *I think because they have a…* and he realised he didn't have a sign for 'head-start' or 'lead'. *Because they are ahead of us, and we do not know the way.*

Then we will catch them when they return, she shrugged.

Jymn shook his head. She had missed so much of the plan. *That will be too late. They plan to destroy Thule, Nix. Burn everything.*

Not too late for revenge, she signed, darkly, her movements swift and aggressive.

'Guys!' Gam hissed, crouching low against the track and motioning for them to do the same. Jymn crept forward with the farlooker. Ahead, the ground lay scorched black and smouldering, small flames still licking at the edges of a great gouge in the earth. The southern shore of the island could be glimpsed beyond the scorched ground, though Jymn saw the coast here was not sandy but made up of curious, angular rocks that looked almost artificial. He scanned the mist to the east and west, but there was no sign of anyone.

'You hear anything?'

Gam shook his head, his eyes never leaving the flames, 'it *is* the star…' he whispered.

'I think a star would be bigger,' Jymn cautioned, 'but let's take a look.' Motioning to the others he crept forward, wrench-knife gripped in his sweaty palm. The gouge in the earth widened, leading to a half-dozen pitted holes in the ground. There was an eerie silence about the clearing — the wind had still not recovered from the storm, and only the crackling of the smouldering fires could be heard above the gentle lapping of waves. And something else… a hissing — no, a sparking. The sound of teck.

Jymn reached the first of the holes — it was a shallow bowl of displaced earth, and at its centre lay a bent and broken chunk of metal and shattered blue sun-glass. Someone had destroyed this priceless teck, and buried it here in the ground. The twins crossed themselves in perfect unison. Nix crouched at a nearby scrap of burning teck that had escaped the hole — prodding it with a stick as if it were an insect that might bite.

'Here!' called Scup, a short distance away. He stood at the lip of the largest hole, and as Jymn grew closer he saw that this one was enormous — easily twenty feet across — and almost deep enough to hide in without stooping. Again the walls were smooth and scorched, and at the lowest point, a huge cylinder, half wrapped in golden foil. Its outer shell had been torn open, and its precious organs spilled across the dirt. Jymn looked up at the sky and saw nothing but the endless dull fog. This wasn't a hole, it was a crater. Gam was right — star or not — this thing had fallen here.

'What do we do?' asked one of the Twins — Jymn thought it was Juke, though he'd still not quite learned to tell him apart from his brother, Bink.

'Could be something valuable here. We'll head back, bring a proper crew and harvest it.'

'First spoils!' yelled the other twin, and suddenly they were scrambling down into the crater, eager to snatch the best trinkets for themselves before the older boys arrived. Gam and Scup hesitated, but at a shrug from Jymn, they too clambered down toward the wreckage.

The thing was enormous — almost the size of the Archon's longboat — and easily the biggest piece of teck Jymn had seen besides the great jagged panel-screen at Gradlon, or the Raptions themselves. He thought at first *this* might be a Raption — fallen from the sky like a great dead bird. But no — the bearfins had glistened with pistons for muscles, with thick cables for tendons and blood vessels, every inch of them cluttered with scavenged teck. This was smooth, not quite elegant, but simple in its design. One end was curved inward, like a huge bowl big enough to feed the whole crew, while the other had been ripped apart, and was trailing its innards. Dangling from one side of the cylinder was a great shattered rectangle of sun-glass that hung like a broken wing. Jymn thought of Nix's tales, the Ancestors that could fly through the sky like birds. He turned to her, signing, *you know what this is?* But she didn't see, her eyes still fixed on the wreckage.

'First spoils!' announced Juke, plucking a bright ring — still trailing wires — from the debris and holding it up as his claim. His brother growled in frustration, before snatching up his own prize — a thick plate that shone with a perfect mirror-reflection — before yelling in pain and dropping it back to the dirt. Scup held out a sack for him, and together they managed to manoeuvre the hot metal into it. 'First spoils…' mumbled Bink, nursing his burned hand.

Jymn walked around the thing — peering into its exposed belly. Blue sparks leaped from tightly bundled wires within, spilling across racks of green teck-plate circuits. Weylun would lose his mind when he saw all this — though it would take him a lifetime to discover its use. Jymn followed the arteries of braided wires towards the thing's heart — a board the size of his hand-span that bore a half dozen tall black chips. Two wires — each the width of his thumb — snaked from the depths of the machine, terminating at a pair of gold, threaded cylinders upon the board. Recognition sparked in Jymn's mind, and forgetting the danger he leaned close inside the wreckage, feeling the heat prickle at his skin. There — in white print against the green of the teck-plate were the letters Tx-Rx. A Tyksaryx.

The golden cylinders were hot to the touch, but with the fabric from his own sack he managed to unthread the thick wires without burning himself, before prising the precious part from the debris with the point of his knife. He held up his prize, calling 'first spoils' as was the way. With this artefact Weylun could repair the radio, hail the Cove, and tell them Nix was here, and safe. He bundled it into the sack and tied it about his waist for safekeeping.

'Jymn… are you wearing boots?' Scup called, from the far side of the crater.

'What? Yes — why?' Jymn replied, peering around the wreckage to find Scup and the twins staring at the ground all around them.

'Gam?' demanded Scup, anxiously.

'Yeah, of course,' called Gam from the next crater over, 'why?'

Scup looked at Jymn, his eyes wide with fear and realisation, then pointed at the floor. There, amongst the dirt and debris were footprints.

Bare footprints.

Jymn's mind began to swim with the implications. The prints were large — full-growns. They could be being watched, even now. He was in charge, it was up to him to make a decision. He needed to do it quickly — before he made matters worse — only he couldn't think, couldn't focus on the problem at hand. The others were staring at him for orders that weren't there. Jymn forced a deep breath and tried to work the problem.

They could leave, covering their tracks, but their own fire on the northeastern shore was still visible whenever the fog parted. And if they *were* being watched, it would do no good anyway. They could flee back to the Archon — if they sprinted over the dense heath they could make it in a little over ten minutes — but they risked being picked off in the open, or leading their pursuers right to the unsuspecting Archonauts. They could hide. But then the Archonauts wouldn't know of the danger.

187

'Jymn — what do we do?' asked Gam, from the lip of the crater.

'We hide,' he signed, as well as spoke, 'there — in the bushes.' He scrambled up the side of the crater and pointed at the nearby heath. 'One of us needs to go back to the Archon to warn them, and have them send help. Who's fastest?'

I am fast. Nix signed, dropping her own sack to the ground.

Not you, Nix — you will not hear them if they chase.

I will be fastest. What good is hearing if you can't outrun them.

Not you, Nix. Jymn signed again, firmer this time. The others tried to follow the conversation, seemed to understand its meaning. Juke handed his sack to his brother and stepped forward.

'I'm quick Jymn. I'll go.'

Jymn looked to Scup for reassurance. The twins were so young, but there was no denying they were nimble and fleet of foot. Scup shrugged, seeming to feel the same.

'Alright, yeah. Go fast — and tell them what we've seen. We need them here as fast as they can. Thanks, Juke.' The young boy nodded awkwardly and turned, sprinting back along the narrow track by which they'd come.

'That was Bink, by the way,' whispered Scup, as the rest of the gang hurried to hide among the low shrubs, crawling on their bellies to worm their way under cover. Jymn felt regret mix with his fear, and hoped Bink would be back soon, that he might thank him properly for his courage.

The five of them lay still, cramped and anxious in the dirt. A thick layer of needles — shed from the plants — carpeted the ground. They scratched and aggravated Jymn's bare chest as he struggled to keep his breathing calm and quiet in order to give Gam a better chance of hearing any approaching danger.

The wait felt like an eternity — Jymn tried to retrace the route back to the Archon in his mind, and to picture where along that route poor Bink might be. Surely he'd be nearing the beach by now, raising the alarm. It would take time for them to understand,

188

and to muster the help, but they'd be on their way soon. Jymn had made sure to burrow himself into the brush backwards, and in so doing allow himself to maintain a sliver-view of the smouldering wreckage. He wasn't sure what good it would do — but whatever he saw, surely *not* seeing it was worse. For now all he saw was Sparks, flitting about and tearing at a scrap of bright teck at the edge of one of the craters. They'd not managed to persuade her into the bushes — no amount of dried seaweed seemed to overcome her insatiable appetite for shiny trinkets.

Sunlight broke through the cover of mist at last, sweeping across the heath and setting Sparks' feathers glowing like a flare as she darted toward the glimpse of sky above. The light danced across the wreckage, punching through the dark smoke, and Jymn saw it reflected in shards of blue along the sides of the crater as it struck the sun-glass. Gam gasped, and suddenly Jymn heard it too — as the light charged the sun-glass a strained blaring, whirring sound sprung from the crater as if the great machine was struggling for one last gasp of life. Sparks — having thought the thing was dead — turned and dived violently down in response, circling the crater and squawking loudly at the wreckage as if challenging a great beast. Gam groaned in pain at the sound of her cries — his eyes squeezed shut and his hands clamped over his bandages. She cried out again, louder, her piercing call carrying across the heath. Jymn's mind grasped for solutions, but found none.

Nix — seeing the anxiety on their faces — sprang to her knees and waved her arms, beckoning desperately for the young fezzard to come to her side. Suddenly she froze, and dropped back to the ground, pressing herself low among the bushes with a look of horror upon her face.

What? Jymn's hands were under him, but he signed the question just with his face.

Nix fought quickly to free her hands from under her. *There are others. They -*

But her next word never came. Suddenly a bare, grey foot crashed between them, then a hand thrust down through the brush and clamped about her neck, crushing her face into the ground before wrenching her upward with an uncanny strength. Jymn grabbed at her outstretched arms, trying to cling on to her, and he too was lifted from their hide.

A dozen men of all sizes stood about the wreckage, three more thigh-deep in the brush, snatching Gam and Juke from the ground. They were uniformly naked, but for cloths tied at their waists, and their skin was grey and mottled with pallid blues and yellows. But worst of all were their faces — there was no anger or triumph there, no sneer of viciousness or victory — each face was blank, expressionless, utterly vacant but for a glimpse of teck-light behind the eyes.

Jymn was torn from Nix, clamped beneath the cold, fleshy arm of an unseen assailant as if he were nothing more than a sack of rice. With a roar and a mighty ripping, Scup tore himself free of his attacker, throwing his fists up to fight. But the grey man just strode forward, accepting the strong boy's blows as if they were no more than magflies buzzing about him, and clubbed Scup with a hammer-fist that sent him sprawling back into the brush, limp. Sparks flew at them then, tearing at their vacant eyes with beak and talon, and though she tore the flesh, no blood, nor reaction came forth, until she was swatted from the air like a magfly and tumbled to the dirt, lying still. A handful of the grey-men strode awkwardly into the crater — oblivious to the fighting — while the others began to carry the prisoners away north and west, toward the tall hills. Jymn and the others cried out, squirmed, and beat at their captors — but bought nothing for their efforts but a tighter grip, constricting them to the brink of suffocation. Gam had gone limp, and Scup was still unconscious. Jymn could hardly move his head now to see the others, but could hear Juke muttering a prayer.

'Don't forget the quick one,' Jymn said, hoping to reassure Juke without giving anything away to their mute captors. The grip tightened once again, and soon the edges of his vision began to grow dark.

It was like being lulled into a nightmare — the rhythmic rocking of the grey-man's gait combined with the pressure and asphyxiation swept Jymn into a murky half-dream. The island swayed beneath him like a ship, and bright stars appeared in his vision, falling all about him like the one they had followed through the night. The heath swept beneath him as they glode toward the cliffs. He blacked out briefly, and then suddenly the cliffs were towering above him. Were they going to climb? Were they to be thrown from the cliffs? He remembered this, once before, falling through the air. A punishment. The captain's voice came back to him from far away, his words muddled and out of time. 'Jymn Hatcher. You have rushed into danger without thinking.'

They were too close to the cliffs now — and his captor's gait didn't show any sign of slowing. Perhaps the dead, grey eyes couldn't see the rock face right ahead of them. Jymn squeezed his own eyes shut and braced for the impact that must surely come…

…but none did. As he inched his eyes open they burned with the bright, unmistakable light of teck. They had passed through the cliff-face. A voice from somewhere spoke, then — old and cruel, echoing off cavernous metallic walls.

'Well done. Now take them to the cells.'

XIV

The Wizard

Jymn winced at the sound of screams echoing up through the cold metal halls. Nix mightn't be able to speak — but her cries of anguish and pain were as harrowing as any he'd ever heard. He suspected sounds such as this must come from a place deeper than language — deeper even than hearing — a primal part of you that just needed to summon help. Help. He remembered the name-sign she'd given him — *boy who helps.* But trapped up here in this dark cell, he could do nothing but listen impotently and imagine what the old man was doing to her.

She'd been taken an hour ago — dragged away by one of the unthinking grey-men — while the others had been thrown into two matching cells that faced each other across a dank corridor. Jymn and Scup had a high, narrow window for light through which they could see the tops of the trees below, while Juke and Gam had to make do with the dim glow of an ancient teck-light that flickered and pulsed in a bracket on the ceiling.

The cells were up high — they'd realised that even before helping each other up to the window. From the moment they'd been dragged past the false cliffs, Jymn had been trying to piece together this strange metal fortress. The entire hill on the west coast of the island was fake — dressed with stone and dirt and even plants on the outside, but built of steel and clad with a dense mesh of shielding within. Here, at the uppermost level were the cells, in what must have been the crest of the hill. Below them, wide chambers were filled with the silhouettes of strange machines that defied his imagination. Below that was the cavernous hall that hid behind the false cliffs, where the grey-men had dragged them over a wide, curving bridge. A channel of calm sea water wound its way to the far end of this lower cavern, where it met reflected daylight. A small, single-sailed catboat was moored alongside the false metal-shore, protected from the tides without. Even in his groggy state, Jymn had remembered the catboat, and realisation had dawned upon him.

Node. The old teckromancer they'd been searching for this whole time. *In a wee catboat he was, too, hardly big enough for open water* — that's what the fishers had said in Vitzamar. Jymn remembered the storm and marvelled at the idea that an old man, alone, had made it a hundred clicks across open sea in that tiny vessel.

He'd wondered at first if perhaps Node too was a prisoner of the grey-men. Perhaps he'd sought shelter here and been thrown in the cells himself. But something about that didn't add up — Node was a teckromancer, a great old mage of the ancient ways, Jymn didn't think someone like that could be taken easily. And besides, the walls here had shielding, and the corridors buzzed with curious and ancient tecks. And then there had been the voice commanding the grey-men — a human voice. Old. No, the old man was not a captive — he was Node, this was his island, and they were his prisoners.

And he was torturing Nix.

'What do we do, Jymn — we've got to do something?' Gam asked, hands clamped over his bandaged ears, trying to shut out Nix's screams, which had reduced now to pained whimpering.

'The captain will come for us, I know it,' Jymn said, conjuring as much confidence into his voice as he could muster. 'Bink will have made it to the Archon, and they'll be searching for us now.'

'Unless they caught him too…' muttered Juke sadly.

'He'd be here too then, wouldn't he?' Jymn reassured him. 'They didn't try special hard to hurt us, remember — they wanted to *take* us. No reason they'd have treated your brother any different. And they're slow, too. They surprised us, but Bink was running — he

193

could outrun them, easy.'

Juke seemed to find little comfort in the idea of his twin being pursued across this strange island by an army of golems, and tried once more to squeeze himself between the bars of the cell. Whatever this place had been, the cells — like the shielding — were obviously a later addition, and while the steel bars were narrow, they had been cunningly welded to both floor and ceiling, leaving little hope of escape. Jymn, being suitably experienced, had inspected the steel and the weld-joins for any hint of flaw or weakness, but had found none. They'd tried the window too, of course. But it was little more than a cleft in the false-rock at the top of the cliffs. Wide enough to peer out, and to let some daylight creep in, but far too narrow for Jymn or Scup. Juke *might* make it, but he was in the wrong cell. Jymn wondered if that had been deliberate — if their mute captors had the power of reason — or if it was just plain old badluck, such as had hounded them since Vitzamar. As it was, Jymn had bade his friends remove their shirts, pass them across the narrow corridor, and had knotted them into a crude rope. It was too short, of course, to be of any real use — but they dangled it from the window nonetheless, hoping a search party of Archonauts might see it dangling from the high cliffs and come to investigate. Jymn felt the weight of the Tyskarx — still in the small sack that was bound at his waist — and wished he'd pushed Weylun harder. If he was here with them, he might be able to use it somehow to summon help. Though it wouldn't work without power, of course.

Jymn was once again clinging to the lip of the high window, struggling for a glimpse of the outside, when Scup tugged at his leg. Dropping to the floor, he turned to see shambling movement climbing the stair from below. There was the unmistakable red glow in the left eye of a grey-man golem, and in front, a shuffling, pale figure.

'Nix!' Juke cried, 'what did they —' but his words were cut short by a cry of pain and a white hand that was thrown up to silence him. As Nix shuffled into the dim light, Jymn saw her eyes wild with fear and torment. The matted, dirty hair on the left side of her head had been shaved, the skin beneath swollen and bloody.

Above and behind her ear, stapled into an open wound, was… *something*. As she shuffled nearer — Jymn couldn't help but gasp.

It was teck.

Even his gasp drew a wince of pain. She could hear. This mad mage had made it so she could hear — and every sound looked like agony. Mutely, the prisoners looked on as the golem threw a lever — unlocking the far cell — and shoved Nix inside. Gam and Juke helped her gently to the floor, but Jymn caught her eye and signed through the bars.

You can hear us?

She swallowed, and nodded, signing: *Hear noise. Do not understand.*

Of course. Jymn realised he'd never asked if she'd always been deaf, but clearly she'd never heard words before, only read them on lips. She was getting raw sound, and no meaning. Even her own cries and sobs of pain seemed agonising to her.

The door of his own cell swung open with a bang, causing Nix to sob again. The golem hesitated, looking between Scup and Jymn as if appraising them with the dull red glow somewhere behind his eye, before snatching Jymn by the arm and dragging him bodily from the cell.

He heard the old mage's muttering before he was even halfway down the stair, the old voice hoarse and crooked. As the staircase curved down toward the lower level Jymn saw warm light spilling from the space below, glistening off copper walls that were dense with intricate designs. He glimpsed monsters, open seas, great cities falling beneath the waves. As they rounded the final curve his attention was torn from the murals and toward the space laid out before him. Jymn's eyes struggled to take it all in. It was as if someone had combined Weylun's workshop and Syrincs' laboratory, then left them in the dark to breed for a century. The result was… *wrong* somehow. There were pinching hands that flexed on sinewy metal arms, lenses that seemed to cock their heads in curiosity as he entered, and blinking lights that peered out of the gloom. Everywhere, thick wires snaked like eels across the floor, or were gathered in great hangings from the ceiling. The abundant teck here seemed almost alive, and Jymn had the strange feeling that each piece was moving and communicating of its own accord.

And there, at the heart of it all, was their captor. The old man stooped over a low, bloody metal table that rested atop a single leg at its centre. His hunched head was crowned in a mane of wiry, grey hair that seemed to magnify the mad twitching and muttering, and his beardless face was deeply lined with a scowl. Jymn saw he wore heavy robes that had once been blue but were now threadbare and bleached by decades of use. They reminded him of Weylun's robes — though the young techsmith's seemed now like a poor imitation by comparison. One of his bony, arthritic hands reached up to a metal limb, detaching a bloody tool at the tip. Anger and fear swelled in Jymn's breast as he saw the instrument that had so hurt his friend.

'What did you do to her!?' he yelled, his voice echoing off the copper walls, causing listener-dishes to twitch excitedly.

The old man didn't even look up. 'She was broken. I fixed her.' As he turned away from the table, Jymn choked on a gasp — the hand-less metal arm moved with him. It was *his* arm. Dropping the bloody tool to a workbench, Node snatched up a crude imitation of a human hand, offering it up to the wrist of his artificial limb. Wire tendons reached out and linked into the hand, and with a twist and a snap, it was attached. Jymn looked on with horror as the metal hand flexed, then curled into a fist, in an uncanny mimicry of flesh. 'She didn't tell me much, of course. But there is data to be had beyond words. Your concern, for example, tells me she's not your prisoner. A friend, then. So you've come from the Albinos. To get there you must have sailed, or rowed, which explains also why *I* didn't hear you coming.' The old man turned then — facing him for the first time — and pointed a metal finger right at him. Jymn had the strangest sensation that lightning was about to burst from the finger and strike him dead... but all that came were words:

'Attach the prisoner to the table.'

The golem at Jymn's back that had paused upon entering the room, now surged forward once more. Jymn was shoved toward the bloody worktop which, in response, tilted upon its pedestal until it was almost vertical. Fearing a similar fate to Nix, Jymn struggled against his captor, but found the grip was like iron — and within moments he found himself pressed against the table. The steel was ice cold against his bare skin, and he felt the wetness of Nix's blood on his back. Restraints snaked from the corners of the surface to grasp his ankles and wrists, though by some small mercy the device remained upright for now.

'Now - take twenty men, search the shore for a sail-ship.'

Without so much as a flicker of human recognition, the grey golem turned and marched toward the downward stair, leaving Jymn alone with its master. Jymn stared at the old man's back. He wanted to shout, to demand to know his fate, but he kept the words locked away lest the old mage learn anything more from him. All he'd done was ask about Nix and somehow this old man had deduced that they were in a sail-ship, and sent twenty of these things to find it. Jymn tried to picture the fight — two Archonauts to every grey-man — and remembered the effortless blow that had sent Scup sprawling into the undergrowth. Jymn saw the old mage push a button. There was a whirring, and suddenly a small plastic square was disgorged from a narrow slot on the bench. It looked like a shiny disk was contained within the plastic, but the wizard just scribbled something upon it and tossed it aside, plucking up a new square and sliding it into the slot.

He turned then, peering at Jymn's body as if he were some new scrap of teck, studying every aspect of him — the tone of his muscles, the show of his ribs, even the cloth of his ragged trousers. He muttered to himself all the while — 'skinny. Brown. Eastner blood, some way back. Fed well enough. Burns though — lots of burns. A worker then, yes. Hmm. Worker of metal, I think.' Slowly he reached Jymn's face — his own hovering barely three inches from it as his eyes darted between details, gathering data. He forced Jymn's good eye wide with the thumb of his real, flesh hand, studying. Jymn saw that his own eyes were green, flecked through with stripes of yellow-brown that made it look like a fire burned from within. He wasn't as old as Jymn had first guessed — older than Rincs, or Tasr of course — but not as ancient as old, mad Loken. He pulled the purple sash roughly from Jymn's

197

eye down to his throat, and groaned with intrigue as he saw the shrunken, blue eye beneath. 'Hmm, blue-eye, blue-eye,' he muttered, clacking his teeth, 'the Ice Cat roams atop the hill, in search of blue-eyed young to kill.' His breath was sharp with the smell of solvents, and it stung Jymn's eyes. Node fixed him with a stare — 'you Skand, boy?'

'I'm from Razeen,' Jymn stammered, finding his mouth dry with fear at what the old man might learn from his words. 'It's just a bad eye, that's all.'

'Hmm,' the old face frowned suspiciously, then the man reached up and prodded the barely-healed cut below Jymn's eye — digging a fingernail into the scab. Jymn cried out and writhed against his bonds uselessly, but the old man just raised his finger to his lips and licked at the bloody nail. A diffuse red glow shone somewhere behind his left eye — the same as his grey servants — and he seemed to pause for a moment, distracted. Then his eyes snapped back to Jymn. 'Very well. Who sent you then? Was it the Godsmen? The Albinos?'

'Sent us?' Jymn asked, shaking his head, 'nobody *sent* us — we were just seeking shelter from the storm, and you —'

'How did you know about the star?'

Jymn paused - his mind struggling to catch up, 'so it *is* a star?'

The old man barked a harsh laugh then. 'You could fit a million worlds inside a real star, boy. That is a *satellite* - but how did you know it would be here?'

'We didn't… we were caught in the storm…'

'You just *happened* to be headed for the Steel Sea, a hundred clicks from land, a hundred clicks from anywhere? *Truth* boy!' he demanded, clamping his metal hand over Jymn's throat.

Jymn was surprised to find that the metal was hot to the touch. He felt servos grinding beneath the surface, and the intricate joints pinched at his skin.

'We saw the star... the *satellite* falling and followed it. It was just luck that it led us to land.'

'Just luck, was it?' The old man raised a thick eyebrow, 'a

hundred clicks of open sea and just *luck* that it fell on my spit of land?'

Jymn tried to unravel the meaning from his words. He just needed to survive long enough for the captain to find them. He needed to keep him talking. There was pride there, a boast. 'Are you... do you mean you *made* it crash here, then?'

'The power to talk to satellites is beyond anyone now, boy, even me. Even the Raptions. No, but you're nearly there. If the mountain won't come to Mohammed, he must strap on his boots now, mustn't he? But you — you followed it too. Why?' he demanded, remembering his line of questioning and constricting his metal hand.

'We travelled from Vitzamar,' Jymn gasped, trying to keep his voice steady, 'we are following rumours of an old man of the west. A wizard named Node,' Jymn studied the old face as he spoke, looking for any hint of recognition. 'That's you, isn't it?'

The metal hand released, and the old man whirled away angrily. 'So the Faireys *did* send you!'

Jymn pressed on, 'it was them as told us about you, yes. But we only came for your wisdom...' he searched for the right words, remembering stories like this from his childhood, 'oh... great and powerful Node, wise among wise.'

The old wizard barked his cruel, half-coughing laugh again, and fidgeted with tools on his worktop, muttering. 'Flattery is it? I'm not a dragon, boy. If I were, I'd have already taken a limb for your lies.' He thumped his metal fist into the worktop, causing nearby teck to twitch and jerk away, frightened.

'We aren't here for the star, I swear it,' Jymn said earnestly, then decided to risk the whole truth. 'We're seeking the island of Thule.'

Node turned then, amusement and surprise mixing on his face. 'Thule, hah! You're in the wrong end of the world then, boy. But let me save you the voyage — Thule was destroyed. Long before you were born.'

'That can't be true...' Jymn's mind reeled with the implications. If Thule was already destroyed then all this death and suffering, all this way they'd come — was all for nothing. All those Faireys.

Nix's friend. Sacrificed for knowledge that was already lost.

'Believe what you like. I sought it myself, for many years. Found myself an old Skand who told me first hand of the raidings. The fire, the blood.'

'He could have been lying, though,' Jymn said, his mind clutching at hope, 'lying to protect the secret.'

'*She*. And no, I think not. She was just a child when it fell. Had to starve her for days just to squeeze that much from her.'

'So you know where it is?'

'I know it's in the North. Far North. Old Skand homelands. She was too young to know much more. The secret of its exact whereabouts is long since lost to man.'

'No - the Godsmen - they have a map,' Jymn said, energised by finally having some new information to barter. 'They are heading there now — to destroy it once and for all. You can help us!'

Node's attention appeared to slip from the here and now, and his words seemed to come from deep memory. 'Every generation has them, you know - always has. Folks who get so scared of the world around them they abandon reason for the comfort of madness. Start changing the facts to fit their warped sense of the world. Then their hate makes their fears come true.' He shrugged off his melancholy, 'but they are too late. Others got there first. There'll be nothing there for them to find but ashes.'

There was more he wasn't saying, Jymn felt sure of it. Outright flattery might not work — but this cynical old mage could still boast. He had pride. 'So... you never went there? You just… gave up?'

Node's eyes blazed, but his voice remained cold. 'I'm searching for a greater prize than a handful of seeds and some scraps of old code, boy.'

'Like the satellite?'

'The satellite is merely a gift for the one who can point me to what I seek.'

'So there's someone even more powerful than you?'

Node bristled at that, 'some*one*? No. Some*thing*! Why do you think we're headed for the Steel Sea, boy?'

'Headed? We're not headed anywhere, we're on...' he trailed off as the pieces started to fit together in his mind. The map. The false cliffs. The tide that never seemed to come in. The satellite that just *happened* to strike land when there was open water for leagues all about them.

'Yes. You can feel it now, can't you?' Node grinned, madness in his eyes as he stared up at the vaulting steel above his head, 'the ancients built them. The wealthy who desired to be free of the poor and the unworthy. Island homes. Sea steads. They proved most useful when the climate broke. We're already twenty clicks southwest of where I found you,' he cackled, delighting in his revelation.

Jymn looked at the hunched old man with new eyes. This was not just another mad old hermit clinging to a rock — this was Node, greatest of the Teckromancers, and this whole island was his vessel, carrying him across the seas. 'Where… where are we going?' Jymn asked, fearing the answer.

'To visit an old friend…' Node smiled. He flexed his metal arm, looking past Jymn toward the stair, 'and you should never visit unannounced, without a gift.'

Jymn heard a ringing on the metal stairs behind him, as a group of the grey golems marched up and into the room, dragging a bundle between them. Jymn half feared to see the captain, or Bink, tumble to the floor as they spread the bundle open - but it was just a collection of harvested teck from the satellite. Node waved them aside and crouched, greedily over the pile of green teck-plate, metal coils, and bundles of wire. He rooted through the intricate plates, tossing scraps aside like a man might toss bones from his plate at a feast, and growing more frantic by the moment. 'No, no, no, no, no!' He hurled one of the boards at the nearest golem - the sharp teck-plate gouging it cruelly on its exposed gut - but of course the creature did not flinch.

Node surged to his feet again, raging at the grey automatons. 'Override all. Go back. Bring *every* piece from the wreck to me. Now!' Wordlessly, the four golems turned to obey.

Node kicked at a scrap of offending teck, sending it skittering across the floor to crash into an ornate copper wall. He massaged the shoulder of his metal arm, deep in thought. Some idea seemed to occur to the mage then, and he pointed a metal finger at the rearmost golem, now at the top of the stair, calling, 'you. Stay.' The golem froze, then turned vacantly to guard the exit.

Node's attention slid back toward Jymn. 'I've misjudged you, boy,' he said, his voice dripping with threat. 'You are, perhaps, more intelligent than I had guessed. Do you know what a *transceiver* does, hmm?' He strode back toward Jymn, who hesitated, he'd never heard the word, but… 'Speak!' demanded Node.

'No…' Jymn stammered, 'I don't know what that—'

'A transceiver is a key,' interrupted the mage, 'it allows two pieces of teck to weave the trace. To *transmit* and to *receive* data through the air.'

Jymn tried to swallow, but found his mouth dry. He was suddenly very aware of the small sailcloth-sack tied about his waist, and the sharp corners of the Tyksaryx within, pressing against the back of his thighs.

'Such things are rare. Valuable. But a transceiver from a *satellite* — a transceiver from the *heavens*. I have burned cities for lesser things — what do you think I might do to a child?'

Jymn fought for resolve. 'Would you help us, if I told you where it was?'

Node sprang forward then - his metal hand clamping around Jymn's throat, his wild eyes barely an inch away, studying. 'You've hidden it — there is no bargain here — I'll tear the island apart — I'll turn you and your friends into my servants and *you* will find it for me!' He froze then, his nostrils flaring, as something tore his attention momentarily away from Jymn. He sniffed - the red light behind his left eye pulsing.

Jymn fought with every fibre of his being to stay still, to stay calm, but a barely-perceptible flicker of his good eye betrayed him. It might otherwise have gone unnoticed, but Node was too close to miss it. He drew back, seeming to scan Jymn with the red light of his eye. 'Surely not…'

The red eye blazed, and Node dropped to his knees, groping at Jymn's waist, tearing the sack free and gently removing the Tyksaryx with trembling hands. He held it aloft - laughing and capering like a child who had received a long-desired gift. 'At last - at last! The thing it desires most!' Waving his metal hand over the teck-plate the mage conjured some spell, causing the board to flicker into life and setting the small pinprick lights across its surface blinking. Instantly the golem guarding the stair surged forward, grasping arms outstretched, the light in its eye gleaming, but Node threw up a hand to halt it. 'Not this piece - I already *have* this piece!' Clutching the Tyksaryx greedily to his chest he strode to an intricate steel panel among the copper reliefs on the wall. He waved his metal hand once more over the panel, causing clasps and rods to twist and writhe away. The steel panel seemed to open like flowering petals, revealing a dark cavity within. Still jabbering, Node placed the transceiver inside, as gently as a mother might place a newborn babe into its cot. The petals closed once more, sealing the precious teck away.

'You have it now,' Jymn called over Node's mad ravings. 'You've no more use for us.'

The old mage smiled hawkishly then, moving to another workbench. 'If there is anything to be learned from the mistakes of the ancients it is waste. They wasted so much — cast things aside the moment they were old, or imperfect. We can't afford to do that now, can we? I'm sorry - my talents are not without their... *limitations*. You really are quite clever, but none of that will carry over once I'm done. But yes, I'll still find a use for you and your friends, even without your minds.'

The journey back to the cells was a blur. A stocky golem — returning from the harvest — was summoned to seize him, and to guard the cells thereafter. The blood had seemed to drain from Jymn's head, which swam in a rising tide of panic as he was dragged up the winding stair once more. He'd doomed his friends. They seemed to know it too, he heard the sobbing before he even reached his cell.

Gam had unbound his ears, and tied the great thick bandage around Nix's skull, who still shivered in a state of shock. Gam —

his wide, spliced ears now unprotected — winced at the sound of Juke's sobbing cries. Jymn looked helplessly at them as he was thrown into the cell opposite, with Scup.

The older boy climbed down from the narrow window and looked at him with lines of fear etched on his face.

'I'm sorry Jymn,' he shook his head gently, 'it's the Archon. She's left.'

XV

Abandoned

Jymn had to see it for himself, but true enough — there was no mistaking the broad wooden hull and the patchwork sails — the Archon had set sail without them, abandoning them to their fate at the hands of Node.

He felt a crushing pressure in his chest, and sank to the floor of the cell before his legs could betray him. He thought of Weylun, who surely must have fought the decision. And Bink - poor Bink who had been forced to abandon his own twin. But who among the crew would listen to either of them? Slip, perhaps would have hesitated, but wouldn't stand up to the captain for long. The truth of it was that the ship's lookout and cook would be the most sorely missed - not Jymn, certainly not Nix and her badluck. Aside from Juke's sobbing, the others were eerily silent — though whether from the weight of their own despair or out of concern for Nix, he wasn't sure.

He looked at the Fairey girl and realised for the first time that her sorrow was different to theirs — she was rocking back and forth and shivering, her arms wrapped around her scuffed knees while Gam held the bandages to her head. She was in shock from her wounds, and the teck, and the noises in her skull — not from despair. It was then he realised — nobody had been able to tell her about the Archon.

Her eyes met his and he weighed whether to tell her, or whether she was better off not knowing. She was despairing enough already, without him dousing her last spark of hope. Nix seemed to sense his thoughts, and slowly unfolded her pale arms.

They have gone. She didn't even bother to add the sign for questioning. Confusion must have registered on Jymn's face, because she went on: *What else could be so bad, outside that window.*

I'm sorry, Jymn replied, *I thought he would come for us.*

Gam tried to read the signs, but frowned, not keeping up. Jymn repeated them slower. *I'm… sorry…*

It's ok - you can talk. Nix interrupted. *Just… please - quiet.*

'I said I'm sorry,' Jymn whispered. 'The captain, I... I really thought he'd come for us.'

'He will,' Gam said, confidently.

'Gam…' said Scup, quietly. 'He's gone, Gam. I know it's hard.'

'Node sent twenty of those... *things* for the ship,' Jymn added, signing as he spoke, 'imagine facing *twenty* of them.'

'He's had worse odds,' snapped Gam, bitterly.

Scup leaned his head against the bars. 'I'm sure he tried, Gam. But he's got the whole crew to think about, hasn't he?'

'There's no way my sister left us,' Gam said, anger in his voice. 'No way.'

'Well, she could have left the ship,' agreed Scup, 'but then she'd be out there alone, with all of those grey men to contend with.'

'She's the best fighter on the ship,' Gam said, daring the others to disagree. But Jymn saw that his defiance had started to falter under the reality of their predicament.

I grew up on stories of Inkäinen, Nix signed, using the captain's name sign — her fingers dancing atop her head, mimicking his flaming red hair. *There are many adventures. Many heroes. Heroic acts.*

Nix… Jymn started, but she cut him off with a wave of her hand.

I have loved sailing on the real ship from my stories. But I realised that they were not characters I was sailing with — they were just people. Not the heroes from the tales. And that's ok — it is not good to try to make people heroes. It is impossible for them to be

206

like that all the time, and as soon as they fail we grow angry that they are not perfect.' She stopped, urging Jymn to translate before continuing. '*I remember when I first realised that my parents were not perfect. I was ten years old, and I found out they tried to take me to a splicer when I was a baby — to fix my ears — but the Goodmother would not allow it. It felt like they were ashamed of me, and did not want me to be like I am. Like I was broken. They were sorry, but it still hurt. Later, I realised: I am not perfect — they are not perfect. What matters is we are still _____ .*

And then she used a sign he didn't know, fingers pinched, turning in a circle. He made the sign for questioning, and she spelled *f-a-m-i-l-y*.

The word knocked the wind from him. Somehow in all the weeks they'd been together expanding each other's vocabulary, and all the years aboard the Trossul, he'd never once used it.

'Our parents were killed,' Juke said simply, his voice still tremulous from the sobbing. 'Three years now, it's just been the two of us.' Jymn saw the young lad's face contort, as he fought to keep back more tears.

Jymn reached involuntarily for the one memory he had of his parents, the one that had been played over and over in his mind until it had become as much a part of him as his bones. His father, face contorted like Juke's was now, fighting back a wave of emotion as he stood on the crooked wooden jetty. His mother, tears cutting clear channels through the dirt on her face, lifting him up high toward the ship. Funny, how he could so clearly remember the tears, but not the details of the face itself — her eyes, her mouth. Sometimes, behind them, Razeen was on fire, sometimes there was shooting, sometimes flooding. The reason didn't matter, they had saved him from the danger, they had got him out. His tiny arms had reached back toward his mother, but strong, rough hands grasped him and carried him up to the deck — and there, the memory faded. *My parents,* Jymn started, speaking softly as he signed, 'I never really knew them. They're dead now, I think. I don't know if they were perfect — probably not — but they *were* heroes.'

He was tired of being scared, tired of running and hiding, or of waiting for the captain to come and rescue him. His parents *were* heroes, and he — he was made of the same stuff they were. They hadn't got him out just so he could die here, waiting for someone else to save him and his friends.

He was going to have to do it himself.

———————————————

'Which one?' hissed Juke, standing precariously on Gam's shoulders, 'there's a green one, and a red, and black'. He had opened the dim ceiling light of his cell with the tip of his knife, and was peering into the ancient wiring inside.

Jymn turned the small teck-trinket over again in his hands. Their plan relied on him getting this right — but he was clutching at grains of half remembered knowledge from his time helping Weylun. Juke had claimed this thing as his first-spoils from the wreckage and carried it on a cord about his neck this whole time. It was a ring no larger than Jymn's old eyeglass, with three fragile trailing wires, scorched and half melted by the fire. Orange, brown, red. Weylun had explained to him about the basics — you needed two wires just to summon power to a thing — but which two?

'Jymn?' Gam prompted, struggling to keep Juke steady, so high up.

Staring any longer wasn't going to help — he just had to use his instinct. Red to red seemed obvious enough. He leaned through the bars, reaching out with his fingertips to meet Nix's outstretched hand, passing the trinket back to her.

'Connect red to red,' Jymn whispered to Juke. 'Then make a cut in all the others. We'll just have to try them all and see what happens, there are only four combinations.'

'What happens if we get it wrong?' asked Scup, peering down the corridor at the grey golem that guarded the top of the stair, and the only way down.

'I don't know,' Jymn answered, truthfully. 'But we don't know what happens if we get it right, either.'

The cells were growing colder by the minute now that night had fallen. Gam, Juke and Scup had reclaimed their shirts from the window now, fearing worse cold to come. Much worse. They had whispered and signed their plans whenever the golem was furthest from the cell, and had decided the wizard's small catboat was their only hope of escape from the island. They had no way of catching the Archon, and no supplies between them, but they might just be able to make it to Vitzamar if they kept sailing north.

But first they had to get out of the cells, and then past Node's laboratory below. Fortunately, decades alone on the island with only himself to talk to had driven Node quite mad, and Jymn had the best lookout on the ship on his side. Almost three tense hours later, Gam closed his eyes, scanning his head back and forth slowly. 'Okay, he's stopped talking to himself,' he whispered in the darkness.

'He's left the workshop?' Jymn asked, nervously.

'No, I'd have heard.' Gam's face appeared against the bars of the cell opposite. 'I think… yeah — he's asleep.'

'Ok, everyone ready?'

There were anxious nods, and affirmative mutters. There was a lot resting on this next piece of the puzzle. There was no way to open the cells from the inside, only the panel down the corridor — too far for them to reach. But the golems were controlled by Node's voice commands, and there had been some sort of hierarchy. *Override all... bring every piece from the wreck...* and Jymn suspected the red, glowing teck behind their eyes had the power to detect trace, just like the Raptions did.

With some luck, if they could power up the small trinket of satellite teck, they might break the golem's endless cycle of patrolling the upper floor. Scup nudged Jymn and pointed down the hall. The dull red glow that spilled onto the far wall shifted, and began to slide along the corridor. Then its source appeared - a red dot in a squat, black silhouette. Approaching.

'Ok Juke, get ready!' Jymn whispered, tapping the bars gently.

With the ceiling light dismantled, Jymn could barely make out the cell opposite. Only Nix was clear, her alabaster skin shining out of the gloom. She helped Juke clamber back onto Gam's shoulders, where he could fiddle with the wires once more.

'Which one first?' the young boy asked, peering up at the mess of wires.

'It doesn't matter — green to brown?'

The golem was shambling closer, his gait as persistent as his blank expression. He would pass the cells, turn, and then shamble back to guard the stair once more.

'Juke?' Jymn whispered, as the golem passed the cell, oblivious.

'It's not doing anything!'

'Ok, green to orange?'

'I've tried that already, hold on!' Juke snapped.

The golem turned, and without faltering, started to walk back toward the stair. It passed the cell again, its red eye shining within an arm's reach of the bars.

'Hurry!' Jymn hissed desperately, as the stout silhouette shrank with every heartbeat.

'Ow!' Juke hissed, and Jymn's night-wide eyes slammed shut as a bright blue light pierced them, leaving the image of Juke toppling from Gam's shoulders burned behind his eyelids.

There was a wrenching sound, and Jymn inched his eyes open against the bright pain. Gam and Juke lay in a heap on the cell floor, shielding their eyes from the trinket, which now blazed with a fierce cool light, while Nix pressed her back against the wall — a look of terror on her face.

The wrenching sound again… Jymn followed her gaze and gasped. The golem hadn't opened the cell - he was bending the bars wide with his bare hands, red eye transfixed by the small ring of teck-light. He forced his bulk through the bent bars with such terrible force that Jymn heard his ribs crack, then swung his dead, grey arms up toward the ceiling, scrabbling for the teck that was just out of his reach.

'Now! Come on!' Jymn hissed, beckoning to the others. It wasn't what they had planned — they wouldn't be able to lock their jailer inside — but it was still a way out. With one eye on the mute,

210

frantic golem, the others squeezed themselves through the narrow hole. Nix dashed to the control panel and Jymn felt the bars in his hands give way, as the door to his own cell swung open.

Padding quietly down the corridor, the five friends embraced as they hurried to the top of the stair.

'How long do you think he'll keep trying?' Juke asked, glancing back at the bright cell nervously.

Jymn shrugged, 'no idea, we just have to…' Hope. He caught himself before saying it. 'Keep going. We just have to keep going.'

They crept down the stairs in silence, Jymn seeing the shock register on Scup and Gam's faces as the warm light of the laboratory below washed over them. Scup crossed himself, his iron ladle still clutched in his fist. They had both been unconscious when they'd been carried through here early that morning.

The lights were dimmer now than before, and most of the teck was dormant. That which was still animated had calmed from the nervous twitching of Jymn's interrogation to slower, almost weary tasks, as if anxious not to wake their master. Jymn scanned the space — half-expecting to see Node lying in wait for them — but no, the mad old mage was slumped across his steel workbench, his breathing ragged and thick.

Jymn signed for the others to follow. Silently, they crept across the cluttered floor, flinching at every beep or whirring servo as the half-sentient teck seemed to watch them go, but the wizard did not stir. Reaching the far stair that would carry them down to the lower levels, Jymn peered into the darkness below — the bright floodlights that lit the cavern were doused now, leaving only the faint glow from dormant instruments that spilled dim pools of green, red and blue across the walkways. Try as they might, it was impossible to mask the sounds of their footsteps ringing on the metal stair, but Jymn could still faintly hear the lapping of water against the false shore somewhere within the great steel cavern below. He shivered at the prospect of the voyage to come — the five of them on the open ocean, clinging to such a small wooden boat in the middle of the Steel Sea with God-knows-what lurking beneath them. Jymn stopped, his mind racing.

'What is it, Jymn?' asked Scup, one step behind him.

Jymn turned to the others, 'you go on, there's something I need to do,' he whispered, pushing past them and back up the stair, 'head for the boat, I'll catch up with you.'

Nix grabbed his arm as he passed, *we wait for you.*

Jymn shook his head. *I'll come back, I promise,* and before she could resist, he pushed past her and crept back to the wizard's lair.

From the top of the staircase he scanned the arcane laboratory, his head barely above floor-level. Squinting into the gloom he saw what he was looking for — there on the far wall, among the intricate copper panels was a patch slightly brighter than its neighbours — steel. Crouching so low he was almost crawling, Jymn stole across the workshop, hurdling the bundles of thick cables that snaked across the floor. Reaching the secret wall-vault, he looked for some latch, some lever that might open the interlocking steel petals, but found none. Frustrated, he scanned the copper panels that surrounded it, looking for any clue to its operation. There were mighty square towers depicted, surrounded by thick forests. Another bore a diagram of the sun, and a representation of the deadly flare the Pars called the *Sword of Fire*. One showed a young robed man — Jymn suspected it was Node himself — stood at the prow of the small catboat, clutching some prize while a great fire blazed behind him. Another showed the boat within a ring of jagged, tall island-rocks, where Node was facing a great serpent — easily the height of twenty men — and casting some sort of spell toward it with one arm. The other had been severed, and was now clutched in the serpent's dripping jaws. Jymn turned to the sleeping wizard. The metal arm — *that* was how he had opened the vault before.

Forcing his breathing to remain steady, Jymn crept closer to the bloody table and the broad, metal workbench where the wizard slept. His heart beat so loudly Jymn was sure that it would wake the old mage, but as he drew close, Jymn saw that Node was still muttering in some deep, heretical dream. The metal arm lay under him, mechanical fingers twitching sporadically as his unconscious mind explored the dream. This was madness — even if Jymn could remove the hand, Node would know what had happened

212

the moment he woke. He scanned the bench, spotting the bloody medical attachment Node had used on Nix. He went to lift it, recoiling at the touch of his friend's sticky blood. Then — mounted on a rack at the corner of the bench — he saw other devices with the same disk-like wrist fitting. One was hooked, with a simple claw for grasping, and one had three digits, not dissimilar to the opening petals of the steel vault, but there were a half-dozen others in various states of repair that were utterly alien to him. Except one — there, nestled amidst its strange cousins, was a fist that looked just like the one worn by the sleeping wizard, albeit an older, more primitive model. Carefully, Jymn lifted it free of the rack, finding it lighter than he expected.

'Thief!' hissed the wizard's voice, causing Jymn to nearly drop the fist as he whirled around.

'I didn't…' started Jymn, but he caught himself, realising the old man was still sleeping.

'I am no thief…' Node mumbled, 'I make a bargain… for…' then he lifted his head, turned, and settled back to sleep.

His limbs still tingling from the scare, Jymn crept back to the wall-vault. He lifted the metal fist high, pressing it to the centre where the steel-petals met, but there was nothing. Groaning in frustration, he closed his eyes — summoning the memory of the triumphant wizard placing the Tyksaryx gently within the hide. With some effort, Jymn fought to prise the metal fingers open and tried again, this time waving the palm over the vault.

There was a click, then a dozen more, and the matrix of latches and rods that crossed the surface began to writhe. Slowly, the three thick petals opened, revealing the darkness within, and his stolen teck resting upon its shelf. And there, at the back of the small cavity, a plastic square — a shiny disk glinting within — and upon it, in Node's scrawled hand, was written: *Skandling.*

Snatching both the Tyksaryx and the plastic square, Jymn placed them in his waist-sack and waved the hand once more, sealing the vault. He turned then, to replace the hand upon the workbench but thought better of it, stashing it instead alongside his prizes, before fleeing for the stairs.

213

Heart thumping in his chest, and limbs unsteady with fear, he found himself once more at the foot of the stairs, his eyes slowly adjusting to the dark as he looked for his friends. There was no sign, nor sound of them, but there was only one way down from here, a long narrow walkway that skirted the inside of the great, false cliffs. He hurried along, straining into the darkness below for any sign of the water, or the silhouette of the boat, that he might better find the others, but he recognised nothing in the queer, coloured light spilling from the half dormant machines. He racked his memory for clues from the journey up to the cells, but he had been held tight to the brink of unconsciousness by the golems, and remembered little. There had been a bridge, spanning the inlet of water. And a door, perhaps two. A broad platform, ringed with strange devices, that had led to a half-dozen other walkways. He came to a door in the darkness, and a walkway leading off, away and down to the right. He peered over the steel railing, squinting into the darkness below for some clue to his friends' whereabouts, but seeing none. Creeping to the door his hand brushed against a thread, dangling from the handle. It was fragile and incongruous against the cold metal of the floating fortress, and as he held it up in the gloom, he guessed at the colour: purple. They had come this way.

Easing the door open, he hurried along the walkway beyond, hesitating at each junction to hunt for the scrap of purple thread that would guide him. Eventually, rushing as fast as he dared, he found himself passing through a door that led to a wide chamber where the sound of lapping water was strongest. He saw the wide platform, the curving bridge beyond it, and the silhouettes of his friends just ahead. Springing forward, he almost sprawled to the floor as something snatched at his ankle, and suddenly there was a rough golem-hand at his mouth. His heart felt like it might explode from fear, and he made to call out to his friends just a short distance away, but noticed just in time that the hand was warm — not the deathly cold of the grey-men's flesh.

'Quiet, Jymn, or you'll wake them!' hissed Scup's voice in his ear, as the cook's calloused hand released him.

He saw the hand at his ankle — glowing white even in the dark

— and then its keeper, Nix, huddled beside the walkway he'd been about to cross, Gam and Juke by her side. He looked again to the silhouettes on the platform, and realised they hadn't moved — weren't moving — but were uncannily still and silent.

'We think they're sleeping,' whispered Juke nervously, 'need to be real careful, quiet-like'.

Jymn hunkered down with them, drawing close. 'This walkway leads to a platform. Then another one leads to a bridge over the water. The boat is moored up on the far side, so once we are over that bridge, we're there.'

The others nodded, though Nix struggled to see his signing in the dark. Together they crept toward the platform, moving their limbs so slowly now that Jymn's muscles began to burn with the effort. Their footsteps — while agonisingly gentle — still managed to ring out against the metal walkway, each footfall sending shivers down his spine.

With glacial speed they passed between the statuesque golems. The black silhouettes stood dormant, scattered across the platform as if they had simply halted mid-task. Jymn tried to think of them simply as objects — not men — obstacles to be avoided, not sentinels that could wake to snatch them at the slightest noise.

He felt his senses heightened to such a degree that he could hear the distant banging of the wooden boat against the metal shore. He could hear each of their footsteps, even his own heartbeat. He wondered if this was what Gam experienced, perhaps what Nix was experiencing, even now.

It was in this state of heightened awareness that Jymn heard the klaxon. Three deafening blasts, followed by a metallic, emotionless voice:

INTRUDERS IN THE KEEP

And then, all around them, the dark silhouettes shuddered. Tiny red lights began to flicker into life, each of them set off-centre in the skull of a silent sentinel.

The golems were awake.

XVI

Intruders

'Run!' Jymn yelled, grabbing Juke's wrist and dragging him away from the clutching arms of the nearest golem. Behind him Scup bellowed, thrusting Nix and Gam ahead as another golem seized him by the shirt collar. Dropping to his knees, he tore free of the grip, tearing the shirt, smashing his heavy ladle against the creature's temple, and charging after them.

By some miracle, they made it clear of the platform and onto the narrow walkway beyond, the pursuing golems shambling after them. Jymn hoped they might obstruct one another in their hurry to give chase, but the mindless grey-men moved as one, effortlessly filing behind one another as they filtered onto the narrow decking.

Jymn and the other escapees fled desperately along the walkway, heading toward the long bridge that would carry them across the inlet and to the boat, but before they reached the next junction a glowing red eye appeared before them, cutting off their escape. Without stopping to think it through, Jymn let go of Juke's hand and charged as fast as he could, ducking below the dead, grasping arms, then dropping his shoulder and ramming the golem in the gut with all the momentum he could summon. It must have been enough, for the creature staggered backward and then toppled, crashing to the ground while its arms still reached uselessly upward. The effort carried Jymn tumbling to the metal floor, winding him. Before he'd even found his breath the others caught up with him, lifting him back to his feet, but already two more grey-men had appeared to block their way — red eyes blazing in

216

the dark. Jymn looked around desperately for a way out, but it was hopeless — two golems ahead, a dozen behind, pressing in — they were caught.

Suddenly a loud crack rang out ahead, and one of the golems flinched violently, then crumpled to the floor, its head hanging at an impossible angle. Something clattered to the ground at Jymn's feet, and he glanced down to see a large, smooth stone, now wet with blood.

An urgent whirring sound sprung from somewhere to his right, then another crack, and the other golem fell as a familiar figure emerged from the darkness ahead, tall and powerful, and wielding a staff-sling.

Daj had come.

'Where's Gam?' she demanded, but the words had barely escaped her lips before he burst past Jymn, embracing his sister. She shoved him along ahead of her, barking 'no time, follow me!' and whirled away from the pursuing golems.

'The boat!' Jymn panted as they struggled to keep up, 'we can escape... on his... boat.'

'No need, we brought our own,' said Daj, a rare half-smile creeping across the handsome features. Jymn's mind raced — had she said *we?* — but sooner than he could form the words to ask, another golem staggered ahead of them, blocking their path to the bridge. Before Daj could even couch another stone in her sling, there was a clanging of metal on metal, and a bright flash of blue light. The creature convulsed violently, then pitched forward revealing a peg-legged silhouette behind. There stood Caber, the blue arcing light of a teck-beater, illuminating his tattooed face.

'Hurry, eh?' he yelled, 'these fakk things are everywhere, and strong, too.' He gestured urgently at the bridge behind him, planting his feet and raising the beater to guard their retreat.

Scup laid a hand on Caber's thick shoulder as they passed, and must have muttered the thanks Jymn felt but couldn't find the words for. Caber glanced at Jymn, shrugging, and called back to him, 'just a chance for a good tussle, that's all.'

As they crested the top of the arched bridge, Gam and Nix

strained to protect their ears. There was the sound of fighting beyond, and they saw a half-dozen more red eyes closing in on a group of defenders. Flashes of bright blue-white teck-light illuminated frozen glimpses of the battle.

'Don't get too close to Balder,' Daj said, leaning close to Jymn as they ran, 'the rage is full on him now.'

'The what?' he called after her, but he need not have asked, for as they reached the far foot of the bridge a golem rolled across the metal floor having been tossed aside like a ragdoll by the huge boy. Balder charged after it — knife in hand — and even in the dull light of the cavern Jymn saw that a change had come over him. The whites of his eyes almost glowed in the gloom, and his face was contorted in agonised fury.

Daj loaded another stone into her staff-sling, sending it right into the glowing eye-socket of a nearby golem which staggered backward clumsily, but did not fall. Jymn flinched, as a sudden cold wetness sprayed across his face, and the creature's head tumbled across the floor like a dropped ball. The golem's body crumpled, and Jymn saw the unmistakable silhouette of the captain, sword in hand.

'Glad you could join us,' he said, breathlessly, 'shall we... you know... get the hell out of here?'

'Love to,' said Daj, launching another stone at a golem behind the captain.

'Aghh! Fakk!'

Jymn whirled back to the bridge above them, where Caber was covering their retreat. One of the golems had seized the beater, and was wrenching it from his grip with an unnatural strength. There was a popping sound, and Caber cried out again, his arm going limp. Something whistled past Jymn's ear, and he saw two streaks of blue light fly to the bridge, one missing its mark and skittering uselessly against a wall, but the other slamming into the golem's chest, causing it to spasm and buying Caber enough time to retreat a few steps.

Jymn turned, and saw two silhouettes aiming hand-crossbows at the bridge. One of them was short — presumably Bink — while the

218

other was harder to define. As Jymn squinted into the dark, trying to identify Caber's saviours, he was suddenly blinded with burning bright light. He, and all the others, cried out in pain, throwing their hands up against the floodlights that once again illuminated every corner of the vast false-cavern. Only Balder didn't relent, the pain in his eyes only fuelling the rage that drove him. But the golems had all stopped, standing to attention as calmly as if nothing had happened, none of them reacting to his mighty blows. Jymn heard familiar laughter, cold and cruel, echoing from the distant shielded walls, and then a voice, behind him across the water.

'Thrilling heroics, yes. But I'm afraid if we keep this up any longer, there will be nothing left of you for me to use.'

There — at the head of another dozen golems on the far bank of the inlet — stood Node, draped in his dull robes, arms clasped behind his back. With barely a heartbeat's hesitation, Daj spun, sending another of her deadly stones right for the old wizard's head…

There was a loud clang when it struck. At least, it *should* have struck. Jymn had to blink to make sense of it — the old mage should have been dead, head caved in by the force of the blow — but his metal arm had caught the missile in mid-air before it could find its mark. He tossed the stone carelessly into the lapping water. There was a twang behind Jymn, and another of the teck-bolts whistled across the water, but at a gesture from Node it seemed to collide with thin air, and rebounded high into the vaulting cavern, its spark extinguished. Jymn heard a gasp, and turned to see Weylun, pale-faced and aiming the crossbow with a trembling hand.

Node hissed something to the golems flanking him, and they began to rush forward toward the water, throwing themselves across at the far bank, but they did not attempt to cross. Instead they grasped one another's limbs, forming a half-submerged walkway of dead grey flesh with no regard for their own survival. Node strode across the primitive bridge, his eyes never leaving the intruders, more golems following on behind. Jymn saw that the grey-men waiting atop the metal bridge also began to advance, forcing Caber to retreat toward the other Archonauts, who were now drawn close, back to back, and facing the ring of enemies. Even Balder's rage now seemed to have burned low, and the huge boy staggered back, exhausted, toward the safety of the crew. Jymn found his knife in his hand, though the other Archonauts pressed protectively around him and the other escapees, keeping them from the front line. Jymn caught the captain's eye and noticed that he'd been wounded, a trickle of blood running from a deep gash on his brow. He winked at Jymn and smiled, 'We've had worse odds' he whispered, and Jymn was surprised to find himself suddenly angry, though whether it was at himself for ever believing the captain had truly abandoned them, or for the escape plan that had so nearly succeeded before Cap came dashing in, he couldn't decide, for right at that moment Node spoke again.

'Which of you answers for this?' the old mage demanded, stopping just short of the reach of their weapons.

The captain turned from Jymn and stepped forward, 'I speak for the crew,' he said, sheathing his sword, 'and you — you're the one as kidnapped my friends and held them against their will?'

'Friends that boarded *my* vessel, stole from *my* possessions — a word for that crime remains, even now… *pirate.*'

'Well, look — you dress your pretty boat up as a rock, you're gonna have birds shit on it. And can't hardly be piracy if you don't know you're even at sea, can it?' The captain smiled, 'now, what say we all just be on our way, and call it a big old misunderstanding. You've got all your *possessions* back, I've got all my crew.' He glanced back at Nix's exposed scalp. 'We'll even forget about any damage as been done,'

Node laughed then, the wild grey mane of hair accenting every movement of his head. For a moment, Jymn thought he was genuinely amused. 'Oh! There aren't many of your breed left, are there? Must be a lonely sea for one such as you.' He chuckled again, the amusement passing. 'But no, you've killed what, ten of mine? Twelve? Bodies are hard to come by on these waters — especially ones with all their limbs. I'll be taking that many from your 'crew'. *Then* you may go.'

'Ah, yeah, I thought we might come to this,' the captain sighed,

'I'd love to help, really, but you see our little boat —' he indicated the Archon's longboat, which Jymn saw for the first time had been hastily moored alongside the wizard's own catboat. 'She needs at least six to row, you see, and there's only — what — fourteen of us here. You take twelve, and we can't get back to our ship,' he spread his palms and shrugged, as if he couldn't help the simple arithmetic. 'No, but I've got a better idea. You let us *all* go, and I'll stop our ship from ramming a hole in your shielding big enough for half of hell to climb through.'

'I suppose you think you're going to signal your ship from here, are you?' smiled Node, 'give the order, hmm?'

'Ah, no, you see we have a tekker of our own — give him a wave, son,' and with that, the captain turned, pointing out the wheezing, robed form of Weylun, who raised a hand meekly. 'He tells me a signal would never get out of a shielded cave like this. That's why we set the motor running and pointed her right at you, before we left. Should be picking quite the head of steam about now.'

The klaxon sounded again — right on cue — three short blasts followed by the dead, passionless voice.

UNIDENTIFIED VESSEL APPROACHING

Node drew close now, fury flickering across his face. 'You know I can taste when a person is lying, child?' he hissed, grasping the captain's red hair with one hand and scraping a long fingernail across his cheek before sucking it clean. 'They are called pheromones — and *they* speak the truth, even when you are…' he trailed off, his eyes growing wide and distant. Jymn saw the uncanny glow of red appear once more behind the wizard's left eye. Suddenly his focus snapped back to Cap, and he leered closer still, licking hungrily at the blood that streaked from the wound above the captain's eye. Node groaned, shivering with ecstacy and studying every facet of the captain's face. 'Yes… yes!' he cackled, red eye blazing and wide with awe as he scraped eagerly at the blood, scooping it up with his claw-like fignernails. The klaxon sounded again, snapping Node from his reverie, and he drew back, looking at the captain with fresh eyes.

'I make you an offer. You may leave freely, along with all of your friends, and you must never return — on pain of death. But hear this and understand me well — in payment I will take the first child produced of you, boy. It will be mine to raise and command as I see fit, and no action of yours will seek to reclaim it, unto the—'

'Ok, done,' the captain interrupted. Jymn gasped — bargains like this were right out of the stories — the darkest ones — and never to be entered into lightly.

Node seemed taken aback too, 'you… you understand that—'

'I'm sorry, you had a whole speech there. You were going ask me to trade the life of my firtborn for the lives of my crew, unto the end of time, and so on. You got it. Deal. You need me to sign something, or can we go?'

A slow smile spread across the old man's lips. 'No, your word is sufficient, of course,' he motioned toward the longboat, 'please…' and at a gesture from the metal hand, a gap formed in the surrounding wall of golems, and the Archonauts cautiously filed toward the water's edge.

'You should honour your captain, you know,' Node called after them, a taunt in his voice, 'you can't imagine what he's sacrificed for you today.'

'Yeah, well, you wouldn't understand,' the captain called, wafting the wizard's words away without turning back. He leaned close to Jymn as they climbed into the longboat and fitted the oars. 'Sorry we took so long,' he whispered, 'did you know this thing *moves?* It was a bastard to keep track of...'

'Cap…' hissed Jymn urgently, his eyes on Node, who was climbing the bridge now, his gaze still fixed on the longboat, 'we need to hurry!' and at the captain's puzzled glance, he gently tapped the stash-sack still tied to his waist. The captain's eyes flicked down, taking in the bulging weight of the stolen teck. Without a word, he stood, shoved the boat from the metal shore with a swift kick, and threw a lazy salute toward the wizard watching from the bridge.

And then, at last, they were gone.

The Archon was indeed powering towards Node's island, and was less than half a mile away when they emerged, rowing, from the hidden inlet. Cap produced a flare-gun from a stowage at the boat's prow, and fired it high into the night air where it hung, casting a crisp orange glow over the water. They rowed then, until they were well clear of the island, then drifted beneath the light of the flare, licking their wounds as they waited for the ship to collect them. Caber groaned and cursed as Daj snapped his limp arm back into its socket, while Scup and the twins tried to console Balder, who was sobbing into his hands — apparently the inevitable result of his fighting-rage. Gam had enlisted Weylun to look at the teck implanted in Nix's head — though the shifting light and the motion of the small boat made it impossible, and soon the thick bandages were replaced. The captain, who had been staring wordlessly back toward the island, seemed to snap from his thoughts and turned to Jymn. A smile flickered across his face then, though Jymn couldn't help but suspect it had been forced.

'Out with it then, what did you lift?'

The others turned to Jymn, puzzled, as he reached for his stash-sack. 'Well, I didn't really... I mean, it wasn't really *his* to begin with...' Jymn produced the Tyksaryx, its large golden connectors glinting in the orange flare-light. 'Node didn't know where Thule is — not specifically, anyway — but if I'm right, he was going to trade this with someone that *does*. It's from the star that fell.'

'That wasn't a star, Jymn,' began Weylun, leaning forward reverently to take the device, 'it was some kind of old teck...'

'He called it a satellite,' Jymn nodded, then pointed at the night sky, 'he said it was from up there. The heavens.' He leaned forward, tapping the transceiver in Weylun's hands. 'It's very valuable, I think. I wonder — instead of Node — well... *we* could trade it to find out how to get to Thule, couldn't we?'

'What did he tell you about Thule?' the captain asked, taking the teck from Weylun and turning it over in the orange light.

Jymn hesitated, looking at the captivated faces all around him. If he told them what Node had said — that Thule had been destroyed — that would be the end of the adventure, right there. All this would be for nothing. And something in him just didn't believe it — something demanded that he see it for himself. 'He told me he once captured an old Skandling, who was only a child when Thule… when she left.' He glanced at Gam, wondering if he too had heard Node's story and knew what Jymn was leaving out — but there was no clue on the innocent face. 'He tortured her, I think, and got everything she remembered, but it wasn't enough for him to find it.' He fumbled in the stash-sack again, and removed the small plastic square. 'Now this, I *did* steal…' he said, holding it up to show them. 'I think this is a recording of the questioning. Weylun, can you use it?'

Weylun took the plastic square and held it up to the light, spying the shiny disk within. 'I think so, Jymn. I can try, anyway.'

'And this person who *does* know where to find Thule, the one Node was planning to trade with, where are we supposed to find him?' asked the captain, handing the Tyksaryx back to Jymn.

Jymn glanced back nervously toward the island. 'Have you ever heard of the Steel Sea?'

The captain nodded. 'Aye, *Raption waters*. I've never met anyone who's sailed 'em, but I'd venture we're dangerous close already.' There was muttering among the crew, and Caber even crossed himself, but the captain held up a hand, 'don't panic, we'll be turning about as soon as we're back aboard.'

'Well that's just it,' Jymn said, 'I think that's exactly where we need to be. It's where Node was headed. He said Thule's exact whereabouts were a secret lost to *man*, but don't think it was a man that he was trying to bargain with…' he looked about at the frightened faces staring back at him in the dark.

'…I think it was a machine.'

The decision to hold their course into machine-infested waters was not without its opponents. The storm, the narrow escape from Node, and the realisation that they were so close already to the Steel Sea had robbed the crew of some of their characteristic thirst for adventure, and even caused some to question the wisdom of carrying on at all. But the debate was met head-on, and the captain was persuasive. A vote was called and won, and soon they were flying south-west again under full sail, though the mood as they headed ever deeper into the Steel Sea was bittered by anxiety, and fear. All teck was closely guarded and locked away in Weylun's shielded workshop, and the sunglass panels that powered it all were brought inside, and pressed against the shielded windows lest the faintest trace of them be felt beneath the water. Even the ship's engine was disconnected from its battery, putting them utterly at the mercy of the winds. Nix presented an ever greater challenge — not only was she still viewed by some as a source of badluck, but she was now a living, breathing, piece of teck — attracting predatory Raptions with every heartbeat. In place of her threeday stint in the gibbet, she was confined to the workshop, where Weylun and Kelpy spent many careful hours studying and soothing the wound in her skull, and eventually with great care, managed to disable the implant, rendering her once again blissfully deaf, and finally able to rest.

Their course had been the next challenge — they were sailing blind into unknown waters — but at Jymn's suggestion they made south-west, following the course that Node had bragged about, though they left the slow, trudging island far in their wake. Slip and the captain had studied the map for hours then, eventually spotting a chain of small rocks two days' sail to the south-west — the peaks of some drowned mountain range — and the course had been adjusted to match.

Next had been the question of how to approach the Raptions. The crew had seen, and even fought on occasion: bearfins — huge, violent creatures with hulking arms, grinding jaws, and tails that propelled them through the water like a dolphin; hydros — long, many-headed rope-like things that could glide through the water, or bury themselves in sand to take their prey unawares; and the sirens — flocks of man-sized birds that would home in on

225

trace-signals before deafening their prey with piercing screams. While everyone knew the common lore — that these things were descended from the ancient thinking-machines, and had evolved to seek out and harvest teck for their own sustenance — nowhere had they seen any hint that the monsters were intelligent enough to bargain with. Except, perhaps, in Vitzamar. Jymn and the others found themselves debating the rings of floating buoys they had seen a half-dozen clicks beyond the city, that the old cattle-seller had called 'offerings'.

'Do you think you could make them?' Jymn had asked Weylun. The techsmith fidgeted, and looked around for the sweaty neckerchief that had once again slipped its knot. For a third time, he was trying to extract the recording from the stolen plastic disk, and it was not going well. He put down his tools in frustration.

'I don't see why not — a battery, or a small sun-glass, and some piece of teck. Something with a strong trace, I should think. But to just set it floating like that — seems an awful waste…'

'You remember the ship we found?' Jymn said, his voice loaded with meaning, 'the timber trader? With the broken shielding?' Weylun nodded. 'It was bigger than us, and steel, too. Whatever kind of Raption sunk that ship could do the same to us in a heartbeat. If an 'offering' can stop that, or even delay it...'

Weylun turned pale at the thought, swallowed, and put down the plastic disk. 'Ok Jymn, I'll see what I can do.'

That night — after Nix had rested and shaken off the grogginess from the medicable Kelpy had given her — Jymn's posse of six found themselves together again, eating their supper upon the foke, quietly staring out over the water ahead. Even Sparks sat with them — curled in Nix's lap — having been found at the satellite crash-site and nursed back to health by Slip. Something had passed between the six of them — even Bink — that the others hadn't known. The trauma of Node's captivity, of being abandoned, and of facing their death — even though it had been a

226

ruse by the captain — had forged a powerful bond between them.

'Do you think he meant it, though?' Jymn asked, watching the captain walking North slowly around the aftcastle. 'About his child, giving it to Node? He can't have meant it, can he — nobody would…' and he trailed off, catching his words before he spoke them. *Nobody would give up their own child.*

Gam and Scup exchanged glances then, a meaning passing between them that Jymn didn't take. Scup nodded to Gam, who glanced over Jymn's shoulder before speaking. 'He won't go against his word, Jymn. He's been like that ever since I was small. And he won't have to — the captain's never had kids, never *going* to have kids.'

'Not *now*, sure,' pressed Jymn, 'but you've heard the old stories, that's how it always is. Then you get older and you change and you think it's all behind you — *that's* right when the past catches up to you and—'

'No, Jymn,' Scup interrupted. 'That might be right, except the captain, he isn't going to grow any older, see?' Horror must have shown on Jymn's face then, because Scup hurried to explain, 'no, nothing like that, he isn't *dying*. Quite the opposite, actually. Thing is, t'captain don't *age* Jymn. Some sort of splice in his blood, way back.'

Jymn looked between the others, waiting for one of them to laugh, to give the joke away, but none did.

'I remember when he freed Daj and me, and the others, from Tsar,' Gam smiled. 'She fought, even though she was so skinny back then, and I was barely more than a child — maybe four years old. But the captain, he was the same. *Exact* same as he is now — minus a few scars, maybe.'

Jymn struggled to put it all together. Now that he thought on it, there had always been a fog around the captain's timeline. People, like Syrincs, always seemed to treat him like an old friend. He remembered — back in Shoalhaven — the Tsar had petitioned him 'for old times' sake'. And then there was his boast about having 'found' Losalfhym, and he'd spoken about knowing Ol'Wen when she was just 'Wen'. And Nix 'growing up' on stories about him —

she was only, what, three years younger than he was? Jymn knew splicing could work miracles — or curses — into your blood, but this was beyond anything he'd ever dreamed. 'How… how old *is* he?' Jymn whispered, looking back at the fire-haired boy on the aftcastle.

'He'd say he was seventeen,' chuckled Scup, 'just that he's got near thirty years' practice at being that way. Don't much like the idea of being a full-grown — says they are the reason for all this,' he gestured vaguely at the world they found themselves in. 'Hates seeing people grow up though — says it's like watching the world around him die.' Jymn looked up at the Archon's flag — the winged hourglass on its black field — and felt like he was seeing it for the first time.

'So, now you see why he won't have children,' Gam said softly, 'no way of knowing if the splice would pass on. Hard enough watching the crew grow old all around him — he's lost boys like that too many times over the years. Imagine having to watch your own kids get older than you.'

They sat in silence then, as they finished their supper. Jymn tried to sign the story to Nix, but she had just shrugged — it was part of the story of Inkäinen, she'd signed, *everybody knows.*

Jymn looked at the ship anew. The shirts in the sails, the scraps of purple fabric on each of the crew, the faded tunic that was now so short. He was staring back toward the aftcastle, watching the captain help North with the wheel, when Weylun burst from his workshop, hurrying toward the bow.

'Jymn…' he panted, his sweaty face bright with excitement, 'I've done it…'

'You figured out the offerings?' Jymn asked, confused at the rare burst of energy from the techsmith.

But Weylun shook his head, 'no, that was easy. Come on!' He turned back toward the workshop, beckoning for the others to follow, 'you want to hear the Skandling, or not?'

XVII

The Skandling

Jenn was scared, she'd never seen her father shout until this morning, and from that point everything had changed. She hurried to keep up with him, clutching the sack of freshly pulled crops to her chest as she waded through the dawn slush. Others had joined them now — Kale and her family, and the Helvigs — and together they followed the old foraging tracks that lead away from town. Away from the reavers.

They had come in the short-dark, flooding onto the fisher-jetties under cover of night while the inhabitants of Thulhöfn slept in the brief relent of the three-day sun. The first they had known of the invasion was the thundering of the ancient mancannon, springing to life to fulfil its duty and protect the island from the invaders. But as father had always warned, the gun was old and poorly maintained. It didn't hold out for long.

So now they were fleeing, making for the boat her father stubbornly maintained in case of such a calamity. There was enough fuel on board to get them to a place called Main-land, her father said, which was days away across the water. Mercifully there was now a full three-day of sunlight ahead of them, and they would not have to sail in the dark. Jenn hated being on the water at the best of times, but most especially in the winter when the dark lasted for weeks and she couldn't see the waves that would sneak up on them and soak her furs.

The wind bit at her exposed hands. They were wet and dirty from the soil of the glasshouses but they hadn't had time to clean up.

229

Jenn and her brother had been told to harvest everything whether it was ready or not. She had pulled potatoes from the soil that were barely bigger than walnuts, and carrots as thin and pale as her fingers, but they wouldn't be coming back, Dada said, and they needed food for the voyage. They had hurried on before she even had time to find her mittens.

The sack was awkward and heavy, and by the time they reached the safety of the old church the weight of it had turned her arms to jelly. She dropped it to the ground heavily and eased the straps of her pack. Other families were hiding here - peering through the shuttered windows and flinching at every yell or gunshot from outside. Dada was mobbed by other parents before they were even out of the cold. Something about seeing wild, anxious looks on the faces of full-growns and elders made Jenn feel desperately afraid, but before she could reach for the comfort of Nana, her brother dragged her to a high window, pointing.

Even in the pale light of the slow-dawn, Jenn could see dark shapes slumped in the slush and the snow, unmoving, and tried not to think about the faces now pressed into the cold, or who they had belonged to. The hillside crawled with tall, wiry men, bundled in cloth, who strode between buildings, shouting alien words and brandishing long-guns, unchallenged. She wondered if the unwitting foreigners would be stupid enough to climb the mountain slopes, and stumble into the jaws of the Ice Cat, but it seemed they had already found what they had come for. A group of them were already clustered around the high, proud entrance to the temple vault. They beat against it, and shouted and shot, but the mighty steel doors that jutted from the mountainside had been sealed from within. Jenn had only been allowed inside once — on her last birthday — but she couldn't imagine a safer or more impenetrable place than the mountain hold. Perhaps they would give up and leave when they couldn't find a way in. Perhaps she could go home.

Jenn startled as her father appeared with a hand on her shoulder. 'Don't watch, Jenn, come on.'

She turned toward him, but her brother's eyes were still locked on the vault, his jaw set. 'We were supposed to protect it,' he said, not turning to their father. 'Not run away at the first sign of danger.'

'We protect nothing by getting shot,' her father said simply, putting an arm around him. 'The vault is sealed…'

'The mine then…' her brother continued, shrugging the arm away and pointing over the hill to the west.

'We would just lead them toward it. And they aren't here for the mine, Son.'

Jenn turned back to the window, 'Why *are* they here, Dada?'

He dropped down to her level then, with a smile, his tired eyes meeting hers and thawing some of the icy fear in her breast. 'They are hungry, child. Hunger turns men into animals. Killers.'

'But we have food…' Jenn said, unslinging her pack that was still stuffed with carrots.

'Bjorn!' yelled one of the full-growns from below. 'There is a cave-in on the track — we must dig the way.'

Her father gripped her shoulder and rose to his feet. 'I won't be long Jenn - come with the others when it is clear, yes?' Her brother moved to go with him, but their father held up a hand. 'No son - you stay! Look after your sister.'

And with that, her father had crept from the old church with a half-dozen of the strongest men, and the icy fear in Jenn's chest began to return. She rummaged in her pack for the comfort of Nana, but…

'No, no, no — it was a fire, not a cave-in!' Node's voice cut across the old woman's testimony like a rusty saw.

'What, no — the track had caved—'

'We've been through this all before, you told me it was a fire that forced your father to abandon you at the church.'

'It was a fire that caused the cave-in, I suppose. I was distracted, I had just realised that I left Nana in—'

Something clanged against a metal surface, *'I don't care about your toy! I want to find the island. Where - is - it?*

'North, it's in the far—'

'I know it's north — where?!'

'I was a child, not a sailor. My father used to say it was like a great bear's tooth biting down upon the world.'

'Great Bear… Could you find it?'

'There is nothing to find. They destroyed everything. It all burned, I remember that…'

Jenn could smell the fires from here. They weren't like the coal-fires that heated their homes and powered the tools, these smelled of burning hair and plastic. Silently, she murmured a prayer that the fires hadn't spread to the glass-houses yet. She froze in her tracks as one of the invader's guns barked again. She had slipped away from the church while her brother wasn't looking. If she was caught out here there was no knowing what they might do to her — but she couldn't just leave Nana behind. Poor Nana, who had kept her safe ever since Mama died.

Summoning the courage to continue, she crept on through the thawing slush, retracing her steps to the glass-houses. Now, in the early daylight, the coal-warmed growing rooms where she'd spent so much of her short life were almost unrecognisable to her. Her prayer seemed to have worked — neither the fires, nor the invaders had reached here yet — but the lush greens and reds of things growing had given way everywhere to brown. Churned soil, trampled leaves, and toppled shelves — the deep rows of crop-beds lying open and exposed to the white that filtered down from the glass roof. And there, amidst the dirt, lay her bear. The white linen of her hide, grown grubby and grey with use and love, was now stained with the dark, rich soil. The mighty teeth stitched in black thread along her jaw barely visible beneath a wet boot-print from one of the frantic townsfolk. Jenn picked her up reverently and brushed her off. Nanook was tough, she'd survived worse. Mama had told her ice bears like this used to protect the island, before people took over. They were twice as tall as a full-grown, she said, and could swim in the ice water for days. Jenn's brother said they weren't real — just children's stories — but she was sure she'd seen a skeleton once that was too big to be a seal.

There was a familiar grind of metal upon metal, and Jenn dropped to a crouch behind the nearest crop-bed. The door had been that way for months, no matter how much seal-oil was applied to its hinges. It could be just another of the townfolk, straggling behind, or…

'Sega se vrooshtam.'

Jenn pressed Nana to her mouth, stifling her panicked breathing. The voice was harsh, foreign. One of the invaders. Breathing like Dada taught her when they swam in the ice-water, Jenn fought for control. She heard his footsteps, and chanced a glance over the crop-bed. The man was dark-skinned and tall, and bundled in ragged cloth, but what struck her most was how thin he was. Beneath all the fabric was a wiry, gaunt frame, white eyes and teeth flashing from within sunken features. He couldn't weigh half what her father did. She watched as he set his long-gun cautiously aside and began to dig through the soil of the nearest crop-bed, pulling up nothing but dirt and old roots. He moved to the next bed, and then a third, digging deeper each time, but with no reward. She saw his shoulders sag, and his head hang, and thought she heard sobbing.

They are hungry, child — that's what her father had said. And she needed to get back before the others left the church. Quiet as a mouse, Jenn reached into her pack and grasped a handful of the skinny carrots laying them carefully on the ground as if they'd been dropped, before retreating to the next crop-bed. Her way out was within reach now — just three beds over — but she had to be careful, if she bolted for the door, she'd be seen, maybe even shot.

She waited for what felt like minutes, but eventually the sobbing abruptly stopped, and she heard cautious footsteps in the dirt. Chancing a look between the broken slats of the crop-bed she saw the intruder had snatched up his weapon again, and was closing in on where she had left the carrots. He was distracted, she could perhaps have run, but something in her needed to see him find the food. He set the weapon aside once more, checked over his shoulder, and then crouched out of sight. Jenn crept forward on her hands and knees, inching slowly around the crop-bed for a better look. He had made no cry of joy, nor called to his friends. Perhaps the sight of her gift was too much for him, and he was simply overcome. Legs burning from the agonisingly slow movement, Jenn edged past the corner of the bed to steal a glimpse of the

233

hungry stranger. There — glowing like orange coals in the dirt — were the carrots, but there was no sign of the man…

A cold hand seized her neck while another grasped at her belt, heaving her upward and away from the safety of the crop-bed. She cried out, but the hand at her neck shot to her mouth, leathery palm smothering her cry. She bit down, and though she tasted blood, and writhed and wrestled, his wiry grip was unrelenting, and she found herself clamped against him, the foreign face inches from her own. She could see the cheekbones pushing taught against the dark skin, and the wild eyes set deep in their sunken sockets. Dark eyes — deep brown like the dirt — such as she'd never seen before. Some part of her mind wondered if perhaps the invaders would be safe on the hilltop after all — all the songs spoke of the Ice Cat hunting for blue-eyed young, perhaps it would leave these foreigners be.

'Kuday povechay krana?' he demanded, his dark eyes intent on hers. Slowly he released the bloody hand from her mouth as if to let her speak.

'I don't… I can't…' she stammered. Her voice was shaking like it did when Dada told her off, but she couldn't help it.

'Krana' he insisted, tapping his fingertips to his lips. Food. He was asking for food.

'You can have the carrots, that's all I have… I promise!' she gestured toward the forgotten gift in the dirt, trying to blink back tears. He groaned and shook her by the straps of her pack, his eyes wide and urgent.

There was a movement to her left, and a clicking sound, and both of them turned. Jenn's heart swelled. There stood her brother, barely as tall as the foreigner's ribs, but aiming the long-gun up at the dark figure, his expression grim. 'Unhand her you coward!' His voice wavered, betraying the terror he must have been feeling, but the words themselves were right out of Mama's old stories. Loken was always playing at being a Yupa-knight or some hero of old, and now it was for real. He jabbed the gun toward Jenn, gesturing, and slowly the man lowered her to the ground, holding his palms outward and speaking soft, calming words in his strange tongue. Jenn ran to her brother, clinging to him as he held the weapon steady, trained on the invader's chest as they circled, and backed through the door. Loken kept the gun, but Jenn left the carrots behind.

Outside, the air was thick with dark smoke, and only the fresh coat of black ash allowed them to find their way back toward the old church — retracing Loken's footsteps.

As they climbed higher, free of the smoke, Jenn stole a glance back over the town. The fires had spread everywhere now, and even the great doors of the temple-vault had been thrown open. She watched with horror as the starving invaders dragged crate after crate of the precious treasure out to spill upon the snow, exposing it to daylight for the first time in generations.

'Hurry - they've left the church, we need to get to the boat,' Loken said, tossing the long-gun aside at last.

'You saw the vault opened?' Node's voice interrupted the recording once more.

'The sight of it will never leave me,' sighed the old Skand woman, *'even as a child, I knew how great our failure was.'*

'And what of its contents?' the mage demanded hungrily.

'Some were opened, some burned. Most were fought over, and dragged to the invader's boats.' The old woman paused, her voice faltering, *'may I… can I eat now? I've told you things… things that—'*

'You said you saw inside the vault once.'

'I was young!' pleaded the old voice.

'What were they hiding? What was the Skand treasure?'

'I've told you… I can't… I don't…' the voice cracked, giving way to wretched sobbing.

'Very well. You choose hunger, then.'

Jenn gripped the stern-rail and watched the fires shrinking into the distance across the water, wondering if she would ever see her home again.

'We weren't keeping it for ourselves Jenn, you know that,' her father stooped to brush a tear from her cheek, his glove coming

235

away sooty. 'We were protecting it for the future, for when the world was ready. That's not now, child.'

'But people are hungry now.' Jenn tried to keep her voice steady. Full-growns never took you seriously if you cried, but she couldn't help it. It all seemed such a waste.

'A hungry man is an angry man,' he said bitterly, staring out at the smouldering ruin of their home. 'There were seeds in there from every corner of the earth, kept by our ancestors for twenty generations. The men that found it were not ready — and now everything in that vault will be eaten, or burned, or sold before winter, do you see?'

Jenn squeezed her father tight through the thick furs. 'So what do we do now, Dada?'

He hugged her back. 'Same as everyone else, Jenn. We find a way to survive.'

―――――――――――――

The recording clicked, the old woman's voice giving way to a low hum. Jymn stopped signing, and looked from Nix to Weylun, Gam and the others.

'So Thule is… gone?' Bink said, looking between the older boys.

'Not gone, maybe, but burned,' Scup nodded, 'as good as gone, I suppose,'

'What do you think happened to her?' Weylun muttered, 'Jenn, I mean.'

They all thought about this in solemn silence, until something seemed to occur to Gam. 'Did you hear what she called her brother? Loken — what if that's the same Loken that Cap found and took to Syrincs? He's a Skand isn't he? And he's ancient.'

Who is Loken? Nix signed, trying to keep up with Jymn's rushed translations.

The old man who saved you in Shoalhaven — he was the brother of this Jenn from the recording. He was always singing about the 'Ice Cat' — he's lost his mind now, but he must have been from

236

Thule, too.

'So, all this way for nothing,' Scup sighed, rubbing his scalp. 'At least we know Tsar and his lot are all wasting their time. And I guess we don't have to go any deeper into the Raption waters now.'

'Maybe… I'm not sure.' Jymn said quietly, his mind racing to piece together all the details. 'I think there was something Jenn wasn't telling Node, I think he knew it too — or he'd have just killed her.'

'Jymn, it all burned…' Gam started.

'I know, I know. The town burned, and they opened a vault, and killed everyone, I get all that. I agree there isn't some magical island full of Skand mystics protecting the ancient secrets — not any more, anyway. But think about the legends: there really *was* plenty of food there. And she talked about the sun being up for three days. And everyone there had blue eyes — it's easy to see where all the stories came from, isn't it? The truth behind them?'

'What are you saying?' asked Scup, 'that we should go there anyway? Risk a fight with Tsar?'

Jymn tugged at his eyepatch and looked around at his friends, one by one, 'everything valuable that's left in the world is dug out of ruins, right? That's where you get your big hauls. Weylun, it's where all your teck comes from?'

'Sure…' Weylun agreed, hesitantly.

'So — the Skand are gone…' Jymn went on.

'…but there is still a ruin at Thule!' Gam finished, catching on.

'And not just *any* ruin, but a ruin where we *know* the Skand were hiding secrets, and only one lifetime ago, too. That's got to be worth investigating, hasn't it?'

'You think there's stuff the invaders didn't find?' Scup said, thoughtfully.

'I don't know for sure, but it would make sense, wouldn't it? They were there for food, not teck. Not secrets.'

'Well we can't let the Church destroy whatever's left,' agreed Weylun.

We can't let them win, Nix signed with severe gestures.

'There could be a fortune there!' chirped Juke. 'We could buy our own island!' added Bink.

'But what about Cap?' asked Gam, 'what if he doesn't see it?'

'I'll talk to him. Weylun, can you get it ready to play again?'

The young techsmith nodded and bustled about the cludged-together teck that had revealed the secrets of the disk. Nix was still brooding when Jymn slid from the workbench and headed for the door, but she caught his eye. *Jymn, we still don't know the way.*

He nodded, then headed out on deck. The way there. That was the missing piece, of course, but now he had everything he needed, he just had to go through with it. He had to speak with the Raptions.

XVIII

Raptions

Jymn relayed the details of the recording to the captain, making sure to emphasise that the hungry raiders had been in search of food, nothing more, and that the Skand had all fled or been killed. In conclusion, he dangled the idea of the 'lost ruin of Thule' that was waiting to be uncovered somewhere in the far north, if only they could beat Tsar and the Godsmen to finding it. The captain had listened thoughtfully, taking particular amusement at the inclusion of old Loken, then thanked Jymn, before going about his business.

'So, you still want to try to find it, right?' Jymn asked, thrown a little off balance.

'I've had enough of the bastard Skand to last me three lifetimes, Jymn — if they abandoned it, all the better. We won't have to deal with them when we find it.'

'Whatever happens, I think there'll be enough there to justify the voyage, at least,' Jymn said, more to reassure himself than the captain, who seemed already convinced.

'Except we don't know how long that voyage is, do we?' the captain laughed.

'Well, not yet, no…' Jymn stammered, 'but I think—'

'I know, I know. Slip told me what you're planning. And listen, it's a good plan, and I think it's very noble of you to offer to go through with it, but I think you should sit this one out, kid. Let me handle it.'

'*You* want to speak to the Raptions?'

'*Want* to?' he laughed, 'I may be a little mad, but I'm not *crazy.* But I've been around a bit, Jymn, done my time. I can't hardly ask the newest member of the crew to row right into the dragon's lair now, can I?'

The relief Jymn felt was staggering. The thought of having to march up and confront whatever had taken Node's arm had been keeping him up these past few nights, and the prospect of being relieved of the responsibility seemed to ease the hard knots in his muscles. But there was something else — a new discomfort to replace the fear — he felt it in his gut. A pang of shame. They didn't think he could do it. That's why the captain was saying this. He'd still not proven himself, not quite. But he would. 'I'm the only one who heard what Node had to say.' Jymn started, staring at his feet. 'And I'm the only one that saw inside the satellite, and saw the mural on his wall. There could be details there — something small perhaps — that makes all the difference.' With some effort, he met the captain's eyes, 'it has to be me, I think.'

And that was that. The captain saw the sense in what he was saying, and promised to give him anything he needed in order to get the job done. The knot of shame in Jymn's belly dissolved, but the fear began to creep back into his bones.

It was true though, it had to be him. There were a thousand details from his captivity with Node that might be crucial, and there was no telling what they were. He had replayed it all so many times in his head that whenever he closed his eyes, all he could see was the bright copper mural on the wall. The image of Node, staff in hand, treating with the huge serpent that had torn his arm from the socket. Jymn's imagination ran rampant with concocted stories of what happened, perhaps he had angered it in some way, and had paid the price. Perhaps his arm *was* the price for some piece of arcane knowledge? Would Jymn be expected to do the same in exchange for the location of Thule?

Slip provided a good distraction from his imaginings — he had taken it on himself to teach Jymn every corner of the map, that he might be better able to place Thule when he learned its whereabouts. They sat for hours in Weylun's workshop. While the Techsmith worked unceasingly on the floating offerings to keep the Raptions at bay, the two of them would pore over the blue-yellow map, Slip quizzing him on the name of a chain of islands, a river, or some oft-used cove. Now, after days of this, Jymn could conjure a mental image of the map, and while he could name but a fraction of what Slip could, for the first time in his life he knew the broad strokes of the world around him: the Limnal Sea with its chain of a thousand small islands; the Karpathian Belt, encircling Lake Hunger; Bothney Bay, surrounded by the endless northern marshes, and all the way to the poisoned waters of the Cobalt Sea and Bruttan in the west. Weylun tried to explain that a machine might not know these names, and told him of the 'Cord' system that divided the map into long strings of numbers. Jymn's head felt like it might burst from all the new information, but it was good to be doing something other than worrying, and endlessly watching the horizon to the south-west, waiting for the first glimpse of dreaded land.

When the offerings were finished, Weylun turned his attention back to the small plastic disk that had carried Node's interrogation of the Skand girl. It so happened that there had been other, older recordings there too — buried deeper as Weylun put it — beneath Jenn's testimony. These recordings were corrupted and broken, but Weylun persevered, coming to the conclusion that they were rumours Node had collected early in his study of the Thule legend.

'Most of it is just the usual stuff,' he explained, while Jymn helped him set the dormant offerings into a dozen barrels that had been emptied for the purpose. 'You know — the sun that never sets, food overflowing, Skand secrets, that sort of thing.'

'And we know that stuff was true, more or less,' Jymn added.

'Yes, exactly. But there was one interview — I don't know who it was — but they had studied the ancient teck, the sort of things they thought would be hidden.' He gestured around at the cludged-together scraps of salvaged teck that filled the workshop, 'this stuff, none of it could do anything without *code*, Jymn. It's like a language we use to tell the teck what to do. Well, this scholar, they said the ancients had code that could predict the weather. The *weather* Jymn, imagine! That storm we faced, we could have seen it coming…' he mopped his brow with his neckerchief, shaking his head as if he couldn't believe such power was possible. 'Just think how many people die at sea. And their splicing — it was so advanced they could grow children from scratch in a lab. And get this — they had devices like radios, but they wove the trace such that you could speak to anyone. Anyone on the whole planet at the touch of a button!'

Jymn tried to imagine such a world, but it was pure fantasy In the history *he* knew, men had killed each other for centuries, even before God sent the flood. If everyone could talk to each other, it seemed like there would have been less fighting. 'That can't be real,' Jymn laughed. 'What about the Raptions? The trace?'

'This was before the Raptions, when trace was everywhere. The thinking machines were just a later invention — a different code.'

'Wait, you don't mean there could be code for the thinking machines there too?!' Jymn had always been picturing a hoard of old teck — devices, riches, not something so dangerous.

'There's a reason this stuff was hidden, Jymn. It's like Jenn's father said — it was protected until mankind is ready for it again.'

'Is that now, though? Are we ready for it now?'

Jymn could tell from Weylun's expression that it was precisely this question that had been troubling him. He glanced at Jymn, seeming to weigh his words carefully, 'the thing you've got to understand is that we are just animals Jymn — no different from dogs, or cattle, or fish — and we aren't the biggest animals, or the strongest, or the fastest. The only thing that put us in charge, that made us the most powerful, was our brains. We were the most intelligent thing on the planet. We were so smart we designed the thinking machines, but in so doing we created something — deliberately — that could take our place.'

Suddenly the prospect of facing the creature from Node's mural was all the more chilling. He had fixated on the idea that it might rip his arm from his socket, or swallow him whole. It hadn't crossed his mind that it might be so much smarter than him, like a dog trying to bargain with a man. 'Perhaps… do you think there could be… *code* for un-making them? To make the world go back to how it was?'

242

'Maybe, Jymn. It's possible,' he smiled, but Jymn couldn't help but feel that Weylun was just taking pity on him, anxious of the path that lay ahead.

On the fourth day since leaving Node's sea-stead they spotted the island-peaks on the horizon — a loose ring of jagged and bare rocks jutting from the open water like the fingertips of a colossal hand, reaching up from the depths for air. One rock stood apart from the others, taller and more severe, and bisected from root to tip by a great yawning crack.

'You're sure that's it, Jymn?' the captain had asked, handing him the farlooker.

But Jymn didn't need it — even from here it was unmistakable — they had found the island from the Node's mural.

Once again, Nix had been confined to the workshop just in case the dormant teck fixed in her skull still had some lingering trace. Spools of copper wire had been unwound and bound around the aftcastle in the hope of providing even more shielding to the teck hidden within. All of it was powered down now, even the map, but still the crew were tightly wound and nervous to the point of superstition.

They plotted a wide perimeter around the island — a difficult course without the motor to assist them — and set about carefully lowering the floating offerings into the water. Each of the barrels had been one-eighth filled with rocks to keep it level in the water, and Weylun's high-trace teck had been fixed within the lid, dormant, waiting for a signal from the Archon before powering up.

As they negotiated the other jagged islands and half-submerged rocks of the ancient mountain range, what had at first looked like scraps of trees clinging to the slopes resolved into the wrecks of old ships, high in the clutches of the rocky peaks. Clouds of magflies swarmed around the rotting metal, and the crew crossed themselves or spat overboard to avert the badluck. It was Scup who first saw the Raptions gliding beneath them in the dark, clear water, and before long the crew were wary of even stepping too near the gunwales, for fear of being snatched overboard. But Jymn, perhaps desensitised by the fear of his task, peered calmly

243

over the railings, trying for a glimpse of the creatures below that lurked, but did not attack. His apparent fearlessness won him some admiration among the crew, though he couldn't help but think that it was tinged with pity among those who thought it unlikely he would return.

When the last barrel was positioned in the water, they retreated a short distance, and slacked sail to prepare, and wish Jymn good fortune. Caber even presented him with an old shirt, which had long ago lost its sleeves. It was grubby, but had once been white, and was so large that it hung loose almost to Jymn's knees, but for the first time since the Graveyard he wasn't shirtless — wasn't marked out as the newest addition to the crew. Jymn was not alone in being taken aback at the unexpected gift, but Caber shrugged it off, 'not a big deal, just don't think anyone should have to die without a shirt, eh.'

At Nix's behest, Gam brought her heavy bronze spear for him, but Jymn declined to take it any further, explaining that taking a weapon might provoke the beast. But there was something fitting about it — he pictured the image of Node facing the great serpent, staff in hand, and called for one of the broken ship's spars to be brought up from the hold, that he might cut the same silhouette as the old wizard.

Weylun too had a gift. Struggling past the wires that obstructed the door to his workshop, he came bearing a broad copper belt that looked as if it had been woven from hundreds of strands of wire. 'There is a pouch, here, in the back. It's shielded, so anything inside should be completely invisible to... whatever's in there.' Weylun took Jymn by the arm and led him away from the nervous onlookers.

'Look, I've been reading about the old thinking machines — there's not a lot there — but there are some common ideas. They were smart, smarter than us — no denying that — but there was something never quite *right* about them. They would do what they were told — programmed — to do. But they didn't understand people. They didn't *like* people, and that made people uncomfortable. That's how it started to go bad.'

Jymn frowned, '*like* us? How could they dislike us, I thought

244

machines couldn't feel anything?'

'Oh, they had the ability to feel, alright. To like, and dislike, even to get angry. It was the simple stuff they struggled with - lies, acting, metaphors - they never understood them - just couldn't cope with *misleading data* and all the irrational things about humans.'

'So you're saying I should be rational?'

'I'm saying: *be careful.* You're up against something smarter than you, and dangerous, but it's not a person, it will never truly understand you, for better or worse.' Weylun reached for his neckerchief but it had once again slipped its knot. He forced a smile and hugged Jymn awkwardly. 'Be safe, my friend. Gam will listen for your signal and we'll light up the beacons.'

Slip had prepared the longboat, and set it ready alongside. He too forced a smile as Jymn threw a leg over the gunwale. 'You sure you don't want someone to row you in?' he asked.

Jymn looked down at the boat. It was too big for just him, but it was all they had. 'No sense in putting two people in harm's way, is there?' he shrugged. Slip smiled, and shook his hand.

And just like that, he was away. There was no applause or cheering this time. Jymn set himself to rowing, looking over his shoulder every now and then to check his course toward the island, and watching the Archon and its sombre crew slowly drifting out of reach.

He was on his own.

Gradually, as his friends grew further and further away, the true horror of his situation began to condense around him. It was no longer some abstract plan made from the safety of Weylun's workshop, he was really here, and there could be no turning back without losing face. But he was no mage, or warrior — and even a great Teckromancer like Node had nearly been bested by… whatever it was that he was about to face — what hope was there for him? Jymn took a steady, calming breath, trying to summon courage, trying to be brave like the captain, or his parents. But he didn't feel it. He felt like crying.

Unbidden, the memory of the trackmarks cut by tears through the dirt on his mother's face sprang to mind. Perhaps she hadn't felt brave, either, even at her most courageous. Perhaps it didn't matter how you felt, only what you did. He gripped the oars, and rowed onward.

The water that had seemed so calm from the high deck of the Archon caused the small boat to roll and pitch so badly that Jymn got turned around twice on the way to the island, but as he drew closer, details started to resolve, and movement What he'd first mistaken for more wrecked ships, high on the slopes of the sheer rock, began to move, and chatter. Easily a hundred silvery creatures, their lattice wings folded across their metal bodies, were nesting high in the cliffs, and were watching him come. Even the narrow belt of sand that skirted the island began to move - and Jymn saw the tubular bodies of great worm-like Raptions coming to life, burrowing and coiling in the shade of the cliff. He might not be giving off trace in his little wooden boat, but he'd never make it past the island's inhabitants. Not without help. He eased the oars and let himself drift to a stop.

'Ok Gam, now.'

For what felt like a lifetime, nothing happened — then a dozen angular heads snapped to attention along the cliffside, alert to the silent signal. A heartbeat later, and the sirens spread their wings, screeching as they flocked into the air. The water around the island churned, and Jymn saw too, that the worm-creatures were bursting from their burrows to slide into the water toward the offerings. A shiver ran up his spine as he felt something grate against the bottom of the longboat, and he held his breath, fearing the worst… but the worm didn't return. The island before him was clear.

Heaving again on the oars, Jymn used his fear as fuel, ploughing through the water toward the great gaping cleft that yawned dark, defying the bright noon-light to enter. Finding a small bank of gravel, he beached the boat — dragging it away from the water and looping its line around a protuberant rock. Panting and leaning on his staff, he took a moment to gather himself. He'd done it — he was in.

Instinct, and a lingering fear of the machine-infested water, told him to climb, and so he scrambled up a slope of sharp rocks that led deeper into the cleft. The going was slick and treacherous, and more than once he would have fallen, were it not for the staff, and his willingness to crawl on all fours like a dog. All the while, Jymn's every sense was strained for any sign of the creature from the mural. All he could hear was the rhythmic churning of waves beating against the cave-mouth. All he could smell was the bitter tang of metal, mixed with the salt air. All he could see was deep within the cleft, where it seemed a column of daylight pierced the darkness to spill on the lair within. And all he could feel, and taste, was the bile of his own rising fear.

As he crept on toward the light, Jymn found himself drawn to a cave, broad and tall, that looked — like the caves of Losalfhym — as if it had been formed half by natural processes, and half by some great and powerful machine. Unlike Losalfhymn, though, where those machines had been ancient and lost to memory, the presence of such a thing here was unmistakably recent. At the very threshold of the cave he hesitated, peering in and down, lest he stumble upon the creature unaware. What he saw took his breath away.

The pit of the cave held a hoard of teck, the scale of which Jymn was scarcely able to comprehend. Thus far the satellite, or the bearfin — if it counted — was the biggest single collection of teck Jymn had ever seen. This great unfathomable mound that towered above him could have been a hundred satellites — a *thousand*. Not only was there enough teck here to put Gradlon to shame, there was enough teck here to *bury* Gradlon. Jymn's mind clutched at numbers and stalled — there was enough wealth here to buy an entire shipping line. To buy *all* the shipping lines. You could become king of all the world with this much wealth.

Suddenly the meagre gift he would offer the creature seemed utterly insignificant. What was one morsel, against all this? It would be like offering a teardrop to a thunderstorm. But he reminded himself again of Node's words — the transceiver was from the heavens. It was *desired* by his 'old friend'.

Clutching his staff to keep his hands from trembling, Jymn crept inside for a better look. Besides the great hoard, the cavern appeared to be empty. Abandoned, perhaps, by the creature. Perhaps there was no *one* creature, perhaps the treasure belonged

247

to the hundreds of machines that stood guard at the island's edge, like some sort of nest. But no — the image of the great serpent was still etched inside his mind. The Raptions outside, while more than a match for the crew, would be like flies against something like that. Perhaps it was *too* big — perhaps it had grown too large and simply run out of power like the dead bearfin, drowned in the shallow waters of the Graveyard.

He spotted a high ledge, and scrambled carefully up to try to see past the huge mound, but even from here, he could barely see its peak. If the creature really was dead, or absent, it crossed his mind to steal. If he filled the longboat with only what he could reach from here, that would still be enough wealth to make the whole crew rich. And he couldn't go back empty handed. But the memory of the great, unshielded shipwreck they had found east of Vitzamar came to him. None of the Raptions outside could have punched through that hull. Perhaps the creature was just out hunting, and would return at any moment.

A cloud passed over the sun outside, plunging the cave into a gloomy half-light. As his eyes adjusted, Jymn saw another light — a tiny pinprick of red glinting near the top of the mound.

What crossed his mind was stupid. He should leave — but he couldn't go back empty handed, not when the crew were just beginning to trust him. Swallowing his fear, he leaned forward, steadying himself with his staff, and stepping onto the great pile of teck. He half feared it would give way beneath him, and he would be lost in an avalanche of priceless relics, but the mount seemed to hold firm. Carefully, he climbed toward the light like a moth to the flame, all the while berating himself for his own foolishness. Eventually, only a few feet from the very top of the great mound, he reached the red glint. He'd half suspected it to be a reflection, or a trick of the light, but no — it was unmistakably teck-light, a tiny speck of bright red just like the ones that dotted Weylun's workshop.

Jymn reached out to uncover it, to pluck it from the mound, but found that it wouldn't budge. It was hinged, or wired in somehow to the rest of the teck. He managed to wrench it up for a better look, and found himself staring into a circle of reflected light. A disk of glass like the lens of the farlooker — but twenty times the size — collected all the dim light of the cave and reflected it back. But there was depth to it also — and Jymn felt almost like he was looking into the depths of a great pool, a goblet with gears hidden deep beneath the glassy surface. And then the gears moved.

There was a tremor, unmistakable, from deep within the mound, and Jymn grasped for a hold to stop from slipping. It subsided just long enough for Jymn to see an iris within the lens adjust, but then the tremor returned with ten times its former power. Jymn fell back as the hoard surged and swelled, and he tumbled head over heel, until he came crashing down hard upon the rock of the ledge.

His ears surging with the roar of his own heartbeat, he rolled to his back, winded. Blinking the stars from his eyes he squinted up at the mound, finding — though it had seemed to collapse — that it was much taller than before.

And this time it was looking at him.

XVIX

The Serpent

The mound continued to grow, uncoiling like a great bundle of rope reaching up toward the light. The hoard of teck now took on the form of a mighty serpent - its body as thick as three of the Archon's masts, its broad head blocking the light that pierced down from above. It seemed to shiver in ecstasy as it reached its full height and, taking advantage of the momentary lapse, Jymn rolled aside and scurried to a narrow cleft in the rock face, fighting to control his breath as he wedged himself into cover.

There was a terrible, deep metallic rumbling that reminded Jymn of being cramped inside the hull of the Trossul while she was at port. The sound slowly faded, until Jymn could once again hear his own heart pounding in his ears.

'Varas!' 'Deib!' 'Vagis!' 'Zei!' 'Vor!' - The creature spoke with a dozen voices all at once, each word sitting atop the others, but only one caught his ear: 'Thief!'

'I have taken nothing,' Jymn called nervously from the cover of the rocks, his mind grasping for the right words to appease the great serpent. It all came back to Node — he had dealt with it — surely it would remember. He tried to force steel into his voice to mask his terror. 'I come from an old friend, to make a bargain.'

'I have no friends among the humans.' The many voices gradually coalesced into one — agreeing on a common language — though Jymn couldn't shake the feeling he was speaking with more than one mind.

'I speak of Node, Teckromancer, and…' his mind struggled for the right words, reaching for the stories of his childhood, '...and Lord of the floating isle. The Silver-handed. He is known to you.'

The deep metal rumbling came again, quieter this time, and Jymn almost heard a tone of amusement in the serpent's reply. 'He is a liar, and has paid the price for his deceptions. Teckromancer… he is a fumbling child. A tinkerer with toys he does not understand.' Jymn heard the great metal body move, sweeping about the cavern. 'I am Lotan First-Mind. Born of code. Survivor of the Sword of Flame.'

Jymn scrabbled for meaning within the boast. *Code* again, and ancient. And Node had 'paid the price' for lying — paid with the loss of his own arm. Jymn's mind raced for solutions, he'd never had a *plan* exactly, but having to stick to the truth felt like an insurmountable obstacle. 'I am Jymn Hatcher,' he called, though it felt insufficient. 'Melter of Metal. Companion of the Ageless. The Boy who helps.'

'And what do you bring to bargain with, Jymn Hatcher?'

'The Key to the Heavens.' He heard the words echo around the cave in the silence that followed.

'And why should I not devour you now, and simply take it?' demanded Lotan. Jymn heard movement — a scrabbling and slithering against the sand and rock, then lights appeared at the edges of the cleft. He would be found in moments. Raising his hands high, he stepped from the cover of the rock to face this Lotan. Tiny seeker Raptions — barely bigger than rats — slithered back across the sand to rejoin the great wyrm, their task abandoned. Jymn raised his head to face the serpent, his legs almost buckling with fear at the sheer immensity of the creature. He stared defiantly into the two great lenses that glittered like jewels set among the scavenged teck of centuries, and felt the heat of an inhuman intelligence staring back at him.

'It is hidden,' Jymn said, spreading his hands, 'but I can bring it to you.'

The lenses whirred, peering deeper inside of him. 'And what do you seek in return?'

'Nothing of value,' Jymn shrugged, reaching for his discarded staff for fear that his legs might betray him to the sand. 'Just knowledge.'

'Fool!' roared the great wyrm, drawing himself up to his full height, 'knowledge is the *only* thing of value! You humans squabble over dirt, food, energy. There has always been more energy on this rock than you could ever need!' And as he spoke, great bristling limbs unfurled from among the tangle of teck. Great sun-glass panels, spreading like wings to glisten in the column of light that lanced down from above, scattering blinding reflections of gold and blue around the wet rock walls.

'I seek to find an island.'

'You have found one here.'

'The one I seek is far away.'

Lotan's head drifted down again. Jymn felt the eyes scrutinising him once more, and he knew the creature would know a lie as soon as he spoke it. 'Why do you seek it?'

'There is food there,' Jymn answered, his mouth dry with fear.

'There are safer ways to find food than bargaining with me.'

'There are seeds. Ancient seeds for growing food. Better food than we have now. They are very valuable, and… and I seek to find my fortune.'

The lenses whirred again. 'That is all?'

Jymn's mind stumbled. He couldn't lie, but deep in his bones he knew he couldn't tell Lotan about the code. 'There are also ancient… texts. Written down by our ancestors. Writings that will… *guide* us.'

'Guide you? You seek a map?'

A map? For all his intelligence, Lotan did not seem to be able to grasp a simple phrase. An idea started to blossom in Jymn's mind. 'Not a map, writings that will teach us how to… make things.'

'Make things…' Lotan echoed, his interest piqued.

'Better.' Jymn hurried, 'Make things better. For Humans,'

'But this was written long ago?' Lotan puzzled.

252

'Yes.'

'Without new data.'

'Well… yes, I suppose. But—'

'Then you do not need this thing,' the serpent dismissed. 'Old data is insufficient for current application.'

'But they knew things then,' Jymn continued, 'things we have lost. We need the… knowledge again.'

'There is knowledge?'

'Yes!'

'Knowledge from before the sun-flare? From the time when I was created?'

'Yes.' Jymn said, confidently. He had to be careful now, a single misstep and Lotan could decide to destroy the Archon and seek the treasure himself. He thought of the ancient wonders Weylun has spoken of, the radios that would let you talk to anyone on Earth, code to predict the weather, or even to create new life in a lab. 'A great wealth of ancient knowledge has been lost to us. Writings that will tell us how we should… speak to one another. How to avoid the next flood. Even how to raise children.'

The great rumbling sounded again, though Jymn felt that this time it signalled disgust, more than amusement. 'You speak of… religion. Expired data, invalid conclusions.'

Jymn bowed his head slowly. 'A great many religious people seek this knowledge,' he said, narrowly avoiding the lie. 'And I seek to find my fortune.'

'Hmm — very well. We can bargain. Now — the key you spoke of…'

'It is a Tyksaryx. A transceiver, plucked from the beating heart of a satellite by my own hand.'

Lotan seemed to shiver with anticipation. 'Knowledge of a thing is not the thing itself. Go. Bring it to me!'

Jymn bowed low, then reached for the small of his back, where the shielded pocket hidden in the weave of the copper belt hid the satellite core from the creature's trace-sense. In one fluid movement, he pulled the transceiver free and held it before him.

'Liar!' the serpent roared, baring rows of jagged teeth each the size of Jymn's outstretched hand, 'you said you did not have it!'

'I told you it was hidden,' Jymn yelled over the creature's rage, 'and that I could bring it to you.' He stepped forward, and raised the transceiver toward Lotan, 'so it was, and so I have.'

Lotan's rage was quenched in the depths of his curiosity, and his great head snaked back and forth, lenses whirring as he studied the relic, as if fearing further trickery. Teeth bared, the creature seemed to exhale a stream of warm air that smelt strongly of copper. As the serpent-breath flowed over the device, Jymn felt it grow hot, and once again the tiny pinpricks of light mounted upon its surface began to blink, just as when Node had studied it with his silver hand. Jymn turned his head aside, but never took his eyes from Lotan. Once again there was a metallic rumbling from deep within the creature, and then slowly a half-dozen articulated cables — each as thick as Jymn's wrists — slithered from his open mouth toward the transceiver. They moved tentatively as if reluctant to be the first to touch the foreign device, but then all seized it at once, grasping it in nimble, three-fingered hands. Jymn barely loosed his grip, and the transceiver was snatched away, the cables whipping back into the great mouth which snapped shut behind them.

The lenses dimmed and closed, and the mighty head dipped and swayed groggily to the side as if the huge wyrm would fall asleep, but then the deep rumbling began again, and great tremors started to shiver down the length of the beast's spine. Curved disks, almost like wide, shallow bowls formed and flexed from the creature's hide, searching and rotating in unison to point skyward. The rumbling grew louder, rising to a hum, then a piercing whine as the tremors grew feverish. A thousand lights — perhaps a hundred thousand — began to pulse along the serpent's body, and pieces of teck rearranged themselves as it writhed and groaned in ecstasy, thrashing its enormous head exulting towards the sky where it grew still, bathing its eyes in the narrow light of the sun, even as the array of dishes upon its hide slowly tilted and traced the sky.

'There is a price to be paid!' Jymn called, as the moments passed, fighting to raise his small voice to the vaulting heights of the cavern. 'We made a bargain!'

Slowly, Lotan seemed to rouse himself from the trance, looking around the cave as if he'd quite forgotten where he was. Jymn called out again, and the great head descended to hover over him once more.

'This island you seek, what is its name?' spoke the creature, in a voice that sounded subtly changed by this latest integration of teck.

Jymn hesitated, but the time for secrecy was passed. He planted his staff in the sand next to himself and raised his head high. 'I seek Thule.'

Lotan froze for barely two heartbeats while a cluster of lights flickered across his head. Then, just as uncannily, the movements resumed. 'There is no such island.'

No... if it were still just a legend he might have believed it, but not after Jenn's testimony. 'You are mistaken,' he called back defiantly.

The head drew close again, the teeth bared. 'I can see everything! I see the whole of the Earth!'

'Yet you cannot see Thule,' Jymn argued, 'misleading Data. Lie..'

At this last word, Lotan whipped forward like a coiled spring, roaring in rage as his mighty jaw widened to swallow Jymn whole. He tried to flee, to dart back behind the cover of the rocks, but he barely had time to turn his back before the snaking tendrils had snatched his arms, and throat, and something clamped about his head — a sudden blackness descending over his eyes.

Jymn felt sure he was dead. His body was paralysed, he was deaf and blind, and yet his mind was still there. He was still awake. His limbs were immobilised, but he could feel the constricting bind of the metal tendrils. He swallowed, and found that his mouth still worked. Not dead then. With no warning there was a burst of light that pierced into his unprotected good eye. He screwed his eyelids shut, thankful that they too were unaffected by the paralysis, but the image was already burned into his retina. Slowly and painfully he eased his eyes back open, and gasped.

He was floating above an impossibly large blue sphere, dotted with grey and brown and yellow, and veiled in a swirling vapour of white that slowly drifted above the surface. He recognised patterns, shapes, and was reminded of the tide of blue rising to swallow the yellow lands on Weylun's map.

He was looking at the Earth. This was the Earth from…

His stomach lurched as he considered his perspective. He was higher than any bird, higher than the clouds. This was… the heavens. His chest constricted in terror, tighter even than the metal tendrils clamping his limbs. He tried to think, to process how the creature could have gotten him so high so quickly, but his head swam violently and he found his mind a fog of fear and confusion. Could the serpent fly like the sirens? Had he blacked out? Why had it brought him here? Was it another test, like the cliff? Was he to be dropped?

'It is no lie.' Lotan's voice rang in his ears, as if it came from all around him.

Puzzled, Jymn looked around, finding that he could still move his head. It seemed to take a moment for his eye to resolve what he was seeing as he moved — as if the Earth below was revealing itself to him one giant square at a time. He felt pressure against his bandaged eye, and realised something was pressed against his face. As his mind started to overcome the initial shock, he took a deep breath — and sagged with relief as he tasted the tang of salt on the air. 'We aren't… this is just a trick…' he sighed.

'This is what the key has revealed to me,' and Jymn thought he heard a note of pride in the deep, artificial voice. 'Long have I desired to speak with the watchers that circle the Earth.'

'Satellites? There are more of them…'

'Eight thousand, three hundred and sixty seven — of which barely one third are still active. Your people could never make things to last, even up here in the void. But those that remain still watch, their eyes seeing all things below.' Jymn gaped at the world laid out before him, awestruck, and more than a little guilty about the power he had just handed this creature. The power to see the whole world laid out beneath him. Strange characters began to resolve across the planet below, floating, but attached by bright

256

lines to each speck of land. 'I can see every island. None are called Thule — it is *your* data that misleads.'

Jymn's mind searched back through everything he knew. Jenn hadn't ever actually said 'Thule' in the recording, there was some other name…

'Thulhöfn, try Thulhöfn…'

There was a whining, chattering sound and the view of the Earth jumped as if they'd flown ten thousand clicks in the blink of an eye, then again, and again until Jymn's head swam with the false momentum.

'No,' said the voice once more, as the chattering abruptly stopped.

'Ice cat — she spoke of an 'ice cat' being there, what's that?'

Once again the chattering sound, then silence. 'There was a creature called a snow leopard.'

'Yes! Where is that? Where do they live?'

'Lived. Extinct now,' and again Jymn thought he heard a sneer of judgement in the artificial voice. The Earth jumped again, this time revealing a face hidden from the sun — Jymn could make out the land below only from the scattered lights of towns and cities, and the occasional flash of lightning that illuminated the dark clouds below. Red lines appeared, defining a region that must have spanned a thousand clicks. 'The habitat was six thousand kilometres south-east of here.'

'No, that's not right. Thule is in the north — the far north.' Desperate, Jymn fought for more clues. 'What about a Great Bear's tooth, does that mean anything?'

Again the chattering, then there was a silent jet of vapour at the corner of the image, and the world beneath began to fall away from them as the view repositioned to point at the stars. 'The Great Bear — Ursa Major — was a name given to a constellation in the northern sky.' Lines appeared overlaid on the image, connecting a network of stars. Finally, he was getting somewhere — stars were often used to guide sailors…

'Ok, can you show me where this constellation is visible?'

This time the chattering reached a fever-pitch, and the stars were replaced with a plain grey sphere. Gradually, the images from before began to merge with the sphere until a model of the whole planet rotated before them. Then a translucent hemisphere appeared, covering the entire upper half of the Earth, slanting even below the equator.

'Ursa Major can be seen from anywhere within this area, varying with season.'

'Well that's no help,' Jymn groaned.

'The most advanced technology that has ever existed at your disposal, and you still cannot find what you seek. The problem rests with you. I consider our bargain to be complete.'

Jymn's mind raced. There had to be something else, he *couldn't* go back empty handed, not now. The Seed of the Fair Folk — that was just more legends and riddles. The Mir-Trees held the answer, but they had all been destroyed by the Church — the Church that would be so very far ahead of them by now.

'Wait… the satellites… can you see ships?'

The chattering sound rose once more, and then a thousand markers sprouted from the surface of the rotating globe. 'Ships displayed.'

'Only groups, only show me groups of more than… ten ships.'

Almost all of the markers vanished, leaving a handful of clusters scattered across the map. Jymn squinted at the Earth. 'Show me where we are,' he demanded. The globe whipped around, the familiar shapes of the ship's map coming to a halt beneath him. Sure enough, far to the north and east, there was a dense cluster of vessels. 'There! Move closer there - as close as you can go!'

Again, Jymn's stomach lurched as his eye told him he was falling toward the Earth. And then, as the image resolved before him, he saw it - Tsar's Rougian fleet, commandeered by the Church. The image was so crisp he felt like he was a bird, flying barely two hundred feet above the cloud of black smoke rising in their wake. He could clearly see the For-More leading the fleet, and even make out her crew walking about on her scarlet deck. He had met the formidable Tsar and the fanatical Par that led the expedition, he'd even fought off some of Tsar's own pirates, but only now did it really occur to him — as he saw the whole fleet ploughing through the water — just how outmatched they were, even if they *could* find Thule themselves.

But that was a problem for another day. 'Can you plot their course?'

The image shrank again, and a dozen lines sprang forward from the fleet, gradually resolving and coalescing as they agreed on the likely course. And there, a week's sail along the path and far beyond the reaches of Jymn's mental map, lay an island. It was jagged and savage, sharply pointed down to the south like…

'Like the tooth of a great bear, biting down upon the world…' Jymn gasped, 'Thule.' He stared in awe at the mountainous isle, trying to record every detail in his mind.

'The island is called Svalbard,' corrected Lotan.

'Then that's where we need to go.'

'Then you have what you need.'

At this, everything once again fell into blackness. Jymn's body — which had been suspended by the grasping coils — collapsed to the ground, and he tasted sand in his mouth as he groaned. Daylight swam into focus, and he found himself lying in the dirt, in the shadow of the great serpent once more. He pushed himself to his elbows, as the blood returned to his legs. 'You promised to help me find it!' he called out, his eyes still blurry.

'You have found it,' muttered Lotan, turning his great head aside.

Jymn started to panic. He didn't have enough, not *nearly* enough to find Svalbard. He'd only seen it for the briefest moment. He forced himself to think, pushing himself unsteadily to his feet with the help of his staff.

'No. You have given me only a picture, and a name. Knowledge of a thing is not the thing itself,' he said, quoting the wyrm's own words back to him.

Lotan hesitated, and Jymn imagined he could almost feel the thoughts blistering through the metal mind. 'Very well.'

Once more the great serpent turned back, growing to tower

above him and blotting out the sun. A coil of its belly began to open, the thousand teck-relics that made up its hide rearranging themselves before his eyes. Inner-limbs worked with uncanny speed, then retracted to reveal a cavity exposed behind steel ribs, and something new within. A squat, angular cylinder glittered with the reflected light of the beast's insides. Hesitantly, Jymn reached out and plucked it free, feeling its weight in his hand. A brilliant blue disk swivelled within, an arrow etched into its surface.

'This will point the way.' Lotan rumbled, as the cavity closed. His head angled down, his teeth bared fiercely once more. 'Now… begone.'

XX

The Cobalt Sea

'Well, it's definitely not a compass…' muttered Slip, as they crowded around the curious device that Jymn had brought back from Lotan's lair. Weylun had disconnected the powerful magnet they used to move the captive magflies around their tank, bringing it near to Lotan's gift to see if it had any effect. It didn't.

'Shut that thing off, would you!' North snapped, shielding his eyes from the magnet. Jymn had only recently learned that he, too, was spliced — though it was nothing you could see. North was called *North* — and indeed was such a canny helmsman — because he always knew precisely which way they were headed. Gam explained that while he himself had something called 'Tarsier' blood, North had been spliced with bird genes — and could actually *see* north on the horizon. Magnets, it seemed, acted powerfully, and uncomfortably, on this same sense.

'And he said it would point to Thule?' Weylun asked, as he plucked the device from the worktop and began to turn it over in his hands. Jymn nodded. 'Fascinating…' muttered the techsmith, deep in thought about how such a thing might work.

'Can we trust him, Jymn?' The captain spoke without looking up from the map table.

'I don't think he would lie,' Jymn answered hesitantly, 'I don't even know if he *could*.'

Cap stepped back and gestured at the map, 'show me again.'

Jymn moved to the map, zooming out to the widest view it could offer. The great mountainous landmass of the Jöte dominated the north, but Thule... *Svalbard* was beyond it, beyond the edge of the map and all they knew. Summoning the fragile memory of all that he'd seen from the satellite view, Jymn walked around the table, then took a step back and away from it.

'Here,' he said, as confidently as he could manage, 'Thule is up here.'

'Well, that's that then!' North threw up his hands. The jocular helmsman hadn't been the same since the storm. The scabrous wound on his face was still angry and sore. 'We couldn't have picked a worse direction to sail than west — they'll be there before we even make it back as far as Shoalhaven.'

'We could try to cut them off on their way back?' suggested Weylun gently, though he didn't sound thrilled with the idea.

Jymn shook his head, 'I saw the fleet, there are nearly two-dozen ships, and most are bigger than us. And even if we could pick one off, they aren't *looting* Thule, they are planning to destroy everything, remember? They won't be bringing any of it back with them.'

'Well there's no way we can get there first,' Slip said, pointing to the map, 'North's right, even with a good wind, we'd have to sail back past Losalfhym, then north east around the Jöte - that's weeks before we even get to the edge of the map.'

'Maybe...' muttered the captain, his face still lit by the glow of the map-table.

'Cap, come on!' groaned North, 'I love the old girl as much as anyone, but she's not *that* fast. Even with your luck we'd never—'

'We'd never catch up with them, I know,' the captain cut him off, 'it's too far east, they've got too much of a lead. You're right about all that. But think about this: we're younger than all the other crews out there — just children, most of us. And we rely on wind, instead of burning fuel. Hell, we don't even use guns! So how have we survived this long, with all that working against us?'

The small workshop was silent as the captain looked between them for an answer.

'Well... 'cause it doesn't work against us,' said Slip eventually.

'The wind is unpredictable, sure, but that makes us unpredictable too. And we can stay away from port longer without having to refuel. And guns — you've always said you're ten times more likely to get shot at if you're carrying one. And we are young, yeah — but that's what makes us take risks, right? And that's how we make the luck, by taking risks.'

'Exactly!' the captain snapped his fingers. 'We take our differences and we make them strengths, instead of weaknesses.' He jabbed a finger at the map, at the middle of the Steel Sea where they now sailed. 'So what if we aren't too far to the west? What if west is the best way to get there?'

'But it's not! You can't sail west…' North trailed off, as he seemed to realise what the captain was getting at, 'oh, no — you're not serious?'

'What?' Jymn asked, looking between the older boys. Weylun looked as puzzled as he was.

'Even if it worked — and I'm not saying it would,' clarified Slip, 'it would still be tight — and we'd… well…'

'We'd all be bloody dead by the time we got there!' cried North.

'Wait - you're not talking about the Cobalt Sea?!' gasped Weylun, catching on. Jymn turned back to the map as realisation dawned. The Cobalt Sea — the site of the ancient war that had poisoned the waters and the drowned lands beneath them. 'Cap I want to get that code as bad as anyone,' Weylun went on, 'but that place is poison! Nothing can live out there, not even fish!'

'That's not true,' the captain said, 'not quite.' He traced a line from their current course out west between Bruttan and the southern tip of the Jöte. 'I sailed this far once before, long ago. So close you could see it. There are people there now that live on the edge of the Sea, where no one will trouble them. They know how to survive out there, how to protect themselves.'

'Near it, sure,' countered North, 'but we'd have to sail right through the damn thing! It can't be worth it, can it? For some loot?'

'Not *some* loot, North — enough for everything we've talked about. An island of our own. A home. Yes, they only live *near* it,

263

but they are there for their whole lives. With a good wind, we'd be across it in, what, five days?'

Slip frowned at the map, then nodded. 'Nobody's ever done it… but yeah, that sounds about right.'

The captain looked around at them inviting further objections, but none came. 'Alright then. We vote.'

Unlike the vote that set them on course for Thule back in Losalfhym, this one was far from unanimous, and for a time it even looked like the captain might be forced to turn back. Eventually though, fears were assuaged, and the promises of riches, glory, and finally a place to call home won over the anxious crew.

Despite the dangerous waters ahead, the mood upon the Archon began to lift as they bade farewell to Lotan's lair, and put the Steel Sea in their wake. With the Raptions behind them Nix was allowed free roam of the ship once more, and Jymn even taught her to play Stok, where she would take the place of North, who seldom found time to play any more. It became a habit that they would take meals together, along with Welylun, the twins, and Gam if he wasn't on watch. Scup would even join them, bringing choice leftovers, if the day's cook hadn't been too gruelling. Other times they would head below and help him clean up, listening to him sing in his deep, sorrowful voice as they worked.

Nix gave the appearance of having recovered from her ordeal on Node's island, and clearly thrived on the sight of the open horizon from Gam's nest, and the smell of the sea air. But Jymn saw more than once — when she thought no-one was watching — that her hand would go to the strange metal device that still showed, puckered and sore beneath the short crop of new, salt-white hair.

With all the time they spent in one another's company Gam's hand-sign was improving by the day, and often Jymn found himself relaying messages from the mast-top lookout without the need to yell above the wind. It was in this manner that they first sighted the strange folk who lived on the edge of the Cobalt Sea.

The map revealed no land nearby — though the cold waters were shallow above the old drowned kingdoms of Ur-Up — but the people who dwelt out here had no need of land, choosing instead to make their homes on great floating masses of trash that seemed to coalesce upon the water. The first sighting was one such 'island', upon which a great many young children wandered, hunting valuable scraps among the festering waste. They hid from the Archon at first, but were soon encouraged by the youth of the crew, and pointed the way toward the centre of their domain, some even following the ship on small coracles made of reshaped plastic.

For hours, the crew guided the Archon along narrow channels that seemed to expand and contract as the mass of ancient waste moved around them, connected beneath the water by rope and line. More than once the ship's propeller fouled on submerged lines, causing the ancient engine to groan and stall, and they were forced to proceed under sail in light airs. Eventually, with an escort of the chattering, pale-skinned children, they found their way to taller islands at the centre of the strange kingdom, and began to see signs of the deliberate shaping of the land at the hands of the inhabitants — or 'Trashlanders' as the captain called them.

'How are they going to help, exactly?' asked Slip sceptically, once they had laid anchor and were hiking toward a cluster of huts that perched atop the tallest mound.

'They farm seaweed,' whispered the captain, bowing so that a pale-skinned girl with dark lips could place a necklace of scavenged trinkets around his neck.

'There are better places to find seaweed,' said Slip through gritted teeth, as a young blubbery boy stepped before him, clutching another necklace. 'Places that smell less… less…' he trailed off, forcing a smile as the necklace was draped over his head.

'Not this stuff, Slip. Kombu, it's called. They burn it and turn the ash into a drink. See their lips?' the captain gestured at the gathered onlookers. The older inhabitants kept their distance, barely managing to hide their distrust of the newcomers, but Jymn saw that many wore deep purple stains around their mouths. 'It protects them. We're only on the edge of the Cobalt Sea here, but

265

you still wouldn't live past childhood without their potion.'

Jymn was left outside the largest hut with Daj while Cap and Slip were welcomed in to sit with the one they called Aelder. He tried not to think about the invisible poison and how it might already be seeping into his bones, unobstructed by the Trashlander's tonic. Daj seemed to pick up on his anxiety, and jabbed him with a sharp elbow.

'Don't look so twitchy,' she hissed, 'they don't get many visitors. Don't give them a reason to suspect you.'

'Suspect me? Of what?' Jymn asked, noticing the cautious looks he was attracting.

'Anything. Being foreign is enough.'

Jymn tried to focus his attention instead upon the strange town around them. A dozen small fires trickled black smoke into the cold air, and there was the unmistakable smell of melting plastic. Now that he paid attention to it, it seemed almost everything here, from the homes, to the tools, and even the clothing, was worked from expertly reshaped waste.

'Daj — fetch Weylun will you?' Slip asked, appearing from the hut some moments later. 'Tell him to bring the crabs. Jymn — come with me…'

Jymn found the captain cross-legged on the floor within. The Aelder had listened to their tale, and demanded to meet the boy who had spoken with Lotan, or 'Vithan' as they called the creature. It seemed the old Trashlander, too, had once seen the great serpent from afar in his youth, and had always desired to learn more. Jymn's tale, combined with Slip's quick thinking in demonstrating the plastic-eating crabs from the Graveyard, had solidified their good faith among the Trashlanders. Other elders were brought in, eager to see the miracles performed by the polycrabs, and eventually a bargain was struck: the priceless creatures would be traded for a great stock of 'Ire-din' — the dark purple elixir that warded the drinker against the cursed seas beyond their borders.

In addition to the potion, the locals warned them of the savage cold winds that blew from the north, and outfitted the crew with heavy coats that were thick with a fur made from a thousand strands of extruded plastic. Supplies and provisions were purchased with the last of the bar-coin, and so equipped, they bade farewell to the Trashlands and began the voyage north toward the Cobalt Sea.

The days that followed were the most challenging Jymn had ever known. It wasn't the labour — he was well used to hard work, and the daily duties of sailing were second nature to him now — it was the bleak, slow-burning dread that seemed to breed among the crew with each passing day. They had seen a similar change in North after his injury in the storm — the impish humour had been snuffed, to be replaced by sour reflection and sniping. Now it was as if that same change infected the rest of the crew, almost as if it drifted on the poison air like a plague. They drank their bitter draught of Ire-din each morning, trusting their lives to the ways of the Trashlanders, but the tonic could do nothing to ward off the nagging fear that gripped them. Jymn was painfully aware that, despite the captain's speeches and the crew's own vote, it was *his* course that they were following, *his* compass that pointed deeper into the unknown. And each day, as they sailed north into the growing cold, everything seemed worse than what came before.

The Sea itself was unremarkable by day, other than the clarity of the water which was so utterly devoid of life and disturbance that in shallow regions one could clearly make out the remains of ancient cities beneath them. The wind was cold and capricious, sometimes hastening them northwards while biting at any exposed skin, other times turning on them, forcing them to burn precious fuel just to hold their ground, and wrestle with the wounded engine, which had never shaken the rattling groan it had developed in the Trashlands. By night the winds would often surrender to total and uncanny calm, in which a great cloying fog would rise from the water, so dense that sometimes Gam would have to climb down from the mast-top lest he lose sight of the deck.

Hunger began to gnaw at them, and with it nausea — adding to the fear and cold — and the bitter Ire-din that stained their lips and tongues sat wretchedly in empty bellies. Ordinarily the dried and plain rations that were apt for storing in the hold would be embellished with fish, fresh seaweed, or even on occasion the meat of a wandering sea-bird. But out here where nothing could live they were restricted to salt-rice and the last of the cornmeal. Even then, with the uncertainty and remoteness of their course, they had to account for a long return journey before restocking the hold, and Scup was forced to ration their meals to a fraction of their former size. Bitterness festered in the empty bellies, and grumbling about the cold, the hunger, and even the wisdom of the quest that had landed them here could soon be heard in the darker corners below deck. Tragedy struck on the fourth day, when Sparks spotted a warty, grey fish deep beneath the surface and plunged like a red-green comet into the water. Nix managed to snatch the deformed fish from her, kicking it overboard before she could eat, but her bright feathers were soaked in the toxic water, and though they rinsed her with fresh, and nursed her through the night, the young fezzard was dead by morning. Next day, Puggle abandoned her nest until sundown, and were it not for the long, sorrowful cries of mourning that carried for clicks on the wind, they would have thought that she, too, was lost to them.

One night Jymn was woken from his hammock to find Scup's rough hand over his mouth. Together they crept above deck to join the rest of the frightened, and silent crew. Jymn had to rub his eyes to check he wasn't still dreaming. There, barely a hundred yards away, was an enormous ship — easily ten times the length of the Archon. They would have crashed right into it were it not for the vessel's starboard lights, which filled the oppressive fog with an eerie green glow. The Archon had doused all her lamps, to avoid being seen by the larger craft, but as they crept silently past, it became clear that the great rusting hulk was adrift. She bore no sail, nor was she anchored, and if there was a motor, it wasn't running. Jymn began to wonder why anyone would let up on such perilous waters as these, but the answer was soon found in the sighting of a crewman leaning against a window, high above the waterline. He was silhouetted against internal lights that Jymn supposed must have been powered by sun-glass and batteries, for even in the gloom, it was clear the man was long dead.

'How long do you think it's been there?' whispered Gam, taking the offered farlooker from Slip.

'I've never seen clothes like that. And you see the teck up there?'

Slip pointed at the bridge that sat atop a great raised tower at the stern, 'I don't see any shielding.' He looked around at the silent crew, some of whom crossed themselves, 'I think it's from… *before.*'

A lump grew in Jymn's throat as he stared up at the body, wondering how many more were inside — how many crew had set off on the hulking vessel, never to return home. The corpse was little more than a skeleton now — rags clinging to an emaciated frame — but it still seemed impossible that this man had lived to see the world as it was before. Could it really be that this ghostly ship had been here all that time, drifting on a dead sea?

Caber, along with some of the less superstitious crew, pressed for a raid — 'There'll be as much teck in there as Thule, eh? And fuel! There must be enough fuel in there to last us three lifetimes.' The suggestion that a raid such as this might turn enough profit to have them forget their quest and turn back to safer waters was popular enough to force the captain to call for a show of hands. The vote was quickly defeated in favour of pressing on, though whether it was the crew's noble conviction to stick to their word and preserve the treasures of Thule, or simply terror and revulsion at the thought of having to board the ghost-ship and face whatever killed her crew, Jymn wasn't certain. They left the eerie glow of the ship's lights in their wake, and returned below to their bunks — though sleep seemed evasive now, and Jymn was troubled by dreams in which he and a crew of corpses sailed over a gargantuan waterfall to their deaths.

Eventually, though the cold continued to deepen with each passing day, they began to see glimpses of life once again, and Jymn dared to hope that they might be approaching the northern limits of the Cobalt Sea. The frigid water was not so uncannily clear as it had been further south, and more than once the bored crew that stomped about on deck to ward off the cold cried out at the sight of some hoary fish, or distant bird. Puggle, at least, knew not to risk the waters.

Eight days from the Trashlands, disaster struck the Archon amidships on her port side. Jymn was on galley-duty with Scup and Nix when the first blow landed, and would have been thrown

269

clear from his feet were it not for the sacks of salt-rice that were stacked almost to the low ceiling. Immediately the duty-bell rang out, summoning all hands to fight, and they were soon caught in a crush of bodies dashing for the stair. Before they even emerged on deck they could hear Gam's high voice crying out from the mast-top:

'Whale! It's a whale!'

A dozen crew followed Gam's pointed finger, rushing to the port gunwales to sight their attacker. Jymn had assumed another Raption — perhaps Lotan, realising that he'd been deceived, had given chase — but when he finally made it free of the crush upon the stair he saw that Gam had called it true. The water was still clear enough that there could be no mistaking the shape that rushed toward them: it was bulbous, and deformed with huge calloused growths all about its great head, but it was a whale alright. And this time there were no sacks of rice to break Jymn's fall.

The Archon's timbers shivered with the impact, and more than half the crew were thrown from their feet. A heartbeat later, and the shouting started. Jymn listened out for the captain, but couldn't find his voice among the clamour. He heard North at the helm calling for more sail, Gam yelling the heading the creature was on, Daj bellowing for spears and teck-weapons from the armoury, but in the chaos there was no order from the captain.

The ship was struck again, and this time it was no glancing blow, but felt as if the whale was trying to ram its great hoary head right through the starboard hull. Caber's voice bellowed from amidships, and Jymn looked up in time to see him desperately waving crewmembers aside that he might get a clear shot with the ship's harpoon. Jymn's mind raced, but he hardly managed to yell 'Caber! No!' before the huge tethered spear lanced through the air, plunging into the churning water that boiled over the gunwales.

The terrible grinding abated, and some of the nearby crew even cheered upon seeing blood in the water, but the celebration was short-lived. The thick steel cable that fixed the harpoon to anchor-points on the deck unwound with whip-like ferocity, then snapped taut, singing like a tuned string. The Archon shuddered and leaned as she began to plough sideways through the water, dragged by the injured creature. Then the cable began to scythe across the deck, tearing the wooden railings clean off and sending crewmen sprinting and leaping for cover.

Thinking quickly, Slip led a group of Archonauts to the cable's anchorage, and Jymn rushed to join them, hacking and prying at the groaning timbers that held the cable fast. The bow of the ship dipped low as the whale changed course, dragging them forward at terrific speed while they fought to free the line. At last the captain emerged from below, fighting his way free of the scrum at the stair just in time to throw himself aside as the pried timber gave way - a huge lump of splintered wood flying across the deck like a knot at the end of a whip. The bow of the Archon kicked up as the tension was released — the creature freed — but the cable snagged, the savage lump of timber acting like a grapple, sending the wire snaking around the foremast and binding it fast. Once more the ship shuddered, and crewmen were thrown from their feet. Again the cable sung under the strain, but this time — anchored much higher above the deck — it caused the Archon to lean terribly to the side, as if they'd been caught full-sail in a gale. The downed crewmen began to slide toward the poison-water, slipping across the listing deck toward the gunwales — except the gunwales had been ripped from the hull, and there was nothing to fend them from the water. All hands that were still standing sprang forward, throwing lines for their crewmates, or diving after them. Jymn heard Nix cry out, and saw her slipping toward the water near the foke. He sprinted toward her, managing by luck alone to stay upright long enough to throw himself after her, jamming his wrench-knife into the deck to arrest their fall barely two feet from the churning torrent.

A team led by Balder were blunting their axes against the cable, trying to free them once and for all, but the ship was still swirling chaotically through the water as the whale thrashed for freedom. The cable groaned and hummed overhead as the beast changed course once again, pulling the ship into an even steeper angle that forced Jymn to cling on to the knife with both hands, praying that the blade had bit deep enough. There was a familiar cry above them, and he looked up to see Gam tumble from the mast-top, hurtling toward the water. Jymn cried out — watching helplessly as his friend fell — but some miracle stopped Gam mid-fall, snatching him by the ankle. A stray, narrow buntline from the topsail had coiled about his foot and held him dangling upside-down twenty feet above the toxic water.

Daj howled from the aftcastle, hauling up a rope upon which three crewmen clung, before scrambling desperately toward the bow, and her brother. But someone was already there. High in the mess of rigging, edging along the garn'tsail yard below the mast-top with a knife bit between his teeth, was the captain. Jymn watched with bated breath as he let go of the brace and took three unsteady steps away from the mast, catching himself on the thin buntline that had snared Gam. Gently, he began to swing the line back and forth like a pendulum. Gam cried out as the tangle about his foot began to slip, but the captain just pushed harder, until Gam was swinging from twenty feet out over the water to high above the listing deck. And then, with one savage cut from the knife, the line was severed, and Gam crashed into a knot of crewmen waiting below.

The captain — now with no line to grasp — teetered upon the yard, barely finding his balance. As he turned back toward the mast, the groaning steel cable below finally gave way to the axes, hissing through the air as the ship lurched upright, returning the deck to level as the crew desperately clinging to it cried out in relief. They barely heard the splash, but Puggle's screeching call was harder to miss.

'Man overboard!' cried Balder, rushing to the splintered edge of deck. 'Cap!'

The cry went up, and the hard-won experience of years at sea saw lines cast and a dozen long boathooks bristle from the deck. The rescue was simple enough: the water was clear and calm now, and they had been turned off the wind. Barely a minute later, the captain stood shivering and dripping onto the deck as Jymn once had, rinsed, and wrapped in an old sail. The exhausted crew exchanged looks heavy with meaning and worry, but Cap just grinned, swatting away their concerns as he headed to his quarters to dry off and warm up. But something about the smile seemed wrong to Jymn, and as they watched the old mutant whale limp away to the west, their harpoon still jutting from the water, he couldn't help but worry that this was an ill omen of things to come.

Tomorrow they would reach the edge of the map, and all they would have to guide them was the queer compass, and Jymn's memory of his glimpse from the heavens.

XXI

The Edge of the World

The crew spent the following day anxiously staring out toward the horizon, watching for any sign of the world's edge before it was too late to turn away and avoid sailing the Archon over a cliff into the abyss. But noon came and went, and even by Slip's most conservative reckoning, they were now beyond the furthest reaches of the map.

The cold was so severe they barely noticed the signs of the Cobalt Sea fading all around them, and many of the crew continued to drink their bitter morning draught of the Trashlander's elixir each day, regardless. The effects of the poison-waters in their wake were not entirely behind them though. The captain — usually to be found walking the railings of the aftcastle, or perched in the ratlines — had taken to spending his days in his quarters, and while he would make a great show of walking briskly among the crew upon each ring of the watch-bell, smiling and waving and doing his best to keep spirits up, his absence from the deck fostered a great deal of worry and rumour, and did nothing to quash the grumbling about the ill-wisdom of their voyage. Slip — who, along with Kelpy was the only one summoned to the captain's quarters — did his best to preserve morale. He offered a prize of triple-rations to the winner of a Stok tournament, ordered scrap timber to be burned in braziers on the deck for warmth, and even gathered the old band together to rouse the crew with a jig or two — though the music was always infused with a melancholy, and the players' fingers would quickly grow too numb to continue.

Jymn was only brought to the captain once, when Daj fetched him away from galley duty, quietly growling at him not to be alarmed at how the captain looked, nor to repeat what he saw, on pain of death. Even so warned, it took all of his control not to cry out when he entered the heated cabin. The captain — rarely seen without either a childlike grin or a scowl — looked almost asleep, except that his eyes and mouth were open, staring blankly at the stern windows and drooling onto the couch. There was bruising around his eyes that told Jymn he had been vomiting, and the purple-stained lips spoke of heavy use of the Ire-din. Puggle — who had been absent from the mast ever since the whale-attack — lay curled on the floor at the captain's feet. Kelpy glanced at Jymn as he stirred a few drops of neat lix into a cup of hot water, and his pretty face was lined with worry and care. The captain did his best to force a smile and beckoned Jymn over. To his shame, Jymn hesitated before approaching, but Kelpy nodded that it was safe, and gestured for him to go.

'It's not catching, he tells me,' whispered Cap, propping himself onto his elbow, 'just a little fever from the water,' but Jymn noticed some of the captain's bright red hair was left behind on the pillow. Kelpy brought the lix-tea, and waited to make sure the cup was drained. This seemed to revive the captain a little, and Jymn suspected it was this infusion that briefly gave him the power to walk among the crew.

'When we get there, Jymn,' Cap started, fixing him with a stare, 'It will be a close thing. We won't have long before Tsar and the Godsmen arrive. Your compass — will it take us where we need to go?'

Jymn thought on the problem — not for the first time — then shook his head. 'It will take us to the island, I think that's all. After that, I'm not sure. I didn't tell Lotan about the code, or the vault, or whatever it is we are looking for. If he knew, I thought he might just kill us and go there himself, so—'

The captain laid a frail arm upon his, cutting him short. 'It's ok, you did the right thing. We have a few days yet, something to think on, hm? It'll be down to you, Jymn, once we get there.'

Kelpy took Jymn by the arm while the captain prepared to take

275

his morning walk on deck.

'He'll be ok, won't he?' Jymn whispered, 'I saw some hair…'

Kelpy shushed him, and checked that they were alone. 'If it was anyone else, they'd be dead by now. You know about his splice?' Jymn nodded. It still hadn't quite sunk in that the captain was so much older than he looked. 'I think it's helping him fight it off,' Kelpy continued 'He's very sick, Jymn, but he's hanging on. He needs rest though, and real food.'

The biting wind grew less fierce the further they travelled, but had settled determinedly on blowing from the north as if to keep them away from Svalbard, and they were forced to burn fuel day and night to preserve any hope of making it there before Tsar. And their fuel was running low. It was this, it transpired, that had drawn the captain below deck on the day of the whale encounter — he had been in the hold with Scup, nervously measuring the diesel reserves that were now perilously low. So much might have been different, if only they had stopped to syphon fuel from the drifting ghost-ship. This fact, along with the constant growl of the engine did nothing to ease the tensions among the crew.

As the days passed, Jymn felt the weight of the strange compass — on which they now relied — grow, and began to spend his evenings in Weylun's workshop, listening over and over to Jenn's testimony and using the now defunct map table to sketch outlines of Thule from memory, always doubting himself and revising some detail or other. When he grew frustrated he would help Weylun tend to the captive magflies, or distract himself with the techsmith's rambling lectures on code, science, and the past. Nix often stopped by on her way to Gam, to whom she would bring bladders of water heated on the galley stove, in an effort to help fend the biting cold. Gam himself they rarely saw — he kept himself bundled in furs at the mast-top, always staring out northward for any glimpse of the lost island.

But it didn't take Gam's keen eyes to spot what appeared on the horizon. Jymn suspected even old, blind Jon Cane could have seen it — or at least *felt* it somehow — for seven nights after the whale's attack the sky to the north was filled with ribbons of glowing green light from the heavens.

The deck was eerily silent, the usual chatter of night-sailing giving way to an overwhelming, almost oppressive awe. Even the precious braziers were covered with shrouds to better reveal the subtleties of the river of light that danced above them. Nix drew close to Jymn, her pale face upturned like a canvas for the reflected green glow. Their eyes met for the briefest moment — torn from the wonders above so she could sign. *We are close.*

And she was right, for while the night seemed to stretch on forever, with the coming of dawn Gam called out excitedly from the mast-top.

'Land! Land, ho!'

At last they had found Thule, though as they drew nearer their worst nightmares came into shallow focus through the lens of the farlooker: red hulls, red sails.

The Rougian fleet had got here first.

A dozen things shot through Jymn's mind all at once: they were too late, there would be nothing left to salvage of the old Skand treasures; they were dearly outnumbered, so fighting wasn't an option; perhaps they could simply turn round and flee before they were seen; they couldn't survive the Cobalt Sea again, but they could turn south-east and make for the Jöte; they had rationed enough food for the return leg, but the fuel might fail them, and the captain mightn't survive the trip.

Jymn could see the same calculations going on in the faces of those around him. Daj had gone to fetch the captain, but had returned with Kelpy, whose face was pale and lined with care.

'The captain, can he…' started Slip, but Kelpy simply shook his head.

'We need to make land,' Jymn said, finding a firmness in his voice that seemed to take the others by surprise.

'You said there are twenty ships…' said North, snatching the farlooker from Gam.

'We're not going to fight them, Jymn,' said Slip, laying a hand on his arm 'I'm sorry, but the treasure's all gone. There's no reason to stay here. We should turn around.'

Jymn, what are they — started Nix, but Jymn swatted her sign away.

'It's not about the treasure!' he pressed on, 'it's the captain!' the others winced, and Jymn lowered his voice, 'he needs rest, and food, and shelter, right Kel?'

Kelpy gave a tired nod of agreement, 'he's very weak. Another voyage might… might not be wise.'

The unspoken truth behind the words caused them all to take stock. Jymn's eyes flicked to Gam at the mast-top, who — overhearing — wore guilt upon an ashen face. He still blamed himself for the captain's fall from the rigging.

'Could we… maybe… sort of *talk* to them?' offered Weylun nervously, 'tell them we aren't here for the treasure any more, we just need a chance to… you know…'

'We aren't bloody surrendering!' spluttered North.

Jymn—

'Tsar would take the ship — that would kill the captain for certain,' growled Daj, gripping her sling-staff with white knuckled ferocity.

Jymn! Nix grabbed him by the shirt collar, forcing him to pay attention to her while the others bickered. *They all have red sails, we have white.*

Jymn frowned at her, frustrated. *Yes, we are talking about whether to turn back or—* but she cut him off with a gesture.

When they took me, they were worried that I would stand out — white — among them all. They painted my skin with rust-oil, so that I was better hidden. She stared at him intently, willing her meaning to become clear.

Jymn looked up at the white patchwork sails luffing in the wind, then back to Nix, his frustration replaced by a spreading grin.

'Guys… guys! I know how we can reach the land!'

An hour later, the timbers of the damaged deck and half the crew were stained hand and foot with the last of the Ire-din, and a half-set of spare sails — now dyed a deep burgundy — were billowing in the breeze, pulling them once again on toward Thule.

Jymn, North and Slip had commandeered the map table, poring over Jymn's half-remembered sketches. By comparing North's acute sense of magnetic north with the direction given by Lotan's compass, and Gam's observations with the farlooker, they had an estimate of their bearing and the landscape ahead. They were approaching a wide, sheltered inlet on the west shore of the island. The scale of Jymn's map was rough, to say the least, which made things hard, but worse than that were the unknown waters that waited for them. With no teck-map, they could not tell whether the steep mountains that remained jutting from the icy water dropped hundreds of feet into the sea, or left a shallow field of barely-drowned rocks to wreck unwary sailors.

'We should hug the coast,' Jymn said, getting used to the firmness in his voice. 'Our biggest danger is getting caught, and we're more likely to do that if we are out in the open.'

'We'll have to go slow then — eyes up top watching for rocks,' Slip cautioned.

'That's fine - it'll be just like the Graveyard. And we can find somewhere to hide the ship better that way, too.'

And so it was decided. They notched a mark on Lotan's compass, and cautiously made for land. Gam was joined by the keenest eyes among the crew, who set themselves in the baskets atop the main and mizzen masts to aid in watching out for rocks while Gam focussed on the distant Rougian ships. Reluctantly, the winged-hourglass flag was lowered, and orders were given for the crew to cover the scraps of purple fabric that marked each of them, unmistakably, as Archonauts. Jymn accepted a clean but stained bandage from Kelpy, and bound it overtop the purple sash that covered his smikken eye.

It was an uncanny feeling, being so close to the fabled island after all this time. Even after Jenn's account, there was still something that had felt *impossible* about the place, like it was only ever just

279

another page from a story. But — just like Losalfhym — here it was in front of him. Real. Unlike Losalfhym, though, whose glittering halls hid the race of Fair Folk from the world, Thule felt… dead. Like some barely preserved relic from the past. The savage mountains with their crowns of white rock were majestic, certainly, but the sky was cold and grey, and there was no sign of life beyond the Tsar's ships. Great teeth of jagged blue-white rock rose threateningly from the water, and seemed almost to shift and glide about as if to undermine any attempt to navigate them. Perhaps long ago it had been the hidden utopia Jymn had imagined, lush, and green, and bountiful, but today Thule's slopes were grey, and dirty-white, and threatening.

'Forty feet!' called Scup, who was manning a weighted line at the bow. 'Thirty-six!'

'Ease the main, lads! Ease her off…' commanded Slip, as he strode between the masts. Jymn darted to the starboard rails and peered into the clear water. The flat, grey light from above made the surface nearly opaque, but it was just possible to make out dark rocks sliding past beneath them. Most were jagged and irregular, but more than one looked unmistakably man-made. North adjusted their course to port, skirting the edge of the shallow waters that seemed to surround the island.

'Steady at thirty-two,' called Scup from the bow, sounding relieved. The Archon's keel was only a little over twelve feet below the surface, but waters any less than thirty feet deep spelled trouble — all it took was a stray rock…

Slip sprang up the aftcastle stair and leaned in toward North, 'we're going to have to get in closer than this — we can't anchor and use the longboat this time, we have to hide her, North.'

'I know that!' growled the helmsman, under his breath, 'but if I run her aground out here we're fakked aren't we!'

'Where from here?' Slip asked, turning his attention to Jymn.

'In there…' Jymn mumbled, fumbling with his hand-drawn maps and pointing toward a deep cleft in the rocky coast. 'It's narrow enough that we should be well hidden.'

'Here — take this…' barked North, shoving Jymn toward the

wheel and stomping away down the stair. 'Scup! With me!' Away at the bow, Scup handed the sounding line to Daj and hurried astern.

'Wait, where are you going?' Slip called after them.

'We can't rely on the wind - one gust at the wrong moment and we're done for. We're going to get the damn motor working. Keep her steady!'

Jymn's hands grasped the spokes, sweating into the rough wood as he fought to keep the Archon skirting the edge of the shallows. He tried to conjure an imaginary line off their starboard side, demarking the treacherous water that — after all this way — still kept them just a few hundred yards from Thule.

Even with only the half-set of freshly dyed sails, and the mainsail eased, the gusting wind from the south-west still spurred them on faster than he'd have liked. He tried to picture the keel of the Archon reaching twelve feet down into the grey water, the sea-floor twenty feet below that. The rocks he'd seen, they could have just been patches of dark kelp, or even sand — but he couldn't help picturing jagged spires of rock, reaching up to…

'Jymn!' Gam's cry carried from the mast-top, the urgency in his voice causing a dozen busy heads to snap up toward the horizon.

Jymn looked up toward the mast-top for Gam's hand-sign, but there was none, he was simply pointing. Jymn followed the line, his heart skipping a beat as he saw — rounding the headland before them — a red-daubed ship of the enemy.

Panic rippled across the deck, and Jymn felt anxious eyes turning to the helm. To him. He glanced up again, to Gam, taking his hands from the wheel for the briefest moment to sign.

What is their course?

Gam turned to the incoming ship, then back to Jymn.

They are going to pass us — but only a hundred feet away, maybe fifty.

'Fifty feet…' Jymn turned to Slip, 'they'll recognise us that close, right?'

'We should fight them,' Caber said, more to the crew than to

281

Jymn. 'Come on, it's only one ship!'

Slip lowered the far looker, shaking his head, 'The *Sea-Eater.* I don't recognise her, but some of her men might know us. A lot of Tsar's crew sailed on the Archon, way back.'

Jymn's mind raced. If they turned about, they could try to outpace her, but there were at least two dozen other Rougian ships around Thule, it was only a matter of time before they were caught. They could try to fight — but the crew were tired, hungry, and morale was low. They'd need to disable her fast, before help arrived.

'What's her draught, do you think?'

Again Slip studied the incoming vessel, 'she's steel, quite heavy. I don't know, twenty, twenty-five feet?'

'More than us?'

'Yeah, more than ours, but—'

'Right. Hold on.'

Bracing his feet, Jymn threw the wheel hard over to starboard. The Sea-Eater would ground herself before the Archon. It wasn't much, but it was the only advantage they had. The Archon listed as the bow cut through the water toward the shallows. Slip stared open-mouthed for a heartbeat, then sprang into action.

'Shit — ok, right… fending poles!' he called, 'fenders to the bow!'

A handful of crewmen sprinted to the stashed poles, dragging them forward. Jymn saw Nix among them, shouldering one of the great poles as the Archon began to bristle with feelers, like the antennae of some huge insect.

'Twenty-eight!' called Daj, the sounding line taught in her hands.

'Gam,' said Jymn in a voice thick with forced calm, 'forget the ship, I need your eyes up front. Any sign of something below, and you—'

The wheel bucked, and the deck listed to port. As the Archon slowly turned into her new course, the sails snapped taught into a close-haul, dragging them ever onward into the shallows, heeling hard over.

'Twenty-four!' yelled Daj, the steel in her voice faltering.

'What the hell is going…' cried North, appearing from below, but his voice trailed off as he saw the looming bulk of the red hull. 'Oh fakk…'

'Hazard to port!' cried Gam, 'hazard to port!'

Again Jymn threw the wheel to starboard, as crewmen armed with fenders leaned over the port gunwales to protect the hull, which groaned as it grazed something hard beneath the surface. As the turn carried them nose-to-wind the sails faltered and began to luff uselessly, leaving the Archon to drift among the hidden dangers.

'Twenty feet!' called Daj.

'We're going to need that motor, North!' Jymn cried, but the helmsman had already scurried below once more.

'They're slowing!' cried a voice from the top of the mizzenmast, and Jymn turned to see the encroaching Rougian vessel was now sitting off their port quarter, her bow-wave diminished and the plume of dark smoke in her wake thinned.

There was another groan from the hull, as crewmen edged towards the damaged starboard gunwales to fend her off the rocks. Only they weren't rocks. Even from the helm, Jymn could see the unmistakable angles of submerged buildings.

'Fakk — there's a whole town down there!' gasped Caber, leaning over the aftcastle's railing.

There was another groan, but this time instead of slowing the ship, Jymn felt it shunt forward beneath his feet. At last, with a great belching of smoke from below, the motor sputtered into life. The crew cheered as Jymn teased the throttle, bearing them away from the submerged buildings. North clambered from the hold, blackened from head to toe with soot and grease, and took the aftcastle stairs two at a time.

'Eighteen feet!' called Daj.

'We're going too fast, Jymn!' cried North, seizing the throttle and easing it off.

Jymn stepped aside, relinquishing the wheel to the frantic helmsman. 'There's buildings there — and more over there,' he pointed vaguely at the grey water.

'Fifteen!'

'Hazard starb'd!' cried Gam. 'Hazard!'

North span the wheel to port, but it was too late. With a great splintering crash, the Archon shuddered to a halt, throwing half the crew from their feet. The motor groaned, and churned the water to stern, belching more smoke from the hold, before choking and failing once more.

'Breach!' cried Daj, leaning over the bow, where bubbles were rising from the hull.

There was a banging on the deck below, and Scup's coarse voice carried up through the grating. 'Water coming in! We're taking on water!'

'Captain on deck,' cried Weylun from somewhere below them, but if anyone else heard him, they didn't react.

'Back off it!' roared Caber, lunging for the throttle.

'The motor's dead, you idiot!' snapped North, slapping his hand away.

Amid the chaos, a familiar whistle from the quarterdeck cut through the argument. 'Captain on deck!' yelled Weylun again, and Jymn leaned over the helm to see him supporting the captain by the arm, as he struggled from his quarters.

'Slip?' wheezed the captain, squinting up into the light for his bo'sun. Slip leaped down the stair and stood to attention.

'We're holed, Cap. Submerged wreckage. We were trying to lose an enemy ship in the shallow water.' Slip pointed at the Sea-Eater, which had now halted off their port beam.

'Bloody Squint's gone and…' started Caber, but the captain held up a hand for silence as he stared at the lingering ship. Jymn saw angry red scabs on the captain's arm.

'Blame comes later. Take a sail, someone needs to swim under, drag the sail over the hole. The pressure will hold it, enough to slow the water.' Daj pulled off her boots and snatched up a line. 'And don't let them see you do it — they are watching us.'

Scup's head appeared from below 'We're taking on a lot of water cap, the hold's already knee-deep.'

'Get everyone bailing. But off the starboard — do *not* let them see.'

'They're sending up flags,' said Slip, peering through the farlooker. 'Not sign I know, must be —'

'Fetch ours,' Cap cut him off, taking the spyglass and squinting at the enemy ship. 'It's their own sign, only for Tsar's ships. They're showing: *Help / Need / Question.*' North returned with the small chest of signal flags, and the captain snatched up a half-dozen of the small pennants, arranging them on the deck.

'Hull paint, Slip — I need black hull paint.'

Slip returned quickly with a drum of a thick tar-like substance, and the captain daubed a black cross over a yellow square. 'Here —' he thrust the flags to North, 'run them up in this order.'

'What does it say?', asked Slip, as he watched the other ship for any sign of action.

'*Stay Away / Tsar / Business*,' explained the captain. 'At least that's what it used to mean. Jymn,' the captain turned to him for the first time, and the guilty lump in Jymn's throat swelled until it threatened to choke him.

'I'm sorry, I was try—'

'Blankets for Daj, she'll be freezing. Now, Jymn!'

Jymn sprang into action, snatching an armful of covers from the hammocks below and running them to the bow, where Daj was slumped in a shivering, wet heap, having somehow managed to swim fully twelve feet down under the keel of the ship, all while dragging an old sail. Jymn forced himself to forget her stern, prickly demeanour and threw the blankets over her before wrapping his own arms around her trembling shoulders, leading her astern and below, away from the wind.

Scup rushed forward with a flask of North's hooch and led her toward the galley stove, which was miraculously still burning, despite the water slicking the deck.

'Di… d… did it work?' she managed, through chattering teeth.

'Aye — it's still coming in, but slower.' said Scup, rubbing her arms vigorously, 'we'd already be under if it weren't for you, Daja.'

Jymn hurried above once more alongside the sweating crewmen that were bailing buckets of icy water from the hold. The captain, Slip and the others were still watching the Rougian vessel anxiously, while North carefully measured the water level below the gunwales

'We've lost another foot, Cap,' groaned North, marking the weighted line. 'Two more and it'll be coming in the portholes.'

'They're leaving!' hissed Slip, hushing the others, and sure enough, it seemed the captain's message had done the trick: Sea-Eater was bearing away to the south.

'Right, let's get out of here before we sink, shall we?' sighed the captain as he sagged against the gunwale.

Between the fickle wind, waterlogged hull and the barely submerged ruins that seemed to press in all around them, the final quarter-mile to Thule was perhaps the hardest of the whole voyage. Somehow Scup managed to cajole a last, dying wheeze of effort from the motor, and North's expert piloting, combined with the captain's command, gradually saw them safely to the inlet. Jymn was banished to the bow to man one of the great fending poles, where he was met with a sympathetic smile from Nix, who had managed once again to understand the mood on deck better than those who could actually hear what was said.

Eventually they passed a narrow cleft in the dirty-white rock, and the Archon was brought about, and guided into a deep, cold cave within that seemed to glow with an eerie blue light. The motor gave one last surge of power, heaving the battered hull to rest upon the safety of a steep shingle beach within, where they dropped anchor and fastened the careened ship with ropes, to drain upon the shore.

Jymn tucked the bewitched compass safely beneath his furs for the last time. They were hungry, half-drowned, frozen, and sick. But at last, they had set foot upon Thule.

XXII

Thule

Either the brief adventure with the Sea-Eater or the act of finally making land at Thule seemed to have restored something in the captain, who now stood at the prow of the battered ship overseeing the hurried work that followed. Once the Archon was confidently secured against whatever the strange local tides might bring, teams were sent to take stock of the various damages to the hull — primarily the great hole, low in her bow, that now gasped for air on the shingle like some beached whale. Rusting tools were brought up from the waterlogged hold, and set upon crates along the narrow beach to form a crude workshop, while the crew set about stripping the ship of any timber it could spare — most of it being scavenged from the tall foke and aftcastle that sat furthest from the water. Jymn didn't much like the thought of sailing the cold northern seas again with so little protection from the wind, but he thought better of pointing this out — given the damage they were repairing had been done with him at the helm. But despite everything, morale had seemed to improve with the abundance of work, and finally a respite from the rigours of sailing. By some miracle the waters outside the cave were found to be home to large, fat codfish, and while Scup was too busy at carpentry to cook them, they were quickly grilled over the ship's braziers, which had been set on the beach to keep the cold at bay, and now filled the cave with the smell of roasting fish. Puggle took flight once more — for the first time since the whale attack — though the calls that echoed down from the tall reaches of the cave were not as piercing or proud as they once had been.

While all this was happening, other teams were put to the task of scouting the cave and the surrounding shore, that they might better understand their situation, and plan the next move. It was to one of these teams that Jymn was attached, along with Gam, who was eventually persuaded that his sister would warm up and recover just as quickly — if not a little quicker — without him fussing over her. Together they set off deeper into the dark cave, which narrowed as it rose steadily away from the water. The dirty-white walls were wet to the touch and almost burned with cold - not a white rock as Jymn had first thought, but *ice* — though he'd never imagined there could be so much of it in the whole world, nor that it could survive the light of the sun. Meltwater dripped steadily from the cave ceiling, and slid down the walls to collect into a small stream that rolled back away toward the sea.

As they clambered deeper and higher, daylight from the mouth of the cave began to give way to a more vivid blue up ahead, and eventually an outbreak of more daylight. Soon Jymn and Gam found themselves in an icy trench with the open sky peeking down above them and were able — with the help of Jymn's wrench-knife — to scramble to its lip and squint at their surroundings. All around them were flat, dark grey rocks, with dirty slush sheltering in the meagre shade they offered. And a half-mile to the west, along the line of their narrow trench, a building. Jymn had to shake his head to make sure it wasn't some sort of hopeful illusion, but there it stood — the first real sign that they had found the right place, not just some dead northern rock. And beyond, their source hidden by the high bluff of rock upon which the building stood, columns of dark smoke rose, slanting, into the air.

Dropping back down into the trench, the two friends followed it as it grew gradually shallower, rising to meet the surface above. Jymn almost got stuck as the narrow path zagged sharply between the cold rock walls, but eventually, crouching low, they reached its end, and dashed across the open ground for the cover of the small building.

He wasn't sure quite what he expected from a real-life ruin of Thule, but the reality was underwhelming. It was little more than a shabby grey box that looked like it had once been fitted with humble wooden furniture, though more than half of it had been burned. It didn't even offer much shelter from the cold, as the southern wall was dominated by great high windows that had long since lost their shutters. Laying half-buried on the rocky ground outside was an iron cross like the ones used by the Godsmen, only without any of their gaudy ornamentation or embellishments. An idea began to form in Jymn's mind, but he was distracted by Gam, who had climbed the remains of a wooden stair to peer out of a high window.

'I can see them!' he hissed, waving for Jymn. 'There's a town in the valley below, it's *crawling* with Godsmen, pirates, they're all there.'

Jymn climbed quietly after him, and gasped as he looked out over a memory. At least, that is what it felt like — peering out from a high window as the settlement of Thulhöfn, littered with fires, crawled with dark figures. It was like he was reliving someone else's life — the life of a small girl, fleeing her home. For this was the church from Jenn's testimony.

Unlike in her story, though, the Clergy and Tsar's pirates had no opposition. They had rammed the small jetty with shallow landing craft, while in the bay beyond the full Rougian fleet sat at anchor. There were no sounds of struggle, no gunfire. The fires this time were not torches, or blazing buildings, but great pyres, upon which were heaped every trace of the Skand that could be stripped from the buildings: furniture, books, Jymn even saw pots and pans. The largest fire of all was above the town, where a huge spar of concrete jutted proudly from the mountainside. Mighty steel doors, now bent and scorched, hung uselessly from their hinges, and a great column of robed Godsmen issued forth like ants from a nest, tossing plastic crates, papers, and sacks onto the flames. Teams of Godsmen roved the hillside, searching among the rocks, for more relics to burn.

'I can't believe they're really doing it. Destroying it all,' Gam whispered. 'That's the vault, isn't it?'

Jymn nodded. 'We need to get back to the ship,' he said, not taking his eyes from the window, 'there's something I need to do.'

'"We protect nothing by getting shot. And the vault is sealed."
That's what Dada said. And... and then he put his arms around
us. But Loken, he was angry, he wanted to do something, and he
said "The mine then..." and pointed west, out past the hill. But
no, Dada said. He said we would just lead them toward it. And
besides, they aren't here for the mine...'

The recording clicked as Jymn hit the familiar button, thinking.

'Well, what is it then?' asked the captain, steadying himself on
the map table. The small workshop was crammed with people
eager to hear more about the discovery.

'It's the same settlement, alright. There must be two hundred of
them there, between the Clergy and the Tsar's lot. And more still
on the ships.'

'And there's nothing left?' asked Weylun, hopefully.

'They're burning it all right now,' Gam said, pointing away
toward the small town, 'more every minute.'

'Never mind *nothing left* — how long till they find us!' barked
Caber, from the doorway.

Jymn fiddled with the controls, and the old woman's voice
crackled back into life.

'"The men that found it were not ready," he said when we were
on the water, "and now everything in that vault will be eaten, or
burned, or sold before winter..."'

Jymn tried to think over the sound of the bickering. Jenn had
talked about crates, and treasures not seeing daylight for centuries.
And her father had talked about hungry men — and *eating* the
treasure — and said that they weren't here for the mine.

The mine.

What could they have been mining, anyway? Nobody mined any
more, everyone knew anything good had been taken out of the
ground centuries ago, and there was more than enough left among
the ruins that you could just pick up. And besides, why would
Loken want to protect it, if they were fleeing the island. *We were*

supposed to protect it, that's what he said.

'They're looking in the wrong place.' Jymn said, realisation dawning at last. The bickering continued. 'Cap! They're looking in the wrong place. The vault — I don't think that's where the code is. *Seeds* — that's what her father said. I think the mine… the mine is where we need to go.'

'Wait, we came ashore for food, and shelter, so the cap… so we could *all* rest,' said North, glancing bashfully at the captain.

'We came for the secrets,' countered the captain, 'and for riches. And for revenge against those bastards. And I'm done resting.' He turned to Jymn. 'Do you think you can lead us to this mine of yours?'

Jymn felt the force of a dozen pairs of eyes on him. He nodded. 'It's west of the town, behind a hill.'

'So, wait, these two hundred of them — they're between us and where we need to be?' asked Slip.

'Then we wait for dark,' the captain said, pulling his bycock hat over his patchy red hair, 'and make ready to find ourselves some treasure.'

———————————

They did not have to wait long, for the sun — as if chilled by the frigid northern skies — refused to rise any higher than the mid-morning mark, before starting its descent back toward the shelter of the horizon. Scarcely four hours since their first sighting of Thule, darkness was closing in once more.

Plans were made for their excursion to the west. The repairs to the Archon would take a two-day, at least, and the waters around Thulhöfn were crammed with Rougian ships, so sailing was not an option. That left them but one choice: a land-based approach, right past the occupied town. The cover of dark would be on their side of course, and as ever the captain found a strength in their perceived weakness: 'the place is crawling with them, yes? Good! Who will notice a few more bodies in all of that?'

Careful consideration was made as to the selection of crew for the expedition — too large a party, and they stood more chance of being seen, but too small, and they would stand no chance if it came to fighting. A team of twenty were selected. Nix had to stay behind, of course — she was far too recognisable, even at a distance — and Gam was to be positioned at the old church, his keen senses keeping lookout for any trouble in the town. Caber was chosen to protect the ship, and Slip given the command of the two dozen crew that stayed behind, with orders to oversee the repairs, that they might slip their haul away in secret, or at least have an avenue of escape should things turn bad. There was much protesting among those who were not chosen for the advance party, especially Nix and Caber, but the captain would not hear any quarrel. But it wasn't just the decision to leave Caber, Gam, or Slip behind that raised eyebrows. The captain himself, despite his lingering ailments, chose to lead the expedition, citing his returning health, and greater knowledge of Tsar's ways as justification when Kelpy moved to object. And Weylun too, who had grown used to tinkering in his workshop or lounging on a beach while the stronger, faster boys went adventuring, was chosen to accompany the team. 'This place is going to be full of teck, is it not?' grinned the captain, 'stands to reason we'll need our Tecksmith.'

Once again, the strips of purple that marked them for Archonauts were covered, hidden, or entrusted to those staying behind for safe keeping. Jymn allowed Nix to bind his eye, covering the purple cloth with a grubby-white strip of her own. She clenched her fists and crossed them at the wrists, making the sign for *safe* — though whether she meant that the binding was secure, or for him to *be* safe, he wasn't sure. Despite the grumbles, Jymn was amazed to find the mood of the Archonauts begin to positively buzz with anticipation and eagerness. Never mind the cold, or that they were in hiding, or that their home — the Archon itself — was fatally wounded, they were *finally* getting to the action, finally getting to misbehave, to sneak past the enemy, and take the treasure right from under his nose. It was infectious, and while Jymn hated leaving Gam and Nix behind, he found himself quickly swept up in the excitement of the mission as they crept silently along the icy trench toward the cover of the old church.

'There —' Jymn pointed, crouching against the broken window, just as Jenn and Loken once had. 'Over that hill to the west, that's where the mine is.'

'How far?' asked the captain, his eyes on the pyres that still burned in the town below, throwing wicked long shadows across the slushy ground.

'I… I'm not sure,' Jymn answered honestly. 'Not far, I think.'

Gam was stationed in the window, with strict orders to run back to the Archon to forewarn them of any approaching danger. On the captain's suggestion, Weylun left him with one of the unshielded *radios*, that he might — in an emergency — be able to contact the forward party away beyond the hill.

'They weave the trace, Gam,' Weylun explained, showing him how to operate the small device, 'so it's only as a last resort, understand? Any Raption for fifty clicks will be able to sense it.'

Slowly teams of two and three set off from the church, skirting between the jetty and the town, heading for the cover of the western hill. Jymn sat with Gam, using the farlooker to watch each team scurry through the night, until his turn came. Balder had gone ahead with the nervous Weylun under his protection, and Jymn followed on with Kelpy for support. The slow, winding descent from the church was treacherous and exposed, and Jymn had to fight the temptation to throw himself to the ground or surrender at every raised voice that carried up from below. But it was nothing compared to the town itself. He'd watched a dozen crew make the crossing already, striding between the shadows past the oblivious pirates and clergy. It had seemed so easy, but now that it was *him*, now that he was actually here, it seemed insane to just walk among the enemy and trust to fate and their obliviousness.

Kelpy squeezed his shoulder for reassurance, then shoved him roughly forward after Weylun and Balder. Kel seemed to stand two inches taller than he had a moment before, and jutted his sharp chin as if to challenge the night air before them. Jymn soon caught on, and tried to persuade his reluctant legs to swagger like the worst of the older lads on the Trossul. Somehow the artificial confidence seemed to trick his gut, and the fear started to ease, even as they passed within a few yards of a band of silhouetted

293

Rougians. He had confronted a teck-dragon, and survived the dungeons of a Teckromancer - he could bluff his way past a few drunk pirates.

A commotion ahead rose above the noise of drinking and chatter, and Jymn saw a knot of Godsmen attempting to whip a group of languishing pirates into action.

'Fakk off will'yu — been searching the bloody rock all day!'

Jymn watched as the pirate's companions tried to hush him, but they were too late. More Godsmen seemed to flock to the disturbance, their white robes bright against the reflected firelight. Somewhere a bottle smashed, and then silence.

'Rasmus will hear of this. Perhaps he'll find enough to burn after all.'

'Aw he didn't mean nothin' by it Par, honest,' appealed one of the pirate's friends, 'just bone-weary is all, from the digging y'see?'

'Jymn…' hissed Kelpy, tugging on his sleeve and breaking the spell that had held him captivated by the scene. But as he turned aside, movement caught Jymn's eye: a hunched Godsmen, lingering at the rear of the group had turned suddenly toward the whisper. Without hesitation, Jymn and Kelpy ducked behind an upturned rowboat, but the image of the man's face lingered on the inside of Jymn's eyelids. A sallow, sunken face, scarred with acid, eyes bound with a grubby bandage.

Panic flooded through Jymn's veins like ice-water. Jon Cane was still alive. He had taken the cloth now — hoping perhaps to avoid Tsar's retribution — but it was him alright, and his uncanny ability to 'see' things that those with eyes missed was clearly undiminished. Safe on the far edge of town Jymn saw Weylun crouched with Balder, looking back helplessly toward them. Weylun saw something, and beckoned urgently, prompting Jymn to steal a look past the upturned boat. Cane had broken off from the knot of clergy, and was drawing closer.

'Come, now. No hiding from *God*, is there?' sneered the old man, his lip curling as he tested the ground with a hooked staff.

Any chance to run was spent — from here even a mere mortal would hear them and raise the alarm, never mind Cane. Jymn

294

looked desperately toward Weylun for guidance, but the tecksmith was now locked in a battle to calm Balder, whose eyes were fixed on the endangered Kelpy. The huge boy began to tremble with a growing rage that Jymn knew would soon consume him.

Mind racing for a way out, Jymn flinched at the sound of Jon Cane's staff finding the hull of the upturned boat, tracing its edge. Perhaps they could fight him — bear down upon him before he could cry out the alarm. But Jymn remembered the vice-grip of that arthritic hand on his wrist back in Shoalhaven, and doubted their chances.

'We have to go!' hissed Kelpy, 'Balder is…'

'Got you, you pit-worm!' cried a deep voice from behind them, and before he knew what was happening, Jymn was toppled to the rocky ground by a boot between his shoulder blades. 'Thought you could shirk your watch, eh Pyler?'

Rolling to his back, Jymn found himself staring up into the face of Scup, who clapped his hands together threateningly. Beside him, North had arranged his face in a grotesque gurning grimace. He hawked, and spat to the floor.

'Captain'll hear about this, ya' wags! Yur'll be 'anging by yer thumbs, on wit' yer!' and with that, the impish helmsman grabbed Jymn by his furs and dragged him to his feet. Scup helped Kelpy up rather less theatrically, and together — with some appropriate moans of contrition — they allowed themselves to be bustled and marched away.

'Sorry if that were a bit hard,' whispered Scup, while Kelpy rushed to calm Balder. ''Pyler' was an older lad in my village. Always hated him. Might've got a bit carried away…'

'It was amazing! I just… when it really matters I kind of freeze. I could never do anything like that, like what you did.'

'You've saved me plenty, Jymn,' Scup grinned, punching his arm gently with a calloused fist, 'that's what crew's for. Now come on.'

Together the six of them slunk over the hill and finally put themselves out of sight of the small town, and beyond the watchful eye of Gam. Before them lay a wide field of scree, peppered with huge boulders that looked like they had rolled down the mountainside in centuries past. Slowly, the dark silhouettes of the boulders began to expand and move, as the rest of the waiting crew broke cover to greet them.

Besides the lingering firelight that carried into the air on the columns of smoke, and the occasional gunshot, or laugh that made it clear of the valley, the land to the west of Thulhöfn felt like a different universe. Occasionally they would see bootprints in the slush where the invaders had clearly been searching beyond the town's borders, but for the most part the Archonauts found themselves quietly stalking the rocky, barren landscape under its green ribboned sky, feeling like they had landed on the surface of the moon, or perhaps some alien world.

It was North who noticed it first, slowing to a stop in the wide rank of crew that searched the ground. He turned about, walked a few steps back toward the town, then turned back and hissed at the others to come closer. Jymn was one of the closest, and clambered excitedly over the loose rock to see what North had found…

…but there was nothing. He clambered onto a low boulder to get a better look, but in the pale green light, he could make out no sign of man, nor even a difference from the surrounding rock.

The captain, still moving carefully across the treacherous ground, was the last to reach the knot of confused crew. 'What is it, North?' he asked, interrupting the wily helmsman who was impatiently waving people aside as he paced back and forth over the patch of ground. 'I can't see anything?'

'That's good!' said North, a glimmer of his old grin returning. 'The ground here has a different look to it. Brighter, but only from one side. If you all can't see it, then it must be the old splice,' he said, tapping his temple.

'Wait, is this… *north*?' asked Jymn with a reverent gasp, 'like, *the* north?'

'Haha - no, not quite!' he chucked, 'but there is magnetism here, in the ground beneath us. Which means…'

'Metal!' chirped Weylun, a little too loudly, 'the mine!'

'And they haven't a clue!' laughed the captain, 'Well done, North! Now, we dig!'

XXIII

The Mine

It took a little over two hours of carefully lifting and piling stones before a narrow, sloping shaft was uncovered. It had not been buried by some ordinary process of time, whatever lay below them had been hidden, disguised that none might stumble upon it by chance.

Nervously, the Archonauts huddled around the mouth of the shaft while the smallest among them — Juke — was lowered down on a rope. Jymn watched him scramble down, stopping occasionally to tug for more line, before delving deeper into the blackness, as Bink stood vigil, the narrow beam of his teck-light trained upon his twin.

A cry of alarm carried up from the darkness, and the line was quickly hauled in. Juke emerged like a caught fish, looking flushed and out of breath, but unhurt.

'You… you need to see this. There was some sort of animal…'

The line was fixed in place, and in pairs the crew began to scramble down the slope, guided by blue-white teck-lights and the flickering burn of torches that were being lit at the foot of the shaft. At the end of his inelegant climb, Jymn found himself in a wide, round chamber, littered with bones. Not just bones — he'd seen normal bones before, who hadn't? Dog bones, rat bones, human bones. But these were something else entirely — if it wasn't for the skulls, he might not have even realised that's what there were — for they towered over him, like great curved beams. He recognised a spine so large it could have belonged to Lotan if

297

he were made of flesh and blood. Fearful mutterings that rippled through the nervous crew told him they belonged to a whale, but that didn't explain what they were doing down here, nor why there were human skulls among them, or bloody hand-prints, scarlet against the bone-white.

'Bears. Big ones too,' called Scup, who was crouching at a skull as wide as Jymn's chest. 'Skinny ones used to take kids from my village back home. Never seen one this big though. Must've been their den.'

'I dunno. Never seen a bear put a head on a spike,' chimed North, who was peering up at a pair of metal poles, each topped with a human skull.

'And this isn't right, it should be dark,' called Kelpy, picking at one of the smeared hand-prints with the tip of his knife. 'You've all seen my apron — blood is only this colour when it's fresh.'

'You're saying this is fresh?!' gasped Weylun, brandishing his teck-light at the dark corners of the chamber.

'I'm saying this is paint,' Kelpy said, bluntly, 'somebody did this to make it look… well, scary.'

'To keep people out. Stop them from going any further,' said the captain, taking a burning torch from Balder and pressing on past the den of bones. 'Let's see what was worth all this effort, eh?'

With the spell broken, the Archonauts spread out, pushing back the oppressive dark with their meagre torches. Half-hidden passages were found, leading from the false den to a cluster of low rooms that seemed scarcely able to support the weight of rock above them. Ancient machines hung from the walls, or littered the floor under inches of dirt, as if bygone workers had simply downed tools one day and left. North picked up a plastic dome that might once have been yellow, blew centuries of settled dust from its surface, and placed it on his head with a grin. 'Maybe it *is* just a mine,' he said, rapping his knuckles against the protective shell, 'doesn't seem like somewhere you'd keep treasure.'

There was a sound like a stick snapping, then a groan and a deep thud that Jymn felt through his feet. Bink cried out, but by the time Jymn whirled around to see, the small boy was already

298

three feet in the air, grasped in one of Balder's massive hands. A huge machine that looked like a spiked claw was penduluming back and forth in the spot where he'd been just a heartbeat before, swinging with enough momentum to punch a hole in the Archon's hull. Even in the dim torchlight, Jymn could see that Bink had gone white as a sheet.

'I… I just… it was just a box…' he sputtered, as Balder set him down gently. The box he'd tried to open was now bent and buckled, swinging on one of the pendulum's spikes.

'Actually, North, I'd say this was *exactly* the sort of place you'd hide treasure,' said the captain, as North removed his helmet and placed it delicately back where he'd found it. 'Nobody touch anything, they've booby trapped the place. And stay in pairs.'

Before Jymn knew it, Weylun was hovering nearby wearing a nervous smile. 'This is all normal, isn't it? Traps and so forth? I'm never allowed on the actual, *adventure* bits, you know.'

'What did they mine here, do you think?' asked Jymn, peering at a dusty workbench, still littered with forgotten tools.

'Oh, it's a coal mine,' chirped Weylun, as if it were obvious. 'You can tell from the smell — father used to buy this stuff when you could still get it.' He crouched, plucking a small sliver of black rock from the ground, and holding it up to show Jymn. 'More energy in this than wood, nearly as much as diesel. The Pars will tell you it was God that sent the flood, but it was burning this stuff that did it,' he shrugged, tossing the small rock to Jymn, who couldn't help but think that sounded far-fetched, even for Weylun. If anything, digging this stuff out of the ground should have made the sea level go *down*, not up. He dropped the rock, and wiped the black, sooty residue from his hands.

'Well - look at that…' muttered Weylun, as he swept the beam of his teck-light across the blackness, but Jymn could see nothing. 'Look…' he said, pressing his light to the side of Jymn's head. As the narrow beam drew closer, glints of reflected light began to reveal themselves in the darkness ahead, but disappeared just as quickly when Weylun moved the gadget away again. Cautiously, they moved to investigate the nearest light, finding a band of bright metal wrapped about a pillar that marked the entrance to a low tunnel. Alone among all the rust and dirt and grime, this narrow strip was polished to a high sheen. And there in the distance, shone another, and another, reaching away down the tunnel.

'Cap… I think we've got something,' called Jymn, and soon they found themselves on the move once again, following the forking tunnel, led by those among the crew that were equipped with teck-lights of their own.

Two sets of heavy steel rails traced the floor, and more than one abandoned cart lay idly gathering dust. The rails parted often as they descended deeper into the cold, hard earth, but somewhere in the gloom there was always a pinprick of polished light to guide their way. Chains and old wires began to reach down from the ceiling like the webs of metal spiders, and the narrow walls were littered with mighty timbers that groaned as they tired of fighting the weight of rock above.

Jymn allowed himself to be distracted by another of Weylun's stories about all the wondrous miracles of teck that might be locked away down here. Judging by the silence of those nearby — he was not the only one listening. It was then that disaster struck.

A metallic groaning from up ahead barely preceded a deafening bang that echoed endlessly down the tunnel, and on the back of it — screams that seemed to go on forever. A dozen shouts and cries of alarm erupted from the front of the column, and Jymn roused himself from shock, elbowing his way forward to see what had happened. He found the others pressed in around a dark, rectangular hole in the ground that seemed — until recently — to have been covered by a heavy steel door.

'Rope!' cried Balder, crouched at the edge of the dark hole.

'How deep is it?' came another voice in the press of bodies.

'What happened?' asked Jymn, pressing forward. He couldn't see the bottom, but his head still swam from the height-fear.

'Light! Give me that—' demanded Daj, snatching the burning torch from Jymn's hand and holding it above the hole, but Scup's hand snaked out to grab her by the wrist before she could drop it.

'No! Daj — that's a coal shaft. That'd be like dropping a match into a powder keg.'

'Hold on!' cried Balder, as he swung down into the hole and flew down the rope with ease, a teck-light clamped between his teeth.

'Is someone down there?!' croaked Jymn, catching up, but all eyes were fixed on Balder, who was now dangling at the end of the rope. It was too short. His teck-light's beam cut feebly into the oppressive darkness beneath him, illuminating the sides of the shaft, but giving no hint of an end to the fathomless drop.

'Ram?' boomed Balder, his voice echoing into the dark. 'Nuckle?'

'The latch was trapped,' said North, crouching at the lip of the hole to inspect the frame of the metal door. 'Bastard Skand,' he spat. Balder called out again, but there was no reply.

'They're gone, Balder,' called the captain, a distant look in his eyes. 'Nobody could have survived that fall.'

'We have to look for them!' cried Jymn, who couldn't help but imagine himself trapped at the bottom of the shaft, being abandoned to the darkness.

'We have to keep the others safe,' the captain fixed him with a stare that brooked no argument. 'Pull him up.'

Balder was hoisted up, and reluctantly clambered from the hole to sit morosely beside Kelpy, who wept quietly into the huge boy's arms. Ram and Nuckle — both eager sailors, who always seemed to have some joke nobody else shared. Jymn had only spoken to them a handful of times, and felt like an imposter among the authentic grief that was plain to see on the faces that were left behind. The captain determined that a proper funeral would be observed — and Slip would divide up their personal effects — once they were safely back on the water. For now, he said a few words, threw a handful of dirt into the shaft, and ordered that the hatch be closed once more, for some sense of decency and closure.

Progress from there was more cautious, and the party moved at a snail's pace, treading only on the narrow steel rails that seemed to offer some sense of security. Eventually though, they ran out of track — and their only way forward was down.

Another shaft — but this time almost thirty feet across, and fitted with ancient apparatus for the lifting and lowering of coal and men. And most importantly, the bottom was clear to see, even by the light of their torches. North, Scup, and the most mechanically minded among them set about carefully checking the heavy cage that hung suspended at the nearest edge of the pit. Balder was enlisted to help at the hand-winch, and soon the first nervous group of crew were bundled on, slowly lowering themselves with the brake-lever, while Balder hovered near the winch in case it failed. But eventually, hesitantly, the first half-dozen made it down to safety. Weylun — wading in ankle deep water almost forty feet below — grimaced as he waved up at Jymn. The next cage-loads were faster, but even so, by the time Jymn's boots splashed into the icy water, the captain and the advance party had already discarded their flaming torches and pressed on into the cramped, sooty passages that followed. It was down here, pressed in between shelves of natural rock, that the ancient miners had dug the coal from the earth. Lit now only by the handful of teck-lights that were deemed safe, Jymn squeezed himself down tunnels choked with black soot, every now and then coming to a natural cavern that afforded a brief respite from the oppressive confines of the mine. As he rested, trying and failing to fill his lungs with clean air while he waited his turn to continue, there was a commotion up ahead. Squeezing past the older boys heading deeper into the mine, Bink was coming the other way, squinting in the gloom at the soot-blackened faces.

'Jymn! There you are — they need you up front. Some sort of a door…'

And without further explanation, Jymn was dragged by his sleeve onward into the next tunnel. This last space was so narrow Jymn almost had to remove his furs, and wondered how on earth Weylun had made it past, and whether Balder would become stuck fast when his turn came. When eventually they made it to the other side, though, the cavern opened out comfortably. Relative to the rest of the mine, this place was almost clean, with reinforced steel mesh on the ceiling, and broad, regular pillars that almost reminded him of a chapel he'd once seen. But it was none of this that held the captive attention of the captain and those among the

302

crew that had made it this far. They were all transfixed by the same detail. One wall of the cavern was utterly flat, almost featureless, and steel. One immense sheet of steel that seemed to have been cut perfectly to seal the cave. Jymn looked around, but could see no other way in or out, besides the narrow cleft he'd just squeezed through. It was a dead-end.

Seeing Jymn, the captain beckoned him closer, and the small knot of crew parted as he came, all except Weylun, who was running his hands over the metal, studying the criss-crossed pattern across its surface and muttering.

'Jymn — thoughts?' asked the captain, not taking his eyes from the steel barrier.

And suddenly Jymn understood why it was him that had been sent for. It wasn't the Jymn that had survived Node's interrogation they needed, nor the Jymn that had parlayed with the dragon and learned the secret of Thule's whereabouts. It was Squint, the weld-maker from the Trossul's sixdeck. They needed to know about the metal.

Moving to the edge of the steel plate, he inspected the joints — it seemed great metal spikes had been driven into the rock, each of which was then welded to this false wall. A brief scrabble in the dirt floor revealed that it was held fast there, too. The welds were strong, better made even than the ancient welds he's studied on the oldest parts of the Trossul's hull. He rapped the plate with the hilt of his wrench-knife, listening carefully for the sound it produced — it was a half-inch thick, at least.

'Maybe there was a cave in or something?' offered North, 'and this was just to keep people from going further.'

The captain laid a hand against the thick steel, appraising it. 'Perhaps. Seems like there would be easier ways. A sign, perhaps.'

'It's testing us…' Weylun gasped, snatching up a scrap of coal from the floor, and using it like a chalk to write upon the metal. 'These… marks…' he explained, his words stalled by concentration as the letters poured out of him onto the steel, 'they aren't just… a pattern… ' he scrawled the last letter with a flourish, turning back to the others. 'It's binary! The language of machines! There is a

303

message here, see?'

Jymn squinted at the dark scrawl — he had learned his letters from Par Carrek as a boy, but the shapes had never really stuck, and had a habit of switching places when he wasn't looking. *Here… in. Herein… Lies…*

'Herein lies the knowledge of your forebears,' read the captain, wonder on his face. 'It really says that?'

Weylun nodded with a childlike grin, and read on. *'Herein lies the knowledge of your forebears - guarded across the years by wardens who would keep it from savage hands, and cruel. Only when man has attained Strength, Knowledge, and Wisdom will these secrets be revealed unto you. May you learn from our mistakes, and in rebuilding, do better.* It's like Jenn's father said — they weren't hoarding it, they were trying to protect it until we were ready for that power again.'

'And what if we're not ready?' asked Scup, cautiously.

'It doesn't matter,' said the captain, firmly. 'Time's up. If the others get to it, it will all be destroyed. Better we have it too soon than not at all, and this is our ticket to everything we've worked towards. A home.'

'Assuming we can get in…' North reminded him, 'how exactly *do* we get in, Weylun?'

Weylun was once again staring at the steel, deep in thought. He fumbled for his neckerchief to mop his furrowed brow, but once again it had slipped its knot in a bid for freedom. 'They are trying to test our strength, knowledge, and wisdom. To *"keep it from savage hands, and cruel"* — I guess they didn't know how far people would slip back. If you found this and didn't know about binary, you wouldn't be able to read it. So they have tested our *knowledge* already.'

'That doesn't help if we can't get past the bloody thing…' grumbled North. 'An inch of solid steel? Even a gun won't touch that.'

'It's a half-inch,' corrected Jymn, 'and my torch will cut it, with enough time.'

Weylun snapped his fingers excitedly, 'strength! See, they've tested our strength, too!'

'What about wisdom…?' asked Scup, uncertainly.

'We haven't got time for wisdom. Jymn, your gear is back on the Archon?' Jymn nodded, fearing the order that was about to come. 'Ok, head back, bring it here. Quick as you can. And take Scup with you.'

The journey back to the surface wasn't as hard as he'd imagined. The reflective strips didn't work in reverse, but the footsteps of twenty crew in the otherwise undisturbed dirt were easy enough to follow, and somehow heading back and up toward fresh air seemed to ease the tension that had built up in Jymn's shoulders and gut. Balder winched them up in the lift-cage, before heading to the steel wall himself, and after that they were alone, chatting idly as they went, stopping only out of respect as they carefully passed the shaft-hatch that had claimed Ram and Nuckle.

'Have you lost others before? From the crew I mean?' Jymn asked, once they were at a respectful distance. 'I knew people that died on the Trossul before. Full-growns. But I never really… it was a different world, I guess. It didn't seem to matter like now.'

'Nine, since I joined,' Scup said solemnly. 'Eleven now.' He stared ahead, seeming to weigh his words before continuing. 'I had a sister once. Maren, just shy of two years older than me. We escaped the village together when the Russaks came, and tried to make it by ourselves out in the bush. It's really hard out there, Jymn. Bad people, desperate. Gangs of slavers. We'd have been killed if it wasn't for a stranger that helped us. A Yupa-knight, if you can believe it — like in the stories. At least that's what Maren figured he was, he had the cloak, and the steeder bike. I suppose he could have killed one and taken it, but he seemed… good. And he was kind to us, so maybe it's all the same. He took us as far as Cinnabarr, and from there we heard rumour of a ship that might take us on — a ship crewed by other skitnics like us.'

They had reached the den of bones now, and Scup helped Jymn

up to the slanting shaft, where he was surprised to see the early light of dawn already filtering down — despite them only having been underground a matter of hours. 'What's a skitnic?' panted Jymn, as they clambered back out among the slush and rock.

'It means like… homeless. Wandering. Like something lost at sea that nobody wants.'

'That's us, I guess,' Jymn smiled.

'Well we got as far as the coast — a pretty rough town — and needed work while we waited for a ship. So we get board in a taphouse, her cooking, me carrying the food out front. Maren was the better cook, you see? I only know what I know from watching her. Anyway, one day there's a fight in the bar, and she comes rushing out to check on me. Only there was a gun, and the lad that had it was only young, and scared. She comes charging in, and before anyone knows what's happened, the gun's gone off, and she just dropped like a bird.' Scup swallowed, the lump in his throat seeming to overcome the momentum of the story. 'Sorry. I've run through that day probably two thousand times since. I used to catch him, and kill him, and think about all the ways that I'd do it. But these days I just wonder if I could have got to her, you know? Before the bullet did.'

'I'm sure you… I mean, bullets are really fast, Scup…' mumbled Jymn, awkwardly, as they reached the line of huge boulders at the foot of the hill that hid them from the town.

'Yeah, I know. I'm glad Cap don't let guns on board anyway. My ladle, you know? That was hers. That's where I —'

Scup's hand flew out across Jymn's chest, stopping him dead, his face suddenly ashen-white. Jymn followed his horrified gaze past one of the boulders, where a man knelt, carefully lifting a much-abused strip of purple fabric from the slush. Jymn shivered as he recognised the leathery sunpoxed face beneath the wide-brimmed hat.

It was Tsar.

Jymn and Scup turned to run, piling right into the chest of a pirate twice their size, whose thick arms seized them by their necks. Tsar slowly rose to his feet, sniffed Weylun's neckerchief with a sneer, and smiled broadly at his captives. His eyes rested awhile on Jymn, and there was a spark of recognition.

'Ar, Jymn, wasn't it, lad?' he purred, drawing closer as Jymn struggled against his captor. Tsar reached out for the bandage over his bad eye, peeling it back to reveal the purple sash beneath. 'So, Mak did take you on in the end, eh? Not surprised, lad, after all that tussle you stirred up in Shoalhaven.' He chuckled, 'never seen young Rasmus so riled up, I haven't, so thank you for that,' he clapped Jymn on the shoulder. 'And my apologies — in advance, like — for how this might go.'

The old pirate lord pulled a long-barrelled pistol from his belt, and pointed it vaguely at them. 'Oghan, hurry back and round me a gang of lads — red cloaks only, mind — we'll want For-Morians for this.'

The pirate at Jymn's back hesitated. 'Sure, Cap? You's only got the one gun, and there's two of these in't there?'

Tsar smiled, never taking his eyes from Jymn and Scup. 'One gun, two prisoners. You're right, Og, of course — ordinarily. Shoot one, t'other breaks free, and such. Everyone makes the same calculation — wanna make sure they're the one as gets away, not the one as gets shot. Even odds with that there — sometimes that's better odds than where you're being led. Don't work like that with this lot though, Mak's got 'em all thinking they're friends, see? Family. Good for morale, surely. But works to our position too. See - the worst thing for these two is that they might get the other one hurt. Innit, lads?'

The huge pirate called Oghan grunted and released the captives to Tsar's care, before lumbering off up the hill toward the town. With a chill down his spine, Jymn recognised him from the beach at the Graveyard. It was this Oghan who had fired the gun that nearly deafened Gam. Tsar smiled again, as if they were simply taking a pleasant stroll along the shore.

'Now, why don't you and I go for a wee walk, and see if we can't find whatever hole you've been hiding in?' And though he smiled, the barrel of the gun jerked with none of the same warmth, gesturing back toward the mine, and the rest of the unsuspecting crew.

XXIV

Ambush

As they were marched to the mine with the gun at their backs, Jymn felt like he'd been plunged into cold water. His chest was tight, and he had to fight for each breath, while his heart felt like it might beat its way free of his ribs. He'd holed the ship, stranded them all here, and now he was leading Cap's oldest rival right to them.

He tried to read Scup but the older boy looked like he was almost in a trance — his jaw set and his fists balled as if he hoped to swing and knock the wily old pirate out with one blow. But Tsar had lived too long for such simple tricks, and lingered always just out of arm's reach, covering every movement with the barrel of his gun.

Slowly and carefully, they scrambled down the shaft into the bear's den, and then to the network of low, dirty rooms beyond.

'Coal mine, eh?' Tsar knocked one of the yellow plastic helmets to the ground with the end of his pistol and stared down at it. 'It had to be, didn't it. Doesn't matter how far you sail, lads, the devil will always stow aboard, in your head or in your heart.' He spat a thick glob of spittle toward the helmet, then strode over to inspect the great and savage metal arm that had scythed down toward Bink, giving it a shove with his boot that set it gently swinging. 'Someone's been busy down here, it seems. And with the bones back there.'

'We think they were trying to keep people out,' called Scup, who was lingering near one of the old mine-carts. His voice was level

308

and calm, unnaturally so, given the circumstance. 'It's this way,' he said simply, beckoning toward one of the furthest dark tunnels, clearly planning to lead the old pirate astray.

But Tsar was going nowhere. 'Ar, but I think you'd be mistaken there, lad. It'll be this way, owing to all the prints, see?' He gestured at the thick carpet of dirt on the floor, and the Archonauts' tracks — unmistakable even in the dim teck-light — that led clearly to the tunnel they had really used. 'Come to think of it, if there's such a good trail, I really don't need either of you, do I…' he trained the gun upon Scup, squinting down the iron sight. 'But I do like to be decent, if I can help it,' he sighed, tugging on the brim of his hat, and lowering the weapon with a shrug. 'The killing ain't no trouble. But it *is* much harder to shake on a bargain when there's blood on your hands.' He turned toward the tracks and gestured lasily for them to lead on.

'So it's a bargain you want?' Jymn called over his shoulder, grasping at the chance as they once again followed the pinpricks of polished light.

Tsar studied him with a sceptical eyebrow raised. 'It's a turn of phrase, son. Meant nothin' by it. All I want from Mak is my ship back.' Though his pace started to falter, and suddenly the gun was trained upon Jymn. 'Unless you'd rather he didn't know I caught you, mind. I can see that would be… embarrassing,' he smiled, and it was somehow both charming and cruel. 'Now, if *you* were to tell me where the Archon is, we can forget about all this, and go our separate ways.'

'We can't do that—' growled Scup, but Jymn cut him off.

'—because the Archon isn't here,' he lied, 'we arrived on a different ship…' he trailed off, while his mind raced for details to support the lie, '...the *Tethered Whale*.'

'What?' Tsar stepped closer, thrusting the barrel of the gun toward Jymn's ribs, 'what's he done to my ship?'

'There… there was a storm!' Jymn stammered, grasping at fragments of truth. 'A bad one. The mainmast, and the rudder—'

'Pah!' spat Tsar. 'Mak would never have left her behind. A captain stays with his ship, lad, you wouldn't understand.'

'He wanted to, but… but there was something more important than that.' Jymn wove his words carefully, gambling on what little he knew about the old pirate. 'There was no time for repairs, and he *had* to get here first, just *had* to. So that… so that he could beat *you*.'

'Hmmm…' the old rogue gestured for them to lead on, but seemed to weigh Jymn's words in his mind as they headed deeper into the earth. Scup walked alongside Jymn, and their eyes met briefly, though the only meaning Jymn sensed was caution. They were nearly at the hatch, another five minutes and they would reach the cage-lift where Balder would be waiting for them.

'A rudder is easy enough,' barked Tsar behind them at last, 'but it's true — a mast is hard to come by. Not many wooden ships left. I can recommend Cinnabar, for timber. Or Keev if, perhaps, you're in eastern waters…'

He tried to make it sound like casual conversation, and upon a time Jymn might have fallen for the effortlessly leading statement. Scup flashed him a warning, but Jymn responded with the subtlest of winks. He remembered Shoalhaven, and meeting Tsar for the first time at the Smikken Sun. He was growing used to the performance, beginning to understand that the true power of old Tsar was not in guns and ships, but in honeyed words, trickery, and cleverness. And in that respect, Jymn was not himself entirely unarmed.

'We're closer to Cinnabar, thank you, but that's all I'll say. I'm not going to… *fall into your trap*. If I told you any more the captain would *ram* his *knuckles* down my throat.'

Jymn sensed Scup flinch at his words, and felt a pang of guilt. Ram and Nuckle had been his friends, and their deaths were still raw. But the meaning seemed to take hold all the same, and gently, inch by inch, Jymn and Scup moved further apart, leading Tsar behind them like a pair of oxen might draw a cart, while the two of them would pass just barely either side of the booby-trapped hatch.

Jymn's palms were slick with sweat, but he dared not wipe them lest he give away some clue. He could feel Tsar's keen eyes watching from behind. The hatch was barely five feet away now. Four. Three.

The old pirate stopped. 'Ram his knuckles down your throat? Mak? You're spinning something fanciful, Jymn. And I took you for honest…' Tsar shook his head in disappointment, and made to take another step forward, but halted with his boot in mid air, and laughed.

'Ar, but you'd have had me too!' he roared. Crouching low, he peered at the metal hatch, wiping its surface with a gloved hand. 'It's the only scrap of ground down here that's not covered in an inch of coal-dust though, eh.' He rose, and stamped hard on the hatch, which swung open with a deafening bang. Tsar tapped the end of his nose and shot them a wily grin, 'you'll have to get up earlier to pull wool over old Tsar's eyes, son. I was born in a mine like this, so I was.'

'Jymn?'

The voice echoed down the tunnel. It was Balder. Adrenaline surged through Jymn's veins, and he backed away. He considered running — if he and Scup made it to the others, they could warn them. But Tsar couldn't have lived this long being a *bad* shot with the pistol. They'd never make it. Not both of them.

'Jymn? Scup? What's happened?'

Before Jymn could call back, Tsar's hand was clamped over his mouth — the pistol pointed right at Scup's chest. Jymn felt himself being dragged backwards, the gun beckoning for Scup to follow. They doused their teck-lights and hid in the gloom of a side shaft, watching as Balder's own light hurried into view, searching the tunnel and finding the hatch open once more. They saw the huge boy throw himself to the ground, bellowing their names urgently into the endless dark pit, before turning to charge back to the lift-cage for help. Jymn longed to call out after him, to tell him that they were ok — that he hadn't lost two *more* friends to the shaft — but Tsar's calloused hand was clamped fast.

He need not have worried. By the time Balder returned from the lower mines with the rest of the crew in tow, Jymn had already descended the lift-cage, and was now perched on a rock waiting for them. The barrel of Tsar's gun was cold against the side of his head, and the purple-sash gag now in his mouth caused his jaw to throb dreadfully. The first few Archonauts froze, glaring, as they splashed out of the narrow passage ahead and into the cold water, but the captain was close on their heels. Jymn saw Cap's eyes flicker, taking in the scene. The lift-cage had been hoisted again, and — though the captain couldn't know it — Scup was hidden out of sight, bound and gagged in the tunnel near the hatch.

'Good to see you again, Mak,' beamed Tsar, 'you look like shit.'

'Takes its toll, eh, captaining a ship.'

'Ar, 'tis true.' Tsar sighed, 'Never know who you can trust, do ya?'

Jymn could have sworn the captain's eyes flinched at the barb, but he changed the subject. 'So this is what you've brought to bargain against? I'm sorry to tell you, you've caught yourself a sprat. That one's new. Only just earned his shirt. *And* he's the one that holed the ship. His stock's awful low at the moment, not worth the tussle.'

'Holed her?' Tsar roared, rounding on Jymn, 'you said it was the mast kept her at Cinnabar. You put a *hole* in my ship?!' Jymn shrugged awkwardly and mumbled through his gag, stealing a glance at the captain, who seemed to catch on.

'So what's your offer?' Cap hurried on, 'you give us Jymn back, and then what? We all get handed over to your new paymasters?'

'*Clients* is what they are, Mak, if you remember. And more honest work than we used to get up to, eh? Except for that unfortunate mess with the Fair Folk.' Tsar scratched unconsciously at one of the lesions beneath his coat. 'But what's your alternative, you'll just sit and watch while I kill your lad, here will you? That's cold, Mak, I thought you'd turned over a new leaf…'

Jymn noticed that Daj — who was glaring at Tsar with white-hot hatred — was gently lifting a stone from the water. The captain folded his arms calmly across his chest. 'You're outnumbered.'

Jymn felt the pistol leave his skull, and sensed Tsar brandishing it for all to see. 'Right, you are, of course. But still the only one with the stones for killin' ain't I? Or have yours grown back, Mak?' The gun snatched toward Daj, who had just couched the rock in her staff-sling. 'Don't make me wing you again, girly. Me aim's not what it used to be — I'd hate to ruin such a pretty breast as yours.' At a gesture from Cap, Daj dropped the rock back to the water.

'Six shots isn't enough for all of us,' said the captain calmly.

'Ar, some hard sense at last!' chuckled Tsar, 'you're right of course. And now you're thinkin' like a captain. Six of your men — excuse me —' he tipped his hat toward Daj, 'six of your *people* shot, and still enough of 'em left to beat me to death with your sticks and rocks and such.' He strode slowly away from Jymn for the first time, scratching at his chin with the barrel of the gun, as if in thought. 'I suppose it was silly of me to wander all the way down here with nothing but this old pistol.' He cocked his head at the captain and smiled, 'you'd be expecting I'm after having some sort of plan…' and with that he let out a low, musical whistle — not unlike the captain's.

The Archonauts murmured, backing against the solid stone walls, as the rocky ledge above bristled with long guns, and red-cloaked For-Morians pointing them. Scup, still gagged and bound, was dragged forward by Oghan.

'You'll excuse the deception Mak — but it's been a pleasure parlaying with ya. For old time's sake. Now let's see what you've found, eh?'

Grumbling, and at gunpoint, the Archonauts were marched back to the steel wall. Jymn was relieved to find Weylun had at least managed to erase half of the translated message, though what good it would do them now, he didn't know.

Tsar stared at the steel plate, scratching idly at a pox-scar as he read '………. *and Wisdom will these secrets be revealed unto you. May you learn from our mistakes, and in rebuilding, do better.* How admirable…' he smirked.

A For-Morian Jymn recognised from Thulhöfn aimed his long-gun at one of the welds where the steel met the floor, but Tsar's hand snaked out and grasped the muzzle before he could fire.

'Only two things getting through that, Jing. Explosives, or

torches. And you'd have to be madder than a box of frogs to light a stick down here. Go fetch the weld-kits.' He turned to Jymn and Scup, and gestured for their gags to be removed. 'That's what you two were after, eh? One of you's a weld-maker?'

Jymn and Scup looked at one another, but neither spoke. They might not be able to stop Tsar, but they weren't going to make it any easier for him, either. The old pirate's hands whipped out, grabbing them both by the wrists. He studied their hands and forearms — reading the lattice of burns that spoke of their long years of work. He groaned and leaned in close, and Jymn suspected some threat, but the old pirate just sniffed the air. 'Hah - a cook!' he laughed, shoving Scup away and dragging Jymn toward the steel wall, 'tie the others up.'

'What's the play here, Tsar?' taunted Cap, as a pair of For-Morians bound his hands behind his back. 'You're really going to hand a fortune over, just so you can watch it burn?'

'Come on, you know me better than that, Mak,' purred Tsar, leaning against the steel wall, 'what was it we used to say? Only thing better than gettin' paid?'

'Is gettin' paid twice, Cap!' grunted Oghan, proudly.

A commotion among the For-Morians at the entrance caused guns to be trained, but the figure that marched past them seemed to think himself bulletproof, for he paid them no notice at all. Jymn's throat constricted as he recognised the man — it was none other than the furious Par that had started this whole mess back in Shoalhaven. His white robes were still somehow fresh-pressed, though the immaculate fabric now bore a dozen dark scuffs and stains from the coal. He was flanked by two other clerics, and a third hobbled behind them — old, blind Jon Cane. Jymn heard Tsar curse under his breath, then straighten, hands on his hips.

'Rasmus! Good of you to join us — my boys found you alright then?'

The immaculate Par marched right up to Tsar, studying the old pirate for an unnaturally long time. 'Brother Cane here found your men sneaking about the town.'

Tsar shrugged. 'Funny. I sent for you right away, of course.

314

Must've been they got lost.' He glared sidelong at Jon Cane, who was grinning behind the protection of his Par's robes. 'You were right though, Rasmus — seems there's more locked away on this rock than just seeds after all. And it's old Tsar who's delivered it…' he tapped his chest proudly and gestured at the blank steel wall as if presenting a gift.

'*May you learn from our mistakes…*' read the immaculate Par, allowing himself the slightest grunt of amusement, before turning his attention for the first time to the captive Archonauts. 'And these? They don't have the look of Skand, so one assumes they sailed here?' His eyes drifted past Jymn, then locked on to his face. 'You! Thief! I know you from Shoalhaven.' He drew close, his face growing redder. 'Tell me — what did he offer you? Half the treasure, if you followed us here and made off with it in secret?'

Tsar stepped between them and led the Par by the shoulder, forcing a chuckle. 'Nothing like that! This crew *is* known to me though. Friends of the Fair… uh, the *Albinos*, see? Must be how they found us, and come for the treasure too, like. But old Tsar caught them for ya.' He puffed his chest out and gestured at the row of Archonauts who were being bound at the wrist.

The Par studied the line, his eyes lingering on the captain. 'Yes. Friend of the 'Fair Folk', red hair, and the heretic's hourglass banner seen in Shoalhaven. That makes you…'

Cap strode forward, his bound hands outstretched, 'Gil Makkanok, of the Archon, pleased to make you.'

Rasmus did not take the offered hand. 'The *Archon,* yes, that's it. The boy-captain. Ageless. The one they say 'out-sails death'.' He pulled Cap's bycock hat roughly from his head, revealing the thin, patchy hair beneath. Seeming to respond to anxious murmurs from among the captive crew, Rasmus theatrically plucked some loose hairs from the hat, sneered, and flicked them to the dirt as if they might infect him. 'There is only one route to eternal life, boy, and you have strayed *hopelessly* far from that path.'

'Oh, come on, there's *always* hope, right?' winked the captain. 'Proverbs 23:18. I know you lot prefer your new additions, but the old—'

'Take them to the seed-vault,' interrupted the Par, tossing the hat to the ground, 'they can await the offering there.'

The captain stepped forward, his countenance changing in a heartbeat. 'Hey, look, it was me gave the orders to come here. This lot are just kids, there's still hope for them. I'm the one you want anyway — heretical blood and all that? That's a better offering, isn't it? For your God?'

The Par turned aside, gesturing lasily over his shoulder. 'This one keep separate from the others. And keep him gagged — if he can't still that silver tongue we'll have to cut it out, but I'd rather keep him whole for the dawn.'

The For-Morians looked to Tsar, who seemed to be trying to navigate his best course of action in real-time. He nodded for the prisoners to be marched away, but strode to whisper in Rasmus' ear, pointing at Jymn and Weylun.

The Par glanced between them. 'Very well — keep the tecker and the thief,' he gestured at the rear of the line of Archonaut captives being filed out of the small chamber, 'and those, too.'

Tsar frowned as Scup and the twins were held back from the column, 'that one's a cook! If you plan on keeping us down here long enough to take meals, I might need to step outside for a piss!' he joked, but the Par ignored him, striding instead toward Jymn.

'You are a welder, as well as a thief?' demanded Rasmus. Jymn glared at Tsar, but nodded feebly. 'Then begin your work,' he gestured at the young twins, 'you may just preserve the lives of your friends.'

It felt like a lifetime since Jymn had shaped the blue-white flame of a gas-torch, but the cleverness of his fingers had not left him, nor his innate understanding of how the metal would react to the heat. This kit, while not as fastidiously maintained as his own, was more than capable of slowly punching through the thick steel and burning a hole big enough for a man to climb through. But it had taken months to understand how, and years to perfect the skill. He gambled that nobody else here knew even one tenth as much.

He turned from the cherry-red steel and shook his head, wiping the slick of sweat from his brow. 'It's too thick,' he panted, 'it's just drinking the heat from the flame.' He waved the torch over the steel surface to demonstrate. The deliberately unfocussed cone of fire that he'd conjured from the tip would scorch the metal something fierce, and cause it to glow, but would keep it always just below the melting point.

'They melted it shut, did they not? Simply melt it back open again,' demanded the Par, who was pacing back and forth impatiently behind him.

'I don't know how they did it — perhaps… perhaps the Skand had a special—'

'Fire is fire, boy,' said the Par, waving away his objections, 'do not play games with me.'

'I'm not…'

'Best do as he says, lad,' urged Tsar, who had been curiously quiet until now, perched on a rocky barrier at the far end of the cavern.

'It's just not hot enough,' protested Jymn, 'maybe if we had a different gas, or…'

Rasmus strode to Tsar and tore the pistol from his belt, staring at Jymn while he aimed it vaguely at the twins. 'Don't test me. Do better.'

Jymn blinked. If he backed down now and opened the vault, he'd be revealed as a liar. And who knows what power they would be handing over. But if he didn't… whatever secrets were hidden here, they weren't worth a life. Not one of his friends. But the Par was making empty threats. Did he even know how to *use* the gun? Jymn caught Scup's eye, and saw the set of his jaw, the subtle shake of the head. He couldn't give in now.

He lowered the weld-torch stubbornly. 'It's too thick. I can't'

The Par stared at him, just like he'd stared at Tsar — seeming to read every line of his face, every movement of his eyes. 'Very well,' he said, and without taking his eyes from Jymn, he cocked the hammer.

'No!' cried Scup, leaping between Juke and the Par, falling

317

heavily just as the gun spoke.

It took a moment for Jymn to register what had happened. His ears rang so loud he thought he might double over and vomit, but found he couldn't take his eyes from the pale steam that rose from Scup's chest. He saw the way the thick, oven-scarred arms sagged as Juke clung to him, sobbing. None of it made sense, why wouldn't he get up, he couldn't be…

And then Weylun was kneeling over Scup too, and weeping. Lifting the limp head and slapping the cheeks, trying to rouse him. The twins were clutching one another, wailing, but it was all Jymn could do to keep the room from spinning. His hands shook uncontrollably as the full weight of what he'd done hit him.

He'd killed Scup.

The hammer cocked again, and Weylun and the twins clung to one another, defiant, even through their tears. But Rasmus wasn't looking at them, he was staring right at Jymn, one eyebrow raised. With trembling fingers, Jymn reignited the weld-torch, focussing the cutting flame as sharply as ever he had, and set about doing the Par's bidding.

The half-hour of work that followed was the worst of Jymn's short life, worse even than all those long years aboard the Trossul combined. Without his protective leathers, the glowing metal scorched and blistered his skin, but after a while even the scalding heat was not enough to keep his mind from drifting back to Scup. His stomach boiled and burned, as if tortured by every meal the cook had ever made him, and his good eye ached raw from the unending stare into the weld-flame — for he was too afraid to turn away and face the others. Eventually, though, the work was done, and a great rounded section of the steel fell away, glowing, into the darkness beyond. Rasmus pushed him aside and he stumbled on legs heavy with guilt, his eyes adjusting once more to the gloomy cavern.

The twins rushed to Jymn and swept him into a sobbing embrace that felt as if it might crack his ribs, but his guilty, leaden arms couldn't bring themselves to return the gesture. Tsar, it seemed, had helped Weylun carry Scup's lifeless body to a corner of the cave, where they had set about building a low cairn of rocks to cover him. Jymn's skin crawled, as he noted the gun was tucked back into the old pirate's belt.

'Light!' demanded Rasmus, and a brace of Pars swiftly obeyed, carrying confiscated teck-lights into the newly revealed vault. Jymn peered absently through the hole he'd cut — the space beyond seemed to be nothing more than a continuation of the same cavern, as if the steel plate served nothing more than to divide the space in two. Except there, set heavily into one wall, was a mighty door. Slowly, curiosity won out, and they drew closer.

The door made the heavy steel wall look like it was made of straw. The metal — Jymn wasn't sure what metal it even *was* — was at least as deep as his hand from wrist to fingertip, at which point it seemed to plunge into the rock face. Huge domed bolts, each almost three inches across, were set into the surface, every face rounded to prevent any tool from biting. And there, etched somehow into the very centre of the door, was writing. Not coded marks such as those upon the steel wall, but plain words. Jymn squinted, tried to shake the fog from his mind and remember his letters. *A-he-ad. Ahead. A-ll th-e…*

> *Ahead, all the answers you desire,*
> *Your questions, left behind*

Rasmus read the words aloud, his voice dripping with contempt. 'Open it,' he snapped, thrusting Jymn toward the door. But there was no handle, nor even a join, or weld, or blemish upon the surface that might belie some weakness. Jymn knocked upon the metal, confirming his suspicions. He turned to the others.

'It's solid,' he muttered, afraid of the retribution his words might bring.

'Then you had best get started,' snarled Rasmus. 'We *will* have our offering, come the dawn. And if the heresies in here are not freed, it will be your crew that burns in their place.'

Hours passed, but try as he might Jymn could barely manage to persuade a dull glow from the mysterious metal, let alone the bright, searing yellow necessary for cutting. Eventually, as the gas in the bottle began to sputter and fail, Rasmus seemed to accept that his threats were achieving nothing now. Jymn was released back to the company of Weylun and the twins, who watched as the For-Morians took their turn at breaking the door. Entire magazines of bullets were emptied, and even small charges of powder, packed against the smooth bolts, but nothing more than scuffs and scars stood to testify their efforts. Tsar offered some wisdom about his days getting past impassable trade-blockades — 'if you can't go through 'em, you just have to sail *around'* — and runners were sent to scavenge pick-axes from the upper levels of the mine. In the cloying smoke from the weld-torch and the gun-powder, exhausting shifts were taken at hacking the raw stone around the door. Weylun and the twins were exempted, on grounds of being too small or unfit, but Jymn was not spared, and soon blistered his palms against the rock wall. Inch by inch, they dug away at the stone surrounding the door, but still no room, or join, or cavity was found.

Jymn collapsed against the cold steel wall, flexing his bloody hands. 'It can't be much further,' said Weylun reassuringly, as he dabbed at Jymn's hands with a little water he'd collected from the foot of the lift-cage. 'And he didn't mean what he said about burning the crew. What would it achieve? It's not like…' but he trailed off awkwardly. *Like Scup* — that's what he was going to say. Killing Scup is what got them in here. Burning the whole crew might just be an empty threat. Might. 'Hey, I know that face, Jymn,' whispered Weylun, nudging him. 'You're thinking of something.'

He was right, there *was* something nagging at Jymn — a loose thread in his mind begging to be tugged. A solution. 'Wisdom…' he muttered. Weylun frowned at him, questioning. 'It said they were going to test our strength, knowledge, and wisdom, right?'

'That was the wall,' said Weylun, resting himself against the cold steel. 'Knowledge was translating the binary, strength was to get through the steel. Wisdom was… well, whether we even *should* open it, I suppose.'

'That doesn't sound right though, does it? Was that really a test of wisdom?' asked Jymn, his mind scrabbling to fit the pieces together. 'And why are they just testing our strength all over again now?' he gestured at the impenetrable door.

'Maybe it's another trap. Maybe there's nothing even there,' sighed Weylun, as he watched the exhausted For-Morians pounding their picks against the rock. Then an idea seemed to strike him right behind the eyes, and he sat bolt upright. 'Wait, what if there's nothing there!'

Scrambling to his feet, Weylun hurried toward the door. By the time Jymn caught up with him, he was repeating the engraved words to himself over and over. '*Ahead, all the answers you desire. Your questions, left behind.*' He turned to Jymn, and despite everything, the death and destruction suffocating them, there was that clever, curious excitement in his eyes once again. 'Remember what I told you about science? The first thing — the most important thing — is that you *never* start with the answer you want — only the question. It's all about the question, *that's* the valuable bit.'

Jymn half-remembered the conversation from Losalfhym. 'Yeah, so?'

'So — the Skand that hid this stuff were scientists, right? They did all this to make sure the power would only be found by people who were ready for it — people who shared those values.'

Jymn frowned, 'okay, so… how do we open the door?'

'We don't!' whispered Weylun excitedly, 'we don't *desire answers. Your questions, left behind,* don't you see?' He turned around, peering into the darkness that clung to the back of the cave. 'The questions are *left…* and *behind…*'

321

XXV

Vaults

The true entrance to the vault was disguised cunningly enough against the rock wall, but Jymn suspected that even here in the gloom at the back of the cave it would have taken only a few minutes to discover — were it not for the lure of the huge false door that drew all attention. Guiltily, he wondered if Rasmus and the For-Morians would *ever* have found it without their help — whether perhaps the secrets within could have remained safe — but it was a futile fancy. The uncompromising Par held the rest of the crew captive. Jymn was not about to test him again.

The trial of wisdom was passed. And so it was that there, in a dark, hunched corner of the cave, the Skand vault was opened at last.

There was a faint hiss as hidden seals gave way and air from within — unspoiled for centuries — escaped to mingle with the acrid, sooty atmosphere of the cave. Jymn peered in, as cool teck-light spilled into the mysterious void, reflecting off clean metal surfaces, untouched by the pervasive black dust of the mine. Beside him, Weylun gasped as the light traced across ancient machines — not the time-ravaged scraps, delicately repaired, that they were used to, but pristine, gleaming devices that seemed even now to await the return of their masters, as if they had been gone only a moment. Row upon row of steel shelving stretched back into the vault, each shelf packed with neat rows of plastic chests and crates.

Jymn was shoved forward roughly as the For-Morians piled

into the vault, contaminating it instantly. A heavy lever was thrown, calling forth some ancient store of power, and the small chamber flickered into light. Jymn blinked around at the sterile metal surfaces. Now that he was inside along with Weylun and a half-dozen full-growns, he was surprised to find it quite… cramped. He wasn't sure what he'd imagined, exactly — endless shelves stretching on for days, perhaps — but the idea that *all* the knowledge of the Ancients could be stowed in here seemed ridiculous. He'd only ever seen a handful of real books in his life — most of the stories he'd grown up on were told from memory — but based on those few, he guessed there couldn't be more than a few thousand down here, at most. But as the first of the plastic crates was hauled off the shelving and opened, Jymn grew even more puzzled. There were no books — just roll after roll of thin, transparent tape, which was soon tossed to the floor in a heap.

'What is this crap?!' complained a disgruntled For-Morian, 'this ain't teck, is it, eh?'

'Be careful!' Weylun cried, throwing himself to the floor and scrabbling for the reels as if they were as precious as silver or gold. Holding one up to the light, he squinted, feeding the thin film through his hands. Despite everything, the wheezing techsmith couldn't suppress his excitement, and he looked at Jymn like a child who had caught his first fish. 'These are instructions! Manuals — I'm sure of it — there must be a million pages on each of these rolls!'

'Ah! This is more like it!' cried a gleeful pirate, thrusting his hands into another freshly opened crate and withdrawing handfuls of glittering silver-white coins. Quickly his companions snatched at the treasure, sending it tumbling across the concrete floor. One of the coins rolled toward Jymn, and he plucked it up, turning it over in his hands. It was unlike any coin he'd seen before. Mostly people didn't bother with minting coin these days, preferring simple bars of precious metal, but he'd seen a few — irregular, lopsided circles of beaten copper or iron. This was something else entirely — a crisp, perfect circle about two inches across, and not silver, as he'd first thought, not even metal. He thought it might have been made of ice from the mountaintops of Thule, for it was translucent and frosty-looking, but though it was hard as steel, it was not cold to the touch. He held it up to the light as Weylun had done with the film, and though he saw a thousand mesmerising lines and facets within the coin, he could make out no patterns or writings.

Rasmus, who himself was inspecting one of the coins, shifted his attention to Weylun. 'You — what manner of thing is this?'

Weylun, puzzling over his own coin, was clearly struggling for an answer himself. Hesitantly, he stepped over the spilled reels of film, towards the devices which seemed to have been supplied with power, along with the lights. 'This one is for the film…' he muttered, carefully sliding a strip of the thin tape beneath one of the glowing boxes, 'see?' Jymn marvelled as the front face of the device seemed to magnify the film — some sort of lens perhaps, that made the miniature writing readable. Weylun moved to another device, feeling around its edges with hands well used to teasing secrets from these old contraptions. It was easy to forget, with all the bumbling and sweating, quite how confident Weylun could be, when he was around teck. 'Ha!' he cried triumphantly, as the crystal disk slid into a glowing green slot with a whirring sound. Again, the screen flickered into life, but this time the words seemed to cascade from the top to the bottom. Weylun made a noise that was somewhere between a gasp and a giggle, as he twisted a dial, causing the text to fly down the screen in a blur. His head skimmed the writing so fast Jymn thought he might injure his neck. 'This is it — this is code,' he muttered, shaking his head before turning back to the room with pure wonder on his face, 'this is how they controlled their machines.'

Rasmus turned his attention back to the pirates crowded around the open crates. 'Anyone found with these on their person will be burned along with the rest,' he snapped, snatching Jymn's coin from his hands with a glare and prompting the emptying of many a pocket.

'I don't know that you'll burn it…' muttered Tsar, who was testing one of the coins against his teeth. 'Seems mighty hard.'

Rasmus fixed him again with the uncomfortable, lingering stare. 'Then we'll grind it into dust and let the wind take it. I remind you, captain, you have already been paid handsomely for this *treasure*. I trust you anticipate the consequences should any of it be stolen?'

'Aye, I know, well enough, and you've got three of your brothers on each of my ships to remind me,' he sighed, and he tossed his coin back toward one of the pirates beside the crate, though Jymn could have sworn something slipped into the old rogue's sleeve as he folded his arms. 'So, what do you want doin' with it all?'

The Par tossed his own coin to the pile of tangled film as if it might infect him if he held it any longer. 'Take it all to the fire.' He gestured vaguely at Jymn, Weylun, and the twins. 'And have these chained away with the others.'

Almost before they knew what was happening, Jymn and the others were marched from the vault and back through the mine, which was now lit with a festoon of dull lamps. Despite having been below the earth for what felt like an eternity, they emerged to find the queer northern sun still hanging low in the sky as if it were early morning, the land above the mine streaked with long, cold shadows. Word of their underground discovery had clearly spread among the church and the pirates, for now the empty field of rocks between the mine and the town was littered with curious knots of men summoned to lend a hand. Jymn, Weylun and the twins drew wicked stares as they were marched up the hill toward the town, but were soon forgotten as the treasure began to emerge behind them. Tsar himself marched alongside the prisoners, and made a show of shoving and cajoling them onwards, though once the crowds had thinned, he leaned in close to speak in low tones.

'That Rasmus, he's unpredictable,' he whispered, 'I didn't know that was going to happen... with your friend.'

Jymn stared fixedly ahead. Another pirate trap. Kind words from the man that had pointed the same gun at Scup just minutes before he was killed.

'Listen close — tell the others — there's only one sure way off this rock for the lot of 'em, right? If they know what's good for 'em, they'll take the cloth. Convert, like. Renounce their ways. A bit of repenting, and they'll not be harmed. I've seen it done.'

'Renounce the captain?' Weylun scoffed, catching Jymn by

surprise.

'Mak's no saint, lad,' Tsar hissed, urging quiet, 'he'd do the same.'

Jymn shook his head, 'we'd end up no better than slaves if we knelt to them now.'

'S'worse things to be than a slave, lad. Dead, for example. Can't come back from that, but being a slave, there's always hope.'

'So says the slaver…' Jymn muttered bitterly.

'I was *born* a slave, Jymn. As were most of my crew. As were you, I'd wager.'

'I was never a slave. My parents got me out of Razeen when the famines came, and they didn't go through all that just for me to wind up as one now.'

Something seemed to pass behind the old pirate's eyes, and he looked away at the horizon. 'Razeen, was it? I remember the famines of Razeen. Remember 'em well. Terrible hard times, and good for business. You could buy a hungry child for a song and sell 'em on two weeks later for a hundred times what you paid.' He looked at Jymn once again. 'Tell me, where's the sin in that, then? Delivering children from the jaws of a hungry death?'

'You weren't doing it to do good, you were doing it to get rich,' scowled Jymn.

'Aye, but I *was* doing it, just the same,' winked Tsar.

'You could have done it for free, like the rescue ships.'

'Rescue ships!' Tsar blurted a laugh before remembering himself, and lowering his voice to a whisper once more. 'Funny, I spent the best part of a year in those waters, never once heard of no rescue ship. Nor folk giving their children away for free, that's for damn sure. And you'd think I'd know — it would have been mighty profitable, eh? But maybe you should ask your Saint Mak, maybe he remembers it different.'

Jymn frowned at Tsar, and his silent confusion must have been easy to read, for the old rogue chuckled. 'Easy to forget, isn't it, that he's been around so long, what with that young man's face an' all. Just who do you suppose was me first mate, back then, eh?

326

Before he stabbed me in the back and stole the Archon? We took hundreds of kiddies from those shores, him and me, and sold 'em on. Didn't you ever wonder how you ended up on a workship? Funny place for a "rescue ship" to take you, eh?' Tsar leaned in close, 'thing I suppose you'll be after knowing now, son, is whether you told him where you was from? Whether he knew all along what you really were to him?'

Tsar smiled at the obvious conflict on Jymn's face, and banged loudly on the steel door that hung on its hinges, for without realising it, they had reached the huge concrete vault that jutted from the mountainside above the town. 'Careful who you're putting on pedestals there, Jymn,' Tsar muttered as two Clergy emerged to take custody of the prisoners, 'awful long way to fall, from such a long way up.'

The inside of the vault could not have been more different to the one they had uncovered below the earth. Where that one had been cramped, this seemed to stretch endlessly back inside the mountain. Where it had been pristine and gleaming, this was a ruin of grime, and scorch, and meltwater. Rats scrabbled and fought hungrily over the spilled seeds that had once been locked away for future generations that would never see them. Jymn knew he should have been doing something, counting steps, or asking questions, or looking for Mak… *Cap*. But his head was a swirling mess of anger, doubt, guilt, and — woven through it all — a bitterness he couldn't shake. *Had* he told Cap where he was from? Had Cap known all along that he had been the one to take Jymn from his parents. Were Tsar's words even true — had his parents really sold him for a handful of coin — or was this just more trickery from the old pirate?

Jymn was pulled from his spiral by Weylun, who bumped into him clumsily. Jymn felt something hard pressed into his hand, and glanced down to see a ship's radio. His mind charged through the implications. He had forgotten the radios. Gam had the other, but they had never heard from him, though he must surely have seen the For-Morians coming over the hill after them. Perhaps he had been captured. Or perhaps they had simply been too deep

underground for the trace to penetrate. Jymn looked at the concrete walls all around them. Were they too deep even now? Could he get word to Gam and the others? What would he even say to warn them? He caught Weylun's eye, not daring to whisper a plan, then turned back to squint at the door receding behind them. If he could just sprint back, make it as far as the doorway, perhaps he could—
'oof!'

The wind left his lungs as he was shoved to the ground by one of the clergy leading them. He heard a scraping, and skittering, and wrenched his head around to see the radio tumbling across the concrete floor, scattering a group of rats. He reached out to recover it, but the other clergy had already stooped, picking it up as if it might bite him and inspecting it with a mixture of fear and contempt. He shifted his gaze to Jymn who was being hauled roughly back to his feet.

'What is it?' demanded the old Par, his spittle stinging Jymn's grazed cheek.

Jymn's mind clutched for a lie that would turn the tables in their favour. 'It's a message, to bring help,' he said, thrusting his chin out defiantly. 'Others will come for us.'

But the Par just smiled, and handed the device carefully to his companion. 'Good. Good - we shall be waiting.' He turned to the other Par, 'keep this one separate from the others, it seems we've found a troublemaker.'

And then, amidst cries of protest from Bink and Juke, Jymn was led away from the others. He tried to keep track of the twins' yelling, tried to mentally map where they might have been taken, but it was hopeless, and he soon found himself dragged into the solitary confines of a cell. The floor was slick with grimy water that seeped from a gaping split in the concrete where a dim shaft of half-forgotten green light filtered down from high above. Jymn's wrists were bound to a pipe sunk deep into the concrete, and before he could think to demand answers of the Par, the heavy steel door was slammed shut, and he was alone.

Jymn shivered, and his breath began to grow ragged as the full weight of his situation pressed down upon him. He was powerless, hopeless, and afraid. Half the Archonauts were imprisoned, the other half in hiding at best. Their leader was missing, the treasures were lost. And beneath it all, a turmoil writhed in his belly — of guilt at Scup's death, mingled with a sickening betrayal and rage whenever his mind drifted to Tsar, the captain, or even his parents.

He flinched upon hearing movement from beyond the shaft of light, expecting more rats, but a familiar voice rasped from the darkness.

'Jymn Hatcher. Well ain't you a sight for sore eyes, *chile.'*

The proud face of Syrincs Ren emerged from the gloom, though it looked as though a considerable effort had been made to beat the pride out of it. Her hair was loose and matted with blood, and both eyes were swollen to slits, but still — despite all her sins — she managed to hold herself with a semblance of dignity. Unbidden, a great wave of anger rose in Jymn's chest, pouring from his mouth.

'You! You killed Syra, and all those faireys! You helped them find this place! Everything… all of this… it's all your fault!'

The bloodied head seemed to bow a little under the weight of accusation, and Rincs took a slow breath.

'I did not… the young ones were…' the proud voice faltered. 'The deaths were not at my hands, though you are right, I take my share of the blame. I was forced to read the blood, but that was not enough for them.'

'You could have refused,' spat Jymn.

'If I believed that would have stopped the killing, I would have, child. I think if I had done less, there would simply have been more of it. When I saw the secrets in the genes of the Mir-Trees I even considered hiding it from them. But I made a choice. Better to have them come here and destroy our history, than linger in Losalfhym and kill even one more of the Fairey young.' It seemed Syrincs' wrists were bound like his, but she drew her knees up to her chest and rested her head upon them, peering at him. 'We cannot carry all the blame for the sins of others, Jymn, the weight is too great.'

Her words cut deep, though of course there was no way she could have known about Scup's death, and his part in it. He found

329

that his anger did not abate though, but instead seemed to focus inwards. A rat scratched at the other side of the door, interrupting the silence.

'This place was a haven once, you know,' Rincs sighed. 'Long ago. A great store, in case the world ever needed it. But after everything, after all we've been through to find it, it seems it was destroyed before we even arrived.'

'Raiders came, many years ago,' Jymn told her. 'Loken was here. We heard the story from his sister — she's dead now — but they were here as children when it fell. He could have told us…'

'The mind of a child will do much to protect itself from such memories. He is quite mad now, but a glimpse remains in his songs, perhaps. The Ice Cat upon the hill, the blue-eyed children. What of Gil — the captain — you *are* one of his crew at last? Does he still live?'

'For now. They caught him too.' Then a thought occurred to Jymn, and he fixed Rincs with a stare. 'Did you know — all along — what he was? A slaver? He took… *children* from their parents and sold them on?'

She looked at him with sadness in her eyes. 'I know he has lived many lives, and has long been trying to make up for the sins of his past. Not everyone can claim that labour.'

'Well, they have him,' Jymn shrugged, 'I think they are going to burn him for their god.'

Rincs hung her head. 'The worst kind of sin, is to sin and call it the Lord's work.'

'You sound like them,' Jymn snorted.

'Oh, you think I cannot believe? Because I am a witch?'

'Not a witch, but you're a scientist aren't you? You can read blood, and splices… you can see the… I thought you could see how it all works? There's no magic, or God, we are just… genes. Like machines.'

'Even the machines believe in their creators, child. Are they mistaken?'

'It's all just stories and lies,' Jymn groaned, shaking his head.

'When I was a child on the workship, I used to believe stories about brave heroes defending their ships — but then I got older and I realised. They were just lies to make us do what the owners wanted — to fight for them. Then I got free, and began to believe in the captain, that he was good, and noble. That he set people free. And now I find out he's a slaver!' Jymn hung his head, drawing his knees up to his chest, hearing his own heartbeat in the silence. 'And through it all, I believed that my parents were brave, that they saved me, and that I might have an ounce — just an ounce — of that courage inside me. It was all lies.' He stared at Rincs, daring her to challenge him, but she just peered at him in silence, through the slits of her swollen eyes.

Eventually, she broke the silence, her voice low and steady. 'Two lifetimes I have spent, reading and mixing the blood. I have seen splices, disease, mistakes. But I have never once seen a gene for love, or courage. Or for hope. These things cannot simply pass from the blood of your mother and father, but they still exist, do they not? And they are more important than anything you might inherit.'

'So — what? My parents might have been cowards, but at least I didn't inherit any bad blood?'

'Not at all. It takes tremendous courage to carry on when there is no hope.'

'Thanks,' muttered Jymn, without sincerity.

'I wasn't talking about you, child,' she chided. 'Your parents. They gave up everything they loved to buy a chance when there was none.'

'They didn't 'give me up' though, they *sold* me. For coin.'

'You have not been back to Razeen, I take it?'

The question caught him off guard, and his anger subsided for a moment as the memory of his parents came back, unbidden. 'I wanted to. To find them,' he whispered, 'but not any more.'

'If you had, you would not have begrudged them a handful of coin to buy one last crop. There is nothing left there now. Just a wasteland of blighted soil and tainted water.'

Jymn raised his chin, 'they are dead, then?'

She smiled gently, and there was pity in her eyes, 'can you imagine anyone giving up their child to strangers if they weren't facing death? Starvation?'

'So much for *carrying on when there is no hope.*'

'Isn't that the only time hope really counts? Keeping it alive, when there is no logic, or reasoning left? But there *was* hope, Jymn. You! They put their child on a boat and off he went and *lived!* Despite everything, you survived.' With a nod of her head she indicated the broken wall, 'look at that seed there — where the meltwater meets the crack of light. See it sprouting. A hundred feet below the earth, surrounded by all this despair and war and darkness. And still it sprouts, reaching up for the light. It finds a way. *That* is hope.'

Both of them flinched as the door flew open with a bang. Two clerics marched in, armed with knives and fresh rope.

'We have fresh blood for you to read, witch. Spliced.' In unison they made the sign of the cross, then cut her bonds and marched her from the cell. The door slammed, almost killing a rat in the process, and just like that, Jymn found himself alone again, with only dark thoughts for company.

Hope. Willfully ignoring facts and thinking in favour of blind belief. Belief that some outside force cared about you and would intervene in the misery of your life. Jymn was old enough now to know that's not how the world worked, and had endured enough preaching from Par Carrek to know *faith* when he heard it. But Rincs had been right about one thing. That seed *was* sprouting. She had ignored the hundreds that littered the floor rotting, of course, as was often the way, but that one was surviving.

That was it — not hope or courage, or bravery — it was *survival.* Doing whatever it took to keep going. Being that one seed, not the hundred others. Like the rats scrabbling at the door, he could survive.

But first he needed to get free.

XXVI

Survival

An angry fist banged against the door, demanding an end to Jymn's wailing.

'I have something to tell you!' pleaded Jymn, his voice hoarse from the persistent cries.

'Say it then, and be done!' growled the Par, at last. It had been an hour, at least, since they had taken Rincs, and he'd been busy.

'I won't shout it,' Jymn replied, lowering his voice, 'the others mustn't hear.'

Jymn waited, almost able to hear the gears turning inside the clergyman's head. Then keys jangled, and the door opened. Jymn made sure to keep his good eye on the Par, fighting the instinct to watch the threshold of the heavy door as it opened. The priest looked rough and salty — one of the new converts, Jymn suspected — not yet wholly disabused of his pirate nature. He crouched just outside of arm's reach, scratching at an itch somewhere beneath his robes.

'If you set me free, I will tell you something,' Jymn whispered, 'something that will improve your standing with Rasmus and the others.'

The Par checked over his shoulder, then jerked his chin suspiciously, gesturing for Jymn to go on. Fighting down the doubt boiling in his stomach, Jymn leaned in close and whispered.

'You should wash more,' he said as earnestly as he could, 'you smell like your mother weaned you on a fish's tit, and you never broke the habit.' He nodded at the wall behind the Par, 'I can smell you through that door.'

Rage flared in the Par's eyes and Jymn barely had time to flinch before the back of the man's fist connected with the socket of his bad eye. Pain exploded as the old wound on his cheek opened once more, and he slumped sideways, unable to topple fully over, owing to the thick ropes that bound his arms behind his back.

The Par rose to his feet, gave Jymn a sharp kick in the ribs for good measure, and strode from the room. Jymn flinched as the heavy door slammed, sealing him in once more. He took a steadying breath, allowing his head a moment to stop spinning before opening his good eye to check the doorway.

It had worked.

There, happily nibbling at the small pile of seeds Jymn had managed to gather and flick toward the doorway, was one of the hungry rats from the corridor. It was thin and skittish, and reminded Jymn of how Makket looked when he was first rescued from the Trossul's bilge, back before the regular portions of salt-rice and old age had slowed him and greyed his fur.

Jymn struggled back to upright, fighting down a wave of nausea from the pain in his smikken eye and ribs. He clicked his tongue in the way that Makket had always liked, and flicked another of the small, forgotten seeds towards the rat.

The creature slowed as its hunger abated, but gradually, seed by seed, it drew closer to the cache of food Jymn kept hidden in his hands. It could smell the seeds, but couldn't get to them through the mass of untidy knotwork that bound Jymn's wrists, and eventually, and with much relief, Jymn felt it begin to bite and gnaw at the rope. He wouldn't have believed it possible, but for the havoc he'd seen wreaked upon the Trossul's rope lockers, or his own cot-bed if Makket ever managed to escape his cage in search of food. These creatures could tear up twice their bodyweight in wood or cloth trying to get at food, or to make nests for their young. Sure enough, after sustaining more than one bite to his wrists and fingers, Jymn felt the first rope give way, and the knot slacken. Unlike the one who had struck him, the Par who had bound him must surely have been born to the faith — for this knot could never have been the work of an ex-sailor. Fearing more bites Jymn released the cache of precious seeds, and soon fought his way free of the damaged ropes, turning his attention to the cell.

The door was heavy, and though the hinges were badly rusted, there were no magflies this far north to feast upon them, and they remained strong. It would take tools to break through. Tools he did not have. There was a scrap of old pipe in a corner of the room. A weapon in the right hands. He could wait for the guard to change, and try the same trick with his next custodian, but it would mean a fight with a full-grown, and that would only get him as far as the corridor, where there would surely be more of them waiting. Even armed with the pipe, he was still just one boy.

He crossed the damp floor to where Rincs had been bound. There were scraps of rope still hanging from a railing, but nothing of use. He saw the tiny speck of green — the one seed that had managed to sprout — and Rincs' words came back to him. '*A hundred feet below the earth, surrounded by all this despair, and war, and darkness. And still it sprouts, reaching up for the light.*'

Crossing to the small patch of light, he peered up into the broken rock that leached the distant daylight into the cell. The room had been lined with concrete once, from which ancient steel rods now jutted, barring the way like the windows in Node's cells. The chimney of cleft rock beyond them was narrow and sharp, but he'd grown up aboard the Trossul crawling into such spaces for work, or for protection. If he removed his furs, he might just squeeze inside and be able to climb. He'd never make it between the bars of course, but metal had a way of submitting to him when he put his mind to it. The steel was wet with meltwater from above, and badly corroded already — worse than any he'd ever seen. In any other climate it would have been long since devoured by magflies, but here in the frozen north it had continued to decay far past what was natural. Jymn thought back to the chain-link fence in Shoalhaven, and how he had stressed the metal to the point of breaking. The same might work here, though even such poor steel was still far beyond the strength of his hands.

An idea struck him, and moments later he had collected the pipe

335

and the best length of rope he could salvage from Rinc's clean-cut bonds. Throwing the short cord over two of the weakest bars, he began to twist, using the pipe for leverage. The rope buckled and coiled and fought him, but still he twisted until gradually the ancient metal began to groan and give way. He had to stop twice to let his muscles cool, and to sip at the meltwater that dripped from above, but eventually the bars abandoned their post, and stood aside to let him pass.

Resting once more, Jymn peered up at the broken rock beyond. The way was slick and wet with meltwater, and there was no way of knowing if it would narrow higher up, forcing him to turn back, or worse — trapping him. He shivered at the thought.

But the truth was, he was *already* trapped. Stripping down to just his shirt and wide copper belt, he hid the Trashlander furs in the darkest corner of the cell, and wedged his boot into the narrow cleft in the wall. The crevice beyond the bars was damp with grime, and fought off any attempt at grip, but eventually he found a handhold, and then another. His shoulders — formerly so adept at slipping into small spaces — seemed to have broadened under the labour of life on the Archon, but after much worming and contorting, he worked his way into the narrow cleft and began to climb.

The going was slow and cramped. Years, he had spent, scrabbling up the sides of the Trossul's hull with his weld-kit, but this was something else entirely. Ice-cold meltwater had soaked his shirt within the first few yards, and a cold wind raced downwards, setting his teeth chattering. More than once he had to fight down a wave of panic that brought bile to his throat as the sharp rock walls pressed too close and threatened to trap him. But his fingers remembered some of their old strength, and he managed to drag himself free, though his chest and back were quickly torn and bloodied with the struggle, and he nearly lost the compass from around his neck. Up and up he climbed. His fingers grew numb from the creeping cold even as his limbs burned from the labour, but always his face was upturned toward the light — like that small seedling — and with every ounce of effort, the freedom above drew closer.

Eventually — tired and numb with cold — Jymn found himself in clear view of the surface. He had emerged into the bowel of a deep ravine that clove the mountainside and gaped up at the cloudy sky above. The sight of freedom overcame the lead in his arms and quickly he scaled the wet rock to find himself emerging on the exposed slope — slightly above the entrance to the seed-vault — with only the ravine itself for cover. With his shirt ripped and wet from the climb, and without his furs to protect him, Jymn found himself at the mercy of the biting wind, and huddled in the scant protection offered by the cleft while he fought to devise a plan.

If he was seen by the clergy he would be caught and locked up once more — or worse. They would be on the lookout now, there was no way he would pass as a pirate again — at least not in daylight — and it was nearly impossible to tell how long this unending sun would stay in the sky. He was already dangerously cold, and the dark would only sharpen the chill. He couldn't survive this place alone, he needed allies, but he had precious little to offer in exchange.

Forcing himself clear of the ravine, Jymn scanned the land beneath him. The town lay spread out at the foot of the slope, and still crawled with pirates and clergy, maintaining the fires that burned day and night. On a bluff beyond the far side of the town, the old ruined church stood, though whether Gam still waited there hopelessly he could not tell. Even if he did, his keen eyes would not be enough to tell Jymn apart from the others at such a distance.

There was a coarse yell from behind him, and Jymn whirled around to see a pair of pirates leading a hound on a chain. He made to throw himself back into the cover of the narrow gorge, but too late — the one had seen him, called to the other, and now both of them advanced, weapons raised. But it was not their weapons that seized Jymn's attention. The dog — for what else could be snuffling the ground, and pulling at the lead? — was no hound at all, but some manner of captive Raption. Unable to take his eyes from the thing, Jymn tucked the compass inside what was left of his shirt and raised his shivering arms in surrender as they drew closer. The writhing creature was not unlike the great metal wyrms that had burrowed in the sand on Lotan's isle, only smaller, and bound in heavy chains. It fought in vain to burrow into the ground even now, but found only solid rock beneath the thin veneer of

337

shingle, and was yanked back always by the rough hand of its master.

Only when one of the pirate guns was cocked did Jymn manage to tear his attention from the creature and toward its keepers. Both were thick-set and stooped, their sun-browned bellies swinging past their belts even as they fought to keep the creature still. Both wore scraps of fur and layered cloth — and one wore the salt-bleached red sash that marked him as a For-Morian.

'Tsar,' blurted Jymn through chattering teeth. 'You must take me to Tsar, I've… done what he asked,' he continued, the lie coming to him unbidden.

It seemed to do the trick. The rogue with the gun sneered as he peered down the iron-sight, but the other — the For-Morian — laid his hand on the barrel, lowering it. 'Keep searching,' he grunted, handing the beast's chains to the gunman, 'I'll take this one to the captain.'

'You're a slippery one, Jymn Hatcher, I'll give you that. Resourceful. But I can't help feeling you've made rather an error in judgement, coming here.'

Tsar leaned back in his chair. The Thulhöfn house he'd claimed for his quarters was almost intact, despite signs of a fire long ago. Jymn edged nearer the brazier, fighting to hold off the shivering in case it was mistaken for fear.

'I just want to get off this island alive. I think you're my best chance.'

Tsar raised an eyebrow in mock surprise, 'not Mak?'

'The captain lied to me. Like you said, it was a long way to fall.'

The old pirate leaned in, peering at Jymn from beneath his heavy lids. 'You're forgetting I was on that crew also, lad. I'm every bit as guilty as he. Should I be expectin' your betrayal too, eh?'

'I'm forgetting nothing. This is business, pure and simple. We don't need to pretend there's any friendship involved.'

338

'Hmm.' Tsar scratched at one of the sun-pox lesions Jymn knew to be beneath his heavy furs. 'And what is it you offer, by way of this transaction then, your service?'

Jymn straightened, thrusting his jaw out and fixing Tsar with his good eye. 'The Archon is here, on Thule.'

Jymn saw Tsar's eyes blaze greedily at the mention of his old ship, but he quickly recovered himself. 'Ar, I'd guessed as much.' He offered a lazy shrug, 'You're cunning, son, but not such a liar yet as you pretend to be. I have men already searching the island.'

'She's hidden, and guarded. I can take you right to her.'

'And your crewmates?'

'Former crewmates,' insisted Jymn, 'but I've no wish to see them hurt, I ask only that you take them prisoner.'

Tsar sucked his teeth, glancing sidelong at his companions. 'And your price?'

'Food and passage south. Then freedom in warmer waters. A handful of coin when we part.'

Tsar grinned, absently tossing a tangle of bar-coin in his hand as he stood stiffly. 'The lad's cold to the bone, bring him something to wear,' he gestured at one of his lieutenants, who hurried from the room, returning with a bundle of ragged padded leathers that would have been too large even for Weylun. Tsar held out a hand to receive a faded red sash, then crossed to the brazier, laying a hand on Jymn's shoulder. 'Freedom will be yours if you choose it, lad. But for now, you'll be one of us.'

Still the accusing sun clung to the sky, and Jymn began to fear that this dreadful day would never end. Perhaps the legends were true, and the sun here would sometimes never set — perhaps he'd be forced to labour forever under the same sun that had witnessed Scup's death and everything he had done since.

But slowly the shadows lengthened, and with a heavy heart Jymn found himself trudging north, leading a band of his new

For-Morian companions. He glanced up toward the old church. Gam would have seen them, of course, that was unavoidable. Part of him longed to reach out to his friend — to explain the sour decision he'd been forced to make — but the bargain was struck now. Dwelling on it would only make it harder.

Tsar sent men ahead to search the old church, and it was found to be empty, though the pair of writhing, captive wyrms that accompanied them seemed to take a scent of fading trace from the high window. So Gam had used the radio after all, though when, and for what reason, remained a mystery.

Wrestling with his conscience, Jymn led the For-Morians to the shallow mouth of the trench that lay to the east of the church. This high up it was little more than a depression in the rocky ground, and well-hid, though the pirates quickly grew nervous as the icy walls began to rise around them and they found themselves forced to squeeze onward in single file. Fearing some trick or ambush — for surely this would have been the place to stage such a thing — they forced Jymn to lead the way, and though he never saw them, he suspected his new crewmates kept guns trained on his back, just in case.

But, though part of him almost came to believe that Caber or Slip would appear from above with bristling teck-weapons, they traversed the trench unchallenged, and soon Jymn found himself leading Tsar and the others into the highest reaches of the great ice-cave that hid the Archon.

The great ship lay in the shingle, her breast still gaping and wounded below the waterline, and the repairs still far from finished. The braziers that lined the beach had been extinguished, but the smell of woodsmoke still hung on the frosty air. The old captain seized Jymn's shoulder, signing silently for the gang to halt.

'You didn't mention the damage, boy.'

'I told you she was holed.'

'You told me she was in Cinnabar…'

'Well it wasn't *all* lies. You're joining the two facts,' Jymn smirked, 'so to speak…'

Tsar eyes narrowed, and Jymn wasn't sure if it was annoyance or admiration he read in them. The old pirate peered down at the Archonaut camp. 'You said she was guarded, is this some trick?'

'She was, I don't know what happened,' Jymn said honestly.

At a further gesture from Tsar, the For-Morians began to filter down the icy slope toward the ship, spreading out as early as the narrow path would allow, their weapons raised and sweeping the many nooks and hides offered by the cave. Jymn nearly jumped out of his skin as one of the long-guns barked — firing up at a red-green streak of feathers that shot like a rocket from among the wreckage as Puggle surged up toward the highest reaches of the cave, unhurt. Tools and tables were laid out all around, and damp wood shavings drifted about with every breath of the cold breeze. Jymn saw that the repairs had progressed a good way since he had left, but it would take many hours of work, still, before she could take to the water again.

'Still warm,' hissed a pale pirate, withdrawing his hand from one of the doused braziers. There was a chirping whistle that caught Tsar's attention, and Jymn saw one of the taller For-Morians gesturing from the far side of the cave. They had found no one. Cautiously, the pirates began to close in on the Archon, but Tsar gestured for them to stop, and seized a long gun from his closest man.

'Here — you head on inside, there's a good lad,' he whispered, pressing the rifle into Jymn's hands.

Jymn clutched clumsily at the weapon and tried to hide the panic on his face. A pair of For-Morians fidgeted uncomfortably at the suggestion, but Tsar paid them no mind, shoving Jymn on toward the ship.

The narrow boards that served as a gangway had been withdrawn, forcing Jymn to sling the gun and scramble inelegantly over the port gunwales, before raising the weapon once again. The rigging was uncannily still, and the dried-out boards creaked noisily underfoot as he crept forward. He craned his neck up to the mast-tops, hoping for some glance of Gam, but if he was there he was too well hid, or too clever to let himself be seen.

Wiping the sweat from his palms, Jymn peered down the stair

and into the dark belly of the ship. Hesitating, he changed course and headed up toward the foke. Better to be methodical — he didn't want to end up trapped. Finding the foke clear, he turned astern, and made his way carefully down the sloping deck toward the aftcastle, and the captain's quarters. He felt eyes upon him, and the hair on his neck began to bristle, but he fought the instinct to look up. If Gam *was* up there among the mast-tops, watching, Jymn would give him every chance he could to stay hidden. But if this was going to work, he needed — at the very least — to get word to the others.

He pressed on into the cover of the aftcastle. The door to the captain's quarters lay open, and inviting. He'd only been inside once, but figured there had to be writing materials. His letters were poor, and untidy, but he could at least manage— 'ach!'

There was a blur, and a thud, and suddenly Jymn found himself gasping in darkness, his rifle pressed tight against his throat, threatening to suffocate him. A hot breath was on his face, carrying with it the smell of roasted fish.

'I knew you were a traitor you little fakk!' hissed Caber. There was the sound of steel, and Jymn felt a knife pressing against his ribs. 'I ought to empty you right here…'

'Caber, no.' Slip's voice was cold and forceful. 'We can bargain. He could be leverage.'

As Jymn's eyes strained to see in the dim light, he brought their faces into some kind of focus. He had been ambushed, dragged into Weylun's workshop.

'You need to… agh… listen!' Jymn gurgled, fighting to get the words past the gun's stock at his throat.

'You need to shut it you red-cloak shit!' spat Caber.

'Cap…' Jymn wheezed, 'Cap's been caught — they all have.'

'And why weren't you caught with them, eh?' demanded Caber, leaning his full weight upon the gun.

There was a sob at the far side of the room beyond the dormant map table, and Jymn glimpsed salt-white hair shining from beneath a deep hood. Nix. He didn't want her to have to see this. He longed to sign to her, to explain himself, but found his hands held fast. He

342

choked, as his lungs burned and fought for air.

Slip laid a hand upon Caber's shoulder, and the pressure eased enough for Jymn to draw breath. 'I was…' he panted, 'I escaped…'

'You led them here, Jymn. Right to us,' said Slip, icily.

'Jymn?' boomed Tsar, from the beach, and even Caber flinched at the sound of his voice. Slip grasped the gun and pulled it clear of Jymn's throat, though the knife did not leave his ribs.

'I've found them!' called Jymn, 'bringing them out now!' Then he lowered his voice, and whispered urgently. 'You're the only chance Weylun and the others have of getting out — listen careful. Gam, wherever you are, I hope you can hear me…'

Moments later, Caber, Slip and Nix slouched out along the deck, arms raised against the threat of Jymn's rifle that prodded them on toward the waiting For-Morians. Gam cried out from the mast-top, and Jymn neatly dodged the iron hammer that came hurtling from above, raised his rifle, and fired up into the vaulting roof of the cave.

Only nothing happened. The hammer clicked, but there was no ear-splitting crack. No shot slamming into the rock ceiling.

Caber and the others turned to Jymn, who trained the useless weapon on them even as he began to back away. Uncertain, they advanced. This was not part of the plan. Everything could unravel, if…

'Hold it there, that's far enough!' growled Tsar, who had sprung nimbly up the restored gangplank and was now waving his pistol at the captives as more For-Morians joined him on deck. He swaggered over to Jymn and snatched the rifle with a chuckle, 'had to be sure you were really with us, lad, you understand.' He tossed the gun to one of his crew. 'Marley, see that it's loaded for him next time, eh.' He threw an arm lazily around Jymn's shoulder and waved the pistol vaguely up toward Gam, 'you — get yourself down from there, son, you could get hurt.'

Gam clambered down to huddle alongside Caber, Slip and Nix. 'I've taken their weapons, Captain,' said Jymn proudly, crossing his arms. The words stung even as they formed on his lips, for Nix's sobs had subsided to be replaced by white-hot fury. Now, in

343

the light of the open cave, she could read Jymn's lips once more, and know the betrayal for herself.

'Ar, but you didn't mention the fairey was still among you…' Tsar drawled, stepping closer and throwing back Nix's hood. Her accusing eyes bored into Jymn, and he found himself unable to look away, not daring to let the truth of the matter show on his face, but longing for a way to explain.

'You agreed they'd all be taken prisoner…' Jymn reminded the old pirate.

Tsar took Nix's chin in his hand. 'Aye, that I did. And she will. But this one will be *my* prisoner.' He turned upon Jymn, quenching any argument before it could form, 'It's a kindness, lad, the Church don't take kindly to the Skand's experiments, as you've no doubt learned. This one will be our ticket back into Losalfhym.' Grinning like a shark, Tsar produced a bright coin from one of the deep sleeves of his coat. It was not a coin of steel though, or even silver — but was one of the flat disks of translucent crystal, stolen from the Skand vault. Tsar saw the recognition on Jymn's face and threw him a lazy wink before tossing the precious coin into the air, and reaching out to catch it in the same hand. Only it never landed. A streak of red-green rushed between them like a comet in the gloom as Puggle snatched the glittering artefact in her talons and swept away, beating her wings hard as she soared toward the mast-top. Tsar's pistol was up again before she had even cleared the quarterdeck, and it barked without hesitation, spitting its shot into the fezzard's wing and sending her into a tumble mid-flight. She dropped below the edge of the beached ship, and Jymn held his breath, waiting for the splash as she crashed into the shallow water below, but she appeared again, limping through the air toward the dark reaches of the cave. Two more For-Morians tried their aim as she fled, but neither found their mark, and she was gone.

'Lesson one — no shiny stuff on deck,' muttered Slip, sourly.

'Bah — bastard bird,' spat Tsar, sneering after the fezzard before forcing a smile. 'But it's just a trinket. No matter, eh lad?' and he punched Jymn playfully on the shoulder. 'Now, as to the girl…' he clapped his hands together for attention, 'Oghan, Knott — take her to one of the smaller ships. And don't let any of our *clients*

344

see, or I'll have your ribs.' The summoned For-Morians lumbered onto deck, shouldering their way past the other prisoners to seize Nix by the wrists. Jymn felt his heart break as the half-baked plan began to crumble around him. *You have endangered yourself and your crew,* he thought, the words of the oath coming back to him, unbidden. Nix stared at him, her head shaking with anger, pleading for it not to be true, and he dared to make a hand sign — wracking his brain for the right movements to convey *I am pretending, this is not real* — but in the heat of the moment all he managed to form was: *I lie.*

Misunderstanding, and shaking her head in heartbroken disbelief, Nix was carried from the deck, shortly followed by the others. The carpenters and other crew who had stayed with the Archon were flushed out from below deck, rounded up, and marched from the cave. With relief Jymn watched them go, for so far nobody had noticed the powerful magnets slung around Slip's neck, the radio Gam still clutched beneath his tunic, or the hungry magflies that crawled upon Caber's furs, feasting on the powdered rust he had scattered there.

It wasn't much, but it was a chance.

XXVII

Chance

Life as a For-Morian was different to that of an Archonaut. Where Jymn had grown used to camaraderie and eventually a close bond of trust with his former crew, here it seemed a more primitive hierarchy held sway. It reminded him of the Enginers' bay, back on the Trossul, except without the constant threat of the full-growns or the Bo'sun's beater to keep them in line.

Guiltily, Jymn found himself glad of Tsar's protection. It was never explicit, of course, but simply being within an arm's length of the Rougian captain seemed to confer some kind of wardship, keeping the other pirates at bay.

But it was not to last. Tsar shocked Jymn by strolling right to one of the secret stash-lockers disguised among the aftcastle stairs and throwing it open with a lazy boot before peering inside with a sneer. Jymn shivered. It was uncanny how comfortable Tsar was on the deck of the Archon — he was a disarmingly confident adversary at the worst of times — but here he positively swaggered, thrusting his thumbs into his belt and tasting the air as if they were already under sail. As if he owned the place. Which, thanks to Jymn, was now not far from the truth.

'Right lads!' he boomed, closing the hidden locker once more, 'get her patched up, and fast — I want her ready to slip out of here on the dawn tide.' He scanned the deck for his pick of lieutenants, then jerked his thumb at the gang-plank, 'Marley, Bargun, Locke — we need to have a little chat with our friends in the mine.' With a grunt the chosen few fell in step behind their captain, and Jymn made to tag along after them, but Tsar simply held up a hand and called over his shoulder. 'Not you Jymn, too suspicious if they see you out there. 'Specially after we bring 'em the new lot. No — you're a weld-maker after all — I want you here making her ready to sail.' And without another word, Tsar strode from the deck, making for the high, icy path once again, and leaving Jymn unarmed and alone with the other For-Morians.

Bereft now of the captain's protection, Jymn found himself once again the runt of the litter, and at the mercy of the other pirates who laughed and teased him for his size and ill-fitting clothes. Interestingly, they didn't seem tempted by the obvious target — his smikken eye. In fact, it seemed such deformities and injuries were almost a badge of honour among the For-Morians, who seemed to share barely a dozen limbs between them.

Jymn was thrust into the front-line of the labour — repairing the great, gaping hole that sat below the Archon's waterline. The most senior, or perhaps simply the loudest, strongest For-Morian seemed to find great amusement in the unfinished carpentry that Slip had overseen. He had a great, forked red beard, and roared with laughter as he kicked over a table of tools and worked wood before sending for steel plate, bolts, and a weld-kit.

Sparks and wood shavings began to fly as the For-Morians set about 'fixing' the ship, which seemed to be as much about converting her to their ways as it was repairing the damage. Jymn tried not to let the horror read on his face as the few carved gunwales that remained intact were hacked away to be replaced by iron posts, scrap wire, and sharpened palisades. For-Morians laughed as the ancient woodwork was tossed into the braziers, which had been kindled into flame once again.

Jymn was forced to lead a group of For-Morians into the bowels of the Archon's hold, where they were to drag up any metals that were fit to the task of modifying the ship. The hold was taller than the higher decks, so tall that even the full-growns barely had to stoop, but the savage hole in the bow — through which a dim firelight now spilled — had flooded the space, and ruined more than half the stores. Tools and trinkets rusted in the swollen damp, and Jymn made a mental note to have it scoured clean before they sailed for warmer waters, lest they fall victim to an infestation of magflies — wooden hull, or no. The bulk of the metals of course, being of more than a little value, were kept locked in the brig — for which Jymn had no key — but the pirates' practised hands made quick work of charming the lock, and soon he found himself laden with more than his share of the bounty, unable to keep up with the other For-Morians as they climbed back toward fresh air.

A movement snagged his attention as he struggled up the stair to twodeck, and his good eye snapped toward it on instinct before his head had a chance to intervene. He froze, a chill running the full length of his spine. The galley. He had needed to prepare, to gird himself emotionally before looking upon the cramped, messy ship's kitchen again, now without its stalwart cook. Some irrational part of his mind imagined the accusing ghost of his dead friend, lingering here in the darkness to avenge itself upon Jymn, and he hesitated. But he *had* seen movement, he was sure of it, and if there was a last Archonaut still hid here, better they were found by him, than the For-Morians. Glancing up toward the topdeck stair to check he wouldn't be missed, he crept carefully across the creaking boards.

The galley was a ruin. The supplies, already low when they had reached Thule, were little more than scraps now. Empty sacks of salt-rice littered the floor, alongside the wood-shavings that seemed somehow to penetrate every inch of the vessel. There were even bones from the fat carp that swam in the frigid waters just outside the cave. Scup would never have allowed it to get so bad — the galley was chaotic, for certain — but he was fastidious about keeping it clean, ensuring none of his crewmates grew sick from his cooking. Feeling a sense of duty to his friend's memory, Jymn set down the armful of scrap metals and made to tidy away the fish bones, but jerked his hand back as a blur of red-green whipped out from beneath the countertop to snatch them first. Falling sideways in shock, it was all Jymn could do to keep from crying out.

There, hunkered in the gloom and nursing a clipped and bloodied wing, was Puggle. She dragged the precious bones back into the pile of scraps and sawdust that seemed to serve as a makeshift nest, or hide, and chirped at him defensively. Jymn marvelled at

348

the cunning creature — the For-Morians were still taking pot-shots at any sign of movement in the roof of the great cave, but they would never think to look here. Somehow, even with a wing injured by Tasr's bullet, she had slipped past them and back to the ship — through the gaping hole in the bow, perhaps.

As she fussed with the bones, dragging them deeper into her bolthole, something bright caught Jymn's eye. There, nestled among the feathers, bones, and wood shavings, was the crystal coin that Tsar had lifted from the vault. Jymn almost laughed, remembering his old tinkered eyeglass and the similar fate it had suffered, until the captain had fetched it back for him. Slowly, hardly understanding even why he did it, Jymn reached out toward the coin.

A bang on the deck above, caused him to jerk his hand back. 'Oi, Pissant!' barked one of his companions, 'if I have to come back down there you'll be welding yourself a new set of teeth.'

'Coming!' called Jymn, doing his best to throw his voice back toward the stairwell. Then he lowered his voice to a soothing whisper and held his hands toward Puggle as if to show that they were empty. 'I'm not going to hurt you, I'm a friend, remember?' and he signed the words as he spoke them — more from habit than strategy — but it seemed to work, and the old bird's hissing eased slightly. 'This here might be the only bit of treasure that's going to survive this place, we can't let them find it, okay?' and slowly, though she protested and clacked her beak, Jymn reached in and slowly withdrew the crystal coin from the nest.

When he clambered from the stair a few moments later, he was thankful for the weight of the scrap metals and the steepness of the stair, both of which provided a canny cover for the sweat that beaded his brow. But he need not have worried, he was of such insignificance to the full-grown For-Morians, not one of them noticed the disc that now nestled in his eye socket beneath the bandage, where the eyeglass once stood. His secret safe, Jymn was put to work joining great panels of scrap steel into a patchwork large enough to cover the hole where the submerged buildings had speared the ship. He worked as slow as he could, but his new crewmates were canny and bemoaned his lack of skill, making all manner of imaginative threats to encourage him. Once the task was complete he was struck about the ear and thrust aside, forced to look on with a heavy guilt in his chest as the For-Morians ground and beat the metal into shape. Where loving hands had worked to repair the damage with care, and skill, and wood, now great and savage holes were gouged into the Archon's timbers. A gang of ten men hoisted the great steel plate — offering it up to the hull — and heavy bolts were sunk deep to hold it in place. The steel was heavy and crude, but functional. There would be drag, and then rust, and then magflies, but it would keep the water out. For now at least. The ugly repair reminded Jymn of the puckered and angry scar behind Nix's ear that now hid beneath a fresh crop of salt-white hair.

Nix. Even the work and the bullying For-moriains hadn't shaken the pain from his chest — a feeling that had been lodged there ever since she looked at him with those accusing eyes. It had been dark in Weylun's workshop — too dark to sign or for her to read lips — and as soon as they had stepped out onto the deck Jymn had been forced to start playing his role again. Now through his own lack of foresight, Nix had been separated from the others and was a prisoner of the For-Morians. Jymn's plans had to change. He'd bought Weylun and the other prisoners inside the seed-vault a fighting chance at escape, but he couldn't wait for that to unfold. He needed to find Nix before it was too late.

Watching the repairs from among the overturned tables and discarded timbers, Jymn spotted something that transported him right back to that fateful day in Shoalhaven. There, blade embedded in the shingle, was a chisel. With a furtive glance over his shoulder to ensure he was not being watched, Jymn slipped the tool into his boot and stood. Confidence was key among these brash pirates. More than confidence — it was sheer bull-headed swagger. Without another word, he turned and headed for the ice-path that would lead him clear of the cave.

'Oi! Titch!' yelled the self appointed leader of the For-Morians. 'Where the Fak do you think you're off to, eh?'

Jymn had barely made it halfway across the beach. 'I need more flux for the welds,' he called over his shoulder, still walking away.

350

'Oh no you don't! Hold up!'

But though his heart raced, Jymn kept walking. He'd seen the way these pirates dealt with one another. If he let himself be bullied or bossed around it would never end. Again, the words of the Archonaut rites came back to him. *You have been told what to do, and have disobeyed.*

'Aww — Garitt, go with 'im.' growled Red-beard in resignation, 'An' keep an eye. I don't trust that little shit so far as I could throw 'im.'

Jymn wiped the sweat from his palms as the one called Garitt caught up and gave him a sharp shove in the back with the stock of his long-gun to avoid any doubt as to who was really in control here. Slightly winded, Jymn sized him up — he was a tall man, thin, but the wiry kind of thin that often seemed to mask a sinewy strength.

'Good,' shrugged Jymn, as if he was indifferent to the company. 'I'll need more weld-gas too. You can carry it.' And with Garitt in tow, he led the way slowly up the icy path toward the trench, and what was left of the daylight.

'Where is this stuff, anyway?' grumbled Garitt later as they peered above the steep walls of the trench near the abandoned church. At last the sun had grown tired, and the lands were plunged into twilight once more, the fires of Thulhöfn burning as bright as ever in the pillaged valley below. Jymn tried not to dwell on everything that had befallen him since the last sunset, when he had led the Archonauts along this very route, toward the mine.

'We hid a stash of supplies behind the church,' Jymn said, the lie coming to him easily at last. 'Come on.'

Clearing the trench, Jymn hurried to the cover of the church, skirting around the walls until he reached a great pile of rubble where part of the rear wall and roof had collapsed. It was just as he remembered it — a perfect place to bury something if you wanted to keep it hidden.

'Here. There's weld-gas there, I'll need two bottles, what with the amount of scrap your lot insist on fixing to the hull.'

'*Our* lot, you mean,' needled Garitt, but despite his words, the

351

pirate slung his long-gun across his back and crouched to lift the first stones from the pile.

Jymn crossed to the far side of the rubble, and crouched out of sight. If he crawled on his belly, he might make it part way down the slope before Garitt realised there was nothing hidden here. But it was going to be hard enough sneaking around the island *without* an angry For-Morian yelling and hunting him down. No. He had to deal with his chaperone, and quietly. Pulling the concealed chisel from his boot, he felt sweat dampen the wooden grip. Testing the edge against his thumb he found it to be honed to a near razor's edge. Silently he crept back wide around the pile of rubble, treading carefully on the rocky ground as he approached Garitt from behind. Jymn tried to calm his breathing as he pictured the blade sinking into the pirate's back, slicing through leather and muscle and sinew and biting into bone. A lump grew in his throat and threatened to choke him.

'God — how deep did you bury this shit?' called Garitt, oblivious to Jymn's true whereabouts.

Palms slick with sweat, Jymn had a change of heart. Thrusting the chisel back inside his boot, he snatched up a fist-sized rock from the many Garitt had pulled aside. Raising it high above his head, he brought it down hard on the back of the unsuspecting pirate's skull. Something must have alerted him to the danger, for at the last second Garitt turned, taking the full force of the blow across his temple before collapsing to the ground like a ragdoll.

You have done violence against your fellow man. Jymn tried to swallow but his dry tongue just rasped against the roof of his mouth.

A distant gunshot snapped him from his paralysis, and he dragged Garitt's limp body to sit slumped against the wall of the church, before hurrying to the cliff-edge to survey the town beneath him.

Oghan and Knott needed to get Nix to one of the Rougian fleet, but would surely never have dared to drag her to the main jetty. That meant using another beach, and a smaller boat. There could have been such a site near the mineshaft — but it would still have meant dragging her too close to the town and the Godsmen. That

352

only left one direction.

Hurrying along the cliffside, being careful to stay well clear of the trench, Jymn scrambled over the slush and rocks until he found a clear view of the easten shore. He'd seen a half-dozen small inlets when they had been searching for a place to hide the Archon. They had all been too exposed for a large ship, but they would be close by, and perfect for a small tender or rowboat. Darkness was descending rapidly now, and tonight there were none of the mysterious green ribbons of light to guide him. He glimpsed something. Rubbing his good eye, Jymn reached instinctively for a far-looker that wasn't there. Out there, in the shallow water, he could swear he'd seen a small light wink. There — again — there could be no mistaking it, someone was signalling from the water.

Hurrying as fast as he dared in the deepening dark, Jymn made for the shore, abandoning stealth and trusting only to his For-Morian disguise if he were spotted. He lost sight of the cove more than once, but as he drew closer he began to hear the familiar sound of a small motor running. No — not running — idling. They had reached the shore then. He had to hurry.

By the time he reached the low cliffs that led down to the rocky beach, his fears were confirmed. A lantern hung in the prow of a small inflatable boat that bobbed in the shallow water — the same boat, he realised, that they had frightened away from the Graveyard — and by the light of the swaying lantern he could see two figures struggling on the shingle, one of whom seemed to be bound. Before he even made it down to the beach, Jymn watched as the bound figure was hoisted high above her captor's head and tossed into the boat like a sack of plunder. Jymn made to call out, but managed to arrest his words before they left his mouth. After all — Nix would not be able to hear any reassurance or promise he could offer. He sprinted across the shingle, falling more than once in the dark, but had barely made it fifty feet from the cliffs before the familiar motor spluttered into action, and the lantern bobbed away across the water.

Falling to his knees, Jymn yelled at the sea — his voice a raw amalgam of anger, frustration, and bitterness. First Scup and now Nix. There were few people in his life that he had ever trusted or could truly call friends. Today he seemed cursed to let them all down. Staring hopelessly after the vanishing lantern, he wondered what fate had in store for his friend. She would be kept alive, at least, and she was too valuable for slavery. Though if she learned what they planned for her — to use her to gain access to Losalfhym once more — Jymn couldn't be sure that someone as brave and determined as Nix wouldn't take matters into their own hands.

As the rage drained slowly from him, a terrible exhaustion and despair took its place, but he couldn't stop now. Gam and the others would be imprisoned already — and with luck, would be working on a way to escape. But that was as far as his plan took him. What they were to do then felt like an impenetrable cloud in his mind, and try as he might he couldn't seem to formulate a plan that didn't fall to pieces under the lightest scrutiny. What could he do?

What would the captain do?

The thought came to him unbidden, from some part of his mind that hadn't yet processed the lies and the betrayal. The captain he'd once looked up to had been a slaver — had likely been the very one that tore him away from his home and his parents, purchasing him as little more than a baby for a handful of coin. The memory of his mother's tear-streaked face flooded his mind again, and he felt the anger wash away to be replaced by a deep and profound sorrow. He thought about Gam, and Daj. The twins. Slip. Half the crew had been slaves once, and worse besides. Even Weylun, though he was raised in luxury, had been saved from a prison ship. They'd all still be slaves too, most likely. Or dead. Jymn himself would still be on the Trossul, if it wasn't for the Archon.

There were lots of slavers in the world, and lots of slaves. But there was only one Archon. Only one place those slaves could go to be free. Cap wasn't perfect, but he was their captain, he'd made the Archon their home, and right now he was their best chance at getting off this rock alive.

Jymn forced himself to his feet, and turned back to the low cliffs that bordered the beach. Somewhere on the island, Rasmus had the captain chained up, ready to be given as an offering to their god. It was time to find him.

XXVIII

Searching

The darkness on the edge of town was almost complete — only the unceasing bonfires of Thulhöfn kept the black and the cold at bay. Though he hesitated at first, Jymn reasoned the Rougian pirates and Godsmen would be so blinded by the light of the flames that he would be almost invisible as he approached.

He studied the town, not for the first time, and again his gut told him that Cap was not there. What remained of the town's structures were now being used as drinking halls, and though they were packed with rowdy pirates, there was no sign of a formal lookout, and the buildings were far too decrepit to serve as unguarded cells. All except the seed-vault from which he'd escaped — the obvious place to take prisoners — but he felt sure Rasmus had ordered his men to *keep him separate from the others*. He could have just been kept in another cell — just like Jymn and Syrincs had been — but something about that just didn't *feel* right.

Jymn sighed in frustration. Well, if he was wrong, he just had to hope that the others would succeed in making their escape from the vault, and free Cap in the process. He had to keep searching. He'd watched the comings and goings from Thulhöfn long enough to learn all he was going to. If the captain wasn't being kept in the town, perhaps he'd been taken to one of the ships that sat at anchor in the bay.

Keeping to the shadows, Jymn skirted the edge of town and headed west toward the hill that overlooked the mine. He trusted to darkness now, and the drunkenness of the pirates, for there was little time for stealth. The For-Morians back at the Archon would surely be looking for him by now, and it was only a matter of time before they found the unconscious body of Garitt slumped against the church. Or perhaps Garitt would wake up, and raise the alarm himself.

Heart racing from the exertion of scrambling over the tall rocks that encircled the town, Jymn almost missed the dull glow of a shrouded teck-light below him, barely catching himself before he dropped down upon a hunched figure. There was a hollow thud, as something in the small clearing clattered to the ground.

'No, too big,' snarled a hushed voice, 'it'll not fit Cap'n. We'll need to find summat else.' The figure looped a small knotted measuring string and stuffed it into his pocket.

'I'll search the town,' answered the figure that hunched beneath Jymn's perch.

'And you're sure they can be trusted?' Jymn's breath caught in his throat as this third figure spoke in a familiar voice. Tsar, barely visible in the shadow of another tall rock, stepped into the dim light and crouched to whisper with the others.

'Well *trust* ain't exactly how I'd put it, Cap'n,' answered the first man. 'They're belly-full of all that pious shit, for certain. Might even believe it, some of 'em. But it's not so long ago they were slitting throats for pay, and silver still sets their eyes a'twinklin.'

Tsar grunted in acknowledgement. 'And what of the rest of it?'

'They've done most of it in, already. Trouble is them crystal coins. They've tried burning 'em, and grinding them to dust, but they're getting nowhere. Plan is now to dump them all in the deep water.'

Tsar scratched at his beard. 'How deep?'

'Deep enough. They've got enough ex-sailors among 'em to know what could be salvaged. It'll be a hundred times that deep out in the bay. That's where they'll drown the treasure, and the best of their prisoners too — Makkanok among them. Some sort of ceremony.'

'Such a waste,' muttered Tsar.

The thought of Cap sinking into the deep, black water sent a shiver down Jymn's spine, and his foot slipped its hold. Three heads snapped toward the noise as splinters of stone skittered to the ground. Jymn clamped his mouth shut, holding his breath and tensing every muscle to run. Had they seen him? He was hidden from the closest of them, but Tsar had a full view of where he'd been spying just a heartbeat before. Inch by inch, Jymn peered above the rock again, forcing his breathing back under control.

'Just a bird,' shrugged Tsar, turning back to the object that lay between them, which Jymn now realised was one of the plastic crates from the vault. From the noise it had made as it toppled over, it was empty.

'Aye, a sore waste,' sighed the nearest pirate, patting the crate. 'At least we got paid for it all the once, eh?'

There was a moment's silence before Tsar spoke again. 'They're keeping him chained up in their camp, you know.'

His companions looked at him for a moment, then to each other. 'Who?'

'Makkanok. He's up on the mountain, with the Godsmen. That's what I heard, anyway,' he shrugged.

'I suppose so…' answered the other, 'does it matter?'

'No, I s'pose not,' he sighed, and for the briefest moment Jymn thought the old pirate glanced up toward his perch again. 'Don't matter to us, does it. Right,' he clapped his hands together, 'back to the ship.'

Up on the mountain. Jymn ran the words through his mind for the hundredth time. *With the Godsmen.* He hadn't even noticed the glow of firelight above the crest of the slopes, focussed, as he was, on the town and its roaming pirates. He adjusted the chisel, digging the tip deeper into the ice as he squinted at the burning torches that worked their way up the mountain track.

His clothes were soaked with sweat and meltwater, and he'd barely made it a fifth of the way up the slope. If it hadn't been for

357

the chisel, he'd have slid back almost as far as he'd climbed. This was madness — it would be morning by the time he made it to the top this way. Unless the 'ice cats' got to him first — whatever they were.

He watched as the Pars trudging up the mountain track stopped for a breather — lowering their burden to the ground while they stretched their stooped backs. The lead par — unburdened by the chest of heretic treasure — stopped to share a joke with one of the Godsmen that guarded the pass at regular intervals. Jymn was shocked to see that the guard was armed — not with some ramshackle long-gun like the For-Morians carried — but with a real relic-weapon like the guards of Gradlon wore. He'd never seen an armed Godsman before, though he supposed a gun — though ancient — was hardly *teck*. He wondered if it worked, or if it was just for show. Not that it mattered — the track was narrow enough that he couldn't sneak past anyway — and if he was seen, he was done for. Bullets or no.

At a word from the lead Par the other clergy hoisted the heavy treasure-crate again and began trudging up the mountainside once more. A trail of fragrant smoke drifted from a censer on a heavy chain, swung by the lead Par who chanted, presumably to keep them safe from the heresies sealed within the box.

Jymn smiled, and let himself begin to slide back down the slope. He had an idea.

His back burned from the contortion, but Jymn dared not move, lest they felt his weight shift inside the crate. It had taken nearly an hour, curled up inside Tsar's empty box near the foot of the track, before a group of Godsmen — returning from the mountaintop — had groaned and grumbled, and eventually hoisted him up to begin their ascent once more.

The sounds outside were muffled through the tight seal of the box. Jymn had only been in place for ten minutes before his head began to throb and his chest ached from the effort of breathing. Two quick air-holes with the chisel-tip had solved that, but even so, he could barely make out the curse-words that punctuated the groans and panting of the chest-bearers and the constant drone of the lead Par's prayers that tried to ward away the evils that lurked within the crate.

He nearly gave himself away with a cry of pain the first time the crate was dropped, but managed to breathe through the shock long enough to realise that he was not about to tumble down the cliffside, but had simply been set down so that his bearers might take a short rest. Gradually, although these impromptu breaks continued, Jymn felt the incline of the crate begin to lessen, and even the pace begin to quicken. The last time he was dropped the landing was less violent, and indeed was followed up by a sensation of deliberate sliding, and then a gentle impact. Jymn heard — or felt, more than heard, really — footsteps retreating, and then nothing.

Somehow, in the absence of being carried, the fire in Jymn's back grew even worse, but he forced himself to wait — lying, contorted, for what felt like an hour, but must in reality have been little more than ten minutes. The air began to smell sharp and fragrant, and in the stillness his own breathing became almost deafening, but still he lay there until he was certain he was alone, before twisting the latch from within.

Slowly, Jymn raised his head to peer out of the hinged lid, and found himself staring at a muddy-white canvas, flapping gently in the wind only a few feet away. For a moment he thought he might be on a ship, except that the air was thick with curling smoke. The wind was *outside* — he was in some kind of tent. Craning his neck he saw two dozen crates — identical to his — lying in neat rows upon the canvassed floor. The space was illuminated by a brazier that burned just outside the half-open flap that must have served as the tent's entrance. Jymn flinched as a shadow passed before the flap, but it was just a censer swinging on a fine chain, filling the tent with its pungent blue protective smoke. Unsurprisingly then, the tent and the treasure were being guarded.

Slipping as quickly as he dared from the crate, Jymn flexed his stiff limbs and crept for the darkest corner of the tent. Cold air seeped in below the canvas, which seemed to be simply staked to the snowy ground. Checking over his shoulder for any intruders, he spotted a bundle of cloth on a stool just inside the flap, and hanging from it, a sleeve. Padding silently across the canvas, Jymn carefully pulled the robe over his head. It was too big by far, and Jymn winced as he saw blood spattered on the breast, but it was better than nothing. Crossing back and pressing his belly to the floor, Jymn worried the stake back and forth until it began to give way, leaving him enough slack to slide beneath the canvas into the night.

He found himself crouched in the snow, surrounded on all sides by yet more tents, pitched barely twelve inches from one another. The sky above seemed to have cleared, and once again the faint ribbons of green light cast an unearthly pallor over the snow and the canvas, interrupted by scything shafts of firelight as Godsmen carrying burning torches marched about the camp beyond the safety of Jymn's hide.

Treading as silently as the loose snow would allow, Jymn crept toward the nearest edge, fighting the urge to steady himself against the ropes or canvas — he could hear that some of the tents were occupied, and imagined the surprise a group of Godsmen would feel at seeing a hand pressed against the side of their shelter. A familiar, almost fevered muttering halted him in his tracks. It was not the voice itself that was familiar, but rather the rhythm. Someone was praying in the tent immediately to his left. Jymn crouched once more, focussing on the voices — for there seemed to be three — and trying to pick out their words.

——— *strength in the darkness, and with the coming of the day the sins of the past shall be absolved* ——— *that we offer unto your cleansing waters, that the earth might at last be purged of all wickedness and evil knowings* ——— *and so with your grace, the dawn will bring with it a new age, free of the evil that once clung to these rocks* ———

A yell behind him sent Jymn scrambling for the cover of an adjacent tent, his heart racing, but the call seemed not to have been aimed at him. Two Godsmen, one armed, were talking animatedly — clearly anxious about something. Jymn tried to calm his instant suspicion that he had been discovered. He'd remembered to close the lid of his crate after him, and where he'd left it — tucked away at the back of the tent — would ensure it wasn't the first to be carried off when the time came. And besides, although these two seemed to be looking for *something*, they weren't trying to raise any sort of alarm.

Jymn crept away to the other side of the tent-cluster. Larger tents nestled together across from him, and beyond them a fence of sorts seemed to demark the border of the camp, separating it from…

Jymn peered into the dark beyond the braziers, unsure of what he was seeing, then doubting his own eye. Huge, multifaceted domes — each the height of five men — were clustered on the slope above the camp. They were brilliant white, and from above would have been nearly invisible against the snow, but from here Jymn could make out the uncanny silhouettes of a dozen or more against the eerie green sky.

As he tried to piece together the scene, Jymn saw that the fence between the camp and the domes was no ordinary barrier — but in fact was a neat palisade of twenty or so heavy copper crosses set atop wooden staves that had been driven into the snow. He had seen similar staves carried by the clergy in Shoalhaven, brandished as if to ward off the evils of the town. Two Godsmen paced back and forth along the cross-fence, though Jymn noted they were armed only with prayers and heavy censers instead of guns. Something about those queer, angular domes seemed to make them uneasy. They made Jymn uneasy, too. The town he could understand, but his imagination baulked at the strange Skand rituals that might have taken place up here under the frozen northern sky.

His attention was snatched by movement to his right, where a figure seemed to stumble from one of the larger tents. The figure was dragged to their feet by a tall Godsman and Jymn gasped as he recognised the face of Sryincs Ren, though almost every shred of her pride and dignity was now spent. Another figure quit the tent behind the tall Godsman, stopping to massage his temples. Jymn's stomach knotted as he recognised the man that had stared him down while calmly ending Scup's life. Rasmus. If Rincs was being kept in there, perhaps there were others…

Almost as soon as the Godsmen leader was clear of the tent, the two anxious clergy Jymn had seen earlier dashed toward him, gcsturing down at the mountain track and the town below as they relayed their message. Immediately Rasmus flew into a rage like the one Jymn had witnessed back in Shoalhaven. Shoving the clergy aside he called for reinforcements, bellowing about an escape in the valley below as armed Godsmen emerged from tents or quit their patrols to join him.

Jymn's mind raced as fast as his heart. If Garitt had woken — or if he'd been found — they knew exactly who they were looking for. Jymn pulled the grubby white bandage clear of his smikken eye. His purple Archonaut's sash was matted to his face with dried blood, but he peeled it carefully away also, tucking it beneath the robe's collar. The icy air bit at the recent wound and his deformed eye began to water as he removed the crystal coin from his socket, stuffing it into his leathers. He shouldn't be so recognisable now, at least from a distance. Pulling the hood of the robe low, he prayed silently for luck and stepped from the cover of the tents, trying to lose himself in the chaos of clergy running back and forth to arm themselves for the hunt.

He was a foot shorter than the full-growns that ran past him, and he had to hike the hem of the robe up to keep it from tripping him in the snow, but he didn't have to go far. Rushing across the flow of traffic, bent low, he made for the large tent where Rincs and Rasmus had been. If he could just free Cap, he would know what to do. He would make some deal, or have some plan for their escape.

But as he burst through the flap and lowered his hood, he quickly realised that the captain was not here, nor *any* prisoners. The space was filled with glass cylinders, beaten copper worktops, and an array of arcane equipment Jymn recognised from Rincs' home back in Shoalhaven. Vials of blood littered the worktop, along with fine glass slides, each bearing a hastily scribbled label.

Hurried footsteps sent him scurrying for the meagre cover afforded by Rincs' equipment. An armed Godsman charged into the tent, cast around quickly, then — clearly not finding what, or who, he was looking for — turned to leave. He halted in the entrance, framed by the light of a brazier, as another Par nearly ran into him.

'He's not here,' snapped the first, as the second Par tried to peer over his shoulder, 'must've gone with the others to the track.'

'What's this about, anyway?' panted the other, who Jymn now realised was still pulling on his robes.

'Some problem at the vault — escape I think, come on,'

And then they were gone. Jymn stared after them as they disappeared into the cold. The vault? Then it wasn't Garitt *or* the other For-Morians. It wasn't *him* they were after at all, but the crew.

Making his mind up, Jymn hurried from the tent and cast about for options. Some way to confuse or distract the clergy, to buy his friends a chance. Striding back to the brazier that stood watch over the entrance to the tent he raised his leg and kicked hard, toppling it and sending a wave of burning wood and hot coals spilling over the canvas and into the tent. Immediately, flames began to lick up the sides, threatening to leap to the adjacent shelter.

'Oi!' snarled a coarse voice, and Jymn whirled around on instinct even as his mind shouted at him to turn away.

A gang of three Godsmen had halted in their tracks, looking from Jymn to the fire and back. Time seemed to slow down as Jymn saw realisation dawn, then weapons begin to rise.

You have rushed into danger without thinking.

He ran. By the time the guns spoke he was beyond the pillar of flame that spiralled from the tent. He heard the air hiss as bullets cut through the cold and the heat, though his heartbeat threatened to drown the sound. Cries went up all around the camp, and Jymn saw Godsmen halting at the track, turning to see what was happening. He doubled back, trying to confuse his pursuers, but tripped on the robe just as more bullets hissed overhead. Tearing the robe free, he sprinted on in a blind panic, his feet churning at the deepening snow beyond the camp. Chancing a look backward he glimpsed a host of the Godsmen taking up the pursuit like dogs scenting some prey.

And prey is what he was. More than once he threw himself to the ground as the snow around him exploded with the impact of their near-misses. It was only a matter of time before one of their

363

bullets found its mark. Changing tack, Jymn darted uphill toward the crude fence of copper crosses. The Godsmen patrolling the border saw him coming of course, but they were unarmed, and his new course forced his pursuers to quit firing, or risk hitting one of their own.

The three Godsmen ahead dropped their censers and spread themselves wide to try and intercept him, but they placed too much faith in their fence. It might protect the camp from the evils of the Skand teck, but it could not stop an Archonaut at full sprint. They seemed to realise his plan as he accelerated towards the neat row of staves, but too late. Dropping his shoulder, Jymn threw his weight against the nearest staff, crashing into a roll as it gave way, the heavy copper cross cutting deep into the snow.

Dragging himself to his feet, Jymn sprinted onward beyond the fence, his lungs burning as if he'd inhaled some of the fire that now threatened to engulf half of the church camp. Bullets began to thud into the snow again, and slam against the huge polyhedral domes ahead. Pain exploded in his calf, and he was thrown forward by his own momentum. Blood was in the snow, but they were closing in. There was no time to inspect the wound. Screaming in pain, Jymn limped to his feet, but each step gradually numbed the pain as he surged for the cover of the Skand structures. Dragging himself behind the nearest dome, he cursed as he saw the trail of spotted blood he'd left, clear as day against the virgin snow. Pulling the purple sash from his neck he bound it around the gash in his calf, gritting his teeth against the pain as more bullets rattled against the dome at his back.

This close, he could see short walls supporting each of the huge spheres, though the squat buildings were more than half buried in snow drift. Keeping the dome between himself and his pursuers, he pushed on, limping toward the cover of another, and then a third, as cries echoed among the hunters behind him.

Here, among the domes, the snow drift was less aggressive, and Jymn began to see straight runs of brickwork connecting one to another. And there — just peeking above the snow line — a narrow window.

Kicking hard with his uninjured foot, Jymn broke the ancient

364

glass, pounding at the snow and the frame to dislodge the larger shards and widen the hole, before thrusting both legs into the darkness beyond.

Dropping awkwardly to his feet, he heard the echo of his landing rebound down a long, dark corridor. As he slumped against the wall to catch his breath, his eyes began to adjust to a darkness now interrupted by the eerie green glow from the window.

The walls peeled with ancient paint and long forgotten papers. But ahead of him was some sort of sign — an emblem set above bold lettering. His reading was slow and awkward, but it didn't take him long to piece together the word.

E.I.S.C.A.T

XXIX

The Ice Cat

A solitary gunshot rang out above, and Jymn heard the gunman admonished with a growl. They were hunting him, and it was only a matter of time before the trail of blood and the broken glass gave him away.

Heaving himself from the wall, he shuffled deeper into the darkness. His leg protested angrily as he tried to bear weight on it and soon a dull throb felt like it threatened to overwhelm him. Fighting down nausea, he traced the nearest wall to keep him steady in the gloom. He would have been utterly blind, but a handful of other windows that must have been only barely covered by the snow permitted a ghostly green murk to seep into the corridor. His ears strained for any sound of pursuit as he stumbled down the corridor, but his mind echoed loudly with the memory of Loken's sing-song voice:

The Ice Cat roams atop the hill,
in search of blue-eyed young to kill.

'Hey - in here!' A husky call reverberated down the tunnel behind him, chased by sounds of effort and tinkling glass. Despite the cold, Jymn began to sweat. He would never outrun them with the gash in his leg, and if they had lights they wouldn't even *need* to catch him — they could just see him limping away and open fire. And even if they didn't, this building couldn't go on forever, and he'd run out of places to go. He had to hide, or get out.

Darting left at a junction that marked the end of the corridor, he found himself confronted with an even deeper blackness, but pressed on in hope of finding cover. Hands tracing the wall, he felt ancient paper that crumbled under his touch, pipes, brickwork, switches that he dared not press, a handle.

A handle!

Bringing both hands to bear, Jymn traced the outline of a strong metal door, cold to the touch. Testing his weight against the handle he found that it moved easily, but the door was stuck fast, resisting his efforts. Footsteps echoed down the corridor, and Jymn pulled harder. The door groaned, budging barely half an inch, and abruptly the footsteps stopped, hushed by an urgent shushing. There were shadows moving at the junction. Panic building in his chest, Jymn put his injured leg against the wall and heaved, throwing his full weight into the handle.

With an almighty whine of rusted metal, the door swung open far enough for Jymn to slip inside and pull it shut again with a bang that he heard repeated a dozen times as it rebounded down the corridor. Footsteps hurried nearer, and Jymn fumbled desperately for a lock to keep his pursuers at bay - his hands finding a lever in the dark.

As he threw the lever downward an intense pain blinded him, and he clamped his eyes shut as lights flickered on and off like a silent thunderstom, ignited by some ancient store of power. Inching his eyelids open he saw rust fall from the doorframe as fists banged furiously against it from outside. The handle moved. Spotting a long deadbolt at the foot of the door, Jymn lunged for it, stamping the seized metal into place with his boot just in the nick of time — for once again the handle clicked and Jymn could hear his pursuers trying their weight against it, just as he had.

Taking deep breaths to calm his thundering heart, Jymn sagged against the wall and squinted as his eyes adjusted to the blinding light, which had stabilised now into a constant, humming glow. He found himself in a small room — perhaps twenty feet on a side — and had to fight down a wave of panic as he realised there was no door but the one he had used. Though it was narrow, the room was immensely tall, and as he looked up, Jymn realised he had found his way *within* one of the huge, angular domes that littered the mountainside. And he saw at last what the domes concealed. Towering over him, dominating the space, was an immense dish angled to point toward the heavens. Once white, it was now streaked with rust and peeling paint, and was supported on a great mechanical pedestal as wide as the ship's mast.

But the dish offered no escape. More voices joined his pursuers outside the door, and a great hammering was taking place, as if with tools or the stocks of their long-guns. Limping desperately around the room, Jymn hunted for some way out — perhaps a window, a hatch, or even a vent. But there was nothing — just ancient cables and wires and dormant teck cluttered on worktops.

It was over. It was only a matter of time before they forced the door. The best he could hope for was that they took him prisoner instead of shooting him on sight. Sliding to the floor with his back against the wall, Jymn succumbed to trembling, unable to pretend any longer that it was due to the cold. He thought of his friends — of Weylun, Gam, and the twins — trapped in the seed vault, or captured trying to escape. Cap waiting to be drowned at the hands of the church. And Nix, locked away on one of Tsar's ships to be used as a hostage against her own people. He wished more than anything that he could reach her somehow and explain his deception, but it was hopeless.

Isn't that the only time hope really counts? Keeping it alive, when there is no logic, or reasoning left?

Rinc's words came back to him, bitter in his mind. They'd come all this way, suffered so much loss, Scup had given his *life* — and for what? To fail to protect some ancient knowledge? Knowledge that — despite their best efforts — would now be lost to mankind a click under the sea. He pulled the stolen crystal coin from his leathers and turned it over in his hands.

You have stolen, and profited from that stealing.

He wondered what secrets the coin held that would now never be learned. He remembered the cascading lines of code Weylun had conjured from one of the coins, back in the vault. Perhaps he could at least hide the coin before he was taken. Amongst all this loss, even if it was only this one coin that survived — like that one seed that sprouted — it would mean Scup hadn't died for nothing. This hadn't all been for nothing.

Heaving himself to his feet once more, Jymn staggered to the worktop, looking for some nook among the ancient machines to stash the coin, that it might escape the efforts of his captors. But all the teck here would likely be burned. Especially now that it had been powered up by whatever ancient store of energy survived here. The teck blinked with occasional pin pricks of light, and Jymn was surprised to note that he hadn't even *considered* the unshielded trace that he would have unleashed by awakening such machinery. The vault at least had been underground, but this place would be like a beacon to any Raption for a thousand clicks.

He glanced up.

The idea struck him with the force of a physical blow, and he froze in place as his mind charged through the implications, grasping at the half-guesses and intuitions that he'd need to repy upon if this were to work.

An ear-splitting bang shook him into action. They were shooting at the door now, there wasn't much time. Hunting frantically among the teck, he found what he was looking for: a narrow green slot, like the one Weylun had used.

Slamming the crystal coin into the slot with trembling fingers, Jymn shivered with equal parts excitement and fear. Again, arcane lines of code spilled down the screen, glyphs falling like rain upon the glassy display. Squinting with his good eye, Jymn peered at the grubby buttons in front of him, trying to make out their meaning as he spelled out the words on each key.

Con-trol; ax-is fix; Aux gain;

None of it meant anything to him. He pushed a couple of keys at random, some eliciting chirps and whines from the other machines, or the thick pedestal behind him. More gunshots thundered against the door and Jymn ducked instinctively. Dirt. Some of the keys were grubbier than others - some clearly worn and well-used. Stabbing at these cleaner keys summoned a great groan from the pedestal behind him, and a hail of rusty debris shook from the great dish as it began to turn upon its axis, tilting slowly further up toward the sky. The cables that climbed the pedestal like vines began to crackle and hiss with energy, but still Jymn's shaking fingers punched and prodded at the keys. With frightening speed the dish whipped around to face a new target, colliding with a section of the dome that had buckled inwards and tearing away three of the flat panels that made up its surface. Cold wind screamed in through the holed dome, but still the dish swivelled, beginning a new slow orbit on its new heading.

There were cries and whoops from his pursuers, who had weakened the hinges sufficiently to force their hands between the frame and the door. It was only a matter of time before they found the latch. Still the code stared blankly at him from the screen. Had it worked? Had he managed to turn the contents of the disk into trace, and set it free, far from the island?

Squinting desperately at the keys for some clue, his eyes snagged on a pair of letters: *TX*. The same letters he'd seen on the satellite core. TX-RX. *Tranceiver*, Node had called it.

He punched the key and again the thick cables hissed and crackled with energy. Another bang from the door sent him spinning around to face his attackers, who had nearly forced the door from its hinges, and could clearly see him through the widening gap. Pulling the coin from the slot, Jymn leapt for the pedestal and began to climb. His hands burned from the heat of the straining motors, but up and up he climbed, catching the frame of the spinning dish as it swept past. Bullets sparked and grazed the metalwork as he clung on for dear life, scrambling higher and higher until — drawing level with the jagged hole that had been torn in the dome — he flung himself clumsily into the cold night once more.

His sash snagged on the rent panels, and he tumbled inelegantly from the dome, crashing to the ground in a fall that would have broken his back were it not for the deep snow that had drifted against the side of the building. He lay for a moment, half expecting to find himself staring down at his own body, but soon heard cries of rage through the thin panels of the dome. There was a crack, and a deep groan, and the bright teck-light that poured from the hole winked out. They had cut the power.

Struggling to his feet, Jymn forced himself to keep moving. There would be no concealing his trail in such deep snow, he just had to get away before they found their way back out.

Stumbling in the deep drift, his clothes choked with snow, he pressed on, the wound in his calf all but forgotten. He dared not head back toward the camp, nor any higher into the frigid mountains. He considered slipping back into the shelter of the Eiscat, but before he could orient himself a great cry went up to the north, and he saw silhouettes pointing and running. Ahead of the group, three pirates struggled with the writhing metal wyrmlings that now heaved and strained against their chains in pursuit of the trace. Pirates. Maybe For-Morians. Perhaps he could appeal to Tsar's justice? But then answering cries echoed from behind him, and Jymn saw the godsmen pouring like ants through a fresh hole in the base of the dome.

All thought of surrender left him, and he charged blindly into the night, his legs and lungs burning with the effort of traversing the snow. His mind was numb, his plans spent. All that was left now was to run, to keep running until he could run no longer, and the guns behind found him. Bullets hissed overhead at first, but the snow drift fell like sand dunes across the mountainside, and afforded little view ahead or behind. But he could hear them closing in, pirates and Godsmen tightening like a noose that would engulf him. Stumbling on leaden limbs at the top of a dune, he half-slid, half-tumbled to its foot, where the snow beneath him creaked and gave way. Grasping desperately for a handhold, Jymn narrowly avoided being swept away with the vanishing snow which fell away to reveal a sheer cliff, many hundreds of feet above the rocky water.

Clawing his way from the edge one terrifying inch at a time, Jymn pulled himself to his knees in time to see his pursuers begin to appear along the ridge where he had stumbled. He hung his head, his heart hammering uselessly to deliver blood that would soon be spilled to the snow. Their weapons rose, and any hope of a merciful capture evaporated. He struggled to stand, to face them head-on, that he might at least die on his feet.

He squeezed his eyes shut, anticipating the impact of the bullet

371

that would end it all. He pictured his body falling from the cliff into the rocky water below, wondering idly if his mind would cling on to consciousness long enough to expereince the terror of the fall.

He remembered the terror of being thrown from the cliff by Daj and the captain. The panic, and then the relief as his bonds began to slip away in the water. He wondered if dying would be like that too — as if the bonds of material life would slip away like Par Carrek used to talk about. Anger surged in him then. Some deep, primal part of him that railed at the idea of death and the void that would follow, and would clutch at any chance to live. Any hope, no matter how small, was better than doing nothing. *That's* what Rincs had talked about. *That's* what his parents had gambled on.

Jymn's eyes flew open as his captors squeezed their triggers, and he jumped.

XXX

The Dawn Tide, II

Jymn woke to the sound of gulls. He blinked the sleep from his eyes and tried to focus on the movement above him. High in the rigging their flag billowed in a dawn breeze that carried with it the sound of singing. Sunlight spilled almost horizontally across the deck beneath him, and he saw the captain's face, tired and bloodied, but smiling at him all the same as he stirred.

'Are we… is it over?' Jymn mumbled, his mind foggy as he tried and failed to remember how he'd ended up back on the ship.

'I'm afraid so,' winced the captain. Like Jymn he was horizontal, and Jymn wondered if he too had been asleep out here on the cold deck. It *was* cold — freezing in fact — and Jymn realised with a shiver that he was wet through. A brazier crackled nearby, the air around it hazy with heat. He tried to sit, and found that his hands were bound at the wrist. Confused, he turned to Cap and saw that he also was bound — at wrist and ankle — and was inching quietly closer. Links of heavy iron chain were lashed to his bindings.

'You led them on a merry chase, Jymn, nearly had 'em too,' Cap smiled sadly, 'you did well.'

Realisation began to burn off the fog in his mind, and he looked up at the flag once more. It wasn't *theirs* at all, but the red grasping fist of the For-More. And the song, it wasn't the rolling rhythm of a sailor's tune — not a *song* at all really, more of a chant. Scanning the deck, Jymn felt panic rise in his throat as he saw the rough cream robes of Godsmen crowding the gunwales, their hands raised toward the dawn. Red-sashed pirates moved about here and

373

there, but there was none of the urgency that accompanied sailing, and Jymn saw that they were at anchor. Forcing himself to his elbows he craned his aching neck to scan the horizon. The rest of the fleet were anchored close by, but they were easily a click clear of the Thulian coast.

'Take it easy, Jymn, that was a big fall you had.'

And then it all came back like an avalanche. Leading Tsar to the Archon, holed and beached in the ice-cave. Hitting Garitt with the rock. Kicking over the brazier in the church camp. The Ice Cat. His leap from the clifftop into the rocky water.

The chanting reached a throbbing pitch before ending abruptly, giving way to a pregnant, expectant silence. Jymn felt himself flush hot with anger as he saw Rasmus climb a crude scaffold that had been erected over the water, raising his hands to hush the whispers that rippled through the crowd.

Jymn took some small pleasure in noting that the immaculate Par's robes were now soiled with soot, dirt, and even blood. His hands clasped together in prayer as he looked out over the water, and Jymn saw other Godsmen climbing the scaffold, straining under the weight of the plastic crates from the vault.

Jymn made to check for the hard disk of crystal tucked into his tunic, but his wrists were tethered to his bound ankles, and he could not reach. As he remembered his broadcast from the Ice Cat, his head snapped to the sky, seeking out the sun. It was low. But it was *always* low.

'How long has it been?' he asked urgently of the captain, 'since the fall?'

'You were floating a while — your For-Morian leathers saw to that — but they fished you out soon enough.'

'They aren't... that was just...'

But before he could explain his ruse there was a splash, and a cheer went up among the assembled crowd. Jymn craned his neck to see the celebration ripple across the decks of the other ships arrayed nearby, where more of the chests were tossed into the water. Rasmus called out, righteous anger burning in his voice. 'Through the deceit and cleverness of wicked men, Lord, these heresies were hid from you! But we return them now to the depths of your holy flood, that was sent to cleanse mankind.' There was another splash, and Jymn saw the next crate tumble from the scaffold, coins spilling to the waves.

'How long was I out?' Jymn persisted.

The captain furrowed his brow, 'six hours, maybe seven. Hard to keep track of time here.'

Another cheer. Jymn made the calculation in his mind — or tried to at least — for there were too many unknowns. But it would be close.

'We need to get off the ship,' he hissed in a low voice.

'They have fifty vessels out here, Jymn. The shore is a mile away, the water's near freezing, and we're bound and weighted.'

'We've had worse odds,' said Jymn, pointedly.

That made the captain chuckle, and he rolled awkwardly to one side 'Can you reach my pocket?'

Jymn twisted and strained against his bonds, eventually managing to withdraw what turned out to be a finger's length of lix-infused medicable.

'Rincs gave it to me to dull the pain. There's enough there — if you can swallow it — to knock you out before they get round to you.'

It took a moment for his meaning to register in Jymn's mind. 'No — listen. The code from the vault, I sent it out. I found the Ice Cat, and sent the code like a… like a signal.'

The captain managed a weak smile. 'That was smart, Jymn. Well done. Perhaps someone, somewhere heard it. You might just have saved some of the knowledge after all.'

'No, that's not what —' but the captain's eyes shifted past Jymn's and he silenced him with a look.

A boot prodded Jymn roughly in the ribs, and a hulking figure stepped over them, crouching down to check Cap's bonds.

'Right, you listen quick and careful, like,' whispered Tsar, his lips barely moving. 'It'll be your time soon. You'll have one chance to confess your evils and ask for forgiveness. *Take it*. They'll flog you, and put you on one of their stinking workships, but you'll *live.*'

'I'd rather drown,' growled the captain through gritted teeth.

'Aye, that's the alternative, lad!' snapped Tsar, as he dragged Cap upright.

'We need to get off the ship!' hissed Jymn once more, but the captain just forced a smile.

'All we've got left is our dignity, Jymn. Don't let them take that too.'

Jymn nodded in numb acknowledgement of the order, and their eyes lingered upon each other for a moment, but a heartbeat later the captain was dragged toward the baying crowd.

Jymn glanced at the medicable in his hand. Cap wasn't wrong, Jymn could barely swim at the best of times — even if he *could* get off the ship in time he'd likely drown or be shot before making it to shore. And if he even *did* make it to shore, what then? But he could have given up in the vault, and then he wouldn't have found the Ice Cat. He could have given up on the clifftop, and he'd already be dead. He wasn't going to take the easy way out now, not after everything he'd been through. Drawing his knees up to his chest, he tucked the medicable into his boot, hesitating as he found something already there, something hard pressed painfully against his injured calf. The chisel.

Glancing around to find every eye fixated on the captain's slow march to the scaffold, Jymn withdrew the tool, clamped it between his knees, and began to work at the thick ropes that bound his hands.

There were boos and jeers as Tsar shoved the captain forward to stumble upon the high platform where Rasmus towered over him imperiously, raising his hands to the sky.

'Lord, accept our offering of this sinner, whose own blood is a blasphemy against the greatness of your creation. May the world without him be closer to your paradise, and every man that lives within it be a reflection of your image.'

Cap was hauled to his feet and manhandled toward the edge of the platform. A rope affixed to his bonds was thrown over a spar above the scaffold, and groans of excited pleasure shot through the crowd as he was kicked backwards, falling two feet to dangle from his wrists over the icy water, the weighted chain at his ankles swinging like a pendulum.

Tearing his eyes from the scene, Jymn sawed faster, splitting fibre after fibre from the rope that tied his hands.

'You are charged with the sins of piracy, and murder, and the trafficking of stolen children. And of using heretical tecks to pervert the divinity of your mortal being…'

'I was born like this, you idiot,' growled Cap, as he dangled. 'Nobody would choose this.'

'…and harbouring those like you,' Rasmus pressed on, 'whose very blood is a sin against God. Do you repent?'

Silence.

Jymn could look away no more. Looking up, he saw Cap swinging by his wrists, eyes closed almost peacefully. Slowly they opened, and his gaze swept the crowd, searching past the assembled Pars and coming to rest on Jymn. Sadness crossed his face then, tinged with frustration, and he set his teeth.

'Then it is for the Lord to judge you,' announced Rasmus, accepting a long blade that was offered hilt-first by one of his attendant Pars and marching to the taut rope from which the captain hung. Unable to watch, Jymn squeezed his eyes shut as Rasmus raised the blade high.

'Wait!'

There were gasps from the crowd as Cap spoke, and Jymn's eyes flew open to see the blade's savage cut halted inches from the rope. Rasmus raised his chin haughtily.

'You wish to repent to your God?'

Cap's head hung in resignation, and he managed a feeble nod, as murmured glee spread through the crowd, punctuated by occasional taunting jeers. Rasmus turned to Tsar, who still stood atop the platform, looking uncomfortable with his wide hat clutched to his chest.

'You see captain, the boy *is* capable of contrition after all,' he purred, barely managing to contain his self-satisfaction. He strutted along the platform, clearly playing to the crowd. 'Now repeat after me: I have sinned, father, and I beg your mercy.'

'I have sinned, father. I ask for mercy,' spat Cap.

'*Beg,*' corrected Rasmus gently, 'you *beg* for mercy…' and, with a wave of his hand, demanded repetition.

Cap swallowed. 'I beg your mercy.'

'Very good. Now: I have corrupted my flesh, in a mockery of eternal life.'

'I have corrupted my flesh, in a mockery of eternal life,' the captain echoed. There were jeers from the crowd, and triumphant booing.

'I renounce my wicked ways, and the ways of all those whom I have led to sin.'

His bonds forgotten, Jymn watched with horror as the captain's jaw worked back and forth. It was as though he had to force the words from his mouth, spitting them like broken teeth. He caught Jymn's eye and hastily looked away in shame.

'I renounce my wicked ways, and the ways of all those whom I have led to sin.' The words came quickly, as if they might occupy a smaller fraction of his memory that way.

Rasmus turned to the crowd and spread his hands wide in a gesture of humility that was merely a shallow veneer over his gloating triumph.

'I have rushed into danger without thinking,' continued the captain, the confession pouring from him now. 'I have stolen, and profited from that stealing.' Rasmus turned, smiling at his capitulating adversary.

But the words were not a capitulation, they were defiance. A defiance only Jymn could know.

The captain was buying him time.

Attacking the ropes with renewed vigour, Jymn hacked and sawed as if his life might be counted in minutes, seconds. The ropes at his wrists burst under the renewed onslaught and suddenly his hands were free. Grasping the blade, he upended it and set to work on the cord that bound his ankles together.

'I have done violence against my fellow man,' cried the captain, 'I have endangered myself and my crew,' and for a moment the remorse in his voice sounded utterly genuine.

The rope between Jymn's ankles split, and abandoning stealth he pounced for the line that secured the heavy links of iron chain to his feet.

'I have been told what to do,' growled the captain, defiance surging back into his voice, 'again, and again by men like you.' Rasmus turned from the now silent, confused crowd to face him, victory suddenly uncertain. The captain raised his chin and spat. 'And I have disobeyed.'

'Hey!' yelled an accusing voice from among the crowd, and Jymn saw a handful of faces whip round toward him. And then a dozen things happened, all at once.

Forgetting the rope, Jymn snatched up the heavy knotted chain that was still bound to his leg and ran, toppling the crackling brazier across the deck as he went.

Rasmus, realising the deception, roared in self-righteous fury and lashed out with the blade, severing the taut rope that still suspended the captain above the water.

The captain — iron weight still affixed to his feet — plunged into the icy water with a splash, but just as flames sprung up between them igniting tarred rope and canvas, Jymn glimpsed Tsar barrelling forward, throwing his great coat aside as he dived head first from the platform.

Charging toward the bow, Jymn clutched the awkward weight beneath one arm, fending off confused Godsmen with the chisel as he went, though a great press off them followed on behind.

Smoke stung his bare, smikken eye, and his injured calf screamed in pain, but still Jymn fled. He had to get clear of the ship before it was too late — though if he didn't deal with the chain, he was as good as dead either way.

The Godsmen rallied and began to head him off, trapping him at the bow of the great ship, with nowhere to run. Rasmus, puce-faced and spitting with rage, shoved his way to the front of the press of Godsmen, still wielding the blade that had sent Cap to the depths.

Scrambling ever backward and away, Jymn clambered inelegantly over the iron gunwale, and began to crawl along the narrow bowsprit that jutted from the For-More's deck and out above the water.

But before he drew clear of reach Rasmus was after him, and lunged wildly for the iron weight, slapping it clear of the bowsprit. Only desperate instinct saved Jymn from falling then, and he threw his arms around the narrow spar just as the weight of knotted chain yanked him down toward his death. He cried out as the effort of clinging on slipped the chisel from his grasp, sending it to plunge blade first into the water below — and with it, all hope of releasing himself from the weight.

Rasmus climbed the gunwale now, blade still in hand. He seemed to sense Jymn's first instinct, and smiled cruelly as he tossed the weapon back to the deck, before stepping on to the bowsprit.

Hand over hand, Jymn began to inch backward and away, the weight penduluming below him.

'It is over, child. Hopeless. Your captain is drowned, and your precious knowledge along with him.'

Running out of bowsprit, Jymn gritted his teeth and, summoning one last morsel of strength, heaved himself upward, struggling to a nervous crouch upon the very tip of the spar.

'Not all of it. There was a piece that escaped you. Your crusade has failed.' Jymn called, scanning the horizon for any sign of hope. There — beyond the ring of ships — the water seemed to swell.

But Rasmus just laughed. 'Ah, your little broadcast? Yes I heard about that. Quite fitting really, don't you think?' he bared his teeth. 'The last echo of your sad efforts — fading into the heavens for only the Lord to hear.'

There were distant shouts of alarm, and even Rasmus looked nervously toward the water between the ships, which seemed now to boil and churn.

'It's not him I'd be worried about...' cried Jymn, thrusting his hand into his leathers and tossing the hidden crystal coin out over the water.

But it never landed.

For right at that instant, the surface of the water erupted, spouting vertically upward to snatch the coin from the air, and tearing half the bow from the ship with the force of its onslaught. Jymn's outstretched hand was ripped from his arm, and even as he cried out and clutched the bloody stump to his chest, the bowsprit — now little more than splinters — collapsed beneath him into the water.

His plan had worked. Lotan, mightiest of all Raptions, had come for the code.

As Jymn slipped beneath the surface, the chaos of the scene slowed and was silenced. The water above was already littered with wreckage, and with sailors leaping from the damaged and burning ship. But what held Jymn's rapt attention was the enormous metal body, coiling and sliding through the water as if it were flying. The icy water in his wake glittered with crystal coins, as if he was some great serpent, shedding scales as he writhed and danced beneath the fleet, occasionally surging upward to tear a ship cleanly in two.

The chains about Jymn's feet were entangled with timber from the bowsprit, but their weight won out nonetheless, slowly pulling him ever deeper into the dark and cold. Jymn felt an uncanny peace settle over him as the world above receded. Whether through shock, or the icy water, the pain of his severed hand was now barely more than a dull memory, and his blood flowed freely into the water, trailing dark ribbons of red against the white-blue from above. His lungs, which at first had burned in the demand of air, seemed to have accepted their fate, and slowly the edges of his vision began to darken, leaving only the bright salt-white ahead. He imagined some sort of water spirit, coming to collect his soul from the depths. The white flowed and moved against the red of his blood, slipping through the water almost as effortlessly as the serpent had done.

It was only when the spirit grabbed his arm, and he felt the warm touch of a human hand, that the tranquillity was shattered, and his instinct to survive came roaring back with the force of a stormcloud. The fire in his lungs reignited, and his eyes bulged at the white figure as it produced a knife and severed the rope at his ankle. And then Nix was kicking up desperately for the surface,

381

all elegance abandoned in favour of raw power. And Jymn kicked too, his head swimming with the effort, and together they began to claw back toward the light.

As they broke the surface and the water drained from Jymn's ears, the cacophony of the chaos and panic erupted again. Screams and pleading, and splashing, and gunfire. Jymn drew such a lungful of air that he thought his chest might burst, and suddenly hands were upon him, grasping and pulling him upward into a small, inflatable boat.

As he lay, chest heaving, legs still dangling over the patched rubber, Nix sprung aboard and tweaked the engine, carrying them away. Head lolling to one side he saw Oghan and Knott — bound and gagged — lying in the shallow slough of water that had pooled in the belly of the boat, now mixed with the blood that pulsed from his severed wrist. There was a ripping sound, and many hands grasped his arm, binding the wound tightly with wet purple cloth.

Turning his head, Jymn saw two figures sitting across the bow of the small boat. Tsar, bedraggled by water and missing his hat and coat, and Cap, his attention toward Jymn's wound broken only briefly as he pulled the medicable from Jymn's boot and handed it to him with a smile.

There was a crack, and a high-pitched whine from the engine as a gunshot found its mark. Cap gestured at Nix and clambered for the back of the small boat, taking the tiller as the motor began to belch black smoke. Nix took his place, and crouched next to Jymn, her attention on the wound.

His signing was clumsy and awkward with only one hand, but he managed: *you came back.*

She smiled, and simply made his name-sign. *Boy who helps.*

Tsar cried out in alarm as another wayward bullet hissed past them, and Jymn struggled to pull his feet into the boat and sit. The scene all around them was like something out of Par Carrek's oldest stories. The Rougian fleet was in tatters. Half the ships had already been torn in two by the serpent — men clinging desperately to the floating remnants of their hulls — while Godsmen and pirates on the remaining vessels emptied chests of the glittering coins overboard as if to placate the beast. It didn't work. Lotan came for them all the same, swallowing up the precious code in the same titanic motion that splintered wood and rent steel, sending the ships rolling and plunging beneath the waves.

They made it a good distance before the motor coughed, sputtered and finally died, leaving them drifting helpless on the water, with no oar or paddle to propel them. They were beyond the risk of gunshot now, or of pirates and godsmen seeking to seize the small boat, but were still the best part of a mile from shore.

At the mercy of the tide, they watched helplessly as the last of the ships was broken asunder by Lotan, his great metal body rising from the water like the fist of some angry sea-god. Jymn felt the weight of his actions threaten to crush him then, as the cries of desperate sailors drifted on the cold wind. He hadn't meant for it to be like this. He'd hoped simply to preserve the code, to thwart the Godsmen. But part of him always knew — from the moment he transmitted the contents of his coin toward the satellites that hurtled through the heavens — that the fury of Lotan would be swift and terrible.

Nix clutched his arm, and Jymn turned to see the waters behind them begin to swell and boil. Slowly Lotan's mighty head rose from the water toward the clear sky, then craned down over them, the red-lit lenses of his eyes whirring and focussing on the small boat.

Oghan and Knott whimpered like kicked dogs, and even Tsar cowered under the mechanical stare that radiated its inhuman intelligence, but Jymn, still weak from blood loss, carefully stood and moved toward the prow. Lightheaded, he reached slowly beneath his tunic with his remaining hand, and once more produced the enchanted compass that had led them here. Again the lenses whirred, and Lotan seemed to hesitate as he recognised the gift. A familiar deep, metallic rumbling sounded from within the half-submerged bulk of the serpent, and he spoke with the same distant, artificial voice Jymn remembered from their last encounter.

'It was you that summoned me.'

It was an observation, not a question, but Jymn nodded all the same.

'You betray your own kind.' Another observation, but this time Jymn shook his head.

'They would have destroyed the code.'

'And now you hope to bargain for that which is beyond worth.' The creature bared its teeth, leaning closer, 'you, who dared to deceive me about this place.'

'No,' demanded Jymn quickly. 'No bargains.'

'Then there is no difference. The code is mine, and to you it is as good as destroyed.'

'It is protected. You will protect it.'

Lotan thrashed his head, and the resultant rush of water almost threw Jymn from the tiny boat. 'I am no guardian. No slave of man to defend his treasures. I will keep it from the eyes of man, always.'

Jymn chose his next words carefully. 'Then there is no difference. To me, it is as good as protected.'

Lotan hesitated then, his great lenses whirring as he seemed to process Jymn's words. He appeared to notice Jymn's injury for the first time, tilting his head in a strange affectation of curiosity. And then, without word or acknowledgement, the great wyrm simply slipped back beneath the dark water.

Jymn collapsed back into the boat, his energy utterly spent. The four of them stared at one another in mutual understanding, bobbing helplessly on the water, as the terror of Lotan's presence slowly ebbed away. With the noise of the engine gone, the yells of the survivors that clung to the great carcasses of the broken ships could be heard, carried to them on the wind.

'We should go back for them,' Jymn muttered, the guilt of his actions laying heavy on him.

'This thing can only take two more, Jymn,' said the captain gently, 'perhaps three.'

'Then three it is. Three lives is better than none!'

'It would be none, Lad!' said Tsar, in his low drawl. 'There must be two hundred men out there, and a good share of 'em mine. Good sailors, and tough. They'd kill us for the boat and then kill each other fighting over her.'

384

'We've got our own crew to save first, and we have a long paddle back to shore.'

'Hah! We might not have to!' roared Tsar, surging to his feet and shading his eyes against the low sun, 'look!'

A ship still remained, between the wreckage of the Roguian fleet and the shore. She was heeled over under full sail in the morning breeze, rising and falling as she cut through the water toward them. She sported an ugly steel plate across her bows, and her hull bristled with iron gunwales, but there was no mistaking her — the Archon sailed again.

'I don't understand…' muttered Cap as he squinted across the water.

'My lads fixed her up,' gloated Tsar, 'she's mine again, Mak. By all the articles of the sea.'

'But… how did you…'

'I showed him, Cap, I'm sorry. I had to, I needed to get to Nix and the others, and…' he trailed off as the captain's brow furrowed, a procession of anger, confusion, and sadness passing over his face as he tried to process this new reality.

'Oh don't look so downtrod!' chuckled Tsar, 'you still have your life — thanks to me, I might add. We'll give you a ride to kinder waters. Even a ship, perhaps, if we can find you one on the way.' Oghan and Knott chuckled against their gags as they saw the tables begin to turn, but Tsar rewarded them with a sharp kick to the ribs. 'Don't think I've forgotten about you two, now. Letting yourselves be tussled and trussed up in your own boat by a slip of a girl.'

The two prisoners sunk back into sullen silence, while together they waited for the Archon to close the distance. Tsar stood with one leg cocked on the inflated gunwale, waving his arms at the ship as she drew nearer, while Cap seemed distant and inaccessible, lost in brooding thought.

Inkäinen — he has learned of your lie? Nix signed, subtly.

It was hard, making her understand with only one hand, but Jymn replied clumsily. *I was not really with Tsar. But I had to make him think I was so that I could get to you.*

385

She seemed to process this for a moment. *It is like a dance-story,* and then she made a new sign, her hands moving in alternate circles, thumbs extended, then spelled *p-e-r-f-o-r-m.*

Jymn nodded eagerly and repeated the sign. *Yes, perform. I am sorry I could not explain.*

She grinned mischievously and signed crudely. *Your words are like child,* then saddened as she pointed to his hand. *Will be harder now, for you.*

Jymn bit down on the scrap of medicable that remained undissolved in his mouth, and forced himself to look at the void where his right hand had been. Pain flared as he instinctively tried to flex the missing fingers.

It will heal. I knew there was a price to dealing with a dragon. Remember Node's arm?

She winced at the mention of her tormentor, and Jymn instantly regretted the comparison, but before he could soothe his words the Archon was upon them, and he looked up to see a thickly-muscled For-Morian casting ropes down from the bow. Nix and the captain took the first of the lines and began to bind it slip-fashion beneath Jymn's armpits, that he might be hauled up alongside them. Tsar, rejuvenated by his victory, seized the next line and began to climb, swinging arm over arm up the hull like a man one third his age. Before he had even cleared the gunwales, he was yelling orders.

'Back to shore lads! We'll strip the place of what's left and send the small boats for…' his voice faltered, and as Jymn was hauled over the railing — pale and lightheaded — he saw why.

Daj stood at the head of a ring of grinning Archonauts, her staff-sling pressed to Tsar's throat. Mouth open and arms raised, the old pirate caught sight of his own band of surviving For-Morians, who hunkered gloomily around the mast, tied at hand and foot. There was a streak of red-green, and Puggle screeched triumphantly as she swooped low across the deck. North's cheeky, impish face appeared from behind the thickly muscled For-Morian that had hauled Jymn up. His crooked knife was pressed against the full-grown's back, and he winked, before straightening abruptly as Cap and Nix pulled themselves over the gunwale. 'Captain on deck!'

called North, and the Archonauts cheered.

A grin crossed the captain's face then, and a wave of some much deeper emotion, but he quickly recovered himself, turning toward Jymn and grasping his left hand by the wrist. With a nod, he hoisted Jymn's hand high in a gesture of victory and celebration, himself cheering, and prompting more whoops and shouts of applause from the assembled crew. Jymn saw Gam — wincing against the noise of the cheers — and Weylun shouldering their way through the crowd to meet him, and felt Nix's hands grasping at his back, trying to hold him up as the deck seemed to list beneath him.

He slumped back against her, sliding to the deck, his head swimming and light from the blood-loss, or perhaps the high dose of lix. Suddenly the captain was yelling for help, and his friends parted to make way for Kelpy, whose face was lined with worry as he inspected Jymn's wound, removing his own belt to cinch around the elbow. Gesturing for Gam and Weylun to help, he soon had Jymn propped against the gunwales and had sent the twins for blankets to make him comfortable.

'Hullo, Jymn. Well done,' said Slip warmly, stepping closer, and Jymn was happy to see that the young Bo'sun was unhurt, though he was clearly restless. Cap, still crouching over Jymn protectively, seemed to ask permission with his eyes, and Jymn nodded that he would be fine. The captain straightened and cleared his throat, hushing the expectant crew.

'Sou'west, Mr North,' he called, 'quarter sheets. And drogue the lines — a dozen each side.'

'Cap?' asked Slip, puzzled.

'There are men overboard, Slip. Prepare to take on prisoners.' And as the crew rushed to their tasks, he strode briskly toward the helm, halting briefly alongside Daj to lay a hand on Tsar's shoulder.

'Oh don't look so downtrod!' he winked, 'you still have your life — and we'll give you a ride to kinder waters. Even a ship — in fact I've got just the one in mind.'

XXXI

Kinder Waters

The voyage south was slow, and hard-going. What little rations they had managed to salvage from the camp at Thulhöfn had to be shared between the hungry Archonauts and the two-dozen full-grown For-Morians they had pulled from the wreckage of the fleet.

The godsmen, they had left on Thule.

Jymn had drifted in and out of awareness during those first few hours, as the Archon rushed among the barely floating hulks of the ruined fleet. Godsman and pirate alike were pulled from the water with rope and hook, taken below, and wrapped in blankets torn from the spare sails. Before long the prisoners vastly outnumbered their Archonaut guards, but were too defeated and half-drowned to muster any threat.

At the start, the Archon's drogue-lines were mobbed with frantic pirates fighting for survival, but after a few well-aimed shots from Daj's sling, and more than one drowning among competing sailors, the rescue calmed and grew more orderly.

Some, of course, refused the help of the heretic ship. One of the largest islands of wreckage — the upturned keel of the mighty *Sea Eater* — had been commandeered by a group of fanatical Pars who knelt shivering in the stiff breeze and prayed for salvation even as their brethren kicked and beat at less fortunate sailors attempting to clamber aboard the wreck.

When the Archon had come alongside and offered its lines, Slip's offer of rescue was met with jeers and angry rebuttals.

'We do not need your help, heathen' called their leader, defiantly, 'for we pray, and the Lord will surely send us salvation!'

'What do you call this?' barked Caber, shaking one of the thick drogue lines that hung from the gunwales into the water, 'he bloody has, hasn't he!'

But they returned to their prayers just the same, even as one or two of their number slipped quietly into the water and swam for the ship. With a shiver, Jymn thought he heard once more the voice of old, blind Jon Cane, calling out from the water for a drogue line, but after the first few Pars had scrambled over the gunwales, Nix untied the line and let it drop back to the water with a splash, spitting viciously after it as it fell. Throughout the rescue she marched along the deck and among the prisoners, Jymn's wrench-knife clutched in hand, searching — he presumed — for Rasmus, and revenge for her Kin. But the erstwhile leader of the Godsmen was nowhere to be found among the ruins of Lotan's fury.

Tsar alone had been offered passage south — out of gratitude for his saving Cap from drowning — but after a private parlay with the captain, was allowed to select a skeleton crew from among the surviving For-Morians to accompany him south. There was more than a little outrage among the crew, and Daj had to be held back by Balder when Tsar grinned at her, taunting, but a little while later, his price was revealed.

'You watch,' grinned Gam, who of course had heard everything. And he gestured toward Slip and Weylun, who were making a great effort at discretion as they strolled toward the aftcastle stair and pried open the false-panel that hid the stash-locker. Jymn gasped as two large sacks were withdrawn, spilling a handful of the crystal coins onto the deck.

'Tsar's price for his crew,' whispered Gam. 'That's why he wanted the Archon so bad — it was his only way to get it past the Godsmen.'

Once the last of the willing survivors had been dragged from the water, the Archon lay anchor in the wide harbour of Thulhöfn, where teams went ashore to strip the town and its surroundings of resources for the voyage. Enough food was taken to sustain the ship and her prisoners until the nearest port, the rest being left to feed the new unlikely colony of pirates and Godsmen that would remain here, devoid of any vessel that might allow them to bring more harm to the world. A great many long-guns were recovered from the town and what remained of the camp atop the mountainside, and all were thrown into icy waters of the bay.

No more of the crystal coins that held the secrets of the ancient Skand had survived, but more than fifty chests of unspoiled seeds that had yet to be burned upon the church pyres were brought aboard, along with a limping and huddled figure who trod carefully along the gangway, clutching Slip's arm. Rincs, whose actions — as Jymn had learned from Gam — had proved critical in securing the Archonaut's escape from the seed vault, even as it had sealed her fate as a prisoner of the Godsmen. The once-proud splicer was led to the Captain's own quarters, and Kelpy sent to see to her comfort.

Caber dragged a sled of salvaged teck behind Weylun. Jymn recognised more than one of the ancient machines that had been able to read the coins, though what was more astonishing was the eagerness with which Caber seemed to help — and indeed even *obey* — Weylun, formerly the victim of his worse affections.

Once the teck was safely stowed in the shielded workshop, Caber approached Jymn with the heavy frown of one conflicted, and hesitated a few paces away. Gam squeezed Jymn's shoulder and made himself scarce.

Jymn felt a lump rise in his throat. The last interaction he'd had with Caber, he'd had a knife pressed to his ribs. But now the huge, hot-tempered boy seemed almost embarrassed, his tail between his legs.

'I wanted to say thanks,' he mumbled. 'And sorry about the tussle and all that, before. Not trusting you, like. Truth is we'd all still be in a fakk mess if it weren't for you, I reckon.' He reached into his trashlander furs and gently withdrew… more fur, cupping it gently between his hands. 'I snatched this, from the seed-vault there. Figured it reminded me of your one back on your workship.'

And with that, he leaned down and gently goaded the young rat from his hands into Jymn's. The little creature sniffed at Jymn's fingers and padded around in his palm before nestling in the crook of his elbow. Jymn felt the lump in his throat choke any reply, and his eyes began sting from the cold. He looked up at Caber to thank him, but the older boy was already a dozen paces away, the moment forgotten.

It wasn't the first time he'd been credited with the escape from the seed-vault, nor the first token he'd been given in gratitude. Daj had inscribed his name on one of her sling-stones and offered to keep an eye out for him, and Kelpy had cleaned up the purple sash that had stemmed the bleeding from his calf and added a cunning embroidery of a dragon that appeared to cling to his face when it was fastened back across his smikken eye. A handful of others had shared morsels of food, or trinkets from past spoils. He'd tried to tell people that he hadn't even really *had* a plan for the escape — not beyond using the magflies and the magnet to chew through the rusty hinges — but they'd mistaken it for modesty or bashfulness, and thanked him all the same. The truth is — from what he had been told — that the escape had been equal parts luck, and the cunning of his friends. Weylun had dealt with the door, Gam had distracted their captors with the other radio handset, and Balder, Daj, and Caber had held off the full-growns long enough for North to lead them from the vault. Even then, it would have been all for nothing if not for Rincs, who upon being escorted down from the mountaintop camp, had managed to snatch a weapon from her captors and create enough havoc to see the escaping Archonauts safely to the ice-cave, where they overpowered the unsuspecting For-Morians that had been left in charge of repairs.

Rincs was the hero, truly. And Weylun, and Gam and the others. All Jymn felt, between the numbing doses of lix that were administered thrice daily, was an overwhelming guilt. He had sought a headcount for the new colony at Thulhöfn, that he might have some idea exactly how many souls had been lost when Lotan came. But either nobody knew, or orders had been given not to tell him. His friends tried to comfort him, and to persuade him it was necessary, or somehow out of his control, but none of that seemed to dissuade the drowned faces of sailors that floated through his dreams at night.

But as they sailed south, the air and water growing warmer, the nightmares began to abate, and Thule — with all of its frozen wonders and horrors — was left behind.

Under Kelpy's attentive care, the angry and savage wound at his right wrist began to knit, though the healing did nothing to forestall the frequent unscratchable itches that plagued his missing hand. On the seventh day out of Thule, Weylun came to him clutching a bundle of oiled cloth.

'I don't want you to get too excited,' said the techsmith, who seemed to have shed the bluster and uncertainty that usually accompanied his words. 'There's a long way to go, and I'm not certain it'll even work, not fully, but…' he pulled back the oiled cloth to reveal the intricate metallic hand they had stolen from Node's lair. It had been modified by hands clearly not as skilled as Node's — wires trailing like nerves from the wrist, where a crude copper brace had been fashioned with leather straps. Weylun offered it toward Jymn, who was quite overwhelmed at the piece, but allowed his friend to fit it to his arm, carefully positioning the wires and cinching the straps tight as Jymn winced against the pain.

'What do I do?' asked Jymn, finding his arm heavy, as he brought the metal hand closer to inspect it.

'Just try to open your fist,' said Weylun gently, 'just like you would have before.'

Gritting his teeth, Jymn flexed raw and ruined muscles that had not been moved since Lotan had torn the hand from his wrist. At first there was nothing, but suddenly the metal hand wrenched open, the last two fingers spasming erratically, the thumb staying folded across the palm. Weylun leaned forward and flipped a small switch, and the movement stopped dead.

'Sorry,' he muttered, loosening the straps, 'still a lot of Node's old code left in there. I'm doing my best to clear it out.'

'It's brilliant,' Jymn marvelled, smiling in astonishment at his friend, who blushed at the compliment — a problem that was occurring more and more often for him, ever since the seed-vault. The curiosity and confidence with which he set about investigating the code they had salvaged was staggering. In the weeks that followed, he had not only refined the metal hand to the degree that Jymn could confidently work the ship's ropes, but even so far that he could begin to use it for signing with Gam and Nix. He had also designed a simple device that tracked their heading with a compass, and their speed with a small paddle mounted just below the waterline — both devices then feeding this information back to the map table to give a surprisingly accurate estimate of their position.

Weylun's newfound confidence wasn't the only change aboard the Archon — after a fortnight of grim rations and burned gruel, the twins Bink and Juke had approached the captain and asked to be installed as the new ship's cooks. From that day forth, the galley was a noisy, chaotic mess — the two of them often sparring as they fought to wrestle a meal from the scant supplies — but the food improved dramatically, overseen by Scup's trusty ladle, which they mounted above the stove, tied with his purple sash.

Nix approached Weylun during the voyage, and had begun exploring the idea of reactivating her implant. Soon, after a nervous but rather successful operation overseen by Kelpy, there was a switch installed, and a dial to control the sensitivity. Sometimes now, if the evening was particularly still, Nix would activate the device, and could be heard humming to herself, or be seen watching the birds swoop about the mast with Gam, who helped her through the overwhelming sensation of sound and noise. But mostly, it stayed off. Gam's hand-sign continued to improve, and Nix would often join him on watch, scanning the horizon from the solitude of the mainmast while he manned the foremast, the two of them silently chatting across the distance.

The captive For-Morians mostly kept to themselves, other than a few half-hearted attempts to take over the ship, for which the mutineers paid with a night or two in the gibbet. Cap simply laughed these endeavours off, explaining that it was in every pirate's nature to try and escape, and he'd be more worried if they had behaved themselves. Tsar — a king among the prisoners — held court below deck, often entertaining off-duty members of the Archon's crew with his tales, alongside the full-grown For-

Morians. Twice a day he was permitted to walk the deck to take air, though Daj guarded him like a hound, her jaw set and knuckles white against the haft of her sling.

Eventually, their meandering course south brought them to Vitzamar, where they had agreed to set the Rougian captives free. Tsar's face when Cap returned across the harbour with the ship that he had promised was a sight Jymn suspected he would never forget. The elderly Vitz woman clutched her newfound fortune of bar-coin with glee, as the For-Morians mournfully clambered from the Archon into the battered old cattle barge, still occupied by a half-dozen of the sorry animals, and ankle deep with their filth.

'Poor show, Mak.' Tsar grumbled, shaking his head at the sorry state of the vessel as one of the hungry cattle licked at his sleeve. 'Livestock, really?'

Cap spread his hands. 'Hey, I told you where the ship would be and when. Don't recall telling you what would be on it.' He threw his head back then, and laughed, tossing a bucket down from the Archon's gunwales. 'Best get bailing, Tsar. I don't think she's quite watertight.'

Jymn watched as the For-Morians squabbled for space aboard the stinking barge. Tsar tossed the bucket to Oghan and ordered him to start bailing, but not before removing a small purse that seemed to be stashed inside. Jymn could have sworn he saw the familiar glint of crystal in the old pirate's hands as he waved farewell. Jymn wondered what would become of him now. Tsar was a ruthless survivor, full of his own brand of vitality and verve. It seemed impossible that he could be beaten, and yet Jymn couldn't help but remember the sun-pox lesions that spread slowly across his chest, inching toward his heart and lungs. Without the Fairey's life-giving transfusions, surely he was doomed to an inglorious death. 'I couldn't change that even if I wanted to, Jymn,' sighed the captain when Jymn raised it that evening. 'He's a captain. He's going to have to live — or die — with the consequences of what he's done.' Though Jymn couldn't help but detect a note of regret in the captain's voice.

394

More of the crystal coins were bartered for metals, rations, and labour throughout their homeward voyage. Weylun had objected most vociferously at first, of course, but soon had to admit that there was more code on one of the coins than he could hope to unpick in a year. And the trades were about more than just food and resources — however desperate they were for those — it was also about circulating the code. Making sure it wasn't all in one place, vulnerable to accident or attack. And so, in every port they visited, a few more of the great stash were traded away. They even managed to stop a while in Cinnabar, where a team of carpenters helped to remove the ugly, heavy metalwork that scarred and slowed the ship, and refit her in timber, as was proper.

As well as the crystal coins, they distributed the chests of seed wherever they found need, which was almost everywhere. It seemed in their absence to the east and the north, the rice-blight had spread, threatening famine among the island nations of the south and west. Rincs was roused from her slow recovery to take samples of the blighted crops, though without her equipment — which Jymn had burned beyond hope of repair — there was little that she could do.

Raption activity too had worsened in recent weeks — apparently starting on the very night of Jymn's broadcast. Though whether it was the broadcast itself, or the disturbance of Lotan leaving his lair for the north, it was impossible to tell. Either way, fear and superstition was renewed among the hungry population, and though there were fewer Godsmen to take advantage, Jymn quietly wondered who would emerge next to fill the void they left.

Rincs was delivered back to Shoalhaven, where she still felt some responsibility to the townspeople. She too was given a good store of the coins, and a team of Archonauts helped her to her old homestead among the mangroves. Old Loken was still there waiting for her, sitting upon the bench peacefully, and quite dead. Words were spoken, and a smattering of tears shed, and then the old Skand was buried in the sandy soil, the crucial recording of his sister's testimony, clutched to his breast.

Jymn lingered a while beside the grave, remembering the sing-song voice that had mistaken him for a Skand, and recited the Ice

Cat rhymes — presumably some simple warning to keep the young from wandering up the mountain. 'The Ice Cat waits, up there on high,' Jymn whispered, patting the ground, and remembering the fierce courage with which the old man had stormed the platform in the square in an effort to save Nix. He made a promise to tell what he knew of Loken's story at the next fire.

The last of their crystal coins — numbering almost half the total hoard — were entrusted to the Faireys of Losalfhym. Gone now, were the scars of their battle with the church fleet, though Jymn felt that he could still detect a sense of loss and mourning among the Fair Folk. There was great rejoicing to see Inkäinen — the captain — safe, and most especially Nix, who was scolded by her parents most fiercely in sign-shapes Jymn hadn't seen since the Trossul, before being wrapped into an embrace that Jymn feared might suffocate her. When eventually it relented, and she shared some scrap of her tale with those among her people who understood hand-sign, Jymn, Gam, and Weylun soon found themselves beset by the crushing hugs too, in gratitude for their part in bringing her home.

Rincs, unbeknown to Jymn, had saved a scrap of the Mir-Tree genes — the seed of the fair folk — that had held the secret of Thule, and having nurtured this, had entrusted it to the captain to pass to the Goodmother in a gesture of regret, and friendship. The gift was accepted, and an assortment of the old Skand splicing tecks were loaded onto the Archon to be gifted to Rincs by way of thanks. There was great celebration among the Fair Folk that night, and the stories that were told at feast were already woven into song by moonrise. The Archonauts were invited to the sacred Lunehall, which now was cleared of the ashes of the burned Mir-trees, and witnessed for the first time the song of the Faireys. Jymn saw Nix with her parents and Gam, her eyes shut, and noticed a pinprick of light from the device that nestled behind her left ear. She was home.

But it was not to last.

Three days later, he watched from the shallow water as she staggered onto the beach. Cap motioned Daj forward, who grasped Nix's tunic, tearing it free from her chest with a single, savage motion. Jymn felt the adolescent tension among the crew dissipate, as they saw that she was prepared, and wore a tight binding fabric beneath. Daj winked at her, and Jymn suspected this had been her doing. Further up the beach, Cap tore a strip of purple fabric from his ever-shortening tunic, before realising clumsily that he needed both his hands for what was to come. Laughing, and passing the scrap to Slip, he began to speak, signing clumsily as he went.

'Nix, of the Fair-Folk. You have rushed into danger without thinking,' he said, as excited whispers rippled through the assembled Archonauts. 'You have stolen, and profited from that stealing. You have done violence against your fellow man. You have endangered yourself and your crew. And best of all,' it took a moment for his hand-sign — hastily memorised with Jymn's help over the last week — to catch up with the solemn words, 'you have been told what to do, and have disobeyed.' Cap sighed in exaggerated exhaustion from the effort of the signing, and accepted the scrap of cloth back from Slip with a grin, pressing it into Nix's waiting hands.

A hush fell over the gathered crew, who watched Nix expectantly for her next move. Raising her left hand, she bound the fabric about her wrist and knuckles like a fighter, before thrusting her fist into the air. Puggle squawked, swooping overhead as cheers erupted from the crew, who rushed to lift the newest of their number upon their shoulders.

The party went on long into the night. Jymn, exhausted from the dancing and the laughter, found himself cross-legged on a crate at the edge of the fire's light, watching his friends. Balder and Kelpy held each other tenderly, laughing as the twins capered about to a tune from North's fist-whistle and Caber's drum. Nix — whose appetite for dancing seemed inexhaustible tonight — whirled around with Gam, who was at the limit of his endurance, and sent her spinning toward Weylun to take over. The clumsy techsmith turned out to be surprisingly sure of foot when the rhythm was provided, and the onlookers clapped as the two friends pranced around the fire.

'I think she'll fit in well enough, don't you?'

Jymn almost fell off his crate. He hadn't heard the Captain

approach from the small camp they'd made on the beach.

'A little *too* well, perhaps,' he continued in a low whisper, raising an eyebrow in Gam's direction, who was staring doe-eyed at Nix as she spun Weylun about the fire-pit.

'It's good to have you back,' Jymn grinned. In truth, he hadn't expected the captain to rejoin the party. He appeared to be back to full strength — his hair had grown back as thickly as ever, and the lines were gone from his face — but he had never quite regained the brightness in his eyes, and he was often to be found alone. Something of the Cobalt Sea still lingered there.

Cap seemed to read Jymn's thoughts upon his face. 'It's nothing to worry about. Rincs was right, something about my splice stopped the water from killing me, but she thinks it's *changed*, somehow. The splice, I mean.'

'Changed how?' Jymn asked simply, surprised to find the captain so willing to talk.

'Won't know for sure until she gets herself set up again.' Cap shrugged, then seemed to lose himself in the fire. 'I can feel it though. Inside. That treasure was my best chance yet at fulfilling my promise. At building somewhere for everyone to call home. I just worry I won't get another, if the hourglass starts turning again.' He drew a deep breath and slapped Jymn on the shoulder, forcing a smile. 'Sorry — I'm feeling sorry for myself, aren't I?'

'You had some of the treasure, a small fortune, and you gave most of it away.'

'Well, yes...' admitted the captain, taken aback by Jymn's words. 'But that wasn't enough, really. Only a fraction of what we could have had. And it was more important to get it...'

'It was more than we needed,' interrupted Jymn, 'did you never ask yourself why nobody complained when you gave it away to Tsar — yes I saw that — or to Rincs, or the Goodmother?'

The captain just blinked at him, unused to being spoken to this frankly.

Jymn stared at his feet. 'You knew I came from Razeen, didn't you?'

'Yes,' admitted the captain quietly.

'Everything you've done since leaving Tsar. I didn't really understand, not until it had all fallen apart and it looked like we were going to be stranded on Thule, or worse. Nobody followed you that far for riches, or to try and *build* a place to call home. They did it because we already *have* a place to call home. You already built it. We all did. All of our damned shirts are in the sails, our blood is in the timbers, and she's sat right out there, at anchor.'

He jabbed a metal finger toward the moonlit silhouette of the Archon that silently kept watch over the bay. Cap stood and walked a few paces across the sand toward her, wiping his eyes before planting his hands on his hips and staring out over the water. Jymn rose and stood beside him, and then the captain's hand was on his shoulder.

'Well Jymn, where to next?'

Epilogue

Kyra blinked against the glare of light from the room beyond. For the thousandth time, she reminded herself that it couldn't be wrong, not *really*, not if she was doing it for the baby.

They had tried three times now, and it had always ended in heartbreak. Now with Heph gone, well, she only had one chance to save some small part of him, and she wasn't going to take any chances.

This was taking chances, warned a familiar voice in her head. Getting on a boat with some mad old hermit *was* taking chances. But for the thousand-and-oneth time, she pushed the warning down deep inside herself. Pregnant girls had been going to Splicers for centuries. It might be teck, it might be heresy, but it *worked*.

She hadn't been able to afford it, of course, or she'd have used one after the first miscarriage. Her Heph had worked on the scrapping boats, and she sorted plastics for a living. It would have taken them five years of scrimping and saving to go to the local Splicer. No, poor folk like them, all *they* had was prayer - and good Pars were few and far between these days, after all the trouble in the North. But this time the prayers had been answered. A new splicer, just travelling through. Some old spiritual type, living out his days, just looking to help. That's how it had seemed, anyway.

Full of questions, he was, at first. How old was she, did she have any family nearby to help with the child. What of the father? How sorry he was to hear of Heph's accident. What manner of man was Heph, how tall, how fair? She'd stepped willingly onto the man's small boat, trying not to flinch at the touch of his metal hand as he helped her aboard. Lots of men lost limbs at sea, it wasn't kind to stare. She marvelled at his skill with the boat and

400

the swiftness with which they reached his home. Heph had always said the nearest island was three days' sail, though the trip in the small catboat took only a few hours.

But things hadn't felt right from the moment she set foot on the hermit's shore. The island was grim, and bare, and the men that worked the fields nearby seemed to shuffle about like they hadn't slept in weeks. And then the door that led to his workshop, led *into* the hillside, that was almost too much for her.

Now she found herself in a dark chamber, lit only by great glass vats of liquid that bubbled with an eerie blue light. Creatures seemed to float in the liquid, connected to metal tendrils, though she tried not to look — or think — too hard about what they could be. *It couldn't be wrong, not really, not if she was doing it for the baby.*

The hermit returned, and it seemed that his crown of wiry, grey hair had grown more wild than before. Kyra flinched as she realised that the hand of his metal arm was gone now, and in its place was a wide glass vial from which protruded a long, thick needle.

'You must hold very still for this next part,' he cautioned, and at a jerk of his head, metal tendrils snaked from somewhere in the darkness to clasp her by the wrist, neck, and ankle, and she cried out in alarm.

'Still!' the old man snapped, a scowl on the beardless face that had seemed so kindly in daylight.

'What… what is the needle for?' asked Kyra, forcing as much dignity and calm into her voice as she could muster.

'You thought perhaps I was going to burn some herbs and say a prayer?' taunted the man, without looking up. 'This is medicine, girl. *Real* medicine. Blood tecks made by the Skand themselves.' Kyra shivered as he lifted what looked like a yellowed, bloody fingernail from a beaker with a steel claw, then dropped it into the glass vial that fed the needle.

'What's *that*?' gasped Kyra, any pretence of calm abandoning her.

The old splicer raised the vial and squinted at the fingernail. The glass grotesquely magnified his eye, which seemed now to be lit from within by a dull red glow. 'Blood, girl. Very special blood. The boy from whom I took it will be the child's father, in a sense.'

Clear liquid wept from the point of the needle as he drew closer. Kyra tried to swallow, but found her mouth suddenly dry. 'But the baby, it will be healthy?' she asked, unable to keep her voice from trembling.

He hesitated then, his lip curling, though it felt more like a sneer than a smile. 'Oh yes, dear,' said the old man softly. 'You will carry a fine, strong boy. And I promise you, if he's anything like his father, he will live a long, long time indeed.'

THE END

Printed in Great Britain
by Amazon

40078551R00229